LAUGHTER LEFT OVER

Praise for *The Dancing Finn*

"A delightful, engagingly told, poignant tale. With a gift for image and metaphor that enriches the story, a genius storyteller's art. A girl's hair is 'an unshackled whirl of orange.' A woman bent on conversation 'gleamed at us with carnivorous greed.' This is a constant poetic style both astonishing and admirable. And that comes from a professional (he says modestly) literary critic—or literary cricket, as Mark Twain would say."   ~Robert Detweiler, former director of the Graduate Institute of the Liberal Arts, Emory University, Atlanta, Georgia

LAUGHTER LEFT OVER

RUTH JUTILA CHAMBERLIN

NORTH STAR PRESS OF ST. CLOUD, INC.
ST. CLOUD, MINNESOTA

CREDITS

I gratefully acknowledge writers whose works I quote in the novel:

Thomas Gray: "Full many a flower is born to blush unseen and waste its sweetness on the desert air."
William Wordsworth: "The world is too much with us . . . "
Moslih Eddin Saadi: ". . . buy hyacinths to feed thy soul."
Harriet Beecher Stowe: " . . . they could not sleep for joy."
Edward Wallis Hoch: "There is so much good in the worst of us . . ."
King Crimson: "I've Got a Lovely Bunch of Coconuts."
Hoagy Carmichael and Jack Brooks: "Old Buttermilk Sky."
Unknown: "PorkBellyAcres" and "Old age comes at a bad time."

Portions of this novel have appeared, in slightly different forms, in *Los Angeles Times*, *World Vision Magazine*, "Epic Adventure: Crisis and the Kalevala" (Ph.D. dissertation), and *Dust & Fire, Women's Stories: Annual Anthology of Women's Writing*.

Printed in the United States of America.

ISBN: 978-0-87839-402-9

Published by:
North Star Press of St. Cloud, Inc.
PO Box 451
St. Cloud, MN 56302

www.northstarpress.com

Table of Contents

One

Puzzles

Isak tried to take the two-by-six, but Elsa caught him. She came out to the porch, uphill from Isak, and stood there full of power like a carved wooden lady on the prow of a ship. She piled her arms at her midriff and called, "Put it down."

He would, eventually, but first he peeked at her and got tickled. *Those big bosoms! She's still gotta prop 'em up.*

"You'll break a leg on that thing," she said.

He said, "Ya, well," and fiddled around, taking his time, moving the plank from hand to hand and checking for splinters.

Elsa said, "Maybe you shouldn't go. What if . . . ?" Blinking behind her glasses, she lowered her hands and pressed them into her apron pockets. Her posture said she didn't like reminding him anymore than he liked being reminded. "What if" meant what if he lost track like he did at Sully's house, when he mistook Sully for his mother and actually spoke to his mum—his mum dead twenty years and, anyway, out of reach since he was a boy. What if he got confused. What if Elsa was too far away to help. He leaned back to stare at the Douglas fir canopy a hundred feet up. Hardly any sky showed through, and what little did show had no real color. He leaned the plank on his shoulder like one rib of a tee-pee. Without looking at Elsa, he knew her lips were clamped together in that fierce look of affection. To have something to do, he pulled out his hanky, put it to his nose, waggled it, and stuffed it back in his pocket.

"I'll be fine," he said. "I just want to walk a ways."

Elsa took two gasping, inward-pulling breaths, "*Uh!-uh!*" This frantic kind of sigh came naturally to her and to every other Finnish lady he'd ever met. It signified the petty woes and was harmless. But he wondered what happened to the outgoing air. He thought it might get stuck inside of Elsa and build up and up until one day it'd erupt—like a volcano—right out of the top of her head.

He stood the plank on end, just so, against the garage. She said, "Don't stay long," and went indoors.

A Hills Brothers coffee can hung from his neck and rested on his chest. He tested the cord. It was strong. He patted one pocket of his pants. His hanky and a leather glove. The other pocket: Thesaurus, Swiss Army knife. He was glad she hadn't checked his pockets. She hadn't started *that* yet, anyway.

He picked up the snagger and started down the driveway, a big man made small by tall timber, or, as he preferred, an old man in relics of his pastimes (or past times, he thought he might say)—gray Monkey Ward work pants and shirt, red wool hunting jacket, brown billed cap, safety glasses, metal-toe shoes—all of them shabby to the point of pleasure. Wearing them to a frazzle was a matter of frugality. That, and loyalty. Whistling in a whisper behind his teeth, he turned left at the gravel road he shared with Joe Nichols, passed Joe's house, turned right at the asphalt road, and walked along the shoulder. At sixty paces, he stepped off into the weeds.

A grassy road cut through trees to his left, or the west, came down the hill toward him, and continued on east. This path belonged to giants— towers that reminded him of football players (those-kind narrow waists and bunchy shoulders) or of Vikings (that heroic gaze). They took cable to Isak's place and then stopped a mile farther at the power station, leaving folks higher up to run generators. He was going over the fact that he liked the towers but not the buzz when he remembered the guy who wore a tin foil cap near power lines. Now, *that* guy was *confused!* He thought the buzz was from another planet! Isak puzzled over this for a minute—not sure if the cap was for catching signals or warding them off—and then hustled under the lines to his destination, a meadow an eighth of a mile from home.

Now he stood and let the fears come. Things were bad all right, and not just that business over at Sully's. More and more these days, he forgot what he started out to say, and he got left with his mouth hanging open and no words coming out. Sometimes ideas flew by so fast, all he caught was the tail end, and he might say "tractors" when no one was talking about tractors or "haying" when the last time he hayed was fifty, sixty years ago. He was better off not talking! And jigsaw puzzles? Here's me, he groaned—a guy who hardly needed a ruler, my eye was so good—trying pieces that don't fit by a long shot. And the time I took off to see Ferd? Heck, he's been gone a *lotta* years. The worst time? The helicopter in the house. *Scared the living daylights out of me!* Isak shuddered. *What's needed after a thing like that is a time of quiet.*

Shaking off the bad times, he waded into remnants of summer. Touching his cap, he addressed a clump of unfussy white pellets. "Why, Pearly Everlasting! How-do?" Isak didn't see any miniature violets. He knew why. They came in March, not now. Everything had changed since spring. Back in the spring, the Scotch broom was taller than Isak, squeaky green and full of sass, with blossoms so yellow they could blind a fellow. Now it was shrunken and gray. *Diminished.* The stalks of foxglove were still nine feet tall (*nine feet* tall!), but the tops had bent into scoops, due, maybe, to dodging the sun one day and reaching for it the next. The foxglove still had polka-dots inside the bells, same as ever, but the purple had faded to that old-time color called . . . ? *Rose.* He turned to the ferns. Old age had actually improved them! In the spring the fronds were plain yellow sticks curled at the top like shepherd's crooks, faking shyness but showing their bumpy undersides for all to see. He chased a slippery thought. *Fiddleheads.* Not shepherd's crooks. He had never eaten them, but a person could. Today the fronds were wide, saw-toothed, and high-minded— and *maroon-green,* as if one color weren't enough. He said to one granddaddy fern, "You and me? The older we get, the better-lookin' we get!"

Thigh-high in wild grass, he congratulated God. "Good camouflage! The grass turns that-kind wheat color when it dies . . . (Huh. Did I say *dies?* I meant *dries*) . . . so those yellow elk-rumps blend right in." He checked the ground. No signs of elk. No beds of trampled grass, no black squared-marble droppings (bigger than the deer scat at his feet). He said, "Come evening, they'll be by. Come hunting season, they'll be *scarce*." He rubbed the back of his neck. "They're no dummies, those elk."

Isak listened for coyotes, but it was the wrong time. Nighttime was for coyotes. They kept him awake some nights behind his house, but he didn't mind. They were teaching their young to hunt, and they were not quiet hunters. Whenever they caught something, they yapped and sang—"Hey, kids, over here, we got one!"—and set off choruses from one hill to the other. He played their music in his mind. "Ow-oo-wow, yipe, yipe, yipe!"

Above his head, white stuttered across blue in tidy puffs, a quilt inviting him to stay a while. In his best Gene Autry tenor, he sang, "'Old Buttermilk Sky, I'm keeping my eye . . . (hum) . . . on you.'" *What in the Sam Hill is that word?* He lifted his face to the sun. Barely warm. He tried out words for this kind of sun—weak, tepid, pallid, wan. Turning in a step-pause step, he eyed the thicket behind the meadow. Blackberry thorns—as brutal as steel barbs—protected the hills against easy trespass. Beyond the vines, up a sharp incline, lay a world of vast proportion, home to cougars, bears, elk, deer, eagles, hawks. He *knew* those hills. He had been up there *plenty*-times, had scrabbled up the cliff behind his house, using tree roots as handholds, climbed over ferns and Oregon grape until he reached a plateau of western white pines, a place as hushed and bare of brush as a park at dawn. Higher yet were rivers so tall you had to look *up* to see them! Waterfalls so loud they made you deaf! Six-hundred-year-old burn snags, and living cedars older yet, and lava tunnels so long that no one could find you if you got lost inside them. *You bet* he knew those hills! He had hunted elk up there more times than he could count.

No more, he groused. These days, I'm lucky to hunt berries. If Elsa gets her way, I won't even be doing that.

On a rise behind the blackberries, alders leaned on each other in staggered rows like drunks standing at attention. "They have that-kind mottled skin," he said, "like Finland birch." He clicked his tongue twice, seconding the notion. He was guessing about Finland birch. He was born in North Dakota

4

and had never been to Finland. But he had seen photos. In a roundabout way, the alders reminded Isak that he was a Finn. Being a Finn meant being brave. Finns had *sisu*, courage beyond the norm. *Guts.*

Above the alders, the Douglas firs took over and climbed the hills as far as he could see, blocking his view of Mount St. Helens, which was eight miles north as the crow flies. He shuffled his feet and faced south. The near woods matched the Forest Green in Nell's crayon box. (Where *is* she, anyway?) The valley meandered east to west, nipping at hills on either side. Below him, pieces of the lake signaled to him in silver and peach. He saw dream shapes on the water, skips of light and rounded mountains, jiggles of birds. A man in a boat, or maybe not. A blue haze made the hills seem lazy, or sleepy, like the start of fall. Which it should be about *now,* he thought. He narrowed his eyes at the hills beyond the lake. They didn't have the navy-and-orange plaid of late fall, or the slate blue of winter, or the jillion baby greens of spring, or the solid dusty green of August. He had pinned it! *Early fall.* The hills tucked behind each other to the horizon, paling as they went, first blue-green, then blue-gray, then lighter and lighter gray, holding white logs of fog in the hollows. "Cotton batting," he said, "for cushioning. For when the mountain blows." He chuckled and shook his head. He was just giving himself a tease.

He sniffed. Someone was burning brush over toward town. He listened, heard nothing. Then a meadowlark sang. The song was a convoluted gargle up and down the bird scale, a coded message for Isak. When it was over, it lingered on the air, filling Isak's ears. Nodding gravely, he accepted it as a gift and walked on.

The meadow had been quiet as long as he stood still. Now, when he moved, it erupted in grasshoppers—*noisy* grasshoppers. He tested them. He took a few steps and grasshoppers flew, clicking like castanets. He stopped, and they clung to the stems they had landed on, frozen, like children playing Statue. Intrigued, he stooped to look at one. It was an inch long, light-green, striped in black with delicate red piping on the legs—so fancy it seemed hand-painted. He wished Elsa could see it.

In a ruckus of grasshoppers, he resumed his tour. It was a poor season for blackberries. Too many were hard, small, still red. He liked them big, soft, and black. In one area, deer had stripped branches of berries and left soggy strands of fruit. He went to another spot, picked berries, and ate them. He pulled a thorn from a finger with his teeth.

Then he saw it, a branch loaded with fat, ripe berries. But it was at the top of a thicket that he guessed was ten feet tall and ten feet deep.

He knew what to do. He put the leather glove on his left hand and held the snagger—a broomstick with the hook of a metal clothes hanger taped to it—in his right hand, like a sword. He stationed his feet, took a handful of vines with the gloved hand, and gave a heave with his right arm, swinging the snagger at the branch. He missed. He tried again and missed. The third time, he lost his balance and fell forward into the bushes.

He let go of the stick. Gasping more in chagrin than in pain, he disengaged himself from thorns. After retrieving the stick, he went on to his next plan.

He found an alder limb that had fallen of its own accord. With his Swiss Army knife, he stripped it of branches and twigs. He collapsed the knife and returned it to his pocket. Placing the limb on the blackberry thicket, horizontally, at knee height, he formed a step, or a rung. With the snagger under his right arm, he again took vines in his gloved left hand. He set his right foot on the rung without putting weight on it. He was tired but gleeful. He was conquering the blackberries!

Using the snagger as a cane, Isak lurched upward onto the devised rung. The rung collapsed and he tumbled to his right, landing with his rump on the ground and the rest of him hooked on thorns.

Again he disentangled himself. This time it took longer. He stood back to assess the distance to the fat berries. He saw how high the branch was. Impossible! What was he *thinking?* He pictured the two-by-six, imagined setting it on the thicket and crawling onto it, deep into the bushes, felt himself falling headlong.

He took in a steely breath. "If I'd've been on that thing?"

A movement caught his eye—a panicky movement on a blackberry bush. He stooped to see what was happening. A spider had caught a grasshopper and was wrapping it for storage, zipping around it with a stream of spider glue. Isak was captivated. "Can you beat that? He's hog-tying it!" The grasshopper, ten times larger than the spider, was kicking and stretching the casing, but the bitsy spider paid no attention. It whipped magic string around and around the grasshopper until it resembled a mummy, then affixed it, upside-down and active, to the low edge of the web.

Now the spider could relax. It scuttled to the center of the maze and made itself yet smaller. It sat very still. The grasshopper gave a few twitches but to no avail.

Caught up in the drama, Isak said, "Hoo! That poor hopper is *pantry stock!*" The spider ran down to the bundle and bolstered the bindings. The grasshopper moved, but the spider was sure of its handiwork. It returned to the center of the web where it sat and groomed itself.

Isak laboriously stood up. He was surprised that he still had the coffee can. *I must've held my breath all during that . . . ?* He had trouble knowing what "that" was. Death fight? Defeat or victory? Depends on a fellow's point of view, he decided.

Carrying his snagger, he walked alongside the thicket. Now that he was looking for webs, he saw them everywhere. Some were as big as four feet by five feet. How could a spider jump that far to start a web? With the wind, he guessed. He figured that web-building must be slow work. "Slow is okay," he advised the spiders. "Haste makes waste." On every web he saw the same scene—in the center, a black spider, at the bottom, grasshopper packets.

Isak had never seen so many grasshoppers or such big webs or such poor berries. He had never fallen the way he'd fallen today or made so many mistakes. Life was changing on him, and—for the first time that he could recall—he felt too tired to keep up.

When he got to the driveway, Elsa was coming down the side steps, holding a cardigan around her like a blanket. She called, "I was on my way to find you," and came to meet him. With the matter-of-factness he'd admired for forty-odd years, she noticed the scratches on his face and said only, "Better put alcohol on those." She didn't seem to see that his berry can was empty.

In the garage he wasted time, putting away the snagger, the glove, the coffee can, rehearsing what he would say. "I'm having these what-you-call *episodes*," he would tell her. "Things smother me. They come in too close." He took off his cap, scraped a hand through his hair, returned the cap to his head. Nothing sounded right.

He climbed the outside steps, went through the kitchen into the bathroom, hung his cap and jacket on the double-scoop hooks, used the toilet, then washed his hands with Lava soap, pushing the gritty gray suds under his nails, making concentric squares with his palms, and clapping his hands all different ways as if washing away his confusion. He used Ivory soap on his face, rinsed it and patted it dry. He considered his image in the mirror. He pushed down the cowlick at the crown of his head, but it bounced back. The older he got, the balkier his hair got. At the moment, he had two inches of old-man stubble at the tallest part of him. Elsa had been saying it was time for her to cut it. She was right. He said to the mirror, "I better not say I fell. She'd get to worrying."

In the kitchen he stood with his hands behind him as Elsa took a flatbread from the oven, set it on edge, and cut off a canoe of crust. Steam was rising from the cut—or was that his imagination? She had curled her hair, he noticed. Her dress had purple circles on it. With his eyes closed, he sorted out the smells—bread, salmon, hash browns, snap beans, tomatoes, dill pickles, *pulla* sweet bread, coffee—smells that defined his existence. When he opened his eyes, he saw a horse by the stove. Then it was gone.

But something else was wrong, something more than the horse. He stared at the barometer, the African violets, the table set for two. Who else was coming? He moved around the corner and looked into the front room. Rag rugs on top of carpets. Who else used to do that, put rugs on top of other rugs? The place was nice enough, but *whose*? A Regulator clock on the wall clucked at him, *Tut-tut*, as if guessing his troubles.

Then it came to him. This was *his* place. He should have known! "Every man's home is his . . . puzzle," he improvised, catching the joke.

Back in the kitchen, he tried a little grin at Elsa. "I saw the darnedest thing out there. This spider caught a grasshopper . . ."

It was no use. She had on her sacrificial face, that longsuffering, bemused look of hers, and now that he had stopped talking he heard her saying "Mmm?" at intervals, at nothing at all. He remembered a truth he kept forgetting. His wife took events in stride. To Elsa, nothing could be more ho-hum than a spider catching a grasshopper. He had been spoofed by his own short sight! His wife was practical to a fault. Her practicality kept the house clean but could never encompass his awe. When it came to the wondrous borders of life, the luminous bits that needed time to grow, or were partly hidden, or were funny by themselves, Isak was on his own.

She put bread slices on a plate and took the plate to the table. Other foods were there in serving bowls. "Better eat before it gets cold," she said. She took off her apron and draped it on the step-stool at the end of the table. He recognized the stool, a black metal contraption that squeaked when a person unfolded it. Where Nell sits. *Sat.* Was Nell ever in this house?

Elsa sat on the bench and scooted smartly to the middle. Isak could see his place across from hers. Not a real place. He stood like a child seeking permission. No, he amended, like the master of the house, making up his mind, or . . . ? He ran out of words.

"Matt called," Elsa said. She pried a truant hair from her forehead and poked it into her curls. "He said he has some late squash. If you want it."

"Sure, we could get some," Isak said. Still, he did not sit down.

She sighed. "Uh!-*uh!*" She flicked the skirt of her dress, smoothed it over her thighs. "He mentioned the toaster. I tried to find it but couldn't."

"It's there. In the garage."

"I couldn't find it."

"It's there," he repeated.

Reaching behind her, Elsa snapped off the stem of a spent geranium bloom and set it on the counter, then reached again, this time to her apron, and wiped her fingers. Isak could smell geranium juice. It stayed in his nostrils. Odors like that didn't bother Elsa. That was another difference between them.

"Did you get it fixed?" she asked him. She had that way about her, push, push, did you get it done? When she knew the answer, which was no.

Isak knew what the problem was. The kitchen was too far from the meadow. He couldn't bridge the two. He tasted words for the meadow. *Dangerous solace. Speaking silence.* He needed to go there. Elsa had too many answers, she took away his air.

In an instant, he made up his mind. He would figure things out, yes, but later. First he'd go to the meadow and be heard, have an audience with the Creator, *then* talk to Elsa, maybe even the doctor, about . . . his problem. But for now (and here was the nub of it), he would let Elsa be Elsa. He would honor her sanctuary (the house) and the comforts she provided (the considerable comforts she insisted on providing) and keep that other sacred space (the meadow) to himself.

Heavy with his secret, and astonished at feeling twice rich, he said, "Not yet," and sat down to eat Elsa's food.

Every day after noon dinner, they rested, Elsa on the bed, Isak in the recliner in the front room. On this day, for once, she wasn't watchful. She was snoring when he left.

When he got to the bush with the fat berries, he set the two-by-six on end and lowered it to make a gangway. He stood back to gauge the distance.

"Heck," he said, "I can get to those, *easy.*"

He had crept four or five inches on hands and knees—the coffee can clunking the plank every time he moved—when the two-by-six tipped and dropped him through a hole in the vines. He felt the bone snap before he felt pain. He had time to register: left leg, thigh bone, *femur.*

An image came forward to mingle with the terror—himself climbing blackberry bushes, the same trick he had tried today. He saw his many errors. It was winter back then. The vines were tough and dry, like rodeo ropes. He wore leather gloves on *both* hands, and hip waders, and a quilted jacket. He crossed the thicket on a whim, to see if he could do it, not to pick berries. It wasn't even berry season. Besides, that was a long time ago, when he was just a pup.

More images jumped in before he could stop them, Elsa waking up, going to the front room, finding him gone.

Before the spinning dark could take away the meadow, he said, "She'll be worried. I'd better head home."

Two

Add Salt

Nell stirred odds and ends in a basket meant for fruit—firecracker, ferry schedule, toothpicks, hair band, swim card, receipts, pennies-off coupons, nail file, flea collar, bottle of bubbles. Not there. She drew a small wooden box toward her, lifted the lid and found a jumble of recipes either written on three-by-five cards or snipped from magazines and folded into lumps. She took out an ice cream booklet. It fell open to "Summer Picnic Vanilla." She made a sullen face. The last time we tried *that*, it came out slushy. And salty. The family's falling apart! We can't even make ice cream anymore.

She pulled two other recipe boxes her way and lifted the tops. More recipes, topsy-turvy, the result of six years on the move—storage units (lock it and forget it), furnished rental homes (four years in Manila, two years on Hook Island), and the unpacking process itself (children yelling, "Lookit!" and streaming items through the air). Jed was ten and maturing fast, the owner of arms and legs too long and too eager, marionette limbs that jumped at unexpected times. When the recipes flew by accident, he knelt as if humbled by such mysteries, gathered the cards and crammed them into recipe boxes, any which way. That was three months ago. It seemed like years.

Drawing out "Hot Lemon Pudding," Nell felt a tickle of interest. There was Jane's Australian backhand on a half-sized note labeled, "Department of Civil and Geological Engineering, School of Engineering and Applied Science, Princeton University, Princeton, New Jersey, 08540." Nell shared a kinship of foreignness with Jane Morgan from Sydney and Olga Olafsdottir from Reykjavik. Nell felt as alien in ritzy residential-Princeton as

Jane and Olga felt in the United States. Dan's teaching assistantship came with an unusual perk, the use of the home of a colleague on sabbatical, a handsome saltbox on a street of shade maples. Nell should have been thrilled. But she was bored. Her immediate neighbors were socialites, satellites in a whirl that sounded to her like death. Committee work and fancy balls? No, thanks! Jane and Olga were artists married to guest lecturers, parked for a year in student barracks. Nell liked sitting in their kitchens with cooking going on and toddlers underfoot. Would she recognize Jane's son, Pip, if she saw him today? He would be twenty-three, same as Max. She couldn't recall the names of Olga's boy and girl, picturesque children with platinum hair and lake-blue eyes. In any weather they wore chunky sweaters with reindeer and snowflakes knitted in. Nell babysat for Olga once and no more. The children screamed and clawed the door until dawn, when their picturesque parents came home and saved everyone further grief. Coffee spots made the recipe hard to read. Nell had never made "Hot Lemon Pudding."

Nor had she made "Jane's Rye Bread, Best Ever"—Jane's breezy title for her own bread. Nell took the bread recipe that was clipped to the pudding recipe and skimmed it for the word she knew she would find. "Add dissolved yeast to other liquids, then fling into 2½ cups rye flour and 3½ cups white flour . . . ." *Fling!* She loved that word. It had *verve.* Dan had learned to appreciate rye bread on the Russian fishing boat he worked on, the summer they met; he claimed he *existed* on rye bread for three months. Nell thought she might bake him some.

Her writing could wait. She would do at least one job from beginning to end. Too much in life was never-ending! At the kitchen mirror, she slid the upholstered elastic band from her braid, re-braided the last inches of hair, put the band back on. She went to the den and got a pen, a bunch of new divider cards (she had been planning this project for some time), and a pack of blank labels.

Nell got settled on a bar stool at the kitchen island and dumped three recipe boxes on the counter. Leaving the recipes in a heap, she wrote new labels for two sizes of dividers, then stood the four-by-six dividers—"Appetizers" to "Vegetables"—in the bigger box and split the three-by-five dividers in half and put "Appetizers" to "Fish" in one small box and "Meat" to "Vegetables" in the other. She added another category to each box and marked it "Miscellaneous."

She turned to the recipes. "Cookie Press Butter Cookies" came up twice. Both cards bore the name "Roz." Nell groaned. Roz could do everything, and do it with style. Roz skied, water-skied, played tennis and racquetball, baked mountain-high bread, traveled the globe, served imported wines, cooked fantastic meals, knew operas, played football with the men. It never *was* a balanced friendship—Roz and Gabe charmed by Dan (classy, mysterious) but baffled by Nell (no style). Too many killer rides in an open MG! Too many haikus in the tops of trees! Nell and Dan later heard that Roz and Gabe had divorced. Nell threw away one copy and filed the other, tapping it firmly in place, leaving the past behind.

"Swedish Pancakes." Steve's pancakes! Amoeba-shaped, heavenly with lingonberries. Dressed in jeans and boots in the Pacific Northwest, she imagined loafers and tweeds in New England, football weekends with Berit and Steve. We *laughed* with the Svensons! Nell was taken aback. How long since we've seen them? Seventeen years. How long since we've laughed with friends?

Disconcerted, she put away "Swedish Pancakes." She picked up "Cuffy's Brownies" and was back at Mrs. Smythe's house in student-Princeton, a state-of-being far removed from residential-Princeton. When Professor Smythe died, he left his wife their elegant three-story home and no money. An uncured gambler, he had lost their savings but managed to save the house. To support herself, Mrs. Smythe turned her house into a labyrinth of furnished flats, elfish apartments favored by students. Nell and Dan felt lucky to get one. There was no bedroom, and they had to walk through the bathroom to get to the kitchen, and once in the kitchen they could hardly turn around, but they loved the place. The main room had a double daybed, a fireplace, a desk, an oak wardrobe, two high walls of windows, and sheer white curtains that multiplied sunbeams. Cuffy and Marcus Corson lived above them in the attic, a rambling set of rooms with slanted ceilings. Cuffy baked something chocolate every day. Cuffy and Nell taught English at different schools, and if Cuffy got home first, the smell of brownies met Nell in the parking yard. Twenty years and three thousand miles from Mrs. Smythe (who was probably dead by now), Nell had a belated miff: Mrs. Smythe liked the Corsons, but not *us*. One day, after inspecting the trash cans in the alley, Mrs. Smythe accused Dan, "You have the wrong amount of trash!" That evening the two couples joked and tried to guess. Did she mean too little or too much? Too much, it turned out. Mrs. Smythe suspected Nell and Dan of having friends stay overnight. The renter she *should* have suspected was Miss Tryon down the hall, a storky, righteous bachelorette who snuck her mousey lover out before dawn, she peeking out to see if the coast was clear, somehow missing Nell peeking back, he scuttling down the steps, hugging his briefcase as if it rendered him invisible. Nell and Dan didn't have friends stay overnight. They just invited friends over for meals, often. *I actually used these recipes.*

She stood up, windmilled her arms, sat back down, and picked up "Snowflake Cookies." Given to her by Mrs. Sorvino, Dee's mother, in Trenton. Nell grinned and pronounced it the right way, "*Treh'*-hn." After they quit partying with Roz and Gabe, she and Dan made a turnaround and ran a street ministry in Trenton's "Italian ghetto." Most of the kids had nicknames—Jacky the Hand, Razz Man. Even the girls had nicknames. Nell and Dan were house-sitting one month in a big historic house, and they invited the Trenton kids for supper. Someone stole the antique silver from the sideboard. The next day, at the diner by the school, Dan told the kids what had happened. Jacky the Hand got out of the booth and stood over the others, spread his hands at his waist, palms down, and shifted them outward, making a vow as wide and smooth as a highway. "The Hand'll take care of it," he said. The silver reappeared the same day. The recipe called for room temperature butter, heavy cream, and powdered sugar. On the card Nell had written, "Lots of work but worth it."

When she picked up "Sigrid's Raised Doughnuts," she was eight again, living in Chalmer, Alaska, and Sigrid and Hitch Albertson ran the rooming house next door. Sigrid was a tall, blonde, flamboyant Swede with a smarty grin and a takeover chin. Nell's mother, Elsa, was a quiet-mannered, brown-haired, moderate-featured Finn of medium height. Despite their differences, the two women were friends. As a child, Nell pretended they made up one person, sort of a combined mother. Sigrid's sister Carol cleaned houses in St. Paul, and when her employers grew weary of their sable coats and crepe dresses they gave them to Carol. Carol had simple tastes, so she mailed the clothes to Sigrid. Sigrid didn't mind that they were hand-me-downs or that other Chalmer women wore clothes more fitting for a fishing town, which is what Chalmer was. She looked theatrical in designer suits and feathered hats. She had a habit of opening the back door at Nell's house and yelling for Nell's mother, *"Halonen!* You home?" When Sigrid left her husband, she also left town, and the two women lost contact. When Nell and Dan got married, her parents came outside to Southwest Washington to live near Nell's maternal grandparents. Sigrid seemed lost forever. On a trip to Alaska, Elsa tried to find her. A woman in line at the Chalmer post office heard Elsa ask the postmaster for a Sigrid Albertson. (He had no record of an address change.) The woman said that Sigrid had left town in the middle of the night, years ago, without telling a soul. (Elsa had known *that* much already.) "Usually," the woman said, "everyone knows everything! But no one knows where Sigrid went." In a final attempt to find Sigrid, Elsa dialed *O* and asked the long distance operator for any Sigrid Albertson, anywhere in Alaska. The operator whispered, *"Halonen!* Izzat *you?"* Elsa put her hand to her mouth, then to her chest, laughed and caught her breath. Sigrid said she was living in Bear Paw, near Sitka, about as far from Hitch as she could go without changing states. She had never remarried, never had children. Talking on the job was against the rules, but Sigrid was a person who flaunted rules. When Nell was little, she learned facts of life from Sigrid that had nothing to do with procreation.

"Deep Dish Berry Pie" appeared next, her mother's recipe. Her mother's pies were legendary. Nell had met strangers who, after hearing her maiden name, Halonen, shouted, "You mean you're *Elsa's* daughter? She sure can bake a pie!" For fifteen years, until she retired a month ago, her mother had baked pies and breads for Portia's Porch, a popular family restaurant in Vancouver. Her fame was justified. She adjusted recipes to make them her own, snuck grated lemon peel into a lemon pie, that sort of thing. She was an expert at anything that went on in a kitchen. Her canned goods were superior; her reds stayed red; her greens stayed green; the quality held up all winter. The one time when Nell tried canning, the tomatoes popped their lids and foamed at the mouth and made a lethal brown mess. But she and her mother did share one talent, pie-baking. When she got back to the States and could buy familiar ingredients again, Nell baked three magazine-cover pies—two apple pies with hilly, sugar-crackled crusts, and a cherry pie with a lattice top. She set them on trivets, expecting praise. Addie, then four, was crestfallen. "Oh," she said. "Are you trying to make pies? Are you trying to be like Grandma?"

Nell got up and filled her coffee cup. Yes, Addie, Grandma is the pinnacle, the standard against which all baking is measured. And you're right. I'll never catch up. She picked up a stack of index cards bound with a rubber band. Menus. Before the children were born, she kept track of lunches and party meals she had eaten at friends' homes and at restaurants. She removed the rubber band. The top card read, "Randolph Coffee House, San Francisco, three courses: (1) lentil soup, small black-seed rolls, wine, green salad; (2) white rice, chopped green onions, almonds, celery, served in bowls on a board; (3) coffee, pastries." Another card: "Cassie's Luncheon for Emily." On it Nell had written, "Shrimp-stuffed tomatoes, artichoke hearts, berry iced tea, *petit fours.*" (*Petit fours?*) She had no memory of Cassie, or Emily, either. She ruffled through the pack. Some cards described meals she herself had served guests. *I wrote down menus so I wouldn't repeat them with the same people! That's how often we had company!* In a studied backhand very different from her natural printing (in red ink, no less), she had recorded what she served the Lindbergs for breakfast. "Strawberries tipped in powdered sugar, sausage links, poached eggs on trimmed toast, cinnamon rolls, coffee." The card gave no hint as to why the Lindbergs had stayed the night. They lived a mile away. She found plans for a wedding supper she had apparently given for Charlotte.

"Chicken curry with three chutneys, crumbled fried bacon, minced hard-cooked eggs, sliced bananas, chopped tomatoes, toasted coconut. Currant rice. Green salad. White wine. Strawberry shortcake." (*Currant rice?*) Charlotte was long divorced and out of touch.

Nell dropped the cards into a three-by-five box behind the divider called "Menus" and returned to the recipes.

"Four Cheese Fondue." Midtown Manhattan, the McNaughtons' walkup. Patty and Jim spent a graduate year in Switzerland and brought back a fondue recipe that called for four imported cheeses. They found the cheeses in New York and invited Dan and Nell for fondue. Dan and Nell climbed six flights up to the McNaughtons' room, stepped in, and were swept away—candlelight and jazz, the city lit up, wine and cheeses blending. The four had to take turns getting to the table, opening and closing the door to let each person climb over the bench—but oh, the fondue! The fun, the conversation! How could two couples enjoy an evening so much, then drift off and never meet again?

It took a while to get past Manhattan. She and Dan met in Anchorage the summer he worked on the Russian fishing ship, and he swept her into a first love/lifetime love and to New York right after the wedding. They lived in midtown Manhattan at the Tetherton Institute, where Dan studied foreign affairs; Nell taught four-year-olds uptown. They lived on floor six at Tetherton, ran laps in the basement, visited friends on floor eight, ate in the cafeteria on twelve, played frenetic ping-pong on thirteen, and sent volleyballs sailing off the roof toward the George Washington Bridge. They witnessed a shooting, chased crowds to see Tito, Eisenhower, Khrushchev, saw their first opera, discovered Birdland and jazz, stood in line for standing-room-only Broadway tickets, moved their VW from one side of the street to the other on alternate days, according to regulations, and got tickets anyway. They saw Princeton in football frenzy and Boonton, New Jersey, in the rain. They were too busy to be homesick, and so Christmas caught them off guard.

The day before the Christmas break, Nell mummied her charges in snowsuits and handed them over to governesses or parents. Wishing her fellow teachers a happy holiday, she hurried down to the street. Crowds pushed her and taxi tires threw slush, but the evening ahead held promise, and she was eager to see Dan.

The concert lived up to expectations. The members of the chorale—a dozen Tetherton students and their spouses, including Dan and Nell—did their best for the conductor, an animated enthusiast who had turned their motley group into a respectable madrigal chorus. First they sang outdoors—Dickensian courtyards, snow, navy blue night. Then they sang in Tetherton's parlor, a mahogany cave stifled in evergreens. Bayberry candles put them centuries back. Burgundy velvet draped out the cold. In high spirits, the singers made it through "From Out of the Wood Did a Cuckoo Fly, 'Coo-coo!'" without laughing, a major feat. The parlor soon reeled with holly-and-ivy songs. The medieval carols were achingly poignant. Nell didn't feel the jolt until the music stopped.

The crowd burst into jubilant chaos, parents pushing toward sons and daughters, hugging, cheering. No one was waiting for Nell and Dan.

They held hands and watched. Until then, she hadn't known the cost of living so far from her parents. She hadn't treasured her upbringing or incorporated its wealth into her new life. Preoccupied with learning new ways, she had effectively blocked out the old. Her parents had waited in vain for evidence that she needed them. That night after the concert, she realized she *did* need them, very much.

Not that things were rosy with them. As an only child, she felt a heavy but undefined duty toward her parents. She called them and wrote them letters, but she never had much to say, or what she said seemed frivolous. She didn't know how to please them.

She held a stack of recipes in one hand and fluttered them with fingers of the other. Stopping at random, she came to "Cobb Salad, Mary's New Year's Eve Potluck, 1966." Nell had brought ingredients for the salad, including a homemade dressing that had never failed. When it came time to set up the buffet, the hostess, Mary Styvesant, a whirlwind chef who ran a cooking school, offered to mix Nell's salad. Nell said okay, thinking Mary would surely do it better than she could. But the salad turned out wrong. It needed . . . what? Thirteen years after the party, she lectured herself: *Stay in control!* Then she smiled, remembering someone else at that party who lost control. A graduate student was sitting cross-legged on the floor, holding a plate of food, packed in among other students and caught up in loud talk, when, unhappily for him, one of those silences that can fall on a crowd, fell, just as he suffered a lapse of alimentary poise. A terrific blast it was. It rebounded off the walls. No one looked at anyone else. Not one word was said by anyone but the offender, who said his one word in a small voice, "Oops." Still, no one said anything. No one laughed about what everyone was dying to laugh about. Finally, festivities resumed. Since then, after a mistake of any kind, Dan and Nell could lean to each other, say, "Oops," and laugh, celebrating the fact that they were together then and were together still.

In spite of side-trips, she made progress. Before long, she could line up three organized recipe boxes. She had another idea. Raising her fist in the air, she said, "I'm going to write a *recipe* . . . (she raised her fist again) . . . for how to get *unstuck!*"

Nell went to the desk, sat down, rolled a sheet of paper into the typewriter, and typed a list of household jobs that niggled at her, estimating the time it would take her to do each one. She typed the names Dan, Jed, Addie and listed activities she wanted to do with each. She typed the names of friends who lived far away, sports she had once enjoyed, new sports she wanted to try, trips she wanted to take. She made a note to call the adoption agency. At the end, she had three pages of notes.

She retrieved a clipboard and snapped the pages to it. Running her finger down her list of friends, she chose Berit. In her address book, she found the Svensons' phone number. Did they still live in Boston? She dialed.

"Hello?"

That voice. Liquid velvet! She would recognize it anywhere. "Berit, it's Nell."

"Nell? I can't believe it. You've been on my mind all week!"

"What are you doing at home?"

Berit made a noise, "Heh-ah-heh." The same laugh! "If you thought I wasn't at home," Berit said, "why did you call?"

"Shouldn't you be at your office?"

"Remember, we're three hours later."

"Oh. Right. Are you in the middle of supper?"

"No, I was running to the store. I came back for my glasses and the phone was ringing . . . . Nell? Are you okay?"

"I'm fine."

"How is everyone?"

"Dan works too hard, but his hair's still red, no gray. Cute as ever."

"The kids?"

"They're great. Max teaches in the Philippines. Addie and Jed keep us hopping at home. We want to adopt another girl."

"Really? You're brave." Berit was a career woman who had never taken time off to have children. "Nell, you sound a little *off*. What's going on?"

Leave it to Berit. She always zeroed in on what was bothering a person. She was a psychotherapist, and her profession sloshed over into everything she did or said.

"Well, the column nags me," Nell said, "so I keep writing. But I feel . . . I don't know—*off*, I guess."

"Off, how?"

"Early menopause? Or the same ol' same ol'."

"Are you sleeping too much? Gaining weight, no interest in sex?"

"You mean depressed. I'm not depressed. I'm just . . . restless. But I did sort recipes today and *that* felt good." She said this with mockery, but it still sounded ludicrous.

"Great! But don't sit there feeling bad. Are you exercising? Taking vitamins? Maybe you need the song."

Berit and her famous advice! In college, Berit told friends who felt bad for any reason to sing "Do Your Ears Hang Low?" until they felt better. It usually worked. On her end of the line, Berit sang, "Do . . . your . . . ears hang low? Do they wobble to and fro?"

Taking the clipboard with her, Nell chinned the receiver and stretched the phone cord into the kitchen. Berit was singing, "Can . . . you . . . tie 'em in a knot? Can you tie 'em in a bow?" Nell made an amazed face at the mirror and mouthed, *It's working.*

"Can . . . you . . . throw 'em over your shoulder like a continental soldier?"

Nell checked to see if she had yeast. She did. She shut the refrigerator door with her boot. Gripping the clipboard, she wrote, "Buy rye flour."

The instant she hung up, the phone rang. Her mother said, "Who were you talking to? I tried three times. Your father broke his leg."

This was something Nell dreaded on a daily basis—bad news about her parents. Compared to the rest of the world, compared even to her children, her parents seemed vulnerable, beyond her ability to protect them. "Poor Daddy! What happened?"

"I found him in the blackberries over by the towers."

"Poor Daddy," Nell said again. "How is he? Is he at home?"

Elsa took in a double inward sigh, "Yah!-*huh!*" She paused as if leaving the phone to make sure that he was, indeed, at home. When she spoke again, she sounded tired. "He's sleeping. We got home an hour ago."

"Who's 'we'?"

"Joe from down the road."

"Mom? You want me to come down? I could bring the kids."

"No, it's okay, we'll be fine."

"Let's think about it, anyway," Nell said. "You must've tried calling when I was talking to Berit. Remember Berit? I've told you about her. My friend in Boston?" She did this too often when talking to her mother, escaped to other topics. But diversion never worked. The words between mother and daughter didn't have enough juice. Mother and daughter dried each other out.

Breaking a small silence, Nell asked, "How did you find him?"

"He was late getting back, so I went to where he likes to pick, and there he was."

"How did you get him home?"

"Well. I got Joe, and he put a mattress in his truck . . ."

"Mom! Jed came in all bloody! . . . Oh, it's just a scrape. I'll call you back."

As she put down the receiver, Nell felt a ping in her chest. Her mother needed to talk, and Nell had hung up on her. Forced to choose between her child and her mother, Nell had chosen her child. Any way you looked at it, her mother had lost.

Three

The Travel Bug

Elsa sighed, thinking this was just like Nell, off on a trot, not staying anyplace long enough to really *be* there. A regular Nervous Nellie. Elsa couldn't seem to find a settled place with her—her own daughter. Even in person, they spoke past each other, into the space around the head, meaning to connect but missing by a hair.

She went to the front room to check on Isak. He lay on his back on the opened hide-a-bed, his left leg encased in a cast and raised to forty-five degrees. He was sleeping with a grizzled frown as if trying to find words to an old song. She went to the kitchen, added water to the tea kettle, set it on the burner and clicked it on. What kind of a night would this be? She recounted the day—Isak passed out in the berry patch, the ride to the hospital, Isak in the bed of Joe's truck, her worry about his pain, the nurses, the doctors, the ride home in the thickest fog she had ever seen, Isak resting his cast on a pillow on Joe's lap, Elsa sitting forward between the men on a few inches of bench seat. At home, Joe helped Isak up the steps, into the house, and into the bathroom, got him into pajamas (Elsa first pinked off the left leg at the knee), opened the hide-a-bed, eased Isak onto it, jerry-rigged the pulley, hooked him to it, and covered him with blankets. Before going back home, Joe started a chart for Elsa, a place for noting the date, time, number of Isak's pills, the effects of medication. What would she have done without Joe?

She tried to guess what this injury would do to Isak. Whenever he was indoors too much, he got fidgety, and even before the accident he had been indoors too much. With his mind going blank the way it did, and his

24

putziness slowing to pudding speed, she had grown impatient. He could come out with the craziest things! Yet, now, with Isak sedated, she missed him. She missed the Isak she first laid eyes on, in the blizzard that hadn't quite arrived.

Elsa and Grace Ann were out in their father's 1932 Ford coupe, taking food to the Talvelas, two miles from home. Einar Talvela was out of work due to injury. When they finished the errand, Elsa foolishly drove on. Newly licensed and feeling brave, she aimed the Ford at Tag Wilson's store, three miles farther. By some miracle, Tag had Florida oranges in the middle of winter, in Alaska! Elsa wanted to surprise her parents with a bag of oranges. Grace Ann pulled off her mittens and took a sandwich from her bag; she was the kind of person who ate nonstop but stayed slim as a rod, whereas Elsa, who ate far less, had a middle-age spread at seventeen. Snowflakes were spiraling downward, one at a time. The road felt cushioned—five inches of snow on a slick of ice. Once in a while, the tires dug through to the ice and spun in place, then caught traction and rolled on.

Snow started falling in earnest. Poufs as big as cats' paws came *down down down* around the car, turning the air furry. Landmarks disappeared. The windshield wipers worked hard, but snow was stacking on the front window. The cleared space got smaller and smaller. Soon Elsa had just a tiny triangle to see through.

She decided to turn back. But she turned too fast and put the car in a spin. In rapid sequence, the girls screamed, Elsa jerked the wheel in the opposite direction of the spin, Grace Ann clapped her sandwich to the wheel like an oven mitt to a pot handle, the car fishtailed, Elsa yelled, "Let go!" and pushed Grace Ann away, Grace Ann yelled, "Watch out!" and the car crashed into a snow bank, bucketed, shivered, and grew still.

Elsa shut off the engine. She said, inconsequentially, "How about that? We're facing the same way we were going!" The sisters laughed in shaky relief at the bump they had endured, the jelly mess on the steering wheel, their good luck at being alone on the road with no other cars to bump into, and the bare-naked fact that they weren't dead.

Elsa turned the key. The motor came alive. But when she shifted into reverse the tires spun in place. She tried again, without success.

The wind gave a few strong howls. Snow flew horizontally at the car. Elsa was starting to worry. How could she get the Ford home to her father?

A truck drove up behind her and pulled beside the Ford. The young man in the driver's seat reached to the passenger's side and rolled down the window. "Need help?"

She nearly yelped. He had urgent features and crystal blue eyes, and a beckoning but guarded look. Elsa took pride in her self-sufficiency, and usually it galled her to ask for help, but she liked the idea of *this* young man doing the helping.

She said the obvious. "We're stuck."

He nodded and drove forward twenty feet, parked, and got out.

Having handed over her problem, Elsa got out and leaned on the nose of the Ford. Snowflakes landed on her eyelashes. She winked them off. She squared her scarf on her forehead and retied it. Squinting in the falling snow, the young man reached into the bed of his truck, took out a shovel plus two planks, and set off toward the Ford. His footsteps squeaked, *hunk . . . hunk.* He slipped once but artfully regained his balance. The flaps of his sheepskin cap banged his jaw as he walked. Like every boy she knew, he resisted buckling his chin strap.

Several feet from Elsa, he glanced up. Again, those eyes! He was about her height—she was tall for a girl, he was medium for a man—and had a wide-built, strong-looking body. She wanted to know if he squinted in every kind of weather, why he didn't buckle his chin strap, where he lived, where he'd been all her life. She wanted to know every last thing about him.

As he started to shovel, Elsa looked into the Ford. Grace Ann was running a hanky over the steering wheel—cleaning off sandwich parts, Elsa guessed. Grace Ann hadn't seen what an apparition this guy was, and he hadn't seen her. Grace Ann attracted boys the way a lamp attracted bugs. Elsa planned to get to this one first.

"Thanks for stopping," she said. In the close acoustics of snow, her voice fell with a thud. "I'm Elsa Sepanen. That's my sister, Grace Ann. We live over there." She waved behind her down the road.

26

He looked up to catch her wave. "I'm Isak Halonen . . . Sepanen? Halonen? At least we know we're all Finns." He smiled briefly with his mouth closed. She inhaled sharply. He had a dimple in one cheek. She *liked* a dimple on a man.

After shoveling for five minutes, he wedged one plank lengthwise behind the front right tire, the other behind the rear right tire. He said, "Mind if I drive it out?"

"Be my guest." She handed him the keys and went to stand across the road. Grace Ann got out and stood beside her.

"Better go over there," he said, pointing to a place farther away. The girls moved to that spot. He got into the driver's seat, shut the door, and took hold of the steering wheel. He lifted his hands and sniffed his gloves.

He opened the door. "Grape," he called.

"Oh." Elsa scooped up a clutch of snow and hurried with it to the car. "My sister. She got a little excited." She crimped her face in sisterly tolerance. Taking his gloved hands in her mittened hands, she scrubbed his gloves clean. The touch of him through wool and leather excited her. His face appeared molded, as if angles had been temporarily pinched in and then had stayed that way. Again he showed the dimple, again causing her breaths to be short and hot.

She crossed the road to stand by Grace Ann. He started the engine. Shifting into reverse, he tried backing onto the planks. The first try didn't work. He got out and repositioned the planks, jamming them farther under the tires. Back in the driver's seat, he accelerated in bursts, rocking the car back and forth, the tires kissing the planks with every rocking. On a final, stronger rocking, he backed the car up onto the boards.

He pulled forward, made a U-turn, and faced the car toward the girls' home. He got out and handed Elsa the keys. She thanked him. She was free to drive off, but she didn't want to. As Grace Ann got into the Ford, Elsa forced conversation.

"Are you visiting around here?"

He nodded. "With a guy from the last job. His folks live on the point."

"Really? Who?"

"Charlie Soon."

"Where are you from?"

"North Dakota."

"That's pretty far away. How'd you get to Alaska?"

He hesitated, evaluating her. "I came for work. I was seventeen."

"Seventeen? *I'm* seventeen." She evaluated him in return. "I suppose you're an old man by now."

"Twenty-nine."

Not bad, she thought. Twelve years between them. He seemed gathered-together as a person, considerate and hard-working. In reality, it was too late for evaluation. She had her eyes set on this Isak Halonen.

But she made sure nothing showed. "You don't look that old," she said.

"So I'm told."

"Why did you leave North Dakota?"

His body gave way, enough to show hurt. "My father . . . We had some trouble."

Elsa wanted to shield him, so she talked about something else. "Why Alaska? Because you like snow? North Dakota must have had plenty-snow if you like snow."

Grace Ann sang from the car, "Ex-*cuse* me! It's *co*-old!"

"I'd better head home," Elsa said. "A bunch of us are skating on the river on Sunday. Why don't you come on by. Around two, even if the weather's bad."

She gave him a stern look. "You're not married or anything."

The planes of his face went into tight formation. "No."

"Good. It's the next turn past the old school road."

"You want me to follow you home, make sure you get there?"

"No, thanks. Just come over on Sunday."

Or the Isak of a month ago, when he made my heart stop. She was in the front room, knitting. He was in the garage. He snuck up the outside steps and opened the kitchen door, backed down, stretched out on the steps, and placed his head on the landing so that just his face would show to someone in the house. He moaned, *"El-sa!"* She came around the corner and saw his disembodied head grinning at her.

That Isak! She held in a smile. She never knew *what* he'd come up with.

He whimpered in his sleep. She could tell that he wanted to roll over, but the pulley wouldn't let him. Reaching under him, she massaged his back as well as she could from that position. She went to the TV and switched it on. The volume was too loud. She turned it down. Dots flitted on the screen, cars, people, a building, barely discernible. She tried the other channel, but it was snowy. Reception was poor in the mountains. Elsa and Isak were lucky to have two channels that worked. Worked *sometimes.*

If she couldn't watch the news, she could knit. She sank into the easy chair, reached over the arm, felt around in her canvas bag, and brought out a ball of red yarn impaled with knitting needles and attached to eight circles of stitching, the start of Nell's Christmas cap. The last time Nell and the children came to visit, Elsa gave Addie some old yarn scraps for a project. Addie found Elsa's bag as well and helped herself to a new ball of yarn. Digging in the bag, she dropped stitches from Jed's Christmas cap. Addie was not the most careful of children, Elsa had noticed. Addie assumed that everything in the world was hers for the taking.

Usually she drank coffee, but when she felt *phooey*, like now, she had tea. Strong tea with milk and sugar made any problem smaller. She stood at the kitchen door window, took a sip of her tea, and sighed an in-sucking sigh, "Yuh- *huh!*" She considered herself an active-type person. Yet here she was, trapped in the house. She snapped on the porch light and held back the curtain at the door window. A light drizzle was fizzing the air, a mist so fine it was hardly visible. The real rains were due any time. *Gullywashers.* Rain-forest amounts of rain. Two hundred inches a year! Buckets of rain for months on end. In Hockinson, where she grew up, just fifty miles from where she stood, she had endured rain for fifteen years. In Alaska, she got a break. But, when Isak retired, where did he retire to? To Cougar, to more rain!

Compressing her lips, she thought about the seasons. The cabin got more sun in the fall than in the summer. In the fall, the sun slanted low and found spaces between trees and made streaks of light on the kitchen floor. The sight of them made Elsa happy, but just for an instant. The sun was only joking. In a few days it would leave, pretty much for good, to make way for the serious rain. If she complained about the rain, Isak would smile at her, cagey-like, and say, "'One misty, moisty morning, when foggy was the weather, there I met an old man, clothed all in leather . . . .'" That Isak! To Elsa, *any* weather was better than rain—blizzard, ice storm, hot spell. Rain made her miss places she had never seen—Bali, Tahiti, Hawaii. Even the names were sunny! This winter would be the worst. No job to keep her occupied. She liked her job so much that she often stayed beyond her shift to clean ovens. Rupert, her boss, would say, "Elsa? You plan on sleeping here? Go home!" Rupert had rules in his kitchen, rules she agreed with. "Wash mixer blades right after using." "Clean up spatters the minute they happen." She was going to miss that job.

The next morning, after helping Isak into the bathroom and giving him privacy, she got him back to the couch and turned on the television. Channel 6 was coming in fine. The local newsman had spiffed up for the camera and slicked his hair. She got a metal TV tray from the bedroom closet, snapped the tray to the *X* legs, laid a placemat over the design (a lotus blossom so big it was indecent), set a spoon and the sugar bowl on the mat, and carried the tray to the front room. She poured Isak a cup of coffee and took it to him. She sectioned half a grapefruit, made Malt-o-Meal, buttered a slice of bread, and delivered the food to Isak. She made another trip with pills and a glass of water. She waited while he swallowed the pills.

He regarded his cast with gloom. "What did the doctor say? How long do I have to wear this?" He seemed argumentative, as if he had never heard the details for himself, as if he blamed Elsa for his broken leg.

"Two months or so. Does it hurt?"

"Some."

She was having a spark of an idea. "The pills will help," she said. "I'll call the doctor and see how long the cast stays on."

After the pills had put Isak to sleep, she dialed the number. A nurse answered.

Elsa said, "Could I speak to the doctor, please?"

"May I help you?"

"Well. My husband has a cast on his leg. When does he have to see the doctor?"

"His name?"

Elsa told her Isak's name.

The nurse said, "And you are . . .?"

"His wife. Elsa Halonen."

"One moment." The nurse went off the phone, returned, and said, "We'll see him in a month and change the cast. In another three weeks, we'll see him again and decide if he needs a brace or another cast."

Elsa looked around the corner. Isak appeared to be sleeping, but he wasn't snoring. She turned her back to him. "Can he travel?" she whispered.

"Could you speak up, please?"

Shielding her mouth with her hand, Elsa said, "Eh, can he go on a car trip? If he rides on a big seat so he can stretch his leg?"

"Yes, as long he elevates the leg. Of course, we have to see him in a month."

She found what she wanted in Seattle's Yellow Pages. She had asked Nell to save old phone books for her. She liked to read the ads; they gave an illusion of travel. After referring to "Automobiles, Used" and "Recreational Vehicles" and not seeing what she wanted, she tried "Automobiles, Parts and Repair" and found a business called The Travel Bug. The pen sketch implied that The Travel Bug cut Volkswagen beetles in half and stretched them into limousines. Elsa wondered where they got the parts for the extensions. From Volkswagen beetle *wrecks*, she guessed. The limousine in the sketch had six windows on each side. The artist had drawn streaks outward from the vehicle, suggesting "shiny, new."

The man sounded joyful on the job. "Travel Bug here! We help you escape!"

"Hello?" Elsa had blanched at the word "escape," afraid, irrationally, that someone had told on her. "Eh, do you ever sell bigger rigs? You know, for people going a long way who need a place to sleep?"

"Sure do!" The man shouted a laugh and talked very loudly. "We're the only ones around these parts who *do!*" Elsa moved the phone farther from her ear. "We sell the big ones and the not-so-big. Where you going?"

"Arizona and Florida," she said, feeling dizzy. This was an audacious claim to make. *Arizona* and *Florida!* "Do you have a van big enough for a bathroom and bunks?"

"You called me on the right day! I just happen to have one! A *bus.* A guy and his wife used it for trips and fixed it up the way you need." The car dealer had a rattly, choppy way of talking.

"Does it have beds?"

He chortled. "Sure it does! Lucky for you I got this one in. We don't get the sleepers in that much."

"Well then." She wasn't sure what to ask. "How many miles on it?"

"About 4,000! That's *all!* That's since the overhaul fifteen months ago. It's a 1959 superior custom conversion. The guy put in a Cat 3208 rebuilt engine and a Fuller TRO 910 transmission and an F-145 Timken rear end and custom bumpers . . ."

She interrupted, saying, "Tires?" She assumed he was reading from a printed page. She didn't understand half of what he said.

"It'll have new ones before you get here, you can bet your bottom dollar!"

"Does it have a bathroom?"

"Yup. And a shower, and a couch that makes into a bed. And a nice radio and new brakes. The paint's got some nicks, but what the hey! It's got a six-gallon hot water tank, air conditioner, custom kitchen cabinets, stereo with four speakers, three forty-gallon tanks and takes a hundred and twenty gallons of fuel . . ."

He *was* reading from a printed page. The list sounded fine, but it could wait. Elsa had to think. She said, "Let's see. Hold on." She stretched the line toward the front room, checking to see if Isak's eyes were shut, if his breaths were going in and out at an even pace. They were.

In a half-voice, she said, "How much?"

"Only fifty-five hunnert! One year warrantee on parts!"

Elsa was bolstered. Over the years, she had saved $11,000. from her restaurant pay. She had a mind to spend part of it.

"I'd like to see it," she said.

"You bet! When?"

Things were going faster than she had expected. "My daughter can come see it with her husband. They're in Wilcox."

"You live out of town?"

"Four hours south. Her name is Nell Sanderson."

"And yours?"

"Elsa Halonen." She felt she was taking a big step, giving her name to a used car salesman.

Four

Merry-go-round

Nell stood in the archway holding a stack of folded towels, pointing her entire person at Dan the way an English pointer points at its prey. Having arrived home late after a dinner meeting, Dan had dropped into his recliner with a Pepsi and the newspaper. Nell had already told him about Isak's broken leg, Jed's skinned elbow, her talk with Berit. Obviously there was more. He had his own news, but he needed to unwind first.

"Mom wants to take a road trip," she said. "They did the Al-Can once but not the lower forty-eight." She aimed her forehead at him.

He said, "And?"

"They're going to Arizona to see Grace Ann and to Florida to see Harald." She turned the towel stack endwise.

"And you want to go with her," he said.

"How'd you guess!" Nell put the towels on the desk and dropped into the second recliner. Clicking the handle two positions back, she extended the leg rest. "I worry about her. All that driving? She wants to buy a bus. Up here. She wants us to go see it."

He watched her massage the bed of muscles deep between thumb and forefinger. Pressure on that spot supposedly cured a headache. But Dan had tried it, and it was excruciating. He suspected that it "cured" a headache by upping the ante on pain so high that, when the pressing stopped, a migraine was a piffle by contrast.

He said, "How long will they be gone?"

"Two months."

"Two months?" Dan let his lashes flap. At times like this, he was conscious of their length. They were too long for any man. But they came in handy for making a point. The point he wanted to make here was that "two months" had a meaning Nell didn't know about yet.

"I know, it's a long time," she said, taking the wrong point. "But you could join us sometimes, and I could teach the kids on the road. Best of all, we'd be out of this house!"

"It's like you knew what was coming."

"Knew what was coming?"

"George wants me in Manila for two months."

She rammed the recliner gear ahead two notches, bolting upright. "Two months?"

"Up to that long. Jay has cancer. A type that moves fast."

"I'm sorry to hear that."

"I need to hire and train a new director."

"I don't want you away that long."

"I know. But it might not take two months."

Nell was silent, then she said, "You could see Max."

"That's the best part."

"But it's like we just got back from Manila!" She waved at the cardboard boxes on the den floor, empty or half-full, labeled, "Desk," "Kitchen," "Odds and ends." The boxes had been in storage for six years. She said, "This stuff used to seem so important. But I'm giving away lots of it. And now, with Mom's trip and your Manila job, I say let's give it *all* away! Let's *move*! We're temporary here, anyway. Just moored overnight."

Pleats formed at the corners of her mouth. "I want out of this house."

They had lived there for three months and never felt at home. The house supposedly had everything a family needed, enough bedrooms and bathrooms, large closets, a fireplace, a nice yard, trees, nearness to schools, parks, stores. But it had no personality, no humor. It looked like every other house on the street—low-slung, beige, *smug*. No humor. They moved in on a sunny Saturday, lugging couches, tables, chairs, lamps, and boxes from a U-Haul truck while the neighbors stayed away in droves. Several times since then, Dan had spoken to neighbor men as they did yard work. They were polite but distant. Nell had felt a similar chill from the women. Then, one weekend, four houses on the block changed occupants. Dan learned that most renters on the block worked for the same company, a firm that sent teams to cities on brief assignments. They knew they would be moving soon, so they didn't bother to make new friends. The reason for the chill was mobility.

Nell said, "Let's start over! Anywhere."

"What about adopting?"

"We'll do that later."

"We'd have to break our lease. Lose a month's rent."

"So what! I'm outa here! I have to check the dryer." She leaped to her feet and left the room, wiggling her bottom and laughing back at Dan.

He stayed in his chair, picturing Nell and the kids and her parents traveling across the country. Ending up, where? For sixteen years he had worked for the Roster Fund, a not-for-profit relief organization. While his office was always in a city, he and Nell liked to live in small towns. In the 1960s, when his office was in San Francisco, they lived an hour away at the beach, in Monarch, a slow-down town where dogs actually took naps on the street. To get there, you drove around mountains, farms, orchards, and sleeping-elephant hills, and when you arrived you found two short blocks that ended at the beach, white Victorian houses, a post office, a general store, a bar, two restaurants. Eucalyptus trees made the air smell medicinal. Roads led uphill to a windy mesa crossed by dirt roads and potholes; cows grazed on cliffs above the ocean; artists worked in hideaways in the trees. Monarch residents were ahead of their time, yet old-fashioned. They shunned goods made of plastic. They ground wheat-berries into flour and baked their own bread. They sprouted alfalfa seeds. They wore clothes they either created themselves or found in free-boxes. They did *tai chi* on the beach. They swam naked in the ocean. They conserved natural resources and urged others to do the same. They posted notes on the town bulletin board: "In these days of drought and sun, we never flush for Number One." They used new words: ecology, antioxidant, hydrogenated, free radicals. ("Free radicals" described the residents rather well, Dan thought.) They named their babies Granola (or did Dan make that up?) and Starlight and Sand (*not* made up by Dan) and earned a living by dipping candles or throwing pots or manufacturing hash pipes. Dan drew the line at hash pipes, but he envied his neighbors who worked at home. He worked in Southeast Asia three weeks out of six. The last time he was in Manila, the family lived there with him. This time he would be alone.

He looked down the hall. Where had she disappeared to?

When they moved to Manila, Max was sixteen, Jed was four. Both had deep-set blue eyes, light-brown hair, and chiseled cheeks. Max played the guitar and Jed played the clarinet, urged on by Dan, who had played the banjo since he was a boy. Both boys played team sports, urged on by Nell, who had participated in more sports than Dan had. There the similarities ended.

Max was a loner and a dreamer. Yet any peer group that met him assumed that he was its new leader. At every school he attended, he was thrust into elected office, only to prove over time that he had no interest in leading anyone, anywhere. He was happiest in a wilderness, hiking by himself or with one or two friends. He could be alone for hours, reflecting on precepts that only he knew about.

By contrast, Jed was an *itch*, curiosity on wheels, always on the move except when examining bugs under a microscope or reading science books, gulping facts about dinosaurs, tigers, whales, bats, marmosets, anything that lived and breathed. He spread his excitement around, shouting, "You gotta see this!" He handled food the same way he handled life, like a good machine, shoveling forkfuls to an internal count.

Then there was Addie, sweet Addie. She was the only one of their children who had inherited Dan's red hair (though hers was a tempered auburn). She was a born collector. As soon as she could walk, she started carrying around her favorite things, which varied from day to day. Now that she was six, the habit seemed set for life. She would be a museum curator, Dan predicted, or an archivist—a grown-up collector of favorite things. She had an eye for detail. It was Addie who first noticed a cloudiness in Pajamas' ears. Nell inspected the cat's ears. Sure enough. Ear mites. It was Addie who applied the drops. She had a magic touch with animals. She was the only person in the family who could give the cat a bath. With anyone else, Pajamas leaped out slopping wet. She once told him to *sit there* in the utility sink while she went to get a flea comb from another room. When she got back, he was still sitting meekly in his bath water. Or a veterinarian, he thought.

Now, another separation. He and Nell made separations bearable by staying current on the phone. Nell took care of discipline when he was away. No stacked-up threats of "Wait till Dad gets home." But family life was a merry-go-round—the hand-push kind, spinning as fast as the pushers could push. Arriving home after a three-week trip, he had to run alongside and find a place to jump on, when he really wanted to fall on the couch and take a nap. When this Manila job was over, he hoped to take the next plane home (wherever home was by then) and, from then on, work only in the States.

His goal was simple. To be with his wife and kids.

* * *

Red's nickname didn't come from any hair he had at present. He was bald except for limp gray tassels that fell to his collar and muttonchops the color of hamsters (the shape of hamsters, too, it occurred to Dan). Red's green suit and string tie called attention to his frame, which was pencil-thin, and his smile gave the impression he worked for pleasure, not for anything as base as money. He shook hands with Dan and Nell, gave the kids a cowering grin, and strode ahead of them, a clink of bones in syncopation. With his back straight, he flapped his elbows near his shoulders and shot each leg forward, heel sharply down, toe sharply up and pointed out—a bumpy walk that somehow kept his head steady. Despite an excess of motion, he made headway no faster than if he had walked the normal way. Dan had seen a walk similar to Red's, maybe in the funny papers.

He whispered to Nell, "Gasoline Alley?"

"The Little Tramp."

Red flapped down an aisle of dented hoods, saying over his shoulder that he had three rigs that would "serve Elsa fine and dandy." He twirled and faced Nell, allowing her a shady grin. "Your mother now? She's a mighty fine lady, mighty fine!" He trembled his tassels to emphasize what a fine lady Elsa was. Executing a military turn, he walked on. Nell sucked in her cheeks to Dan, saying with a look that Red had never laid eyes on her mother so how would he know.

Before a windowless white van that had once delivered bread, Red whirled on one foot and belched. "How about this one?" He banged his chest with his fist. "Ock! Sorry! I get the irps when I get atwitter." Smiling through tears, he opened the sliding door. The Sandersons put their heads inside. Table. Bench. Chemical toilet. The interior smelled rancid. The only light came from the front window and the open sliding door. Everyone backed away, rejecting the van.

"Too dark," Jed said.

"Yeah, too dark," Addie said, shielding the bicycle pump and her Kewpie doll from the darkness of the van.

Red said, "No problem," and bounded down the lane of wrecks. He stopped by a hearse that was dead and gone but living a resurrected life as a station wagon. "I did this one myself!" he said with a showman's dash. The casket slide had been replaced by three rows of seats. Still, the hearse looked like a hearse. The exterior was still black, the windows still bordered in puckered black satin.

Addie gave her father a suspicious look. "Is this a dead person's car?"

Dan said, "Yes, Bumps, it's a hearse." He said to Nell, "You could drive up to your aunt's house in this. She'd think her time had come."

She shouldered him. "You're not nice."

Dan turned to Red. "Let's see the bus."

Red belched. "Okay then!"

The vehicle Elsa had chosen sight unseen was shaped like a city bus, which is what it had been, the exterior paint a faded sailboat blue. Red stood at the door and beckoned everyone aboard. The Sandersons climbed the rubber risers and Dan pulled the fisted handle on the folding door. The door folded shut with an accomplished wheeze. Red pounded on the door. Dan let him in. Red closed the door and placed a carpeted square of wood over the step well, producing foot space for the front passenger. He faced the interior of the bus.

"What d' y' think?"

The front seats were stuffed armchairs upholstered in plum velvet. Windows wrapped the front and sides of the bus, promising wide-angle views of the road. At present, the view consisted of torn-apart trucks. Jed got into the driver's seat and took the flat wheel. He pretended to move it. "We could go to *New York* in this! Let's buy it!"

Addie found two low doors behind the driver's seat and unsnapped the snaps. An admirer of secret places, she gushed, "It has cubbies."

"The previous owners fixed it up when they retired," Red said. "They made the side windows bigger and put in the furniture and drove it up and down the West Coast, Seattle to San Diego!" Dan pictured the previous owners cruising in their armchairs, the Mr. computing mileage, the Mrs. knitting socks—retirees on the lam. They made friends at diners and compared finds, the best ribs this side of the Mississippi, the best burgers.

Addie said, "This is our new transportation!"

Dan said, "'Trans-por-*ta*-tion'? Excuse me, young lady, just where do you pick up that kind of language?" She tilted her eyes at him.

The kitchen consisted of sink, work counter, refrigerator, hot plate, a table, two benches, built-in or bolted down. Straps hung from the ceiling at a height for tall people to hang onto. Canada geese flew in *V* formation on the curtains. On the wall above the table, a cowboy with a lampshade on his head galloped on his horse. Beside him, a wooden owl closed one eye to show the time of day. Beyond the kitchen, the bus narrowed into a hall with closets on one side and a bathroom on the other, then fanned into a living room lined with built-in sofas. The middle sofa, the size of a loveseat, opened to make a bed, Red said. The original luggage racks were still there, near the ceiling. Red pointed at a cot folded and strapped on top of the luggage rack. "That sleeps another one, and the kitchen table makes into a bed, and there's two hammocks you can put on hooks. Sleeps seven altogether!" He pointed out the twill drapes, the new lockers under the sofas. He gleamed at the transformation—from a lowly bus, to this!—as if he and not the previous owners deserved the credit.

When Dan finished the tour, he stood up front and watched the others wander around. Five people fit well inside the bus. As Elsa's appraiser, he felt he needed to notice such things. Nell moved next to him and said, "I love it! I could *live* in it." He used his eyebrows to say, Hold it. It's not time yet.

He asked Red, who was standing close enough to hear any offer to buy, "What are you asking?"

"Only fifty-five hunnert!" With the butt of one hand, Red konked himself on the forehead. "I shou'n't let it go at that price! The guy gave it to me cheap." Laying a hand to his chest, he burped. "You want it, you better take it, it's gonna go fast. We haven't even had it on the lot yet! We're still fixin' it up, tuning it, like that. You're the first ones to see it!"

"Tires?"

"New. Did 'em yesterday."

"The brakes?"

"New! Good, huh?" Red aimed a razzle-dazzle look at Nell and gave Dan a cheeky nod. "The engine's good. The rest is gravy." He took a list from a pocket inside his jacket. "'Two Coleman ducted furnaces,'" he read, "'thermostat controlled, three hot water heaters, two electric windshield fans, new gauges, dash and switch panel, an eighteen-foot awning, remote propane fill . . .'"

Dan interrupted. "Could we get a copy of that?"

"Back in a jiff." Red departed for the shack in his get-along gait.

Nell asked Dan, "Well, what do you think?"

"Not bad."

"'*Not bad*'? I think it's *terrific!*"

"We should call Better Business," he said, "see if the guy's legit."

"You mean *I* should call," she said.

"If you want. And a mechanic to take a look."

Red was back. He handed Dan a sheet of paper. "The guy spent fourteen months fixing it," Red said. "Rebuilt engine, new interior, the works!"

Dan read aloud from the list. "'Fuller RTO 910 transmission, F-145 Timken rear end, Raycor fuel filter, six gallon hot water heater, custom bumpers, Kenwood stereo with four-speaker system, Cobra CB with remote speaker, laundry chute from bathroom vanity cabinet to exterior compartment, foam insulated headliner, dual wheel tire chains, monomatic toilet.'"

He said to Nell, "There's more." To Red, "Gas mileage?"

"Well, you know," Red said with humility, "these buggers eat it right up. But it's a guaranteed eleven miles a gallon. Pretty good for a rig this big!"

Dan said, "We'd want it painted. Do you do that?"

"Nope. But I got a buddy who does."

"How long would it take?"

"Couple days."

"Cost?"

"Say, two hunnert. You want to keep it blue?"

Nell and Dan agreed; blue was fine. "We need to talk to my mother-in-law," Dan said. "What kind of a deposit do you need?"

"Five hunnert. I can hold it twenty-four hours, and give your money back if you can't do it."

"We need forty-eight."

"You got it."

"We need a receipt quoting the price, including painting, stating that the deposit is good for forty-eight hours, and that we get the deposit back if we don't buy."

"Okey dokey!"

Dan wrote the check but hung onto it. "Let's see that receipt."

"You bet," Red said, and he flapped his way back to the shack. He returned with a receipt. The men exchanged pieces of paper and shook hands.

"Call me anytime," Red said with a sly glance at Nell.

The Sandersons got into the yellow Toyota that had broken down twice in the six weeks they had owned it. Dan had bought it from a friend, Sam Grover, and the minute he got it home it had started falling apart—one vital component at a time. Dan was ready to get rid of the car, the house, his earthly goods, everything but his wife and kids, and start fresh.

From the driver's seat of the Toyota, Dan cast a long last look at the bus. He imagined taking off in it with Nell and the kids and driving until they found home.

Five

Bear Paw, So Long

"I've got this idea."

Sigrid had picked up the phone, said, "Hello," and heard just these four words, no greeting. She cleared newspapers off a kitchen chair and sat down, chuckling. "Huh-huh-Halonen! You never did waste time on the phone."

"The phone company gets enough money as it is."

"The phone company was good to *me!* After Hitch? But what're you doing calling on the phone, of all things?"

"Want to go to Arizona and Florida?"

Sigrid had a laugh at her friend's expense. "Ha-have you gone and gotten senile?"

"Do you still have your license?"

"Driver's or hairdresser's? Doesn't matter. I've got 'em both. Why?"

"You could help drive."

Sigrid didn't know how much to admit. "The thing of it is, I don't drive. My knees are bad and they hurt on the clutch. When I do hair, they're fine 'cause I can sit on a stool and tootle around. I had the guy at the hardware fix one up with wheels and it works okay except it trips on the edge of the rug . . . ."

Elsa broke in. "I guess you're not interested."

Sigrid hadn't seen Elsa for years, but she knew how her mind worked. Elsa thought Sigrid talked too much—which was true. But talking too much made Sigrid a good hairdresser. She could talk to anyone about anything for

43

any length of time. "Maybe I'll come anyway and keep you company. When are you going?"

"A week from today."

Sigrid gave a toot of a laugh. "That's pretty soon. How long will you be traveling?"

"Two, three months."

"Could I bring Stanley?" Stanley, lying under the table, came alert at the sound of his name. He raised his head and quizzed her, one eyebrow at a time. When he saw that she wasn't talking to him, he put his head back down.

Elsa said, "*Stanley?*"

Sigrid pictured a soft panic running through Elsa, Elsa thinking, You have a *man*? Sigrid loved to tease Elsa. "He could be the watchdog," she said.

"Oh. Your *dog.*"

"Of course my dog! He's a sweetie. If I didn't bring him, I'd have to put him in the pound and he'd be one sad pooch."

"What kind is he?"

"Black Lab. No fleas."

"That should be okay. Isak is laid up and can't drive. He broke his leg."

"Sorry to hear it! Tell him I said hi. Let's see, I'd have to get someone to water my plants and pick up the mail . . . ." Sigrid put a potato chip in her mouth and crunched down on it.

"Nell's going to help drive," Elsa said. "She's bringing her kids. You can keep them busy."

"Good! I'd like to see her! You probably think of me as pretty peppy. I'm not so peppy these days."

"What's wrong?"

"Like I said, my knees and legs. I have authoritis and my sackerwilliack's shot. I tore a tendon in my knee and it didn't heal right." She put another chip in her mouth. "And I gained some weight."

"Are you eating something?"

"Chips. How about if I go along and do hair? I could cut yours, and the kids' and Nell's. Isak's too—but I guess you do that? And I'm good at maps."

44

"So you'll come-with?"

"Sure," Sigrid said nonchalantly, as if saying she would drop by next door for coffee. Caught up in fusty memories, she said goodbye with only a part of her mind. Elsa's call had brought back the past. The past meant Hitch. Sigrid knew when she met him that he was rough—rough in the sense of woodsy and strong—but his roughness toward her had come as a shock. Eighteen months into the marriage, he lost his roofing job and refused to find work. He sat on the couch and watched TV in a nasty mood. When she urged him to look for a job, he turned on her. She became the enemy. Back then, she was thin and energetic, and for a while she thought she had found an answer— a job for the two of them, managing a rooming house. Hitch could do maintenance; Sigrid could clean rooms and keep the books; by turns, they could answer the lobby bell and collect rent. Within two years, the plan failed. The tenants worked at the fish cannery, and when the cannery closed they all left town to find other jobs. The marriage failed as well. Hitch stormed at Sigrid when the rooming house closed and grew violent at home. She left before he broke any of her bones. She needed work, and Chalmer didn't have many jobs. There were always waitress openings at the Twig Diner, but she knew, even then, that she couldn't take eight hours on her feet. She filed for divorce and moved to Bear Paw, near Sitka, where she worked as a telephone operator. The job was perfect. She could work sitting down. The job gave her security and new friends, including a few installers who liked to flirt. She was still cute, she knew that for a fact, and still young, in her early forties, but she accepted lunch dates and that was it. She enjoyed being single too much to get tied down. After a few years, she felt dead-ended at the phone company, so she went to beauty school. She was curious to see Nell, all grown up, with kids. Sigrid was Auntie Sigrid to every child she knew, but Nell was special. Nell got the whole works—the stories, jokes, lessons that would have gone to Sigrid's child if she'd had one. Whenever Sigrid had coffee with Elsa, Nell came home from school and eyeballed the two, not happy that she'd missed out on the fun. Sigrid told Stanley, "She was jealous as all get-out! She wanted me to *herself.*"

Sigrid asked Cora over for lunch and told her about Elsa's call. She included a theory that she had come up with, based on clues on the phone and in Elsa's letters. "Nothing gets past *me*! I think Elsa's having a midnight crisis, I mean a what-you-call mid-*life* crisis. She doesn't care *where* she goes! She just wants to *go*."

Cora said, "Why?" Cora was Sigrid's neighbor from down the street, a frail, frightened woman who rarely left her house. For Cora, this was risky behavior, visiting in Sigrid's kitchen. Sigrid was proud of her for taking a chance.

"She's got cabin fever, that's why! I can tell by her letters, she's going cracky! She hasn't got any family there any more, and no lady friends to speak of, except at work, and she retired from that job, so she doesn't see them, either. Then Isak breaks his leg and they have to stay inside. That must drive 'em nuts. He likes to be outside, and she hates the rain, and it's going to start raining there pretty soon. Once it starts, it doesn't stop."

Sigrid picked up a metal backscratcher shaped like a curved hand on a stick and pulled it to its longest length. Working it under her blouse in back, she scratched a spot beneath her bra hook. "So we'll go to Arizona and see!"

"See what?"

Sigrid put down the backscratcher and goggled at Cora. Cora could be truly dense at times. "See what life offers," Sigrid said, tossing the words at Cora the way she tossed treats to Stanley, offhandedly, leaving it to the catcher to do the catching. "I'll bet she stays in Arizona. Isak won't go for that, not one bit. He's a fresh-air kind of guy, not one for air conditioning and all."

She shoved away from the table and hoisted herself up, limped to the stove, brought back the percolator and set it on a trivet, and cautiously sat down. In twenty years she had gained eighty pounds. Elsa hadn't said what kind of car she had, but how could *any* car hold a woman who weighed two-thirty, plus a man in a cast, and Elsa, Nell, two kids, and *Stanley*?

Cora stroked the waves in her hair. "I'd steer clear of Arizona," she warned. "I hear it's too hot to breathe. What will you do if she stays? Will you stay too?"

Sigrid waltzed into her first set of lies, going so far as to silently ridicule Cora. (Me? Stay in Arizona? Of course not!) "Nope," she said. "Me and Stanley'll get home some way, by Greyhound, or take the train to Portland and get a plane from there. Yep. It's Alaska for me and Stanley."

"Well, that'd be best, on a plane," Cora said. "Car trips can be tiring on the back end." Cora didn't have much of a back end herself, just a sag in her polyester pull-ups. Sigrid was glad for her own abundance in that regard. She had a built-in cushion.

Cora made motions at her hair, though it needed no adjustment. She said, "How long is your ticket good for?"

"It's the kind you can change anytime," Sigrid said evasively.

After eating half a sandwich, not wanting any cake, Cora got to her feet and prepared to leave. Sigrid stood too and said, "Would you like to babysit my plants?"

"Well . . . Sure . . . I guess."

Sigrid took three spider plants off the window sill and placed them in an empty box that was waiting on a chair. Picking a key from the key rack, she slipped it inside the box. "Here's a key in case you need it." She handed the box to Cora.

"What about your mail?"

"Bill will keep it at the post office."

Cora moved one timid foot before the other toward the front door. "I'll see you then before you go," she said with her usual pettish look.

Sigrid opened the door to let Cora through and followed her outside. She said to Cora's back, "Thanks for keeping my plants."

With a sad little glance at Sigrid, Cora started down the steps, cradling the box with one arm and holding the rail with the other hand, suggesting with her body that Sigrid had burdened her with yet another burden. At the end of any visit, Sigrid could never tell if Cora had enjoyed the visit or not.

Back indoors, she said to Stanley, "Doesn't matter! Me and you are *history.*"

She went to her bedroom closet and held back the curtain. Her closet was a protected joy. She could go there anytime and be transported. She kept promises there! Memory scents. Fairy trips. Safaris. So what if she had to wear a bra that was more battleship than brassiere? She owned a red sari! When she touched the sari, she felt thin and dark-skinned and heard sitar music, *Tring, tra-ee-eeng*. She had a white Egyptian gown with gold trim, a festival dress from Guatemala, silk orange pants from China, a caftan made of rayon scarves. Of her dressy skirts—the black chiffon, the violet crushed satin, and the rainbow rayon—only the black chiffon had any chance of fitting around her (it had an elastic waist). But she caressed them all. They told Sigrid who she was. She was adventurous! Bodacious! Not overweight and lonely. Not lost in anger at Hitch.

She sat at the kitchen table and reached for her pen and notebook. Stanley, who had followed her from room to room, sat at her feet and watched her. When it seemed that she would stay put for a while, he slumped to the floor. To make sure that she couldn't leave without him, and in general friendliness, he put his snout on one of her Hush Puppies.

She started with the regular grinds, her tirades at Hitch, her grief at being childless, her pleas for release from her prison of flesh. She went on to new tugs and beckonings—mostly this trip. All of these, she considered prayers. When she was done, she crumpled the pages. From a cupboard above the refrigerator, she took a metal tea box stocked with emergency candles and matches. She struck a match, set the pages on fire, and dropped them in a brass ashtray on the table. No one smoked at her place—she was allergic to smoke—but she kept the ashtray handy for this purpose.

Now. What-all did she have to do before leaving?

First, don't tell anyone she leaving for good! For sure, she wouldn't tell Cora. Cora couldn't keep a secret. Neither could Millie. Why Sigrid wanted to keep her plan a secret, she couldn't have explained.

When Sigrid said, "Stanley," the dog raised his eyebrows but kept his head down. "The minute Halonen said 'Arizona,' I made up my mind. I need a change! Maybe we'll live in the desert. I'll lose weight and get a tan! Hey-hey! Not anxious, *me*!" Stanley gave her an understanding look.

"*Oh.* The ladies."

Stanley brought his head up and waited to see if she would stand and leave. She didn't. With a whuff, he settled back down.

Sigrid had four regulars, two on Tuesdays, two on Fridays, women who wanted her to do their hair, yes, but also to listen to their problems—*solve* their problems, if she could. Who would take them? Millie? Or Gary at Tresses Unlimited?

She would call them both. She dialed. "Hi, Millie, it's me. Got a minute?"

"Carrie's under the dryer, but *go.*" Like Sigrid, Millie did hair in her apartment, part-time. Three stylists—Millie, Sigrid, Gary—covered the hairdressing needs of Bear Paw. These days, the young girls liked their hair un-permed and uncolored. They wanted trims and no more. Some older ladies, mostly from outside, still came in for perms and a weekly shampoo-and-set. As they died off, the stylists had less and less business.

Sigrid told Millie a fib. "I'm going away for a month and I'd like you to take my regulars. They'd want the same time, same day."

"Where are you going?"

"Arizona. Doctor's orders." Another fib.

"Arizona? That's nice," Millie said—too casually, it seemed to Sigrid. Millie didn't show one bit of concern for the (phony) medical crisis that had prompted a (made-up) doctor to order Sigrid to leave the state (lies, lies). Millie could show *some* respect!

Millie said, "Who do you have?"

"Bertha Ribbicoff on Tuesday at ten . . ."

"I'll be right back." Millie went off the phone to check her calendar. She couldn't keep dates in her head the way Sigrid could. Still, Millie had the right job. She had a body like a couch. As she circled the barber chair, she pressed her belly against the client. This helped Millie keep her balance and caused clients to think of their mothers. Sigrid knew this, first-hand. She was one of Millie's clients. For years, Millie had kept Sigrid's hair in a three-inch puff that flattered her face, which, Sigrid admitted, was flat as a pie tin topside

49

down—a pushed-in little nose and a pushed-out chin. Millie had a way with naturally curly hair. Sigrid would miss her.

Millie returned to the phone. "I can't do it."

"How are your Fridays?"

"Free except for two o'clock."

"Can you take Chicky Lorris at nine? And Gladys at eleven?"

"Wait." There was a pause. "Okay. I wrote them down. When do I start?"

"Next week."

"Oops! Gotta go! Carrie's about to sizzle."

Sigrid hung up and dialed Tresses Unlimited. "Gary? Sigrid. Have a minute?"

"Fire away."

Saxophone music floated over the line, a whiskey and cigarette whine that sounded like someone crying. "I'll be gone for a few weeks," Sigrid said, lying again. "Do you have space on Tuesdays for two regulars?"

"If you'd've called me two days ago, I wouldn't've. But I just had someone leave town on me. Wilma Burlington." Gloomily, he added, "She was a Tuesday. Bill got laid off and they went back to Anchorage." Gary took it personally that Bill Burlington had moved his family away from Bear Paw.

"I have Bertha Ribbicoff at ten," Sigrid said. "Wash and set. Mae Scott at two. Can you do them?"

"Tell 'em to come over."

Sigrid grinned and got Stanley to look at her. She made a circle with her thumb and forefinger, the OK sign—which he took for something good.

Six

Sun Fever

When Elsa and Isak got married, Grace Ann was fifteen and chafing to get out of the snow. If she had been a boy, she would have run away. Anywhere south. Three weeks after the wedding, at the home of her friend Marjorie, she met a couple from Arizona, Mark and Becka Pender. Becka was seven months pregnant, and when she said she planned to hire a mother's helper—a *live-in* mother's helper—Grace Ann nearly burst her buttons. She said, "I'll do it!" Four days later, she left town with the Penders.

Grace Ann was adaptable and bright, and she quickly made friends in Phoenix. Before dating seriously, she finished high school and junior college, earned a degree in accounting, and took a bookkeeping job at a drapery shop. When she met Herb Crenshaw—a contractor helping to spread Phoenix into the desert—she was ready to settle down. When they got married, she kept the company books. Their only child, an angel boy they called Charlie, died as a baby. Grace Ann could not have any more children, so she and Herb put their energies into travel. Every fall they took vacation weeks and went to Europe with a group. Herb died young, from lung cancer, and Grace Ann stayed on at his company. But every time she saw his name on the letterhead she swallowed a gust of pain. She quit her job a month after the funeral.

In that same period, Grace Ann lost someone else she had loved, her neighbor Bernadette, who moved to Savannah to follow her man. Though she was twenty years younger than Grace Ann, Bernadette was a dear friend. Grace Ann attended the wedding and was wooed by Savannah and its promenades of white houses and frilly porches and bearded trees, the marshes and diving

51

birds. But when Bernadette urged her to stay there and live there, Grace Ann said no thanks. She preferred the desert. She did promise to visit. For five years she had flown to Savannah in the spring, when dogwoods made a froth of the town, patted her godchildren as they came along—three boys, born a year apart—and eaten breakfast on the terrace. Each time, she left Bernadette six jars of cactus chutney as a thank-you, plus chili candy for the boys.

Grace Ann made another change after Herb died. It had to do with being a Finn. During her marriage, she hadn't focused on that part of her life. Herb was not a Finn. Grace Ann *was*. She was born Finnish-style, in a sauna, and grew up speaking Finnish and attending the Finnish-language church. Her father raised sheep in the foothills of the Cascades, near Hockinson, Washington, a dairy town named, some said, for a Finlander, Ambrosius Hokanson. In the 1890s, during the Klondike gold rush, Hockinson was a stop on the trail to Alaska. In the 1930s and '40s, when Grace Ann was a child, the frontier spirit was still strong in Hockinson. The old man next door, Helmer Luukinen, bragged, "The road to Vancouver was pure *plank*, and famous people come through here—on their way to Alaska! Like that Klondike Kate? *She* stopped by!" Helmer was a straight-laced member of the old Finnish church, yet he boasted about Klondike Kate, the dance hall queen. "And the Percheron stallions from France? And the Pantages, the theater group? They all came through here, heading for Alaska."

Possibly urged on by Helmer's tales, Grace Ann's father moved his family to Alaska when she was thirteen. His sheep had fallen to pasteurella. Along with other lower-'48ers, including other Finns, he hired on as a fisherman with the Matanuska Valley Project. Alaska was a mother lode of ocean fish, and Finns were born fishermen. In the brief time that she spent in Alaska, two years, Grace Ann learned more about fish than she needed to know. She could identify the artic char, the whitefish, the Dolly Varden. She could tell a chum salmon from a kokanee. She knew that the best bait for halibut was octopus, for whitefish, flies. She once saw a king salmon that weighed ninety-seven pounds, which was about what she weighed at the time. She went ice-fishing and nearly froze her toes. She hated the taste of fish, but her mother cooked fish many times a week. For Christmas they had lutefisk, that dried and resuscitated cod so revered by old-time Finns. The smell nauseated her! To make matters worse, lutefisk—already white and anemic-looking—was served with a bland, disgusting white sauce. When she left Alaska, she was running away from fish as much as from snow—and also from Finnishness, in that she linked Finnishness with fish.

But after Herb died, she reverted to her roots and joined the Suomi Circle, a monthly coffee gathering of Finnish women. The name itself was soothing. Suomi meant Finland, and a circle could enclose her, keep her from being lonely. The founding members were nine Finnish widows living on their husbands' pensions. Originally from Michigan and Minnesota, they had chosen Arizona for their sunset years. On the first Tuesday of every month, they met at Vera Leppanen's apartment, had coffee and cardamom *pulla*, then went to the Tumbleweed Retirement Home and put on a show.

They gave the same basic show each time, but the residents didn't mind. About thirty-five people gathered in the rec room, the wheelchair people up front, the more able-bodied behind them in upholstered chairs, staff aides sprinkled among the residents. A Suomi Circle member, Martha Wostrakowski (maiden name Aho—pronounced *Ah-ho*—a solid Finnish name) called the session to order with a piano chord. The social director for the Tumbleweed, Loretta Cassidy, came to stand in front, an austere presence in pleated slacks and blocky flats. She said, "Let us pray," and the residents bowed their heads, and Loretta launched into a prayer that was like a chant. She started phrases high and ended them low and punctuated petitions with clicks of her tongue. "Oh, Lord, *tsk!* We just come to You today, *tsk!* We just ask You to bless this meeting, *tsk!* We just ask Your blessing on all that we do, *tsk!* In Your name we pray, *tsk!* Amen." Grace Ann flinched each time Loretta clicked her tongue. Every click felt like a poke with a stick and took her mind off praying.

At this point, Jenny Hepponen, a retired home economics teacher, took over as mistress of ceremonies. Jenny was a reedy woman who, despite thirty years in front of teenagers, still got nervous in the spotlight. Dressed in lemon chiffon, she was the picture of sun-belt retirement. For teaching in Michigan, Jenny had told her circle friends, she had invented a uniform of sorts, a coat-dress that she sewed in strong fabrics and dark colors. Now that she lived in Arizona, she made floaty Phoenix skimmers in sunrise colors. Jenny was much admired at the Tumbleweed for her pudding cakes. Setting a cake on a table behind her as a promise of things to come, she turned to the group and twisted her hands together, mentioned the unchanging sunny weather, and expressed the hope that everyone felt well. She then read a joke from *Reader's Digest*, speeding through it and glancing up, flustered, at the end. Most of the residents missed the humor—they wore the same expression after the joke as before—but the circle members gave Jenny a few chuckles. She thanked them without words, with a cringe. Grace Ann felt sorry for her. This audience was tough when it came to jokes, even for someone experienced in public speaking, as Jenny was.

The moment came, the highlight of the show—Mavis Pelki. "You all know Mavis," cried Jenny, extending her arm at Mavis, who was waiting in the next room. Relieved to be relinquishing the stage, Jenny said, "Let's give Mavis a big hand!"

The old people clapped. Mavis came in using walking sticks. She had locomotion problems similar to those of some residents; in her case, childhood polio had lamed one leg. She stood before them, smiling, nodding, patting a hand to her heart. Chunky and pretty in a flowered pink dress, she seemed huggable, like everyone's favorite aunt. She went to the piano, set aside her sticks, sat down on the stool, and tapped the pedals with her good foot. Mavis was of average height. If, during the week, someone shorter or taller than she was had changed the height of the stool, she spun around on the stool until she fixed it. She played introductory notes, then cocked her head and sang, "Little Sir Echo, how do you do? Hel-*lo!* Hel-*lo!*" Her singing style was familiar to the residents—a cheery soprano that vibrated her throat and caught a sob of sincerity in every song. She played and sang "Playmate" and "Yankee Doodle," songs from the residents' childhoods, songs that healed the past no matter what the past had held. Every week, by request, she included "O She's Got Rings on Her Fingers and Bells on Her Toes" and "In the Merry, Merry Month of May." The residents brightened when they heard these songs.

After singing eight songs—including, for the several Finns in residence, a Finnish lullaby—Mavis played a piano solo, "Flight of the Bumble Bee," a tense piece that had residents pressing their lips shut until the final buzz. Now the other circle members went to stand by the piano and with Mavis they sang "Believe Me If All These Endearing Young Charms" and "O Danny Boy." Then, despite an overwhelming Lutheranness among the Suomi Circle members, they ended the program with "Ave Maria"—a moving rendition sung without irony. The rec room tipped with emotion. Residents could be seen drying their eyes. The circle members exited to genuine applause, shaking hands, giving and getting many pats, promising to return the following month.

That was Grace Ann's life—plus swimming at the YMCA on Mondays, Wednesdays, Fridays, and on Thursdays taking a book cart to patients at St. Agatha's Hospital. An uncomplicated existence. She seldom even cooked any more. She had totally lost her touch! When she *did* cook, she might accidentally put cinnamon in a garlicky dish or too much marjoram in the scrambled eggs. If this happened, she just laughed and threw the mess away. She had a favorite booth at Grandee's Café and ate there often. The waitresses called her by name and knew her usual for any meal of the day. When she didn't go to Grandee's, she ate whatever she liked. If she had steamed asparagus for supper and that was all, or corn flakes, what did it matter? She had only herself to please.

But now, with Elsa and her bunch coming to visit, Grace Ann didn't know *what* she would cook. For so many people? So many days in a row?

She honestly didn't.

Seven

Road to Somewhere

Isak knocked on the plaster with his knuckles. He banged it with the butt of his hand. He slid a bent clothes hanger inside the cast and drew it this way and that way, and took it out when it did no good. He bounced his leg, cast and all.

"It itches no matter what I do," he told Elsa. "What's going on?"

She knew he meant her whispers on the phone. She hadn't told him much, only that she was asking the doctor about the cast. She knew he was leery of the calls and her stepped-up speed around the house.

"It's something I'm working on. I'll be gone for a half-hour. You need anything?"

"Just for this itch to stop. Maybe turn the TV on."

She snapped on the television and jogged the antenna. Channel six was coming in, a game show with spinning circles. She pulled on a cardigan, took her keys from the hook, and went outside to the Oldsmobile. Sliding into the driver's seat, she felt out of place. Isak usually sat there. She warmed up the engine, backed the car around and drove out of the driveway, turned left, rolled a short way down the road and stopped. She could have walked, but she wanted Isak to think she was going to Cougar or someplace else.

Through the porch window, Elsa saw Joe napping on the couch. It seemed strange to see him resting. When she knocked he leaped to his feet and drew a hand over his crew-cut. He made a living being quick on his feet. A logger for twenty years, he had survived head whacks, cracked bones, and a chain-setting accident that came close to claiming his life, and finally had been pinned against a truck by a runaway tractor. That last accident ruined his back for logging. Now he sold firewood that he cut from salvage wood and was the first man up for any outdoor job besides logging—or indoor, for that matter—or for any volunteer help a neighbor might need.

He said, "How's Isak?"

"Owly, being inside. We're buying a rebuilt bus to drive to Arizona. Will you teach me to drive your truck?"

If she had said she was flying to the moon in a cereal box, he couldn't have looked more stymied. His flinty face took on gullies as he sorted out what she was saying. He said, "You want the Dodge then. But the camper's on. It's harder to drive with it on."

"Will you do it?"

He took his baseball cap from a hook and put it on. Pressing his left hand to the back of his head, he tugged the bill firmly *down* with his right hand, signaling yes.

Joe's Dodge D200 was muscle-bound, like Joe himself, much higher off the ground than Isak's old Chevy truck (rusting behind their house, beyond repair). She climbed into the cab and listened to Joe's directions, turned on the engine and tried the gears. Easing the truck forward, she practiced weaving around boulders in Joe's field. She did fine with every gear except reverse. Backing the truck, checking the rearview mirror or twisting to look behind her, she could see the camper and that was all; she had to depend on side mirrors to tell her where she was going.

After thirty minutes, she felt she could drive the bus well enough—*if* she could drive it forward. She wouldn't want to try backing a rig that big. Getting into the Olds, she said, "I'll bake you a pie from the freezer. Blackberry or apple?

Joe said, "Either one. Apple, I guess." Since the death of his wife, Ava, four years ago, Joe had cooked for himself and stayed independent. But he never refused Elsa's pies.

At home she got a wistful welcome from Isak. He was utterly dependent. The realization made her sad and roused a small alarm. *If he didn't have me, what in heaven's name would he do?*

"Tell me," he said.

Elsa sat in her knitting chair and told him about the Travel Bug, the bus, Nell, the children, Sigrid, Sigrid's dog, Joe's rig, saying the trip would be good for Isak because he couldn't do anything else with a bum leg, good for her because it would get her out of the rain. "Good for Nell, too," she said. "This way, we can at least *see* them. They got back from the Philippines, when? Two years ago? How often have they been down? Four, five times?"

This was a lot of talking in one stretch. She folded her hands on her lap, signaling her intention to stop talking. Yet she said, "I worry about her. She said Dan might be gone for two months. What if this is a *separation?*"

* * *

Nell took the clipboard to the den and sat on the dead hearth. With her back against the bricks, knees up, she reread her list. Some items were already checked off.

Give notice on house.

Call re: column.

Notify utilities.

Notify trash.

Stop newspaper.

Notify post office, forward mail to Arizona. Buy stamps.

Replace broken door knob.

Steam carpet.

Take bags to Salvation Army.

Call adoption agency.

Buy home-school books.

Take along vitamins.

First aid.

Thread and needles.

Medical ID cards, health records.

Passports.

The hardest part wasn't on the list, saying goodbye to Dan. She tried not to think about it, turning instead to Arizona's weather, to clothes the kids would need or not need. Out of nowhere, she missed the fog of Hook Island. She found an empty page and took notes for a column on fog. Most mornings, fog hid the neighbor islands—or half-hid them—the tops might be visible, or the sides—and Nell did indoor jobs, baked bread, wrote her column, did the bits of housework that couldn't wait for Saturday when the family cleaned house in a whoosh. The fog would burn off by mid-morning, about the time when she went outdoors and ran. No matter which road she chose, the forest was close. On the disk of land that was Hook Island, on any spot not cleared by humans, the forest shot up like a skyscraper. Two clichés formed the bottom level—a "ground floor" truly on the ground and a "carpet of moss" that ran like fur over fallen logs—actually *many* mosses, miniscule fernlike plants. Floor 2: clover, thistles, Shaggy Cap and other mushrooms, hazelnut and fir starters, red berries near the ground. Floor 3: Oregon grape with lavender globes of fruit, like frosted bulbs on Victorian lamps, and spiky leaves like holly. Floor 4: ferns that thrust their arms out, bragging that no other plants could grow faster or be tougher, and blackberry vines that could. Floor 5: vine maples that laced the forest with graceful reachings, beseeching to one side like ballerinas at the barre. Floor 6: broad-leafed maples, hickories, alders. Floor 7: an atrium of cool air hundreds of feet high, mostly trunks branching at levels higher and higher. At the top: cedars and Douglas firs so tall they had clouds in their hair. The forest made a soughing sound, a soft roaring. Nell reveled in the word. Soughing. Speech of wind in monster trees. Or at the edge of surf. On Hook Island she felt at home. Why there, not here?

Nell tucked her feet against her fanny and made pronouncements. She loved wind, wilderness, plants busy growing. *The Pacific Northwest is a green-growing machine!* Whenever it had a chance, say, overnight, it sprouted something green. And not just one green. *Dozens.* In the spring, the greens ran the color wheel of greens; blue-green grasses bowed to the sun, weighted by dew gems along their length; yellow-green skunk cabbage stank up the swamp; even the staid old deacons of the forest, the evergreens, blushed and pushed out eight inches of pale green (which later blended in). Colors appeared sequentially, in small portions, gradually getting the world used to colors again besides green. First came white—in tiny Hooker's fairy bells, spring beauty, queen's cup, and lily-of-the-valley. One exception to the smallness of the whites was the trillium, the size of Nell's palm, three white petals that gradually turned magenta. (Nell liked its other name better, wake-robin. Robin opens his eyes, groggy from sleep, and spies a flower bigger than *he* is. Startled wide awake, he hops-to and gets busy pulling worms.) Next, yellow. Low to the ground, the buttercup and the cinquefoil looked alike except that one had velvet petals, the other, shiny (Nell couldn't recall which). Scotch broom as tall as Nell took over the roadside, neon yellow blooms on long, tangled Merlin wands. Forsythia trees, taller yet, fought for a place in the yellow drama, flicking some branches high and curtsying with others, like divas taking curtain calls. Then came blues and purples, lupines embroidering the borders of the forest, foxglove aiming for Mars, sending up bells as surveillance scouts, miniature violets waiting under fallen maple leaves for Nell to kick aside the leaves, then squirting a scent out of proportion to their size. Spring saved the brashest for last, the reds, in spreading phlox, Indian paintbrush, red columbine . . . .

But now, this trip. There was hope yet. This trip gave a spark to life!

Addie had her favorite items packed. Jed had his tricks and Dan's banjo. They had canvas bags filled with books and games. Nell had phoned Grace Ann in Arizona, an aunt she had seen twice in Alaska, and Harald in Florida, an uncle she had never met, had verified addresses, phone numbers, dates of arrival. She had called her editor, Greg Slocum, and arranged to mail her column from the road. Her first columns, six years ago, were expatriate reports from the Philippines. By the time she returned to the States, she had gained a loyal readership. From then on, the syndicate had let her write whatever she wanted—a nice freedom for a writer. But columns were headstrong! She had to wrestle each one to the ground, pant and struggle, get a finger in the eye for her trouble, and hold it down until it stopped jumping free and making faces. She could do *that* from the road as well as from here.

She went to the desk and found a fish market post card. She wrote:

"Dear Cuffy, don't you love post cards? Everyone can read the news. Here's mine: In the past two days, my Dad broke his leg, Jed, 10, skinned his arm, car repairs cost $1200., I can't balance the checkbook, and the tub stopped up. I put on wooden clogs, got into the tub, tried the plunger. No luck. The door bell rang—the water man saying the water will be off all day tomorrow, second time this week. I sat down to write to you and the standing lamp fell over. The bulb and shade shattered. So what's new at your house? My Mom bought a refurbished bus and we're driving it to Arizona and Florida. Dan and I are moving, but we don't know where to. Are you baking something chocolate? Hi to everyone handling the mail. Love, Nell."

* * *

Sigrid put her woolens in a give-away bag and prepared for her getaway. She spread her white cashmere shawl next to her suitcase on the bed, then laid her costumes and her three dressy skirts on the shawl, rolled the shawl around the clothes and set the roll in the suitcase. She added the clothes she had bought after Elsa called, two cotton blouses, a denim wrap skirt, two T-shirts, three nightgowns, new underwear, white Keds, and fresh white socks. She kept out her new sweat suit to wear on the plane, plus a windbreaker jacket.

She sat at the table and inspected her plane ticket. She wrote a reminder to call the airline and order salt-free food. Millie would drive her to the airport. What time? Elsa had offered to pick her up at the Portland airport. Sigrid had said no thanks, saying she would get to Cougar on her own. But she hadn't realized how far Cougar was from Portland. Later she looked at a map. Sixty miles! How much would *that* cost in a taxi?

Maybe she could take a bus as far as the bus went and Elsa could meet her there.

Do they let dogs ride on buses? How long would the tranquilizer work? What if Stanley was still dead weight when she claimed him? She'd have to wait for him to wake up! How could she let Elsa know she was running late? Elsa would have left home by then.

Humming one tone, Sigrid strummed her lips with a forefinger. She got up to make coffee. Should she take the coffeepot? No. She'd give it to Millie.

Coffee cups? The good sheets?

At her feet, Stanley was sleeping on his side with his legs sticking out straight. She said, "Stanley." He raised his head. She looked him in the eye and said, "Don't believe a thing you hear about quick getaways. There's no such thing."

* * *

Dan sneezed six times in a row, a reaction to the dust being raised in the house. As usual, Nell laughed. His serial sneezing was a source of comedy. She claimed that he yelled his sneezes, unnecessarily loudly, and that he pronounced them different ways. "*Gotcha!*" or "*Rorschach!*" or "*Ah shucks!*" She used this occasion to bring up a current theme, adoption. For two years, ever since they got back to the States, she had been clipping articles on Korean and Romanian orphans, contacting adoption agencies, poring over photos of available USA children. Before they moved off Hook Island, she had even had an adoption agency do a home study. A caseworker came to the island, poked into their lives, asked pesky questions. Nell had kept up her interest in adoption even as they packed their belongings to move to who-knew-where.

He sneezed again. She said, "'*Russia!*'"

He sneezed again. She said, "'*Tasha!*'"

He sneezed again. She said, "'*Sasha!*'"

She said, "You say you want Russian children? Fine with me!"

"We don't need any more kids at the moment."

"Not at the moment. But soon."

She shooed him outside, and he sat on the steps with his briefcase, reviewing obligations. Bills were paid, passports up to date, health insurance in place. For now, the family's official address would be his Seattle office address. He had the Arizona and Florida phone numbers for emergency. Nell would call him every Sunday night, her time, which would be Monday noon in Manila. In his briefcase, he had his passport, work papers, and notes on a Manila orphanage. Nell had heard about the orphanage by mistake, or by Providence. Checking into adopting a child from the Philippines, she dialed a wrong numeral in a phone code. She had intended to call an adoption support group in Oakland, California, but instead she reached, by happenstance, an off-duty caseworker in Green Bay, Wisconsin. When Nell told the woman her story (Nell got the wrong party but told her story anyway), the woman exclaimed, "I know an orphanage in Manila! Good Shepherd Villa! Your husband should go there!" The nuns were very sweet, she said, and they placed children for adoption—in Sweden and other European countries, and in the United States. In his briefcase, Dan had the documents required by the Philippine government—a completed home study (the agency had bent rules to send it with Dan, sealing it with agency stamps to insure that Dan could not read it), a certified marriage certificate, certified birth certificates for Nell and Dan, three personal reference letters, family photos, a medical report for each family member, a statement of reasons for wanting to adopt a child from the Philippines, copies of income tax records, police clearance for Nell and Dan, and assurance from an approved United States adoption agency that a follow-up study would be conducted six months after placement. Dan didn't think he would need the documents, as he didn't expect to find a child. But he was taking them, just in case.

Deek, the weimaraner across the street, whimpered and yapped and leaped at his front gate. If the dog really wanted to escape, Dan thought, he could use his long legs to his advantage, simply get back and take a run and clear the gate. Deek was just complaining. He didn't like being alone. Dan guessed that when he got to Manila that's how he would feel. He suddenly thought about Hook Island, not knowing that Nell had done the same thing just minutes ago. The slower pace had mellowed even Jed, who hated to sit still. Jed could squat for an hour and stare at a tide pool, fascinated by the minute swimmers temporarily trapped there. For Jed the scientist, the shore was a museum of rocks and running birds. For Addie the collector, it was heaven. She collected sand dollars, sea slugs, and shells with residents still living inside them. She once found a seaweed bulb the size of a melon and pulled it home by its ropey tail, the leaves, ragged to begin with, dragging in the sand like laundry gone bad, or flags at a disappointing rally. If allowed to, she would have kept a pail of crabs beside her at mealtime. The town had two gas stations, a post office, a general store, three cafes, two churches. The Sandersons led a quiet life, shopped in Seattle once a month, occasionally held a potluck supper for the neighbors. Dan didn't have to mow the lawn because he didn't have a lawn, just a scrubby slope that bumped down to the water's edge. Island winters were wet and dank, but he missed the slower pace—and Nell's high spirits. Since they moved to town, she had been broody, up and down. Mostly down.

Addie came around the edge of the house holding objects that seemed hard to hold, either bulky or slippery—two egg cartons, two shoe boxes, a macaroni necklace, a life-sized baby doll in a satin dress, and a slew of silk ties that he had discarded. He helped her onto his lap, having to reach around the items to hug her.

"Now don't you get married before I see you," he said.

She smirked sidewise at him. "Dad-*dy*. I'm not *that* old. Will you write to me?"

"Sure. And we'll talk on the phone." Shifting Addie onto the step, he reached into his briefcase and took out a segmented wooden puppet—a smiley Hawaiian toddler in a halter top and grass skirt, standing on a drum. He placed his thumb on the plunger under the drum and his first two fingers around the puppet's feet, then squeezed. The puppet did a floppy hula.

Addie was entranced. "Do it again!" He moved his thumb to various spots and squeezed. The puppet buckled her knees, collapsed into sticks, pulled herself up and stood straight, smiling all the while.

Dan gave the puppet to Addie, who held it with her chin at the top of her pile. He opened the door. She carefully stepped over the threshold and glided into the house.

Jed came outside to see what was going on. Dan took a jumble of metal circles and squares from his briefcase and handed it to him. "The trick is to take them apart and put them back together."

"I can do it!" Jed slammed the pieces in various ways but couldn't separate them.

Dan put his hands on Jed's shoulders. "You'll be the man of the family till I get back." Jed dived into Dan's arms, pressing his head downward on Dan's chest, his habit since infancy. Dan was startled. Jed was suddenly so *tall*. The next time Dan saw his son, how tall would he be?

He found Nell swabbing the kitchen sink as if her life depended on it. He said to her back (and to the mirror: they made a pensive couple), "Are you okay? It's a lot to be in charge of. The kids, your parents, driving, your writing."

She dried her hands and turned and twined her fingers behind his neck. "It's better than going with *you!* Flying all that way again? I'd barely have time to unpack and get used to the heat and it would be time to leave!" He guessed it was exactly what she wanted to do. Go with him.

The time came. Nell kissed him one last time, got into the driver's seat, fixed the mirrors, and the kids slid open the big side windows and called goodbye again and again. Nell started the engine and let it run. Giving Dan a here-we-go smile, she pulled the knob on the folding door. The door wheezed shut—apologetically, it seemed to him. She muscled the bus into reverse and he guided her out of the driveway with hand motions. She backed into the street, pulled forward along the curb, paused, blew him a kiss, and then, too busy to notice him any further, she readjusted the mirrors, looked both ways and drove off. Dan was left standing in the street and waving.

Usually he was the one who drove off and Nell was left standing and waving. Parting was a lot worse for the one left standing. He hadn't known that.

* * *

When Nell was a child, Sigrid was tall, slim, and brazen in hand-me-down silks. Now she was heavy and lame in a pink cotton sweat suit that ballooned around her and made her seem short. Otherwise she was the same, more animated than any three people combined. She still had a coast-to-coast grin and a chin that took over her face. She still laughed in a string of exclamations, "Hee-hee, *you*-ooo-ooo, you bet, yuk, yuk, and then some!"—a commentary that went on until she'd laughed all that she wanted to say.

Sigrid said, "Izzat *you?*" and took Nell into a bear hug. White Shoulders powder puffed from her shirt, the same fragrance she had worn in Alaska. "I've missed you, kiddo! Why'n't you write?"

"Sorry. For a writer, I'm a lousy writer."

Sigrid put her at arms' length. "We'll make up for it. I plan to talk your leg off!"

Turning foxy, she said to Jed, "Aren't *you* the handsome guy!" She reached for his head and clamped it to her chest. From his place of captivity he rolled his eyes at Nell and stretched his neck bands, miming a plea for help. Nell only smiled, remembering.

"This must be Addie!" Releasing Jed, Sigrid sat on a kitchen bench and beckoned to Addie. Addie hesitantly came forward. Sigrid said, "Gimme some love!" Addie let herself be hugged, then moved back and waited to see what Sigrid would do next.

"I have something for you guys." Sigrid took a small paper bag from her purse and shook it. It rang clear, high tones. She pulled out a straight-sided steel bell—about one inch wide and three inches long, strung on a leather cord—and gave it to Jed.

"It's from Alaska," she said. "You wear it to scare off the *bears.*"

Jed hung the bell around his neck and jingled it. "Thanks! Hey, Addie! I can scare off Bigfoot!"

Sigrid brought out a handkerchief bundle. "Addie, these are for you. What are you? Six?" Addie nodded, her eyes on the hanky. Sigrid unfolded it. Inside were six beige starbursts made of what appeared to be stone, an inch in diameter and a quarter-inch thick. Each had two polished holes in the center.

"Guess what they are."

Jed said, "Buttons."

"Right! What are they made of?"

Addie said, "Um. I don't know."

Jed said, "Shells?"

"Nope."

Addie said, "I give up."

"Reindeer antlers! Cut across!" With her pinky finger, Sigrid traced the outline of one starburst. "They find antlers and slice 'em and put holes in 'em and polish 'em."

Sigrid handed the buttons to Addie. "They're yours." To Jed, she said, "You keep the bell. You can take walks with your granddad and scare off the elk."

Nell's father had kept track of Sigrid's antics from a chair in the dining area. He looked sad and out of reach. Nell said, "Are you okay, Daddy? Would you like coffee?"

His eyes flickered yes. He made his way into the kitchen, struggling with the crutches. She wanted to help him, but there was nothing she could do. Setting aside the crutches, he got seated on a bench while Nell poured coffee from the percolator into two mugs. She brought the mugs to the table. He added sugar to his and stirred it in with thirteen dings. The number of dings was the same, but *he* had changed. He seemed vague somehow, as if his mind had gone ahead without him and he felt betrayed. He was too young for this sort of vagueness. She didn't want to lose him to dementia, Alzheimer's disease, old age, or whatever this was.

But she was comforted by the sight before her—her father drinking coffee. There couldn't be too much wrong in the world if her father was drinking coffee.

* * *

When he opened his eyes, he was on the couch, but he couldn't recall how he got there. He took note of the hub-bub—two children twirling, Nell sorting food, Elsa trying to get people to sit down, a big black dog (where had *he* come from?) wagging himself silly, that other lady snorting and laughing and talking at the same time. *That lady is a half-bubble off plumb.* He looked at her again. *Why, she used to live next door! Can you beat that?* He didn't think everyone would fit inside the bus. His cast took too much room. The doctor wasn't happy about the trip, but when Elsa promised to get the cast checked at the right time he gave her the name of a Phoenix doctor. Isak couldn't get straight just where-all they were going, but he would ride along and not complain.

In the meantime, the pain was back. When Elsa passed by in her circling of the room, he asked for a glass of water. She brought it. He sat forward to take two pills.

"Anything else?" she asked. He said no, and she took up her circling again.

Outside, a crow stepped off paces in the weeds. Isak thought: *He's measuring the yard in crow's-feet.* He said the Finnish word for crow, "*Varis,*" adding force to the rolled *r,* smiling, thinking of the dumb-Finn joke that Finns used to tell when he was a boy. One Finn points to a crow and says, "Vat is dat?" The other Finn says, "Dat is *varis.*"

* * *

Sigrid's sister had sent her a bumper sticker to give to Elsa for the trip. It read "FINN WITHIN." Sigrid said, "I dare you," and thrust it at Nell's mother.

Nell's mother, who avoided showiness of any kind, gave Nell a beleaguered look. Nell said, "It's fine with me. The only problem is, when you want to get it off, you *can't!* It's like the price sticker on a notebook. You scrape and scrape, but there's always that sticky stuff left over and it stays there as long as you have the notebook! Picking up *dirt!* I *hate* that!" Realizing belatedly that she was ranting, she stopped. She had come undone over sticky stuff.

Sigrid jabbed her with an elbow. "Re-*lax,* kiddo. We'll put a new one on top when this one wears out."

The sticker went on the rear bumper of the bus, Jed helping Sigrid to get it on straight. Sigrid hadn't lost her powers, Nell was glad to see. Sigrid and her mother had always interacted this way, Sigrid pressing Nell's mother past comfort, her mother protesting, her mother giving way in the end (giving way *some* of the time).

"FINN WITHIN" told the world that a Finn was aboard the blue bus. It didn't say that she had two other Finns with her, plus two half-Finn children, a Swede, and a black Labrador, or that the bus was a means of escape for all except the kids and the dog, who were happy to either stay where they were or go someplace, it didn't matter.

* * *

Preparing to spend a day and a night trapped in planes and terminals, Dan had to mentally shrink. He contracted his kinetic self, took a shuttle flight from Sea-Tac to San Francisco, whiled away a three-hour layover reading a spy novel, flew to Honolulu, spent a four-hour delay (engine trouble) pacing the halls and downing too many coffees. Twelve hours after leaving Wilcox, he boarded a plane that would land in Manila thirteen hours later.

The plane's interior was muted, the air already being sucked out of him. He made his way to seat 5C, slid his briefcase into an upper compartment, and sank into his seat, immediately swinging aside his knees for two Filipina grandmothers who daintily tramped on his shoes, smiled beatifically, and settled into seats 5A and 5B. In the aisle, passengers waited turns to stow their carry-on luggage. They leaned on Dan to let others pass. Steady action went on overhead, loudly or silently. Bins clacked open. Pillows and blankets swung down. Bags and jackets went up. Bins slammed shut. When all of the passengers were seated, one stewardess picked up a microphone and another picked up yellow hoses. One spoke, and the other demonstrated. Emergency breathing. Emergency exits. Emergency flotation. They put away their gear, flipped down little jump seats that faced the passengers, sat down, locked their seatbelts, and smiled in a blank way: See us, so composed? Do we worry about crashing at sea? *Never.*

The plane rolled ahead for suspended moments, rocking gently, turned on the painted lines, slowed, and came to a stop. Dan sat back. This next part of flying he *liked.* The plane started up again and tore along the tarmac, shaking its beams, then did the impossible—floated tons of metal on thin air.

Above the clouds he tried to get comfortable. The airline seat was shaped to fit no actual human body. Far from supporting his back, the seat curved away from his back and made a *C* of his spine. Instead of resting his head, the misnamed headrest forced his head forward like the head of a flying duck. The seat in front of him pressed against his knees. He stuck his right leg into the aisle, giving relief to that one leg, at least. As a diversion, he watched a ritual going on in the galley. Four petite Filipina stewardesses were toiling at a wall of large metal lockers, unsnapping clamps, sliding out locker drawers, looking inside them, shoving the drawers back, pulling out others. The drawers seemed too heavy for the tiny women to handle. As on other flights, he fought an impulse to get up and help. This was their job, he told himself. They did this—whatever it was—on every flight. So he entertained himself by trying to guess what was in the lockers. Or who.

Excellent dark coffee. Shades drawn against the sun. Sleep caught when possible. Shades pulled up for breakfast, artificial dawn. Rouse and step off the plane.

Manila slapped him, oven-hot. The airport was smaller than ever. Passing through customs, he saw Manuel Marcos, the driver for Roster, waiting for him, smiling. Manual was a docile teen-ager who turned into a wild man at the wheel of a van.

Dan's legs weighed a hundred pounds each. His eyes felt full of gravel. He couldn't stay awake. He dozed and woke repeatedly as Manuel zipped through traffic, took shortcuts, bounced through alleys, bumped back onto the main road, horns honking, Manila whirling. In a kaleidoscope of color and motion, Dan caught sight of a small sign set low among bushes by the road. The sign read, "Good Shepherd Villa."

Good Shepherd Villa? *The orphanage!*

He said, "We have to turn around!"

Manuel turned around and drove half a block, eased the van through an opening in a high hedge, and rolled under trees to a Spanish-style compound—an off-white church and satellite buildings connected by canopied walks.

A nun in sandals and a blue-and-white habit walked out to meet the van. She spoke to Manuel through his open window. "I am Sister Mary Clare. May I help you?"

Dan climbed out and shook her hand. "My wife wrote to you. Nell Sanderson?"

"Oh. Yes." The nun took visual stock of Dan. Beneath her smile and her nun's habit, she was a person of authority. "Her letter came today. She asked about adoption."

"Yes. I . . . I'm in Manila on other business."

"Would you like tea?"

They drank tea in a breezeway. Sister Mary Clare told Dan that unmarried pregnant women lived at the villa in a loving environment, received good medical care, and that if a mother could not raise her baby the Sisters placed the child for adoption.

Exhausted as he was, Dan didn't feel up to adopting a child. But he kept the promise he had made to Nell. "We're looking for a girl about four or five years old. We're open to a child with a handicap. We have a six-year-old daughter, Addie, and a ten-year-old boy, Jed. We'd want Addie to remain the older girl."

"I'm sorry, but we place babies only," Sister Mary Clare said. Dan couldn't tell if what he felt was disappointment or relief.

After tea, as they walked to the van, Sister Mary Clare said, "There *is* one little girl who will not find a home. She is delayed in language and has hearing loss, speech impairment, also nystagmus—that is, her eyes jump when she's excited. She is four."

Dan experienced a thump of knowing. "What is her name?"

Sister Mary Clare's face softened. "We call her Laura. She has been with us since she was a baby. She is a sweet child, very affectionate. We would miss her."

He would have to leave that day without meeting Laura. She was on an excursion with a group of nuns. When he expressed interest in adopting

Laura, Sister Mary Clare said, "The director of government children's services prefers to have older children stay in the Philippines."

She reached under her gown and brought out a business card. "But here is the director's number. Call her."

* * *

Stanley lay with his nose on his front paws, keeping an eye on Sigrid. To Nell he seemed a patient dog with no bad habits. Sigrid had her own words for "Down" and "Stay." When she told him, "Give it a rest" or "Don't you dare move," he obeyed as if her version were the real McCoy. Sigrid sat in the front passenger's seat, turning around to kibitz with the kids and make spritzy faces at them. "We could figure out how many hours it'll take, start to finish," Sigrid said, checking the TravelHelper. "All we have to do is, let's see, list the approximate distance from city to city, multiply by 2.5 and divide by 100 miles."

She chortled at Jed and Addie. "Who-hoo wants to do it?"

The children looked up politely and shook their heads and went back to what they were doing. Nell recognized the ploy from her childhood—Sigrid demanding attention when Nell was busy, dangling an interruption and watching her reaction, teaching her (Nell assumed) that life involves interruptions. By glancing at the rearview mirror, Nell could keep track of what went on behind her. At the moment, Addie was coloring in her wildlife notebook and Jed was trying to solve the metal puzzle. Nell's parents weren't visible; they had settled in the back of the bus. The Willamette Valley spread out in all directions, mammoth bare hills in no hurry to get up or down. There was something familiar about this trip, even now at the start—the quiet talk, the buzz of tires, the numb sensation in her ears—the *hum* of a road trip.

Sigrid said, "No takers?"

Reading from a guidebook, she said, "'Salem was founded by a Methodist minister in 1841, Jason Lee.'" Membership in a road club came free with Dan's job. When Nell went to the club office to pick up maps, the agent suggested a TravelHelper, a personalized driving plan—a flip map with a magnified segment of highway on each page. Nell ordered one that would lead her from Portland, Oregon, to Mesa, Arizona, and on to Lake Worth, Florida. The agent had marked pages with a highlighter to show highway construction sites and the shortest routes around cities. The TravelHelper came in a plastic bag with maps, guidebooks, notes on history and places of interest. As the self-appointed navigator, Sigrid had more than enough travel aids.

Nell asked, "How many miles from Portland to Salem?"

Sigrid fluttered pages. "I can tell you how many from Cougar. I add up that Portland is . . . fifty-six miles from Salem." She unfolded a map. "Hah! Says here Portland to Salem is fifty-one miles. I wasn't far off! You didn't think I'd get it, did you? I could sure use some ice cream! But coffee's fine. Mostly I need to stretch." She pulled up her skirt and kneaded her thighs. "Hey, Nell! I've got maps on my legs! If we get lost, we can follow my varicose veins. Blue? Go east! Red? Go west!" She gave in to a fit of talk-laughing. "Hoo-hoo, I'll tell ya, hee-hee, what a life!" She sobered up and said, "Did you know your shins get dented when you get to my age? Say! When you went to the Philippines, what was it like?"

Nell had forgotten this about Sigrid, how she skipped from topic to topic. Anyone listening had to either keep up or get left behind.

"I missed the States," Nell said, "but the kids . . ."

"No! I mean when you first got there. Right off the plane."

"Oh. The *heat*. It's like a furnace! And the traffic is *crazy*. Cars race around like bumper cars and make lanes where there aren't any. They have jeepneys—you know, American jeeps left from the war—and people paint wild designs on them and use them for taxis. A ride in one is like a carnival ride."

"They honk *real* loud," Addie said.

Inflating her cheeks, Sigrid gave Addie an oompa look. "How can you remember? You were *little*."

"Mom says I have a good remembry."

Sigrid said, "Well, honey-cakes, I should say you do."

Jed said, "Nuh-*uh*, Addie. You can't remember. You were just a baby! I saw you when you were born." He laughed rudely. "You were all wrinkled."

73

"And beautiful," Nell said.

Addie asked Nell, "Was I wrinkled?"

"Yes, honey, all babies are. You were, too, Jed. After a while they smooth out."

Jed said, "I'm never going to have babies. They're too much trouble."

Addie giggled. "Boys don't have babies."

"That's not what I mean. I mean my wife."

Addie giggled again. "You have a *wife*?"

"You know what I mean! Babies get in people's way."

Sigrid said quietly, "Like Addie maybe got in your way when she was a baby?"

After a pause, Jed said, "Sort of."

Sigrid said, "I know." She told Addie, "Don't worry, it happens all the time. Brothers say that about little sisters, but later on they're glad they've got them."

In the mirror, Nell saw Addie give Sigrid the same look *she* gave Sigrid when she was Addie's age, an extended look that said, You're weird, but you're okay.

* * *

While Isak slept on the folded-out loveseat, Elsa crocheted on one of the couches. She was thinking about the clerk at the driver's license office. He was still in his teens—or young enough, anyway, to still have acne—and he hadn't developed any noticeable manners. He seemed to wish himself invisible. When she asked him if she needed another license to drive a bus, his mouth went ajar—whether from adenoid trouble or skepticism, she couldn't tell. In a tone that implied she was *way* too old to drive a bus, he asked, "*Why?*" She said, "Because I'm driving a private bus to Arizona and Florida." A flit of envy crossed his face. The poor boy! In that miserable drizzle, who *wouldn't* want to go to Arizona and Florida? It turned out she didn't need extra licensing, but the trip to the office was worth the effort. The boy's awe made her feel robust and free.

74

She turned her thoughts to Isak. He was more lucid these days than he had been for months. Elsa believed the accident had jarred his brain in a positive way. But now he was too quiet. Even a quiet man can be too quiet. The doctor wanted him exercising on the crutches every day, but Isak hated even talking about crutches. It had been all Elsa could do to get him to try them. When he made it to his feet the first time, he threw sinking looks at her. The crutches shamed him, she could see that—the pads at the armpits, the stump-stump way they made him walk. His face said, Crutches! For a man who could do *everything*? In Alaska, friends brought him their broken things—cars, mixers, lawn mowers—and Isak fixed them. When they moved to Cougar, Isak went to the library and learned new skills out of books— furniture refinishing, upholstery work, shoe repair. He could fix anything. He was a fixer by nature. What was he now? Laid up, with his leg in a cast? When his memory first started failing, she fussed at him to stop working so hard. He was retired, she reminded him. He didn't need to keep fixing. But then, being a contrary-type person, what did she do? She nagged at him to keep fixing! She regretted that. He couldn't seem to get the smallest job done. The truth was that, even before the accident, he had lost interest in fixing. He had mostly wanted to pick berries.

She put down her work. Like a moody young girl, she twisted toward the window and tucked one foot under her, put her arm on the ridge of the couch, set her chin on her hand, and stared outside. It was drizzling out there. A fuzz of moisture built up on the glass. When it gathered enough weight, it trickled in a stream to the bottom casing. A blotch of rain hit the pane, *plosh*, reminding her of sprinkling the ironing with her fingers. She realized she had forgotten to pack the Coke bottle with the sprinkler top.

She felt put-upon by rain! Rain made her scratch places where she had no itch. How could a little rain do this to her?

"*No niin*," she said, whispering so she wouldn't wake Isak. "We're not far enough away. When we're far enough away, the rain will stop."

* * *

Isak wasn't sleeping. He was amused that he could fool her after all these years. He had seen her pouting and feeling sorry for herself. It's no good when she has nothing to do, he thought, and when she's around *me* too long she gets buggy. Whenever he got confused or couldn't recall a certain word, she looked at him the way she might look at a stranger. Her glasses got to shining at a time like that. What did she hope? That he would change, and *then* she'd be happy? Change how?

"I'm awake," he said. "Are you okay?"

She forgot to put on a nice face. She still had that concentrated scowl. *As if I'm something under a microscope.* A scientist had to squinch his eyes like that, to examine something small, maybe a germ. Why did Elsa need to examine *him*?

"I'm fine," she said. "Do you want something to eat?"

He saw her perk up when she asked the question. He knew Elsa! The question got her back to being needed and to finding a way through the day.

* * *

Sigrid chortled and pointed at a concrete donkey sitting in a farmyard. "Who-hoo-whoever saw a donkey sit like that!"

"Ferdinand," Addie said. "He sits like that."

Jed said scornfully, "Ferdinand's a *bull*, not a donkey."

Addie said, "I know he is! But they both sit down like that. They're both funny." Nell was glad to see Addie stand up to Jed.

Seated in front, Isak twisted his neck to watch a garage sign disappear. He said, "We had those in our . . . department, too." He glanced an apology at Nell. She guessed that he had wanted to say "town" or "area" but couldn't come up with the term. She admired his creativity in filling in the blank.

She smiled and said, "We did, too. Garage sales are everywhere, I guess. Rest stop, everyone!"

Shifting down and easing off the highway, she checked the mirror and caught a slash of navy, her own eyes. Not bad, she judged, except for the eyebrows. Thick as brushes! She chose the lane for buses and trucks and parked at a diagonal.

She stepped out of the bus and fished in her billfold. As Addie and Jed passed by, she gave each of them a few coins. "Drop them in the can if you want cookies. Stay where I can see you." They ran up the walk toward the coffee shack, Addie carrying her rag dolls. Sigrid came out of the bus and put a leash on Stanley. Walking with a hitch that favored her left, she set off with the dog for the pet potty grass. It took Nell's father several minutes to get up on crutches, travel the length of the bus, hand the crutches to Nell's mother, hold the rail for support, hop down the steps on his good foot, regain his crutches, and assemble himself for going forward. It was hard for Nell to watch. He set off up the sidewalk, her mother walking gamely beside him. Nell said, "You want me to come-with?" Her mother waved over her shoulder, no thanks.

Nell was doing stretches between the bus and an eighteen-wheeler when a bony, overly tanned woman in shorts, about sixty years old, bustled between the two vehicles, calling, "Here, Horsey! Here, Horsey!" A Great Dane galloped up behind the woman, clipped her and nearly plowed her down, nearly knocked Nell into the side of the bus, and ran toward open grass on the longest legs any dog could have. The woman hallooed and ran after him, laughing and shouting, "Bad boy, Horsey!" Nell was glad that Sigrid's dog was Stanley, not Horsey.

On her way to the coffee shack, she looked for Jed and Addie. They were on the playground swings, pumping and racing each other, throwing themselves backward with straight arms and pointed toes, then changing directions by pushing their shoulders through the chains and bending back their feet to clear the sand. Next to them, a woman sat at the high end of the teeter-totter, her hair wisping from its bun and a full-length skirt dangling at her ankles. A bearded man in a bowler hat sat at the low end. She said, "No bumping! Promise?" He said, "I promise." She said, "Are you sure? No bumping?" He said, "No bumping." He scooted forward, kicked off with his feet, and bumped her end, *hard*, on the ground. She shrieked, "You promised!" They rode up and down, the man bumping the woman's end, *hard*, the woman laughing and shrieking.

Nell caught up with Sigrid at the coffee shack. They accepted coffee from the couple behind the counter. The wife, who had a petite body, an ardent face, and harried blue eyes, had permed her short white hair for easy care. Her husband was taller by a head, a beefy man with an overhung belly. The couple wore matching clothes, blue jeans, red sweatshirts, and white baseball caps, like twins on the Fourth of July. He smiled intemperately and offered Nell and Sigrid sugar. They said no thanks.

"So what do you call this place?" Sigrid asked. "On the map it's between Brownsville and Eugene."

"Right you are," he said, beaming at the donation box. "We call it Brownsville. Eugene's down the road. We *like* doing this, serving coffee. Want any creamer?"

Again saying no thanks, Nell looked for the children. They were doing cartwheels on the grass. She jogged her head, trying to get rid of the fuzziness inside it. She took a drink of coffee. She needed to stay alert.

Sigrid asked the couple, "Do you do this often?"

The woman said, "This is the . . . ?" She looked to her husband. "Third time?"

His belly swelled bigger. "Fourth."

Jed ran up to Sigrid and asked her if he could take Stanley. "Sure," Sigrid said. "Just keep him on the leash." The dog checked with Sigrid, eye to eye. Getting her go-ahead, he went willingly with Jed. Addie was sitting on a swing, not swinging but holding her dolls and talking to them. The weather was mild and had a singing quality.

"What are you?" Moving back to see the front of the stand, Sigrid read aloud from the banner. "'Sons of the Vikings.'"

The man shouted, "Sons of the Vikings!"

Sigrid said, "You're Scanda*hoov*ians? Me too! Which one?"

He patted his stomach. "Norwegians. Madge and Jerry Ulman. This here is Madge and I's anniversary year. Forty years! We're doing this to celebrate."

In a shift of stances, and smiling broadly, the Ulmans displayed how pleased they were to be married to each other. Madge inclined her head at Jerry. He expanded his longitude.

Leading with her chin, Sigrid said, "I'm a *Swede*! Sigrid Albertson! The others are Halonens! They're Finns! We're all Nordics!" She moved her head bobble-head style as if the coincidence overwhelmed her. "Halonen! Come meet these people! They're Norwegians! Get some coffee!"

Nell knew that her mother preferred coffee she herself made and that she wasn't interested in meeting people she would never see again. Elsa waved and kept walking.

"You might think it's no big deal," Jerry said, "free coffee. But it takes *work*. Madge here makes the cookies. People come back through here, just to get more of her cookies!" Madge blushed and looked downward, her upper teeth clamping her lower lip.

"All kinda groups take over the shack," he said. "We give out free coffee and cookies, but we get donations. It brings in lots of money. *Lots* of groups try to get in."

He dropped his head and peered left and right, alert for spies from unsavory groups. "We'll be here this week and next week, and, let's see—we were here last week. We should make twelve hundred total!" He raised his brows at Sigrid and Nell, letting them know they should exclaim.

"No kidding!" Sigrid said.

"Good for you," Nell said.

Madge pinned her husband with a stare, scolding him, Nell assumed, for giving too much information. "That includes the other side of the road," Madge said, waffling, "everything together, three stands. And that's before expenses."

Jerry showed his teeth, but his smile had no warmth. He had unplugged any interest in the visitors. "Yeah. We gotta buy supplies."

Nell said, "Well, it's been nice talking to you. Thanks for the coffee." She put a dollar bill in the donation box, swung open the trash can and tossed her cup inside. She looked around for the children. They were running with Stanley on the playground, the dog securely on his leash.

Halfway back to the bus, Sigrid called back to the Ulmans, "I sure wish you the best! We better hit the road or we'll never make it to Arizona."

"*Arizona?*" Jerry yelled, alive again. "Whereabouts?"

"Mesa."

He sounded unbelieving. "We lived there for fifteen years!"

Turned away from Jerry and Madge, Sigrid made a crumpled *pshaw* face. In her love affair with the human race, Sigrid sometimes got slogged down like this and found herself deeper in people's lives than she'd intended to go. But, really, Nell thought, what could *anyone* say to a comment like Stan's, shouted out at the end?

Sigrid said, "No kidding? Well, 'bye!"

Jed and Stanley and Addie ran up and Jed handed Stanley's leash to Sigrid. Nell said to the children, "Now is a good time to use the bathroom."

Addie said, "I already went."

"Me too," Jed said.

They already went? When? If she hadn't seen them go into the rest rooms, what else might she have missed? A kidnapper snatching them? A killer on the loose?

Getting back on the highway, Nell felt shaky. There was a bigness to this trip that she hadn't counted on. *She* was in charge. *She* made the decisions. *She* did the driving. She had let her mother drive once, and she drove well, but Nell couldn't relax, fearing the bus might drift into the wrong lane or off the road. "Daddy needs your company," Nell had said, and that much was true. Just now he was sitting behind the driver's seat, contented as long as his wife was nearby. Nell knew that, other than her mother, she, Nell, was the person he wanted nearby—even if he was shy in her presence. As a child, she had found him easier to talk to than her mother, and she had found Sigrid easier to talk to than either parent. Sigrid was fast-moving back then, and she taught Nell skills that would serve her later on (she said), such as making a bed in no time flat. "You do all the layers *at once*," she confided to Nell. "You don't have to go around and around the bed! Think of all the time you save!" Before Nell was eight she could make a bed Sigrid's way, with Sigrid's help, laying down sheets, blanket, and bedspread in the correct order (Sigrid first flapping them and letting them float into place) and making up one corner at a time. She stood at the head of the bed, mitered the bottom sheet, folded back the bedspread, folded five inches of the top sheet over the blanket, lifted the spread up to the pillow area. Next, she went to the near foot of the bed, lifted away the loose bedding, mitered the bottom sheet, brought down the top sheet and blanket, mitered them, brought down the bedspread, straightened it. She repeated the steps on the other corners. She then came back to her original spot, rammed a pillow into a pillowcase and put the pillow at the head of the bed, whacked it with her forearm and folded it the long way like a hot dog bun, brought the top edge of the spread over the pillow and wrapped it tightly to form a bolster. She smoothed out the bedspread and she was done. To the roomers, Sigrid said, "She could put youz guys to shame! Any o' youz guys know how to miter a sheet?"

When they got back to the bus, Sigrid took the front passenger seat and fell asleep with her head on the side window. In a few minutes, she snapped awake and chafed her face with her hands. "Hey, Nell. I don't know if I ever told you. I've got a genital problem. I get hives if I eat corn."

"*Congenital?*"

"Yah, well, *congenital*. Ever since I was a kid. I can't eat corn on the cob, or corn flakes. Or popcorn." She turned to the children. "Jed. Look at you! I'll bet the girls all think you're cute."

In the mirror, Nell saw him fight off a smile. When he closed his mouth and smiled like that, his freckles grew larger. He *was* cute. All of their kids were. They had taken the uneven parts of Dan's and Nell's faces and fixed them. Dan's chin veered slightly to the right, Nell's, slightly to the left. His nose bent slightly left, hers, slightly right. The kids' faces turned out symmetrical. She took pride in this evidence of teamwork.

Addie told Sigrid, "A girl wrote him *love* notes!"

"Nuh-*uh!*" Jed said. "She didn't either!"

Addie giggled. "How do you know who I'm talking about?"

Nell said, "Whom. I'm talking about *him*, I'm talking about *whom*."

Sigrid said, "Nothing wrong with being cute! You're both cute. Listen! A lot of kids will want to be your friend *just because* you're cute. But you need to choose the right friends! Say to yourself, 'If I hang around this kid, I could end up just *like* him. Ask yourself, 'Do I want to be all ruggedy or voicetrous like this kid?' Your mother used to come to my house when she was little. Did you know that?"

Addie said, "She told us."

Sigrid said, "Let's see, what'd we used to do? Nell?"

"Button-Button," Nell said uneasily, thinking her mother might feel bad being reminded of Sigrid's hold on Nell. As usual, her mother showed no emotion.

Sigrid jumbled items in her purse and produced a party-striped cloth bag, opened it, and took out a shirt button. She got up and told Nell, "Don't let the road cops see me walking around." She walked tender-footed to the kitchen area.

"Elsa, you need to play. You too, Isak." Nell's parents said nothing. Sigrid interpreted their silence as acquiescence. "Put your hands like this, like you're praying." She pressed her hands together near her stomach and pointed them forward. "I'll pretend to give you the button. You pretend you either have it or you don't. But *don't tell!* I'll start with Addie."

Nell couldn't see the details but she knew that Sigrid was sliding her hands down between Addie's, pausing, bulging them as if releasing the button, flattening them and dragging them down and out. Addie gave no indication as to whether she had the button.

Elsa was next. Nell wondered how this would go. Her mother didn't play games! As Sigrid passed her hands through Elsa's, Nell caught a girlishness on her mother's face.

Sigrid went to Nell's father and drew her hands through his. He grinned and said, "I got it," and held up the button.

Jed said, "Grandpa! You're not supposed to tell."

Isak said, "It's a secret, huh?"

"We'll do it again," Sigrid said. "This time, no one tells!"

She repeated the sweeps. No one revealed the button's whereabouts. "Okay, Jed, You guess!"

"I say Grandma."

Elsa showed him. No button.

Isak put on a disinterested face. "It's Grandpa!" Jed said. Isak opened his hands. No button.

Jed said, "You fooled me! How'd you fool me?" Nell's father smiled with his mouth closed. He was having a good time deceiving people.

Addie said, "*I've* got it!"

"Okay, Addie, you're It," Sigrid said. "I'll play this time."

Addie passed her hands through the others' hands. Nell's father raised his eyebrows as if he had the button.

"You can't fool *me*, Grandpa!" Jed said. "I choose Auntie Sigrid."

"Wrong," Sigrid said.

Isak whistled behind his teeth to draw notice away from himself.

"You can't fool *me*, Grandpa," Jed said. "Grandma, *you* have it!"

She didn't.

Addie said, "Grandpa has it." Isak opened his hands to show the button.

Jed said, "Grandpa fooled us! Twice!" Nell chalked one up for this trip. Her parents had played Button-Button.

Sigrid said, "The next game is just for fun. Here are maps of Washington." She handed the maps to Jed and Addie. "Find Indian names."

The children unfolded the maps. "I can't read them," Addie complained. "They're too long."

Elsa whispered to Addie. "Tacoma?" Addie said.

"Right!" Sigrid said. "What else?"

Jed said, "Puyallup! Tumwater!"

Nell's mother put her finger on the map and spoke in Addie's ear. Addie said, "Issa? Issaquah."

Jed said, "Skykomish, Snohomish, Snoqualmie. *Humptulips?* Is that Indian?"

Nell called, "Time to eat the fruit."

California law prohibited private vehicles from bringing fruit into California, and rumor had it that inspectors were being extra strict due to a fruit fly scare. They didn't want fruit flies or fruit fly eggs hitchhiking over the border.

Elsa handed out pieces of fruit. Sigrid peeled an orange, spraying essence of orange, and shared segments with the other people. Jed arranged one on his teeth and made faces at Addie. He did that with apple slices, too, it occurred to Nell. Monkey-face, monkeyshine. Her father peeled a banana, lifting away what he called "banana strings"—the fibrous strips left on the banana when the peel was off—and dropping them in the trash. He broke the banana in two and gave one half to Elsa. Addie peeled an orange in a single loop of peel, which she held aloft for the others to see.

Nell announced, "Four miles to go."

Her mother said, "We still have five apples."

Jed said, "I'm full."

Addie said, "Me too."

Sigrid said, "Let's throw 'em to the deer."

Nell eased into the right-hand lane and slowed the bus. Jed slid open one of the tall rebuilt windows. Sigrid said, "Eeny meeny miney mo, catch a tiger by the toe," and landed on Jed. "Jed gets three," she said. "Addie gets two."

Nell felt her chest constrict. Jed could throw a football so hard that the catcher doubled over in pain. He did the same with baseballs. Addie was four years younger than Jed, not as naturally gifted as he was in sports. Nell hoped this would go well for Addie.

Jed took an apple and stood back. Motioning the others aside, he wound up like a baseball pitcher and threw the apple. It smacked a fencepost— a bulls-eye if he had actually meant to hit it. Taking credit, he raised his arms and gave himself huzzahs.

Addie threw her first apple underhand, a blooper that raked the lower edge of the window frame and dropped onto the road. She said, "No fair. Your arms are longer."

Sigrid said, "Don't worry, hon'. A possum will eat it."

Jed's next apple flew far into a hayfield. He tooted, "Am I good or what?"

Addie took her second shot, her last one. It hardly made it outside. She put her head through the window, came back and flumped onto the bench. "It's on the road," she said. "That's two on the road."

Jed polished his last apple and prepared a grandiose pitch. "How much time?"

Nell said, "*Hurry.*"

Jed handed the apple to Addie. She took it guardedly, expecting him to take it back. He said, "Throw it!"

Addie wound up elaborately, imitating Jed, and pitched it overhand. It landed deep in the field. Everyone cheered. Nell chalked up another one for this trip.

When the inspector bent to the window and asked if there was fresh fruit in the vehicle, six people said, "*No!*" He wished them a pleasant trip and waved them on. Before Mount Shasta came into view, its foothills had to be conquered, gigantic sprawling rises that called for cautious driving. Nell obeyed the rules of mountain driving—kept well to the right of center, even on curves that invited shortcuts, pulled aside to let vehicles pass when several stacked behind her—but even if *she* took precautions, she worried that others might not, that a driver of a big rig might miss a turn and smash into the bus.

When it appeared, Mount Shasta filled the view to the east—snowy, high, and widespread, a solid old woman in a flowing white dress. "It's 14,162 feet high," Sigrid read from the TravelHelper. The people on the bus talked it over and agreed. Mount Shasta didn't pack much punch. They were mountain people, not easily impressed. They had had mountains as next door neighbors! They had looked out their windows at crags and rocky cliffs—at Mount St. Helens, 9,677 feet (Sigrid was reading numbers again), Mount Rainier, 14,408 feet, and the highest of them all, Mount McKinley, 20,320 feet.

So, while mildly interested in Mount Shasta, the people on the bus were not bowled over. "It's not as peaky," they said. "Not as showy."

Yet, for hours, starting when the mountain first appeared and ending when it vanished, they hardly took their eyes off Mount Shasta.

They spent the night at Shasta Lake Campground, buffered by campers and mothered by the mountain. When Nell stepped out of the bus in the morning, she found her mother frying pancakes on a park grill and Jed and Addie roasting marshmallows. Her mother had let them have marshmallows for breakfast! Nell said, "Two each," and asked her mother if she needed help. She didn't.

Nell filled a mug with coffee and joined her father at a picnic table. Sigrid was walking Stanley, he said when she asked. Aspens surrounded the campsite, stripped bare for autumn but decorated a new way. Maple leaves as big as serving platters, dark gold and pliable as cloth, had drifted from someplace high and had draped themselves on the aspen boughs like linen napkins hung to dry. Nell and her father took note of them, smiled and made comments, then sat and drank their coffee.

In the center of California, Elsa gave out the last of the roast beef sandwiches. She told Nell she had plenty-other makings, even for Jed, who liked his sandwiches at full tilt—salami, peanut butter, turkey, bologna, ketchup, jam, horseradish, cheese, mustard, pickles, honey, and hot peppers in one sandwich. Jed's sandwiches were like Jed himself, Nell thought—the whole of life in a single bite.

Nell was having an inward tussle. Before leaving the campground, she had perused the TravelHelper. Her eyes skipped over numbers, highways, arrows, symbols. Her temples throbbed. She had wanted to surprise the kids with a stop at Disneyland, but after locating Anaheim on the map and finding Disneyland in the guidebook and reading about parking regulations, dog kennels, and day rates, she had a screamer headache. She had a few hours yet before she'd have to choose either the road to Disneyland or the road to Mesa. Her mind sawed away but got nowhere. She mentally sang, "Do your ears hang low?" It didn't work. She had the blahs again. This trip had turned into another duty.

"Maw-awm!" In one word, Addie gave warning that she was about to tattle on her brother. Nell wilted. American kids had a skill that came with citizenship—an ability to whine the word "Mom" in a tone that could slice bricks. When other people's children whined, Nell wanted to block her ears. It appalled her when Jed or Addie tried it. The temptation to whine was one drawback to living in the States. In the Philippines, her kids never whined. Of course, in the Philippines, there were other temptations, mostly the privilege in being considered "rich Americans." By comparison in Manila, the Sandersons *were* rich. They had a nice house and more than enough food. They even had a housekeeper; all expats did; it was expected, the giving of jobs to local residents. But Nell and Dan preferred a simple life. In the United States, they drove old cars and bought furniture at yard sales and would never think of hiring a housekeeper. Where, Nell wondered, would they live a simple life next?

"Maw-*awm!*"

"Voice," Nell said.

"Jed's cheating! He took two turns in a row!" The game was Battleship and the table was a war zone.

"You know the rule," Nell said.

Jed said, "I know, settle it ourselves or put the game away." To Addie, he said, "Let's start over."

"You'll cheat!"

"No, I won't. Trust me."

Sigrid said, "Jed, honey, you *earn* people's trust. If you cheated before, why should Addie trust you?"

Jed started to say, "I didn't cheat," and in fact he got it out of his mouth. "I won't cheat," he amended. "Really."

"Better not!" Addie said.

Nell was not being a glorious mom. She felt crotchety. Still, she wanted more kids. She wanted a family like the families in the old Finnish church. They typically had twelve or thirteen children! She wasn't a member of that church, but a friend had shown her a photo and the image had stayed with her. The parents, dressed in black, sat on a loveseat, the mother holding a baby, the father holding a toddler, and ten children stood behind them arranged by height, college students peaking in the middle, toddlers at either end. The girls wore white blouses and plaid skirts and wore their hair in French braids or upsweeps. (Women and girls in that church never cut their hair.)

The boys wore white shirts and dark slacks and had flattop haircuts. (The fathers cut their sons' hair with hand clippers.) Everyone seemed extraordinarily happy, shoulders back, broad smiles. Not a grouchy face in sight! Nell wanted a family that big and that happy.

The migraine clinched it. No Disneyland. The sooner Nell could get to Mesa, the sooner she could crawl into a bed and stay there. As she drove, she mentally wrote her next column. She would blame her headache on diesel fumes, the stinky black plumes that belched out of trucks—the poison blooms of the highway.

By noon, her head was in a vice. She pulled into a rest stop. She had to lie down.

* * *

Elsa drove while Nell slept. Sigrid acted as nurse and overseer. She arranged Nell on a couch, then went forward to see the kids and to assure Elsa that Highway 10 would lead directly to Phoenix, no problem. The steering wheel, a horizontal type of wheel, came up to Elsa's chest. Elsa gripped it honorably at ten o'clock and two o'clock and looked straight ahead.

"You're doing good, Halonen," Sigrid told her.

When Nell woke up, she was feverish. Sigrid gave her a spoonful of medicine with orange juice, then wrung out a cloth in cold water, laid it on Nell's forehead, and told her to scootch over. It took Nell several hops to un-Velcro her cotton top and genii pants from the plush of the sofa. When she had made space for another hip and flank, Sigrid cocooned her in a blanket and sat against her legs.

"Does your chest hurt?"

"No. Just my head."

"The medicine will help."

Relocating her backside, Sigrid folded her hands in her lap. "I remember when you were little and I had a cold. You were so serious! You brought me Kleenex, cough drops, water, hot water bottle. You didn't want me to die."

Nell's eyes misted over—more from sickness than sentiment, Sigrid guessed. She reversed the cloth to the cold side. She said, "I'll sing you to sleep." She used her deep frog voice to sing, "'Froggie went a courtin' an' he did ride, mm-*hmm.*'"

After Nell dosed off, Sigrid went to the front of the bus and told Elsa, "I gave her some medicine I had for tonsillitis. It put her to sleep."

"Isn't that *prescription?*"

"Ya, but don't worry. I take responsibility."

"A lot of good that does if she *dies.*"

Sigrid hoo-hooed to remind Elsa that Elsa was a worrywart. Then she said, "Where are we?"

Elsa let time pass to remind Sigrid that she was a meddler. Then she said, "We just passed Indio."

Retrieving the TravelHelper, Sigrid sat in the passenger's seat and looked up their position. "We're fifteen minutes from the Arizona border." She got up and patted Elsa's shoulder. "Want any juice? I'm getting some from the foodjerator." Elsa said no thanks.

In the kitchen, Sigrid hung onto a ceiling strap and swung above the children. "Did you see Joshua National Park? You like the desert?"

Addie and Jed shrugged and went back to their books, snubbing the desert. They had been traveling in the desert for some time and had spent their oohs and ahs.

"See if you can find any date trees or cactuses," Sigrid said.

"Cac-*ti,*" Jed said.

Sigrid made her face long and jocular. "*You*-hoo-hoo," she laughed, "you're just like your mom! 'Cac-*ti!*'" In a waddle forced by bad knees, she retreated to the rear of the bus.

She sat down and picked up her paperback. Stanley made a circuit until he found the right spot, then sank with an "Unk" and put his snout on Sigrid's slipper. She kept forgetting the title, something about heaven and love. *Paradise Around Us.* The cover painting squeezed at her chest, a handsome hero on a prancing horse, his lady-bride in his arms. Everything trailed—her gown, his cape, her hair, even the horse's tail.

Unsettled, Sigrid gazed at the hero. She was old, sure. But she wasn't
dead.

* * *

Nell kept her eyes closed, hoping to extend the dream. It was the same
dream she had had before—about a house with undiscovered rooms. She knew
the rooms were there, somewhere, behind other rooms, or past the porch, or down
the hill. She called hello in a hollow hall. Was that an echo? A clue to bogus walls?
She wanted more time to search. She wanted someone to stroke her hair. Fever
pictures pressed in—an ice-skating shack, hot-hot stove, skate-walking on a
scarred wood floor, rough kids flirting, her parents when she was little, quiet, not
quite approving of her, or maybe she was wrong about that. Feeling so weak, she
had new empathy for her father. As far back as she could recall, he was huge and
mythical, able to do anything he set his mind to. Officially, he was a heavy
equipment mechanic, a well-defined job. But his *hobbies!* He was a barber,
fisherman, hunter, ocean skipper, weaver, gardener, fiddler, woodcarver, inventor,
knot expert, cobbler, folklorist, historian, jokester, and he had a saying for
everything. "Eat fruits in season, when they do the most good" or "Stick Juicy
Fruit inside those mole holes." He built their fireplace from local rock, repaired
the sewing machine, welded anything that needed welding, measured distance by
guess, and talked down prices at junkyards. He got everything cheap or free, and
he saved whatever he found. He practiced the art of *bricolage* (a term Nell learned
in college)—the making of good things from throwaways. If he needed an angled
tool that hooked a certain way, and if such a tool did not exist, he invented it in
his garage. The words "his garage" meant a rubble dump sorted by mystical means,
one of two identical spaces in Alaska and Washington. Each had a path from the
door to the workbench and was otherwise stacked with junk—davenports, hide-
a-beds, tires, tables, chairs, dressers, car engines, fenders, bumpers, scrap lumber,
broom handles, varnishes, paints, putty, power tools. On the rafters he kept flat
inner tubes, planks too long to stand against the wall, and broken skis. Smaller
items he stored in open drawers, on shelves and on nails in the wall, in jelly jars

and tin cans—fuses, nuts, bolts, nails, buttons, rope, cables, belts, T-shirts, string, knobs, screws, safety pins, needles, thread, paper clips, crayon stubs, one-inch pencils, burlap, fabric scraps, industrial wipe, cans, bottles, bottle caps—all actors waiting for a call. Evenings, he sat at the workbench surrounded by radio, heater, and gooseneck lamp, making magic and singing in falsetto, "Dee-dee-dee." Spectators pressed into the light. A hacksaw said, "How about that?" A watering can: "I never saw the like!"

Nell's father was a happy man. *Before.* Before his intellect started to fail. He was known for his intellect. What would he be without it?

* * *

The Roster Fund took up the top floor of a three-story building, an expanse of waist-high partitions, trees in tubs, teletype machines, copiers, electric typewriters—a sea of industry. Dan's office was on the perimeter, a comfortable space that looked down on the street. He was always on display. The interior walls were glass, and Roster's open-door policy invited co-workers to stop and talk. Dan was a solitary thinker who fought irritation when interrupted. This realization had come to him on this current trip, during his first hour back at the office. He wondered why it had never occurred to him before.

"Your coffee, sir?" Ramona de Guzman stood at the door holding a ceramic cup and saucer. She was new to the firm, an ethereal presence, small-boned even for a Filipina and very soft-spoken. Twice each morning since his arrival, she had brought him coffee the way he liked it, strong, with double cream. She would be an anomaly in the United States. In the States, secretaries insisted on being called administrative assistants but felt demeaned if assisting included fetching coffee. Ramona brought him his coffee without his asking for it and she did it with a waiflike smile. An ex-Carmelite nun who left the convent to get married, she had re-embraced celibacy after her husband died, joined a lay order, and taken this job with Roster. She was polite and efficient, but Dan missed talking to Nell. Ramona was so otherworldly, he thought, that she might float away someday in the middle of a sentence, never to return, whereas Nell had enough bulk and common sense to keep her grounded.

He thanked Ramona, and she left. He felt sodden, unproductive. Usually, after a long flight, he rebounded fast. Not this time. He felt disoriented. Life was distasteful. Beyond the adventure of finding Laura, everything felt wrong, as if his shoes were on the wrong feet. He had an impulse to reverse his shoes, or to reverse *something*. But nothing came to mind. Culture shock, this was. Odd to have it after so many years of travel.

To make matters worse, he couldn't see Max, not any time soon. Max had left a message at Roster, saying he would be away for two weeks and would see Dan when he got back. He was taking his class to Cebu in the southern part of the Philippines for a long-planned study tour.

Contributing to Dan's misery was his housing. To save money toward a home purchase in the States, he had taken lodging in a guesthouse run by Field Workers, a British relief group. The price was cheap for room and board, but Dan felt scrutinized at every meal. Unspoken assumptions ran the place—secret rules regarding when anyone spoke, for how long, how loudly, about what. He had gathered that certain topics were off limits. Others were borderline. He guessed that he had broken every rule at least once. He wanted to find another place to stay.

However, before he could do that, two events happened at the guesthouse.

First, he got food poisoning. Many guests did. The manager was trying urgently to trace the cause. Dan stayed in his room, writhing on the bed or bolting to the bathroom.

Second, he heard taps at his door. He lay still, wishing away the knocker. He heard giggles and more taps. He knew who was there. He got up, wrapped a towel around his shorts, crept to the door, and cracked it open. Nine diminutive nuns smiled up at him. A little girl hopped beside them, her eyes jiggling in excitement. She wore a lacy white dress, leg braces, and orthopedic shoes. Pippy Longstocking pigtails sprang from the sides of her head. They flew every time she jumped. She said, "Hi, Daddy! Hi, Daddy!"

Sister Mary Clare said, "Daniel, this is Laura."

Bent over with cramps, Dan murmured that he was glad to meet her, but, sorry, he was sick, he couldn't ask them in, sorry again. The nuns radiated heat and healing at Dan. Then they swept Laura down the hall, calling with her, "'Bye, Daddy!'"

From his second-floor window, Dan saw the nuns lower the tailgate of an open army truck, climb in, and lift Laura up beside them. As the truck drove off, the nuns crowded the sides, smiling and waving to him, and Laura hopped up and down.

* * *

From her stoop, Grace Ann watched the group get off the bus. They were bedraggled, to say the least. Nell looked sick, and the other lady (the Swedish friend?) was listing to one side. Isak slid down the bus steps on the seat of his pants and hobbled forth on crutches. Elsa walked beside him, bringing his cane. They all seemed in a trance after days on the road. Even the children looked dazed. A big black dog pushed past their legs to reach open air.

They came up the walk and huddled at the foot of her steps, pleading upward like tired sheep, very nearly bleating. Grace Ann felt incidental. Her apartment was what they wanted, air conditioning and showers and whatever home-cooked food she could give them. Not Grace Ann herself.

Belatedly, as if recalling her manners, Elsa introduced Grace Ann to the people in her group.

With a start, Grace Ann recalled her own manners. She said, "Oh, yes. Come in! How was the trip?"

And she brought them inside.

Eight

Flames in the Wind

When Dan felt better, he went to the orphanage to sit with Laura on the swings. She was a winning child, ebullient and talkative. She peppered him with questions. Her words were unique, but her meanings were clear. "You my Daddy? I kleep at your house? You see me in the morling?" He hadn't been able to reach Nell, but he knew she would say, "*Yes,*" to adopting Laura.

He started on the paperwork. In addition to requirements by the government of the Philippines, the United States government required Dan's and Nell's fingerprints, an updated home study, a notarized Petition to Adopt an Orphan, a notarized financial statement, income tax records, Laura's birth certificate, verification of household salary and longevity on jobs, a signed statement from Laura's biological parent(s) relinquishing her for adoption, payment of a thirty-five-dollar application fee. Dan had brought much of the documentation with him, but some requirements couldn't be met in the Philippines. He would have to return the States without Laura. Later, after an updated home study was completed in North Dakota, and after the governments of both countries approved the adoption, he would fly back to Manila to pick up Laura. He hoped to work in a consulting job to help pay for the trip.

A Roster friend from former days, Mike Santos, invited Dan to the island where Mike did volunteer work. On Saturday morning, at a marina in Manila, they stepped into a *banca,* a small tented boat manned by a muscular young man named Darius. Darius inched the *banca* between the docks, avoiding boats moored on either side. Beyond the docks, he maintained the slowest speed and putt-putted in turquoise shallows dotted with heads. The heads, which belonged to men and boys fishing with hand baskets, bobbed in the waves and smiled hello. Safely past them, Darius pushed the speed knob forward and the *banca* roared and skimmed the surface of the water. Dolphins leaped alongside the boat and swam with it. Flying fish flew over the bow. Mike shouted above the engine noise, pointing at islands and naming them for Dan.

He yelled something that included, "Ding dong."

Dan shrugged, not getting the whole sentence.

Mike shouted, "*Ding Dong!* We call Darius *Ding Dong!*"

An hour after leaving Manila, they came within view of Haslin Island. It appeared as an oblong hill covered with trees, the only visible building a European style house on a bluff. "Dash House," Mike said, "built by an American millionaire, Charles Dash. He came to the island three times and went bankrupt in 1930. Now it's a village center and guesthouse. People say it's haunted."

Darius slowed by stages and trolled beside the island. A sandy beach identified itself by smell as a latrine. Around a sharp bend, he eased the *banca* against a high rock quay and killed the engine. Waves ticked the boat against the quay.

Dan and Mike hopped up onto the rock, directly into the company of women and toddlers who had gathered to meet the boat. They stared openly at Dan. He was used to being stared at in the Philippines. A foot taller than most Filipinos—and freckled and red-headed besides—he stood out in any crowd. Mike led the way into the forest, passing houses built on stilts, pigs foraging beneath houses, women hunkering on porches and fixing food. A layer of wood smoke hung in the trees—a familiar presence in Southeast Asia, even in cities. The smell always reminded Dan of summer camp.

Mike stopped to greet a cordial man who was hunkering in front of his house. His face had a yellow tint that didn't seem healthy. As he stood, he moved slowly as if in pain. He offered Dan his hand and spoke his name, Rafael Roosevelt (not *the* Roosevelt, he said with a smile), and gestured welcome to his home, ten steps up the ladder. Like most Filipinos, he was slim and short with brown skin and black hair, but his hair was curly, not straight. While his face paid homage to Spain and China, he looked mostly African.

The three men stepped into the one-room house, displacing an old woman who had been chopping vegetables in the center of the floor. In a single obsequious move, she smiled her way backwards into a corner, taking the vegetables with her. Dan apologized for taking her space. When Rafael spoke to her in Tagalog, she dipped her head and spoke briefly. Rafael said, "She says no, no. She wishes you happiness."

Mike and Rafael hunkered on the floor. Dan sat down and crossed his legs. The family's possessions hung on the wall or stood in stacks at the periphery of the room. Rafael smiled purposefully at Dan and said, "I am American!"

Mystified, Dan looked at Mike. Mike spoke in Tagalog to Rafael. Rafael answered at length in Tagalog. Dan picked up a few English words, among them, "Jersey City, New Jersey."

Mike said, "Rafael's father was an African-American named Timothy Roosevelt. He worked for a shipping company in Manila. Rafael's mother cleaned his office building at night. Timothy met her one night while working late, and after that he arranged to work late quite often. They got married and went to America and lived in Jersey City, New Jersey. Rafael was the only child born to them. His father died when Rafael was a boy, and his mother brought him back to Manila."

Rafael had monitored Mike's translation, nodding his approval. He added a sentence in Tagalog. "His mother died four years ago," Mike told Dan.

"I have many dead," Rafael said in English, eyeing Dan. Speaking again in Tagalog, he relayed to Mike what else he wanted Dan to know.

"His wife died giving birth, three months ago. The auntie cooks and cleans." Mike turned to the old woman, who was working with her head lowered. When she realized that she was being discussed, she bent her head yet lower.

The men went down the ladder and accomplished the maze backwards. Dan saw that for Rafael the act of walking took concerted effort. Past the boat ramp, they came to a building labeled "Clinic." Two old men hunkered outside the door, passing time the way old men in the States passed time outside a barber shop. But American men would be sitting on a bench.

Dan admired the agility of these old men. In the States, people their age couldn't squat like this with their arms on their knees—or, if they *could*, they wouldn't look this relaxed.

These two old men and Rafael were the only men Dan had seen. He said to Mike, "The other men are sleeping? They fish at night?"

"Yes. Rafael can't fish. He has hepatitis A."

"From the latrine?"

Mike nodded. "The others make him stay at home. They give him fish."

Rafael winced a smile at Dan, paying tribute to his kind neighbors.

"His children pick shells from the beach to sell," Mike said. "There's a man who gives them money for shells. They don't earn much, maybe four pesos a day. A kilo of rice costs two pesos fifty centavos. One kilo feeds a small family maybe one meal. A large family? Rafael has a large family."

The school was a one-room plaza with a roof and three open walls. The students sat on benches at long wooden tables. A young male teacher spoke words in Tagalog and the children repeated them in sing-song. The teacher excused them, and they burst out of school like children out of school anywhere, calling and joking, girls in sleeveless dresses, boys in shorts and T-shirts. All of the children wore brightly colored flip-flops. They looked at Dan—at his freckles, white skin, orange hair, and six-four frame—and tittered behind their hands.

Three young versions of Rafael came to stand by their father. In contrast to their classmates who had straight hair, Rafael's sons had curly or wavy hair. They had recently lost their mother, Dan remembered. He wondered how they were managing, how Rafael was managing. Rafael didn't seem strong enough to raise children on his own.

"My sons," Rafael said proudly. "Tell your name and how many years."

The tallest boy shook Dan's hand. "I am Abraham. I am ten years old." The boy was a dignified eldest child.

"Nice to meet you, Abraham. My son Jed is ten, too."

The middle boy had none of his older brother's reserve. With a smile that engaged his whole face, he thrust his hand at Dan. "I am *Isaac*! I am eight years old! I flay music!"

Dan asked, "What instrument do you play?"

"Plute! I fut it in my focket!" Isaac pulled a small whistle-flute from a pocket in his shorts.

Watch out for this boy's *p*'s and *f*'s, Dan said to himself. "My wife's father has the same name as yours. You spell it I-s-a-a-c? He spells it I-s-a-k. In Finland they say '*Ee*-sack.' But we say it the same way you say yours, 'Isak,' 'Isaac.'"

Isaac seemed bored by this rundown of facts. Dan said, "Anyway! Glad to meet you, Isaac." He asked the smallest of the three boys, "And who are you?"

The boy sucked in air. "Jacob."

"How old are you?"

Isaac answered for him. "Seben! His talking is not so good! He says, 'G-g-go away,' like that!" Isaac's taunt sounded cruel, but Jacob seemed not to notice. Rafael looked pained, this pain separate from his physical health.

Dan told Jacob, "Don't worry. When I was your age, I had trouble talking, too." The boy kept his eyes on Dan as if Dan had answers he needed.

Other school children had gathered around the visitors. Dan opened one hand and showed them two foam rabbits, put his hands together, opened them, and six baby rabbits leaped into the air. The children watched, mesmerized. Abruptly, like fairytale children freed from a magic spell, they laughed and scattered to pick up the rabbits.

Mike led the way into the forest, taking a different route this time. School children tagged along, whispering and pointing at Dan, and dropping off at their homes. Rafael's sons walked with importance, having gained the honor of hosting the guests.

Rafael stopped in front of a stilted house and called a greeting in Tagalog. A woman holding a baby appeared at the door. Three small children clambered down the ladder and ran to Rafael, a girl in a sundress and twin boys in nothing at all.

The father put his hands on the little girl's head. Her curls gave her an angelic appearance. "This is Rachel. She is . . . how old?" He gave her a contrived frown.

She held up five fingers. To Dan, she looked more like three.

"Oh *yes!*" Her father raised his eyebrows and chuckled. "*Five.*"

Dan said, "I have a daughter who's six. Her name is Addie." The girl said nothing.

Rafael said, "David. And Jonathan." The twins had taken matching poses at their father's knees. At the mention of their names, they hid behind his legs.

"Hello, David, hello, Jonathan. How old are you?"

Isaac answered for them. "Two!" Each twin held up five fingers on one hand and with the fingers of the other hand separated out two.

"Near three," their father said.

The woman came down the steps carrying the baby. Rafael reached for the baby and gingerly took her into his arms. "Rebecca," he said. Rebecca had a delicate, strained face and seemed frail. Rafael treated her with fondness and a scan of commiseration.

That evening at Dash House, the meal consisted of rice, crawdads, and vegetables, prepared by an immaculate woman who vanished after serving the food. The dining room, situated on the second floor, was designed island-style with no glass at the windows. A hot wind blew throughout the house.

The two men were still eating when night fell like a lead curtain. It shouldn't have surprised Dan. He had worked on other islands like this one, without electricity. But this clunk of blackness always startled him. No ambient light anywhere. Just deep darkness.

Mike lit two oil lamps made of tin cans and rags. The flames flapped crazily in the wind. The men finished their meal and went down to the main room where two small girls huddled at a table, reading by lamplight. They looked up, smiled quickly, and went back to their reading. Mike took a guitar from a closet and strummed it. Dan missed his banjo. It was traveling in the blue bus with Nell and the kids.

Villagers gathered at the windows and looked in at Dan. All day long, he had been followed by villagers. Only when he hid in the Dash House privy, the island's only plumbed bathroom, had he been able to be alone. Now, in response to a signal Dan knew nothing about, adults and children streamed into Dash House, and soon most of the population stood or sat along the walls of the main room. Mike moved his chair to the middle, indicating to Dan that he should do the same. Rafael and his children sat near them on the floor.

In the light of dozens of oil lamps, Mike played his guitar and sang songs in Tagalog. A small girl approached Dan and put her hand on his arm. Her hair was cut in a shiny Sassoon bob, sassy and asymmetrical. She breathed, "I am Clarissa."

She whispered in Tagalog to Mike. Mike said to Dan, "She will sing a song about our homeland, *Pilipinas*."

Clarissa stepped away, took in a lungful of air, and belted out a song in a voice fit for Broadway—a booming, confident, beautiful, stunning voice.

Mike translated quietly for Dan:

> *"When I was young and foolish, I dreamed of a beautiful land.*
> *I traveled far and wide, and after many years I returned to the*
> *Philippines,*
> *land of palm trees, coconuts, mangoes and sparkling blue waters.*
> *I realized how foolish I had been.*
> *I had looked the whole world over, and, all the while,*
> *the most beautiful land was here at home, in the Philippines."*

Dan had never heard such a voice. He was tempted to say, "You could make it *big*! Let me take you to the United States!" But Clarissa's voice was a gift for the islanders, not for the bigger world. He felt privileged to be there and hear it. The words of the song touched him: traveling, seeking, finally seeing.

The music went on for hours. Mike sang. Clarissa sang. Dan and Mike sang. The villagers sang. Dash House shimmered in a bubble, complete in itself, far from the modern world and not needing it.

When Dan went to his cot, sleep came fast. When it was still night, he woke to voices below his room. He got up and stood at the window which in daytime looked down on the beach. Small lights were bobbing—on the water, he supposed. As his eyes grew used to the dark, he could make out shadows, men leaving for a night of fishing, their wives seeing them off. More talk, more laughter. As the boats pulled away from shore, their bow lights swayed. The women stayed until the lights grew dim, then went home chatting. Brave endeavors, Dan thought—men working in the dark, their wives going to the shore when they could be sleeping. This chivalry went on unheralded, night after night, when no outsiders were there to witness it and be awed.

He lay awake sweating and comparing this heat to Thailand's. In Thailand, he would need a mosquito net. Here, he didn't. He imagined a net around his bed—the top drooping and lifting like a silhouette of the Olympics. He tried humming the Olympics. It didn't work. Before the kids were born, he and Nell camped in the Olympic Range in northwest Washington. Hiking down a slant of loose shale, Dan slid out of control. He stopped the slide with one hand and yelped in pain. He found footing and held up his left hand for Nell to see. The pinky finger stuck out at forty-five degrees, an old football injury. Nell gagged. He said, "*Grab* it!" She ground her boots into the shale and took hold of the finger. When he said, "Pull!" she pulled and the finger snapped into place. Dan nearly fainted from pain. They spent the night in sleeping bags but not sleeping. Aspirin didn't help, and they had nothing stronger. Nell told him riddles, knock-knock jokes, anything to divert him. Stars snapped on a clump at a time like lights on a football field. The Olympics made a circle around them, black on midnight blue, spiking and dipping like notes on a sheet of music. Nell said, "Let's sing the Olympics!" She hummed the peaks and valleys and Dan sang, "My finger's killing me, so I'm gonna hug my Nell and forget it, but excuse me a minute while I screeeeeeam." Ever since then, he had carried acetaminophen with codeine, available over the counter in Asia. Now *there's* a travel boon, he thought, over-the-counter codeine.

A gecko made its call somewhere in the house. The first time he heard a gecko croak—a high-pitched yip followed by a gruff growl—he was in Thailand, and he thought a small dog had barked in its sleep. He confused his host by asking him, "Is that your dog?" The man didn't understand. The gecko croaked again. Dan said, "*There.*" The man smiled and said, "Oh!

Gecko." He walked Dan to the next room and pointed to the wall. Near the ceiling, a big green lizard spanned the corner, hanging on by suction toes. Dan was used to two-inch salamanders in the States—beige, harmless creatures. This gecko was a foot long. It ran down the wall and stopped upside-down an inch from the floor. With the complacency of ownership, the Thai man said, "They eat the bugs."

Mike's initial visit to Haslin Island was a month earlier on a work day sponsored by his Anglican church in Manila and the island church called The Way. The leader of The Way, Joseph Santoro, had been attacked by island toughs and was recuperating at home. Parishioners were filling in for him, not an easy job. Normally, it was said, he was everywhere at once, helping anyone who needed help. Mike did what he could to help Rafael. The island had no fresh water. A boat came weekly to sell water, but fresh water was expensive. So, each Saturday Mike brought drinking water plus food for Rafael's family. He did chores with the children, went fishing with them, let them play his guitar. A good way to spend weekends, Dan thought. Mike didn't have wife or kids to worry about. He could spend weekends any way he chose. Then Dan realized that *he* didn't have wife and kids here, either. He would tag along with Mike the next Saturday.

Before returning to the city, Dan and Mike promised Rafael's neighbor, Tala Garcia, to make her a concrete platform. She had hunkered in her yard as they walked by and gestured for them to stop, her smile a mix of flirtation and demand, her teeth black from betel nuts. A childless widow beyond marrying age, she earned a living by raising and bartering vegetables— calabasa squash, kangkong spinach, gabi tubers, bamboo shoots, bok choi. She was a wily trader who talked seasoned gardeners into buying her produce. Her neighbors raised their own vegetables, but Tala Garcia raised fatter roots and greener greens. She was the only woman on the island who harvested coconuts. Bucking tradition, she put on men's clothes and climbed the trees as the men did, barefoot, wielding her knife with abandon and plummeting coconuts to the ground. She envied the concrete at Dash House, the garden walls and walkways, the patch below the basketball hoop. She offered the men eight coconuts apiece for making her a slab for displaying vegetables. The men said they would do it, but for one coconut each. They could bring tools, framing materials, and concrete mix from Manila. In addition to making the concrete slab, they would make a wooden sandbox for Rafael's children.

Back in the city, Mike and Dan canvassed on behalf of Rafael. He needed better care than the island clinic could provide. They wanted to get him into the Mumford Clinic, Manila's premium medical facility. Patronized by expatriates and wealthy Filipinos, it was too expensive for ordinary citizens. Dan and Mike asked everyone they knew for contacts at Mumford, hoping to find someone to help Rafael at reduced cost.

In these ways, Dan was drawn into Rafael's world. Shamed into gratitude, he forgot his gripes about his Manila lodging. The islanders got on cheerfully with far less than what he had at the guesthouse.

He ran into trouble with his petition to adopt Laura. The government director of children's services expressed doubts that Laura's psychological and medical needs would be met in Dan's family. She voiced concern that Dan's work too often took him away from his family. She said she would likely reject his petition.

At the Roster office, Dan offered Mike the job of director. Mike accepted. Dan's work at Roster would be done in two weeks.

* * *

Nell tried to call Dan at the office. The phone rang, but no one answered.

* * *

Dan tried to call Nell at Grace Ann's. The phone rang, but no one answered.

* * *

Nell's migraine was over but she stayed out of the fray, typing away in the spare room, making excuses about deadlines, editors, columns. The apartment crackled with undeclared war. The snippy sisters had a score to settle, and they had made Jed and Addie into game pieces, outdoing each other, moving the kids around and racking up points. The kids themselves were having a great time. Grace Ann took them to places of fun and fantasy—a participatory science museum, the YMCA swimming pool, an old theater that showed silent films—proving that life was not purely work. Elsa stayed at the apartment and fixed food—lasagna, fried chicken, casseroles, cakes—proving that food was a necessity, after all, and *someone* had to fix it since the hostess wasn't about to. Nell thought she knew what had started the feud. Five years earlier, when Grandma Sepanen died, the will left the elder daughter, Elsa, the silver coffee urn, and the younger daughter, Grace Ann, the silver tea set. The tea set was considered the superior gift. How such a trifle could set up this catfight, Nell didn't know, unless it pointed to a bigger hurt—some old gripe that had ripened with age. That was likely *it*, an old gripe. When Nell was a child, her mother had hinted that Grace Ann was the preferred daughter, that she, Elsa, was never doted-on by their parents the way Grace Ann was. Grace Ann was capricious. She won hearts without effort. Elsa was hard-working and dependable, not adept, as Grace Ann was, at playing the coquette.

Now here they were, near retirement age, competing for the hearts of children while acting out their own childhood roles. In this contest of wills they stayed absolutely in character—Grace Ann the whimsical, Elsa the practical.

* * *

The call from Harald changed everything. Grace Ann gave Isak the message when he got up from his nap. "He wants you to call."

Isak said to Elsa, "You call."

She placed the call. Harald shouted, "I'm here in the Twin Cities! I'm going to Nort Deekota to sell the farm! I guess it's okay with brother Isak if we sell?"

"Well, I don't know . . .When?" Elsa had never met Harald, and she knew nothing about the farm except that Isak had grown up there and that she mailed his portion of the property taxes every year. But selling it didn't sound right.

"*Now!*" Harald shouted. "I'm tired of paying taxes! Besides, it's a good time to sell, what with the mineral rights and all."

"Mineral rights?"

He croaked and snuffled, then yelled, "They found oil! Didn't I write? Maybe not. Well, anaway, they found oil and the land's worth a lot!"

"Just a minute." Elsa covered the mouthpiece and said to Isak, "You want to talk to him?"

Isak ran a hand over his morning shave. "What's he want?"

She said into the phone, "We'll call you back. I need to talk to Isak."

"Sure, but let me know! I'll be going to Nort Deekota in a couple days."

Elsa came off the phone and said, "Harald's in Minnesota. He's going to the farm. He wants to sell it."

Isak made a guttural noise like a strangle. The two brothers had the same trait, Elsa noted. They made a choking sound when emotions got high.

"*I* have a say in this," Isak said, "and I say *no!*" He had been sitting, but now he clambered up onto his crutches and made a pronouncement.

"That's where we're going next. To the farm."

* * *

It had been decided. Marcie would go with her dad to help present their side on legal issues. She wasn't a lawyer, but she was persistent. (*Pushy,* more like it. She knew her reputation.) Seated on the floor, she touched her head to her knees and held it for thirty seconds, lay back and did half-sit-ups. Her father hadn't been to the farm for forty years, longer yet for Uncle Isak. Preparing for the trip, she had looked up family records. Isak was born in 1905 and he left home in 1922. It was now 1979. Fifty-seven years since he'd been to the farm. What kind of a man was he? At Grandpa Halonen's funeral, he had seemed quiet. But then, *anyone* seemed quiet compared to her dad.

Marcie had no Halonen blood in her. She wasn't even a Finn. But she belonged to the family in two vital ways. She was adopted into it, and she married into it. After their wedding, she and Adam discovered they were cousins—not blood relations, but cousins. The surprise of it still made her laugh. Adam's mother was born of a tryst in Finland between Grandpa Halonen and an old flame, and she was adopted by an American couple, Adam's grandparents. No one told these facts to Adam as he grew up. It took Marcie's nosy cousin, Kik, to dig them up. Adam was more of a Halonen than Marcie was—even if his last name was Tiskanen and her maiden name was Halonen. *Adam* should be taking this trip, not Marcie. But he was a teacher and couldn't take time off. She was a photographer and could.

She would drive her car, a green second-hand Ford station wagon she secretly disliked. Her father, a dyed-in-the-wool Ford fan, had tracked down this motherly hauler and made it a gift to Marcie, saying it was a steal that he couldn't pass up. She hadn't had the heart to say, "No thanks." She saved her "No thanks" for "No thanks, you guys come *here* for Christmas." Her parents routinely asked her and Adam and the kids to spend Christmas in Florida, but Adam wanted sleigh bells and snow for Christmas, not beaches and palm trees. Her parents had moved from Minnesota to Florida five years ago for her father's health. Overweight most of his life, he was now trim—or as trim as his famous loose skin allowed. He had lost one hundred pounds by avoiding the color white, he told people—whipped cream, doughnuts, sugar—and by walking on the beach with Marcie's mom, Inky. He told people he didn't flap his wings the way Inky did, in that chickeny Olympics walk, but he did fine even with his fake leg. He claimed to feel younger at sixty-six than he had at fifty. He looked younger, too, Marcie thought, and he had more spunk—although he'd had plenty of *that* to begin with.

On this trip, he would need all the spunk he could muster. She had caught wind of Isak's refusal to sell.

✽ ✽ ✽

At the appointed time to call, Sunday night on Nell's side of the globe, Monday noon on Dan's side, she dialed his number. As the phone rang, she toyed with the concept of time. People traveling west gained a day as they crossed the International Date Line. If they kept going west, around and around the world, they could end up old at a young age! Or the reverse. Maybe the Date Line was the Fountain of Youth, and people going east got younger and younger. . . .

No one answered. Where *was* he? Why didn't someone on the office staff answer?

✽ ✽ ✽

Dan tried Grace Ann's number. The phone rang. No one answered. He hadn't talked to Nell since he left the States. Where *was* she?

✽ ✽ ✽

As their mother drove the bus, the children were quiet—worn out, Isak imagined, from being knots in the ladies' tug of war. Elsa and Grace Ann had capped their four-day fuss with a rip-snorting picnic in the park, a project so big it took the two ladies five hours of working against each other to bring it off. He'd never seen meaner faces at a picnic! In Arizona's furnace-sun, they ran the barbeque pit with poker brows, heaving pots from place to place, shooing away offers of help—trying to prove who was the better hostess. Isak knew what was going on, but he couldn't change it. Elsa would never let up. Neither, it seemed, would Grace Ann.

Isak was seventy-four, but he felt seventeen. *I'm going home,* he gloated, *for the first time since I was seventeen!* At rest stops he practiced walking on crutches, planning how to get around when he got to the farm. His brain was ticking like a wind-up clock. He wanted to show the children the farm. Shucks, he wanted to see it for himself! Hear the windmill squeak, see the tank where the horses drank. Did geese still swim in there? He wanted to stand in the barn where the sun streaked in, and go to the field and smell the sage. He wondered if they still kept hogs.

"Daddy, why did you leave home so young?"

Isak was just getting to that, but he wasn't prepared to talk about it. He never knew what to say to Nell. He went blank in her presence. She had been a sunny child, curious about everything. Now she was grown. What could he say to her? Sigrid had bustled him into the front seat and plunked his cast on a suitcase, having no idea he was so sketchy around Nell. He was a captive, so he had to talk.

"Oh, *that*," he said, and he tapped his fingers on his cast. Swiveling his head to the side window, he saw nothing familiar. Just hayfields. No hills to speak of.

"Father," he braved to say, "had a problem."

"What kind of problem?"

He didn't like this line of talk, but he answered anyway. "He drank. Not all the time. But he got crazy when he drank, and Mum closed down."

"How do you mean, closed down?"

Isak's right forefinger captured his right thumb and drew patterns on the thumb nail. "She never held us or anything." He conjured up the skin on her arms as she grew older. Whispery, like crepe. *Rumple-silk-skin.* Why didn't she ever take him in her arms?

"Daddy, that's so *sad*. A mother not holding her children?"

"Bad things happened." He looked steadily out the window. "One day when I wasn't at home, Father got drunk and went to the woodshed. Harald and Esko were ten and eight and they were playing fort out there. Matilda was with them. She was a year and a half."

Isak let out a dry sob. "She liked to hide for fun. She was hiding behind a wood pile. Father was mad at Harald for leaving tools in the field and he shouted and swung an axe at the wood pile and he killed the baby by mistake. He didn't see her behind there."

He had said it. His brain felt overloaded. Too much blood running through.

"Oh, Daddy! I'm so sorry."

"I should have been there! I was working on another farm." He groaned as if hit in the stomach. "Mum never got over it. It got so bad at home, I left for good."

Nell made sounds of sympathy as she drove. It was all she could do; he knew that. There wasn't anything that anyone could do. He looked out the window. Not one piece of land looked like the farm.

"Harald was a silly kid," he said, surprised to be talking to his daughter. "He was clumsy-like and got into people's business, always joking." He focused on the dials on the dashboard. "Esko wasn't the kind to make jokes. He and Father never got along. Esko moved out young too, like me. He died a week after Father died. They never made up. You want an orange?"

Nell said, "No, thanks," her face pocked with concern. He was sorry for passing his burden on to her. He plucked at his one full trouser leg, which had revolved around his leg when Sigrid sat him down and hadn't been right since. He kneaded the pillow against the window and put his head on it.

"Wake me when we get there," he said.

* * *

Elsa had sat behind Nell, knitting, listening to Isak. She had heard the Matilda story twenty years ago, not from Isak, but from Sigrid. Sigrid was a link in a gossip chain between Alaska and Minnesota, and her St. Paul sister had told her about Matilda. The story was famous outside the family. Within the family, it was too bitter for words. Elsa thought about her own family, about that fiasco of a visit to Mesa. Why, that had put her on edge! Grace Ann's lady friends fluttering by? Grace Ann acting like someone Elsa hardly knew? Grace Ann had joined the modern-day times, with her hair pinned up like that, and those club parties. *Voi, voi, voi!* Who could talk to a sister like that—someone who would just as soon fly in the sky as feed you?

But then again, nothing had changed. Grace Ann was simply being herself and so was *she*—Grace Ann with her care-nothing cuteness, Elsa with her common sense.

What had common sense ever gotten her?

Well, *Isak*. It had gotten her Isak! She gained satisfaction from that. At the moment, he was snoring against the window, done-in by so much talk. In the past few days he had talked more than he had for years.

Addie and Jed were doing their schoolwork, inspiring in Elsa a welling of warmth. They had taken to this trip like gangbusters. She said the word to herself. Now *there's* an Isak-word, she thought. Gangbusters. What did it mean? Nell wasn't sick any more, so she could drive. That was a relief. Elsa would be glad if she never had to drive the bus again. Sigrid? Sigrid was . . . Sigrid. And Elsa was out of the rain.

Things were going pretty well. Except for Grace Ann. Grace Ann bamfoozled her. Her aloofness? And those airs? The visit to Mesa had left a coppery taste in Elsa's mouth.

* * *

Nell's father roused, as if from hibernation, and squirmed in his seat. "We're gonna see my home! Wonder if they have dogs?" He angled toward the windshield. "I had a dog named Shep. We went swimming in all kinds of weather. Well, not in snow."

"In what?" Jed asked him.

"In what, *what*?"

"Where did you swim?"

"Oh. The crick. Shep loved that crick! Brother Patrik would come in, then go back out to his books. But that Shep? He'd stay in for a couple hours. Cold? Whoo!"

Hearing her father talk this much made Nell uneasy. A leak had sprung in his normal restraint. She worried that it might drain him of what made him her father.

Addie said, "Did you have cats?" Nell found Addie's face in the mirror. Just before they left Wilcox, Addie had bravely given Pajamas to her friend Tara. When they got to their next place, Nell decided, Addie could get a kitten.

"We had *barn* cats," Isak said with mild scorn, dismissing the idea that cats could be pets, "meowling around the barn when we milked." He turned his top half toward Jed and Addie. "We'd squirt milk in their mouths, then squirt it all over 'em! They got sticky and had to lick and lick to clean their fur." He chuckled like a pranking boy.

"That was kinda mean," Addie said.

"Oh ya? They always came back for more."

Jed said, "Did you have foxes? Or deer?"

"Deer. And elk. Want to know something?"

Nell's stomach twitched. The elk were in *Washington*, not North Dakota.

Her father said, "Those elk like to play! There was this . . ." A sound like shame came to his voice. "No. That's by Cougar."

Nell relaxed. He had found his way back.

"Anyway," he said, "it's steep up behind us by Cougar, and the elk come down at night to graze. They have this path they use. You can see where they put one hoof against a tree trunk and another hoof on a rock and come down the hill." He pushed the heels of his hands through the air. "One day I found another path right next to the first one. This one was smooth and muddy. The elk had made a *slide!* They could've come down the regular path, but they slid down the muddy one, for fun!"

Sigrid chortled, "Sli-hi-iding down on those big bums? Now *that's* a picture!"

Addie said, "You mean the mooses slided down the hill like kids?"

"Not '*mooses*,'" Jed told her. "*Moose.* Besides, he's talking about elk. And it's 'slid,' not 'slided.' And he's just making jokes."

Addie pranced in a seated position. "I *know.* I just like the word. *Mooses!* And I know how to say 'slid.' I like 'slided' better."

In Nell's mirror, Jed looked stymied, like a border collie with no sheep to herd.

Her father said, "That's what they did. They slid down the hill like kids."

* * *

Harald came awake when Marcie slowed the car. She coasted off the highway at the rest stop and parked. These rest stops were new since he was last in the state, forty years ago minus one, the year Fred Rinta leased the farm. Now Fred was dead, and his family didn't want to lease. The farm was back in the hands of the Halonens.

He swung open the door, shifted his seating to the side, lifted out his artificial leg, and brought his sound leg around. What if Isak balks? Who could draw up papers on an oil field? Or lignite? What does a real estate guy know about lignite, anyway? Lignite is coal. Not the greatest coal, but *coal*. Why didn't they just say coal?

Near the coffee shack, a six-foot standard held a map under glass. Harald stood before it and traced his finger along Highway 94, starting at Fargo and going west past Mapleton, Casselton, Wheatland, Valley City, and Eckelson. He came to the spot where he was standing, near Jamestown. A triangle marked this rest stop. He drew his finger farther west. Eldridge. Windsor. Cleveland. At Steele, he aimed south. His heart beat fast. When his finger landed on Kintyre, his breathing came in bursts. In school he had learned that Kintyre—short for MacIntyre—was named for a peninsula in Scotland, that Kintyre meant "the choicest of land." Before the Scots came, Indians lived there. So the main story of Kintyre wasn't Finnish.

But Harald was going to a spot that was Finnish, through and through, and it wasn't far from Kintyre. *The home place.*

* * *

112

Before returning to the front of the bus, Sigrid tossed water on her face and buffed it with a towel. She stared critically at the mirror. The orchid design on her blouse made her more top-heavy than ever. Her face was swollen; too many salty foods. Her eyes were red from insect spray at the last stop. With effort, she took her mind off her less-than-perfect appearance. It was time to get back to her job, the cheering-up of the group.

She affected a choo-choo walk as she approached the children. Stanley, who had shadowed her up the aisle, waited until she sat down, and then he did his flop at her feet, sighed noisily, and nosed up to her slippers.

"So! You guys finish your homework?"

Jed was engrossed in some boy-scientist book. "*I* did," Addie said, attempting to comb a doll's hair, which was a mangled crunch of yellow fiber. Sigrid guessed that the doll had gone through the clothes dryer and come out fried, like Millie's clients did sometimes under the hair dryer. Sigrid sat down and unfolded a state highway map on the table.

She asked, "What's the capital of North Dakota?"

Jed said, "Bismarck. That's easy."

"What Indians live here?"

Jed said, "Apache."

"Nope."

"Sioux," said Nell, "or Lakota, or Dakota."

"Smartie pants." Sigrid turned the map over to a topographical scheme of North Dakota. "Don't look!" She tried to cover a picture with her arm. "What's the biggest *find* at the Pioneer Trails Museum? It's in Bowman. By Montana."

"Give us a clue," said Jed, making blinders around his eyes and looking away.

"I did! I said '*find*.' What's the *biggest find* there?"

"I don't get it," Addie said.

"Here's a hint. Bowman is in the Badlands."

Jed said, "The Badlands have fossils . . . *I* know! Tyrannosaurus Rex!"

"Right. Here's a picture."

Jed said, "We should go there!"

From the front passenger's seat, Isak craned his head back toward the children. "We should go to Morehead and Fargo. But we've got *more ahead* and *far to go*."

Jed hooted. "Addie? Get it? More ahead and far to go? Morehead? Fargo?"

"I got it. I'm not dumb." Addie dragged down her mouth at Jed. "That's a good one, Grandpa. More ahead and far to go!"

Isak said, "Here's a question for you. Why do prairies have potholes?"

Jed said, "They're prairie dog holes?"

"Good try but no ceegar," said Isak. "They're from icebergs." He then made small, ashamed moves with his head. "I meant glaciers. They melted and left holes."

"Glaciers?" Jed gaped at his grandfather. "In North Dakota?"

Sigrid tapped the map. "Yup. A long time ago." She reached forward to pat Isak's shoulder. "Icebergs, glaciers, same thing! Don't worry, I mix up words too, all the time."

She saw Isak aim a look at her. He didn't like being lumped with her when it came to words. Words were *his* bailiwick.

Isak said, "Boom chick-a-boom."

Sigrid cackled to show collusion with him. "My-hi feelings exactly!" To the kids she said, "They're not like potholes in the road. They're *big*, and they fill up with water when it rains—like ponds. If you're in a plane and look down, that's when they look like potholes."

Jed said, "I want to fly in a plane all the time, and I will, when I'm a pilot."

Sigrid said, "So you want to be a pilot. Where do you want to go?"

"Everywhere! South America, China . . ."

"Will your wife and kids be waiting for you to land?"

Jed's face flared crimson. "I'm not getting married. I just want to fly."

"You'll change your mind. Look!" She laughed a short laugh and pointed at a sign in a field. 'PorkBellyAcres.' What a kick!"

"I don't get it," Addie said.

"Bellyache? You know what that means?"

"A stomachache."

"Right. But it also means complaining. So a bellyacher is . . . ?"

"Someone who complains," Jed said.

"Yup. And a pork belly? . . . Hmp. I don't *what* a pork belly is, unless it's just what it says, a pig's belly. They say it on farm reports all the time, 'Pork bellies up, wheat down.'" Sigrid looked to the front passenger's seat. "Isak? What's a pork belly?"

He was sloping slightly toward Nell with his chin on his chest. Like a baby in a stroller, he had simply slumped in place when sleep overcame him.

Sigrid threw her hands into her lap. "Oh, well. Who wants to play Old Maid?"

* * *

As Nell negotiated squared-off roads, her father looked intently out the front window, gulping and swallowing. When he saw a clump of trees on a certain hill, he said, "That's it!" and swiped at his eyes.

She urged the bus up a steep curved driveway and pulled into a wide, quiet farmyard. She stopped and everyone got out and stretched. Nell had expected squawks from guinea hens—the yard birds her father had described. But there were no yard birds, no dogs. The windmill wasn't creaking. No wind was blowing. The house was a white story-and-a-half with a peaked roof and a wing on the right-hand side. A porch along the front of the house had two metal armchairs on it. The barn sat on the opposite side of the yard, down rather far from the house, also white but three times bigger than the house. The painted surfaces on the house and the barn had weathered to nearly bare wood. Outbuildings included a silo, a railroad car, a garage, miscellaneous storage units, and an outhouse. A chuck wagon stood abandoned in the field. Near the house was a fenced vegetable garden, now overgrown. An arborvitae windbreak started behind the house and climbed the hill to a knoll above the road, where it gave way to birches, maples, and other deciduous trees to form a small woods. Infused with sun and rusted by autumn, the trees formed an Orange Julius nimbus. Nell spotted a woodshed in the woods. It seemed to be falling down in slow motion.

Was that *the* woodshed?

A man came striding from the barn, a six-two, florid-faced man in overalls white with dust. He appeared to have climbed out of a grain bin to come and greet his visitors. He went first to Isak and shook his hand, saying, "How-do, come on in, take a load off. I'm Jimmy Rinta."

Jed took off running toward the barn. Addie followed, struggling to corral her patent leather Mary Janes, Nell's evening sandals, the Matchbox car box, and the gingham giraffe. The giraffe looked lost, bouncing in Addie's arms.

Jimmy urged the visitors up onto the porch, opened the front door and hitched his thumb to his left. "Bathroom's there," he mumbled, embarrassed to mention a place as personal as a bathroom. Entering the house, he took off his cap. The hair he exposed was willful and blond, two inches past what Nell guessed was his usual length. Below and above the pressed line left by the cap, his hair aimed outward, upward, and downward, like a heron's nest. He had chapped cheeks, a long upper lip, and vigilant brown eyes. He seemed a gentle-hearted man.

Isak lifted his crutches over the threshold, hopped into the kitchen, and stopped. "It's changed," he said, salivating overmuch. He nodded at a large firewood box to the left of the door. "That's the same. And the stove." Next to the firewood box sat a black cast iron wood-burning cook stove that dominated the kitchen, emoting female strength, the curved legs stating its gender while supporting a heavy body. A long utility shelf, propped on curlicue welded arms above the cooking surface, was a part of the stove. A curved metal lifter for the firebox lids stood in a slot in one of the lids. A white enamel panel decorated the oven door. A black stovepipe came from the back of the stove and went up through the ceiling. Nell's father spent time in front of the stove, sighed deeply, then turned to the next wall.

Nell took inventory along with her father. Window. Stand-alone sink. Curtains below the sink. Open shelves. A work counter, covered with speckled tan linoleum, ran along that wall, skipped over the sink, turned the corner and traveled half the distance to the next corner where it stopped for a window and a pine hutch. The hutch had glassed shelves above, closed wooden doors below, pigeon holes and work space in the center. It looked to Nell like the keeper of history—and a place where a person might also keep the future. "That's the same," her father said, meaning the hutch. A seating arrangement filled the corner—a triangular table with benches on the two walls and spindle chairs on the free side. The floor linoleum was dotted gray, worn thin on the walking paths. The house smelled stale, unused. Nell had an urge to air it out and make it her own.

Isak led a tour beginning at the pantry, a narrow room with counters and shelves on both sides and a pinchy window at the end. The only item stored in the pantry was a black lunch box shaped like a Quonset hut.

"We kept bread in here," Isak said. "No one bakes any more?" He said this to Jimmy, accusingly, as if Jimmy, or *someone*, should have baked bread that day. "And pickles," Isak added.

Uncomfortably, Jimmy said, "When Mom died, Dad stayed on. We wanted him to live with us, but . . . ? My wife brought him casseroles . . . ." Jimmy was a man of few words. He had said this many at great cost. He gave one shiver and motioned the group to the front room.

"The furniture stays," he said. "We don't need it." The front room was low-ceilinged and furnished with a sofa-bed, a recliner, a desk, a rocking chair, an upright piano, and a Ben Franklin stove. For some reason that Nell couldn't pin down, the room had an air of the Old West. The linoleum in here made Nell feel unsteady: green with yellow teardrops that swooped to her right. Initially the pattern seemed lighthearted—quaint, even—but, repeated across a floor that slanted in the same direction, it tended to propel her laterally. She isolated the hint of the Old West, a print on the wall—an Indian man on a pony. The pony was standing on a cliff, hunched, its tail blowing forward. The heads of the man and the pony were bending low.

Sigrid said, "Say! What did your father do here? What did he raise?"

Jimmy said, "Beef cattle. They went to market just before he died."

Nell said, "Beef cattle," thinking suddenly that this farm might be a cash cow. Her mind galloped ahead. *Farming?*

Sigrid asked Jimmy, "Do you live around here?"

"Two miles south. My brother's place is over east. Neville."

"Don't you want to keep this place going?"

"Can't." Jimmy looked shattered. "Can't do both."

Nell said, "That makes sense," though she had no real notion of what farming entailed. Nonstop work, she knew that much. But she wasn't afraid of work.

Isak crutched back across the front room, halted, and yearned upward at a rectangular hole in the ceiling. Stairs without banisters hugged the wall between the front room and the kitchen, advanced to a landing, turned and pressed the outer wall up to the opening.

Sigrid said, "What's up there?"

"Mattresses. Us boys slept up there. Patrik, Harald, Esko." His face pulled into itself. "They're all dead."

"Harald's not," Elsa said. "He should be here any minute." Isak's lips made formations but he said nothing.

"Let's see the rest of the house," Nell suggested.

Hop-stepping to the bedroom, her father caught sight of photos on the piano—graduation and wedding pictures in folded paper frames. He went nose-to-nose with them, then backed away. "Who *are* those people?"

"It's okay, Daddy. They're the Rintas. They lived here a long time." To change the subject, she asked Jimmy, "When is Harald due in?"

Jimmy stood back near the kitchen door, apparently on the verge of leaving. "He should be here by now." He stalked across the front room, wove among the people peering into the bedroom, walked to the bedroom window and looked outside, as if hoping that Harald—or *anyone*—would drive up and let him off the hook. "Eh, I've gotta see to something. You folks be okay? There's coffee, help yourself." He wove among the people again and went through the front room and the kitchen and out the door.

Isak teetered at the door to the bedroom, a small room soaked in sun. He spun on his crutches and crashed into his wife. They tilted, nearly fell.

Nell put her hands on them to keep them on their feet. Isak shouted to Elsa, "Would you *look out!*" Elsa blanched and moved away.

Nell said, "You okay, Mom?" Elsa nodded shortly.

"Daddy?" Her father looked chased-after.

Sigrid said, "Let's have coffee. I'll get the cinnamon rolls from the bus."

Jimmy had set out the basics—cups and saucers, a percolator, a can of Maxwell House coffee grounds, spoons, sugar. Nell's mother handled them with ease. Her father sat on a chair at the triangle table. Nell made busy-work at the sink, meanwhile checking on him. It wasn't like him to snap at people.

But for now life had returned to normal, her mother making coffee, her father waiting for coffee.

After drinking two cups of coffee, Isak maneuvered the raised threshold and made use of the bathroom. When he got back, Elsa said, "*No niin.* You want to rest before they come? Harald and all?"

"Ya. In the bedroom." His face hardened. "We used to . . .? It's all different."

Nell said, too cheerfully, "But isn't it good to be at the farm?" She bit the insides of her cheeks. She had to stop being so glib.

Jed and Addie! Where are they?

She felt a pushing-down on her shoulders, an actual, physical weight of responsibility. She needed to find the kids. She needed to protect them. She needed Dan.

* * *

Hay hook. Brother Patrik got a hay hook in his knee. He yanked it out and went to the house, doused the knee in alcohol, wrapped it, and went back to the field, an act of *sisu* so extreme that even Finns wondered later what had possessed him. He was fifteen at the time. He got to be known as the guy who kept on haying after breaking a kneecap. Isak ran the story through his head. *Now I'm the one with a bum leg.*

Lying on his back in his parents' bedroom, he reasoned out what was wrong. The bed was facing the wrong way. It should be on the *other* wall, so a person could see out the window. The lowboy should be next to it, his Mum's doilies on top. He raised his head. The lowboy and the doilies were gone. His Mum was gone. But she hadn't been here much all along—her body, yes, her self, no. Isak lowered his head. Tears ran onto the pillow that belonged to someone else.

After his nap, he went to the windmill, making his way alone, having convinced Elsa that he would be fine. Jed and Addie had their arms in the tank, dragging currents and causing fret to four white ducks who swam in circles, chuttering, protesting the invasion of their space. They seemed to be pets. Otherwise, Isak thought, they would have flown off when the children came close. He remembered how cold the water was. He touched a finger to it and pulled it back. It *was* cold. He leaned back to see the windmill blades. They were rotating slowly, squeaking. He soaked up the sound of the squeaks.

He said, "How about we go see the barn?"

Addie pulled her arm from the water and wiped it on her jeans. "They have kittens in the barn! Five! They're black except one's black and white. They have their eyes open and they *like* me!" She picked up her dolls and ran after Jed.

The barn smelled of cow manure and bags of feed. *That* hadn't changed, Isak told himself. As before, the floor was scattered with tags of hay. Moving ahead on crutches, Isak took care to find firm grounding. Concrete could be hard on the bumper. He scrutinized the horse tack hanging on the wall. He believed he recognized one harness. Lifting his head toward the hayloft, he asked the children, "You been up there?"

"Sure!" Jed said. "They have this big rope and we can swing out *real far* and jump in the hay! Wanna see?"

"Naw. We did that, too. About broke our necks." Isak took swinging steps across the barn and put his head around the corner. Attached to the barn was a milk-house—a concrete room that smelled of butter. Sun fell to the floor with a cold insistence. He took note of the shiny steel containers—milk cans, cream separator, churns—and concluded that the people here sold

Ruth Elaine Jutila Chamberlin

cream and butter, same as before. In Isak's mind, ladies in scarves were working the churns, not looking up, even though he stared at them for a long time.

He went next to the grain bin—a rail car with a half-open sliding door. It smelled familiar, of rats and oats. Jed and Addie were already there. They took the farm as their own, he noticed, running from place to place like every kid who ever ran here.

Isak faltered in his thinking. *There's something they haven't found yet.*

He got himself across the yard, beyond the house, into the woods at the top of the hill. Jed and Addie had guessed where he was going. They got there before he did.

He accounted for everything. Firewood. Kindling. Sawdust. A chopping block. Wood chips. Spider webs in the same places. Sawdust hanging in the webs.

Someone had cleaned up the blood.

He fought for space in his lungs. Standing as tall as he could, he whirled on his crutches to get away from there.

Right then, Harald and Marcie arrived in a blast of noise. A green Ford station wagon jerked to a stop, curling dust around it. Isak's first thought was: Harald's daughter drives like maniac. So did Harald, starting as a kid on a tractor. Runs in that family, Isak figured. But isn't she *adopted?* She stepped out of the car wearing blue jeans, a plaid red shirt, and cowboy boots—clever-looking, Isak thought, the type who dressed like a cowboy but had probably never met a horse in person. Her hair was long and frizzy, the color of autumn, almost orange. She seemed not to care that it bushed out from her head.

He said, "That-kind hair . . . ?"

She took rangy cowboy steps toward Isak, smiling with no backwardness that he could see. Her eyes were alarming—a clear agate green. She put out her hand and said, "I'm Marcie! You must be Isak!" She looked for all the world like a happy person.

Marcie stepped aside to make way for her father, whose gait was lopsided and bump-along. Isak wondered why he was walking like that. Then he remembered. Harald lost a leg in the war. This one is fake. But is this guy really Harald? This guy is brown from the sun and doesn't look like the fat Harald. But he has the same droopy eyebrows, so it must be Harald.

Harald called out, "Well, if it isn't brother Isak!" He kept talking until he got to Isak, then shook Isak's hand with gusto. Isak had to work hard not to be rocked off his crutches. Harald bellowed at him, even though he was standing practically on top of him, "You old scallywag! You get around on sticks okay?"

Isak said to an invisible cloud of witnesses, "He hasn't changed a bit." His words were loud enough for Harald to hear, but Harald didn't hear a thing. He was making too much noise.

* * *

Watching from the barn, Nell caught the reunion of the brothers— the raucousness of the one, the hold-back of the other. She also saw Marcie, or the woman she assumed was Marcie, disappearing into the house. Nell started for the house. Marcie came outside and loped toward Nell like a distance runner. She was laughing before she got to her.

She shook hands like a roustabout. "You remind me of my cousin Kik! Well, she's *your* cousin, too. Do you know her?"

"No. I remind you, how?"

Marcie analyzed Nell's face and body. "You guys have the same jaw. You're taller, not as stocky. You're a competitive swimmer, right?"

"In college. How did you know?"

"Wide shoulders, little hips. Turn around."

Nell turned around. Marcie said, "I don't believe it! You and Kik have the same rump! Long and narrow, and it boops out at the bottom. *Cute!*"

Nell felt exposed, having her rump discussed, but she liked Marcie's whoop-de-do. "Do they run in the family?"

"Just you and Kik."

In the house, Nell met Harald, a boisterous man so different from her father that she could hardly believe they were brothers. Harald filled the

RuTH ELAINE JUTILA CHAMBERLIN

place with banter and bluster and poked fun at everyone, including her father. No one poked fun at her father. Her father made jokes when *he* was in the mood, but he was basically quiet. People usually honored that fact. Not Harald. She saw something of herself on Harald's face, her eyebrows. She controlled hers by plucking, but they *wanted* to be stormy like his.

Without fuss, taking supplies from the blue bus, Elsa fixed a meal for eight people plus Stanley—macaroni and cheese, cucumbers, tomatoes, bread and butter. The talk centered on tales of the road and sleeping space. Isak, Elsa, and Sigrid would sleep in the bus, Harald on the couch in the house, Marcie and the kids in the attic (Addie told Nell, "Marcie is great, she acts like a kid herself!") and Nell in the bedroom. No one mentioned the reason that people from Alaska, Florida, Washington, and Minnesota had converged on a farm in the middle of North Dakota.

After midnight, Nell got into bed and put her head down. She immediately sat up. *I have to call Dan. He doesn't know where we are!* She took her flashlight and address book and felt her way to the kitchen. Shining the flashlight on the phone, she dialed the international code plus the Roster Fund number. As usual when calling overseas, she quivered from the inside out. The phone rang and rang. No one answered.

She went back to bed. Even though she couldn't reach Dan, she felt giddy. She felt *at home* here. Seventy-five years ago, her Halonen grandparents left Finland and homesteaded this land, built the buildings, planted crops, established fences. She had never met them, but she was getting to know them in this place. Already, in one day, she had stood in the same wind they had stood in, breathed the same dust, and trained her eyes on the prairie to gain a sense of place, as they had. Their hopes were still alive here.

The next morning, she wrote a column on the sense of home, the unpredictability of it—the whack-in-the-chest knowledge that a particular spot was the right one. To her surprise, that spot for Nell—for now—was a farm in North Dakota.

After breakfast, Marcie, Harald, and Sigrid went to town to buy food. Nell washed the dishes, then took a walk with her parents and the children. Jed walked backwards in front of the others, talking with his arms. "There's a big fly in the outhouse! It's like an *alien spacecraft!* It hangs around your face, *bizzz*, *bizzz*—like it's taking *spy pictures* through your eyes!" He and Addie ran to the grain car, the silo, the empty chicken coop, the empty pig pen.

At the windmill, when Nell's father said he wanted to rest, her mother helped him to sit on the rim of the tank. Nell sat beside him to make sure he didn't fall in—and also, if the opportunity arose, to speak with him about staying on the farm. Birds twitted and hopped in the weeds, finding lunch. Her father said, "'Full many a flower was born to blush unseen and waste its sweetness on the desert air.'"

Nell followed his eyes to a solitary daisy by one leg of the windmill. He has a saying for *everything,* she thought. "We had geese," he said, "not ducks." Three white ducks perched on the tank rim across from the human perchers, combing their wings with their bills. "Horses used to drink here. Once we thought Matilda drowned in here. We couldn't find her. But she was hiding behind the tank."

He gave his wife a mystified look, as if asking her why he was talking so much, especially about Matilda. By now, of course, Nell knew how Matilda's love of hiding and Grandpa's love of whiskey led to her death at the hand of her father. By axe. In the woodshed, on this farm.

She invented a danger. "Addie! Careful! There's barbed wire!" She went to the field where the children were. Addie, nowhere near barbed wire, was sitting in the weeds, weaving blades of grass into a bracelet. Jed was collecting stones. Nell stayed with them until her parents were ready to leave. She knew she was being a coward. If her father talked about Matilda, he might erase bad images. But she had squelched him. Matilda died fifty years ago. Her death was still too hurtful to talk about, even for Nell.

After noon dinner, Nell, Marcie, and the kids took another walk, this one a mile north to Jimmy Rinta's place, a prosperous farm set on languorous low hills. Two mountainous white dogs barked them lazily up the path. They were twin dogs piled with fur, less like dogs than sheep in need of shearing. A woman called hello from the side porch. Balancing a wicker basket at her waist, she came to meet Nell and Marcie.

124

"I'm Victoria," she said, shaking their hands, crinkling her nose as she smiled. "You must be Halonens. I heard they're having a get-together." Victoria's body was spare and her eyes were electric brown. She wore her brown hair looped on top of her head; strands of it were blowing loose. Her clothes—a longish cream skirt and a white pioneer blouse—billowed in the wind, and she seemed eager to get the wet items from her basket into the wind as well.

Jed, Addie, Marcie, Nell, and the dogs trailed Victoria to a carousel clothesline behind the house. Putting down her basket, Victoria proceeded to hang laundry faster than Nell had thought laundry could be hung. She picked up a towel from the basket, shook it with a snap, took two clothespins from the pouch of a kangaroo bag on the line, pinned the towel to the line, picked up another towel, shook it, unpinned the right-hand corner of the first towel and clipped it plus the left-hand corner of the second towel under the same clothespin, and repeated the steps, lickety-split, overlapping towels and spinning the carousel. Not much talking went on during the pinning and spinning.

Meanwhile, Jed and Addie did what the dogs wanted them to do—pet them. The dogs enjoyed the attention but took it as their due, sitting at the kids' feet like animal kings, their eyes on the reaches of the prairie. Jed and Addie threw sticks for them, but the dogs ignored the sticks and edged closer to the children, wedging their heads into their hands and forcing them to pet them. If the children stopped petting, the dogs nosed them into action, their jowls getting into the act. Jed said, "Good dog, but you slobber."

After some small talk, Nell said, "We have some decisions to make. I'd like to ask you a few questions."

"Go ahead." Victoria picked up a man's blue shirt, shook it, isolated the terminals of the shirttail seams, and pinned the shirt to the line at those points. The shirt hung upside down, arms "up" toward the ground, subdued and conquered by Victoria.

"If we stayed on the farm," Nell ventured, "what could we raise? We're not farmers, but we could learn."

Victoria's first response was amusement, covered by a considering look at Nell. She stopped hanging clothes and got ready, it seemed to Nell, to set Nell straight.

"My dad knows farming," Nell said preemptively, defensively, "and he knows the Halonen place. But his memory fails. I need to know what we're up against."

With a kind of sympathy, Victoria said, "M-m, yes, winters are tough, and times are hard, and farming's never done." She seemed to take Nell's measure. "But it might work. Jimmy can tell you more. Come for supper tonight. All of you."

Nell said, "That'd be too much! We have a lot of people."

Marcie said, "We could bring food."

"No need. Just come. Seth and Mark would like that. Little-John might be here, might not. He's sixteen. You know sixteen. I told Jimmy that the cat and Little-John are both leaving home—just not together, and not all at once. They show up often enough to keep up residence and get food. They tour the place with a far-off look. Their minds are someplace else! . . . But you guys come. We eat at five."

* * *

Marcie did naturally what Nell didn't do well at all. She played with the kids. Nell liked to buy games and toys, but she let Dan and the kids do the playing. (Board games, for instance, seemed too arbitrary, too much based on chance, even Clue and Monopoly.) But Marcie played any game the kids suggested or made up, even if it meant rolling outdoors in the dust. Today she had a game she called the broom game. Nell was at the kitchen table, writing a letter to Dan, when Marcie came in with Jed, Addie and a broom.

"You have to do *exactly* what I do," Marcie told the kids.

Standing like a palace guard, she held the broom in her right hand with the sweeping end up. She cleared her throat and recited a ditty, tapping the broomstick on the floor seven times. "*Cali*fornia *grapes* are *very* fine *grapes*, but the *grapes* of the *south* are *better!*" At the end, she tapped the floor one more time, crossed her right foot over her left, and didn't move a muscle for three counts.

Grinning as if she had won first prize, Marcie handed the broom to Jed. He pushed out his chest, preparing to show her a thing or two. Nell had seen that look on him since he was two—a certitude that defied all dares. He repeated Marcie's routine to a *T*, the taps, the words, the foot-crossing, the pause at the end.

He proudly passed the broom to Addie.

"Wrong!" Marcie said.

He bristled. "I did it just like *you* did!"

"Watch! And *listen*." Marcie took the broom, cleared her throat, and went through the sequence, exaggerating enunciations and taps to the floor.

"You try," she said to Addie.

Addie correctly performed the words, the taps, the foot-crossing, the last pause.

Marcie said, "Wrong!"

Jed and Addie protested. "We did it the same as you did!"

They repeated the routine but left out the throat-clearing, which, Nell had divined, was the key. After many tries by Jed and Addie and much throat-clearing by Marcie, Jed had an "Aha" moment and cleared his throat.

The ditty made no sense—California *is* in the south, so why the fuss? But it didn't matter. The kids had had a good time. So had Marcie. So had Nell, just watching.

* * *

The minutes before sunrise were murky and foggy, but Sigrid hoped the sun would punch through anyway. She wanted to be the first one up—she needed time to think. But as she looked out of the bus window she saw that Marcie had beaten her to it. Every bit the athlete in shorts and a skimpy top, Marcie was warming up at the windmill tank. She had one foot on the rim of the tank and (impossibly) her head on her knee.

When Sigrid and Stanley ambled up, Marcie said from her cramped position, "Good morning!"

Sigrid asked her, "Aren't you cold?"

Marcie exchanged legs and put her head on the other knee. "Nope. I warm up fast. I run marathons. I train every day."

"You run *twenty-six miles?*"

Marcie nodded.

Sigrid felt weak. "You run twenty-six miles *every day?*"

"No, no! I train at six, or thirteen. I'll do seven today."

Sigrid had planned to take Stanley for a stroll in the field. Compared to Marcie's plan, Sigrid's plan was lazybones. With a smile brighter than the hour inspired in Sigrid, Marcie brought down her leg, reached to the sky with both arms, went forward and touched the ground with her palms. Her legs were shapely, Sigrid noticed, probably from all that running. Sigrid admired legs like Marcie's, curvy down to the ankles. It had been years since Sigrid had *seen* her own ankles. "You know anything about speedometers? Those things you put on your foot?"

Marcie put her hands on the rim of the tank, stepped away and put her head between her arms, stuck one leg behind her and stretched. "Pedometers? You thinking of getting one?"

"Maybe." Sigrid sought the place on the prairie where the sun would appear. "You know how it is. Well, I guess you *wouldn't* know, seeing as how we just met! I thought when Elsa got to Arizona, to the sun and all, that she'd stay there and live. I thought *I* would, too. I thought I'd swim and walk and get skinny. But it wasn't the sun I was looking for. It was something else, I don't know what. But I can start by getting in shape."

Marcie changed legs. "What do you like to do for exercise?"

Sigrid gave Stanley a sideways grin, then laugh-talked. "Oh, heh, heh, jump rope. Hopscotch. Hoo-hoo-hula hoop! I haven't exercised since I was a kid! That's the crust of the problem. When I was married, we had a rooming house, and I scrubbed floors and changed beds—that was my exercise. When we split up, I gained weight and my legs went bad. I need different shoes. And different pants. But not those belly button pants!"

"Bell bottoms, you mean?"

"Yah. Belly button pants. I can't wear those. They're too tight. Maybe I'll wear them when I get back to my *svelte Svedish self.* Elsa now? She stays the same, a little plump but she hasn't changed since the day I met her. I saw this TV show once with doctors on it, and got it installed in me to eat six small meals a day. You know, instead of three big ones? But I went overboard and ate all the time! Hitch was off running and we were calling it quits. I was so chewed up, I just ate and ate. If there's such a thing as chain-eating, that's what I did! But how does it go? 'I'm not fat. I'm fluffy.'"

"Some say it's normal to gain up to ten pounds a decade, from age twenty on."

"Oh yah, ha-ha, I guess I did great till I was forty, then I got ahead of myself! Now I'm *way* ahead. By six or seven decades."

"What does your doctor say? Is walking okay for your legs?"

"Walking's okay. I've just got to *do* it. Maybe if I bought one of those machines for my ankle, it might help. It might motorvate me and get me going."

"For now, I'll run off a mile for you. I'll mark it. Let's see, rocks won't work. Too many rocks. Just a minute."

Marcie ran to the house and came back with a red patterned handkerchief, the kind Sigrid associated with hunters and fishermen. "I'll anchor this with a rock. If you get there and back, you'll be doing great! Just follow the cow trail." Stowing the hanky in her waistband, she trotted away. "Don't forget to warm up," she called. "And *stretch.*"

Sigrid made a few reaches to either side, more like gestures than stretches. She said to Stanley, "Okay, boy, I don't know if you can make it for two miles, you being so old and all." The dog made circles with his nose to the ground, caught a scent and started after it, zigzagging and displaying his dependence on a rabbit or a prairie dog—if not Sigrid—to lead him to his next adventure.

The mist cleared and the sun rose in Sigrid's face. Her mouth went slack in admiration. Alaska had northern lights—the *aurora borealis,* the tall curtains in the sky that scared people, shaking and shimmering red, green, purple—but it didn't have this sort of sunrise. *This* was like a painting done by an excited person, or a hungry one, or an exited hungry person—boiling pots of tomato soup, orange American cheese! The sunrise filled every bit of air space. Sigrid walked more and more slowly until she was standing still, overcome by so much sky.

Stanley came back with his tongue hanging out. She told him, "I think I'm having a prolapse. My feet are shot from sitting on the bus." She waved him away and he lumbered off. As she made her way down a slope to a hollow filled with water, her toes rammed the ends of her Hush Puppies. If she had worn Keds, she thought, she might do better at walking. Hush Puppies were fine indoors, but outdoors they sloshed around and let her feet slide forward. She was tempted to go barefoot. But did they have snakes here? *Rattle*snakes? She looked at the ground and then at the pond.

"Why, this is a prairie pothole!"

Six brown ducks (a *flotilla* of ducks, she thought, reminding herself to tell Isak she'd found the word in a children's book) were cruising the pond, dipping their beaks and shaking their heads as if trying to wake up. Together they went tails-high, heads underwater, feet busy halfway above water, their rear ends popping up and down like corks—a sight that Sigrid found uproarious. In unison, they buoyed back to the surface, took dignified poses, and sailed ahead.

Sigrid sat on a boulder to rest her feet. The ground around her was riddled with rocks. She had to hand it to the local farmers. Before planting any crops, they would first have to clear off tons of rock. She could see raising cattle here, but not wheat or corn.

Climbing out of the hollow, she came upon six of the beasts she had been musing about, cattle—black and white cows being herded by a man on horseback. The man was Jimmy Rinta.

He called to her, "You're out early. I'm late getting the cows in."

"Late for the cows?"

"Yeah. They like to get milked before the sun's up."

"Then why don't they come in by themselves?"

"Because they're stupid critters."

"You've got more patience than I'd have."

Jimmy said, "Cows 're one thing. People 're another. Kids and all? They'd like to drive you nuts." He touched the brim of his hat and rode on.

* * *

In the early evening, Nell took yet another walk with Marcie, Jed, Addie, and Stanley. The others chose to sit on the porch and watch the sun go down. "I want to see what's over there," Nell said, "past the grain car. Maybe we can get through the fence."

"It's not electric," said Marcie. "I asked Jimmy."

"Have you been on farms a lot?"

"Summers. At my aunt and uncle's in Michigan. I miss farms. Man, I miss *chickens!* They get so nervous, like you're going to steal their food! You throw them some corn and they peck at it and look over their shoulders and squawk to warn you off, 'Braawk! Braawk!' My aunt had a rooster who was so vain he'd forget to *eat*. He was too busy parading! I tease chickens. I say, 'Braawk!' right back at them and they get this scandalized look."

Marcie imitated a scandalized chicken.

Nell laughed. "If we stay here, we'll get chickens and you can tease them all you want. I want pigs and horses, too."

"Animals mean work."

"I'm not afraid of work. My mom and I are the same that way. We're better off when we have too much to do."

Marcie stretched her arms before her, to the sides, to the front again. "You'd have *plenty* to do if you stay. Are you serious about it? What do your folks say?"

"Mom likes it here. And it clears Daddy's head."

"I'll play devil's advocate. How would you earn enough to live on?"

"Piecemeal, until we figure it out."

"What if you have an emergency? The nearest hospital must be an hour away."

"I'd drive."

"In the bus?"

"For starters. After that, we'll see. We'd need to get a truck."

Sunset was a sports event in stop-frames, not motions but photos caught in sequence, wrestlers peaking at the height of their strength, a blue-violet brush with violence, purple getting a headlock on red, runners running to the opposite side of the sky streaming gold ribbons, fuchsia tumblers vaulting east to west. The sun clicked downward an inch at a time, then disappeared and left a brown and orange finger-painted tent to cover the earth. Sounds Nell hadn't been aware of ceased for a second, in respect for the passing day, then picked up again, small chirps and rustlings in the brush. She envisioned mama quails settling their young for the night.

Fifty yards ahead, Addie and Jed stood on a rock twice their height. They waved. Marcie and Nell waved. Nell added another wave, one that said come on back.

Marcie asked, "What about your husband? Will he agree? What will he think? What about his work? . . . Listen to me! I sound like Kik. *She'll* ask questions till the cows come home!"

"He'll be fine," Nell claimed without cause. (Dan might actually have a *fit*.) "I'm calling him tonight. I'd like to meet Kik and the others."

"I have an idea! Come for Christmas! For the whole week."

"Seven people? Isn't that too many for your house?"

"Nope, it's big. So is Kik's."

"How's the weather in December?"

Marcie guffawed. "Awful! But snowplows keep the roads clear, unless we get a blizzard."

Nell hugged her arms. "Yipes. Blizzards. We had them in Alaska."

"You lived through them."

"I did," Nell said. "And I'll tell you something else. Blizzards aren't as bad as drizzle. Drizzle is so *piddly*! It goes *on* and *on*! I like real rain, but drizzle isn't really rain. It's just wet enough to be a bother! Half this! Half that! It can't commit itself to *anything!*" She came up short, abashed at her outburst.

"So you want a change," Marcie said. "A challenge."

Nell blew air upward along her face. "Right. Something big."

"Like a farm," Marcie said.

"Like a farm," Nell said.

✳ ✳ ✳

Lorrie Roberson, the real estate agent, was a hefty, hard-breathing blonde who looked startled for no good reason. She shouldn't be running around on farms, she told Marcie. "The dust gets my asthma going and I choke and cough. But here I am, and here are the papers." To the group, she said, "Here's where to sign."

Standing by the kitchen table, she pointed at lines with a cosmetically extended fingernail. "The buyers are chomping at the bit," she said. She was wearing a white blouse and tailored black slacks—and, Marcie could tell, a girdle. Marcie knew natural flesh when she saw it, and Lorrie's hips were too firmly packed to be natural. Lorrie made a furtive tug to her waist. The girdle was obviously biting her.

Isak, sitting at the table, said, "Hold it! I don't want to sell."

Marcie's dad, sitting across from Isak, shouted, "Not sell? What's gotten into you?"

"I don't want to sell," Isak repeated, not raising his voice. "We'll stay."

Marcie saw Elsa's reaction, an animated ripple that crossed her cheeks; Elsa approved of her husband's plan. Marcie had known Elsa for only a day or so, but she already knew that, for Elsa, this was a strong reaction. Elsa sat beside her husband and took in small excited breaths.

Lorrie took in angry, asthmatic breaths.

Harald roughed up his hair, pawing at it with two hands. "Holy moly! I *thought* this would happen! I had an *idea* you might pull this!"

Marcie said, "Dad, don't get yourself in a stew. Blood pressure."

Harald pushed out his lips like a temperamental child.

Nell said, "What about the oil?"

Lorrie shifted her girdle without laying a hand on it, lifting her torso and driving her elbow into her waist, then gyrating it. "There isn't any. I don't know where the rumor started. The only oil is by Williston."

Harald whoofed out a mouthful of air. "Williston? That guy said *Wishek!*"

Marcie saw him doubting himself. He made words without sounds, probably wondering if he had mistaken Wishek for Williston or fallen into wishful thinking.

Lorrie got around to her chosen topic. "But the buyers want to buy! They're Germans from Russia. They've got a group in Hanson and they need more land, and they like your hill. It's the largest one around."

Nell said, "*Germans* from *Russia?*"

"Mennonites, Black Sea Germans," Lorrie said with irritation. She wanted to get on with the important part, the reason she came out to the farm. The signing of the papers.

Marcie asked the questions she knew Nell was poised to ask. "What if we didn't sell? What could we raise?" Nell gave Marcie a pleased nod.

Harald thrust his head at Marcie. "What are you talking about?"

Lorrie glanced around with a town girl's panic. "No, I . . ."

"Used to be wheat," Isak said. "Beef. Barley."

Marcie watched her dad scowl at Jed and Addie, who had just then crashed in from the barn. In response, they laughed. He was a magnet for kids, even at a serious time like this. No child was ever fooled by his gruffness. When he and Marcie first got to the farm, he worsened his limp and went to Jed and Addie and said, "Glad ta meetcha!" and pumped their hands, Jed's, Addie's, Jed's, Addie's, jarring them to their teeth. Since then, Jed and Addie had been teasing him back, patting his arm while he feigned indifference and made ogre faces and asked the universe who was bothering him and calling him Uncle Harald. He wasn't even their uncle! He was their great-uncle, for Pete's sake. "*Great!* Did you get that?" He said he didn't want any foolishness about "uncle." Jed and Addie said, "Uncle, uncle!" He had made it known that he had cartoon movies and a projector and a screen, but he yawned when the kids asked to see them. Last night, he finally showed the cartoons—but only because he was a good guy, he told the kids. Earlier that morning, he had held a hanky to his face like a bandage and whined in a fake Finnish accent, "Brrokka *nokka* all broke!" Marcie didn't speak Finnish, but she knew that *nokka* meant nose. It was typical of her dad to joke about everyday things like hankies and noses. He had a softening effect on people, even on his brother. Isak was quiet, but even *he* loosened up in her dad's presence.

In fact, at the moment, Isak was speaking his piece. "This is the *homestead*," he reminded Harald. "We ran away once, but we can farm it again."

Harald objected. He reached a hand toward Isak and flicked it, flitting away Isak's words. "Hey, hey! *You* ran away. *I* didn't."

Isak's cheeks took on angles, but he stood firm. "We're not selling."

Nell was pop-eyed, enthusiastic. "We can stay! Dan and I and the kids, Daddy, Mom, Sigrid. What can we lose?"

Jed said, "Yeah! Let's stay!"

Sigrid laughed, "*Oh*-ho-ho-*oh*-oh-oh, here we go," her words predicting change.

Elsa seemed to be thinking of something pleasant.

Harald grumbled to Nell, "What do *you* know about farming?"

"Nothing. But Daddy does. He knows everything." Isak laid his head to one side, as if he agreed with Nell but was too humble to say so.

Addie said, "Let's stay! I like the kittens!"

Jed said, "We can jump in the hay!"

Nell said, "We're strong. We can do what it takes."

Isak said, "Wheat curl mite, leaf rust. Hessian fly. Wheat stem maggot."

"What about tractors?" Marcie asked. "Tillers? Harvesters?" She had come to the end of her farm vocabulary. "But Jimmy said he has anything you need."

Isak said, "Too late for winter wheat."

Harald gave Marcie a shrug that depended more on eyebrows than shoulders. He had dropped the idea of selling.

Marcie said to the children, "We'll come visit you in the summers! We'll swim in the tank and fly kites! You've got *lots* of wind for kites."

Lorrie honked into her lily-white hanky, exasperated with this crowd. It was crystal clear that she wasn't needed here, her expression said. In a flurry, she gathered her belongings and left.

Nine

Have I Got News for You

By coincidence, the guesthouse manager knew of a doctor at the Mumford Clinic, a Dr. Stamos, who donated his services in special cases. Clinic fees would still apply, but the physician's fees would be dropped. Rafael had an appointment to see Dr. Stamos in two weeks.

Rafael asked to speak to Dan alone. While the baby napped in the house, Mike took the older children to the beach to hunt for shells. Rafael reached into a leather bag and brought out four sheets of paper written in Tagalog and translated into English. The sheets were embossed with hand-marks and official stamps.

"Take my children," Rafael said without preamble. He handed the papers to Dan. "Take them to America. I will die soon."

Dan could not get Rafael's meaning. He said, "But . . .?"

"I will die soon," Rafael repeated, his smile more suited to an announcement of birth than of death. "I am at peace. I have Jesus. Please. Take the children."

Rafael was giving him his children?

Dan said, "I, I'm honored, but . . . legally?"

Rafael showed him a document that held four signatures. On the lines calling for his signature, Rafael had signed his name.

Dan silently read the document:

"Permission is hereby granted by the Ministry of Social Services and Development, Bureau of Family and Child Welfare (*Kawanihan Ng Kagalingang Pampamilya At Pambata*), Manila, the Republic of the Philippines, for the

137

children of Rafael Irwin Roosevelt (wife deceased): Abraham Matthew, Isaac Mark, Jacob Luke, Rachel Elizabeth, David John, Jonathan Paul, and Rebecca Mary, birth certificates attached, to legally leave the Philippines, upon the death of their father, in the physical company of Daniel Marcus Sanderson, and to be legally adopted by Daniel Marcus Sanderson in the United States of America. This document verifies that Rafael Irwin Roosevelt is a citizen of the United States of America, that he was born in Jersey City, New Jersey, July 6, 1939, birth certificate attached, and that it is his express wish that Daniel Marcus Sanderson be awarded custody of the above-named children."

* * *

In the skinny hour right after midnight, Nell tried not to shake. She was tingly and jumpy, not just because of the flu going around; intestinal flu, the twenty-four hour kind, had made the rounds of the group. The queasiness she felt had nothing to do with the flu. She went over what she needed to tell Dan.

She and the children weren't in Arizona.

They were in North Dakota.

They were going to live here.

Dan was going to be a farmer.

This was not the appointed day for calling, but she had to talk to him! She had gone *way* out on a limb. Despite the sorry state of farming, the failures and bankruptcies, she had decided to try farming. She had told everyone that Dan would agree.

Would he?

Little by little, the group had come to a consensus. The brothers wouldn't sell the farm—not right away, anyway. Dan and Nell would stay at the farm and piece together a living. There were advantages to the plan. The farm felt like home to Nell and the kids. Her father was lucid here. Her mother treated the cook stove as her own. Sigrid would stay for as long as she was needed. Marcie and her family would vacation here, Marcie had announced, and help to harvest wheat (if Nell and Dan ever planted wheat) and ride the range with Jed and Addie (if Nell and Dan ever bought horses) and cook meals on the prairie (if Nell and Dan ever fixed the chuck wagon). Harald said he would rig up a tractor for his fake leg, hitch it to the hay wagon, and give the kids a ride they wouldn't soon forget. He promised to take them fishing and cook them a fish head stew "with the *eye palls* floating in it!"

Everyone was on board. There was just the matter of telling Dan.

She dialed. The phone rang. No one answered. *Someone* at Roster should answer. Did she have the wrong number?

Dan had no idea where she was or what she was up to! At least she knew where he was and what he was up to. *International calls are tricky. Dan is fine. The children and I are fine. I'll do what I need to do, at my end. He'll do what he needs to do, at his.*

* * *

Dan needed to talk to Nell. She knew nothing about Laura, or Rafael, or Rafael's children. The phone rang at Grace Ann's, but no one answered. Where was everyone? He would have thought that, in a group that big, a few would stay back even if the others went out. He let the phone ring twenty times and gave up. He would try again later.

The next Saturday, Mike had obligations in Manila, so Dan went to the island alone. At Rafael's house, the children seemed to expect him to do something or say something, as if he were already their guardian. The twins, who had been playing in the sandbox, stopped digging to stare at him. Rachel stood nearby, holding Rebecca, her hip slung aside to catch the baby's weight. She too stared at him. Dan greeted them and went up the ladder and into the house, dipping his head to enter.

The three oldest boys were hunkered by their father's mat. Rafael's eyes remained closed, his skin bright with sweat. He did not acknowledge Dan's presence.

"Malaria," said Abraham.

Dan said, "How . . . ?"

"How" was immaterial. It was too late to undo the "how." But, still, how had Rafael contracted malaria? Any mosquito that carried the disease would have first picked it up by biting an infected person. Haslin Island had no malaria.

Abraham said, "In Manila."

"When? Why?"

"For the papers." Abraham had overcame his reticence and was speaking as a bold eldest child. "The adoption papers," he said, drilling knowledge at Dan. He knew that when his father died Dan would be his new father.

Dan didn't know how to handle the moment, the sick father, the children, or the matter of adoption. He asked Abraham, "Where is the grandma-helper?"

"She does not like malaria."

"Do you have another neighbor who can help?"

After a pause, Abraham said, "I do not like to ask."

Dan rose to an authority that was newly his. "Abraham, Isaac, Jacob. Come with me." He took them to the neighbor's home where they acted as interpreters. Dan arranged care for the younger children for the next several days.

He and the three oldest boys put Rafael on a stretcher and ferried him onto the *banca*, into the Roster van, and into the Mumford Clinic. The clinic was white and spotless, a welcome sight to Dan.

But whiteness and cleanliness were not enough for Rafael. Four hours after arriving at the Mumford Clinic, he was dead.

* * *

Dan called Grace Ann's apartment. No one answered.

* * *

Nell dialed Roster. This time someone answered, a man who said Dan was out of the office but he had left the guesthouse number for Nell. She left a message for Dan, saying she would call the guesthouse that evening, evening his time.

* * *

The boys went wherever Dan went. At the Roster office, they watched machines tapping words to lands they had never heard of. At the hospital, they endured exams, shots, probing, tests for hepatitis A and other diseases. At the government social services office, they waited as Dan answered questions and filled out forms. At the American Embassy, they waited as Dan filled out seven sets of papers and officials stamped them. They rode with Dan in jeepney taxis, exhilarated by screeching tires, honking horns, swerving near-misses. They walked with Dan on Manila's streets, got bumped by strangers, overrun by bicycles, accosted by vendors selling shirts, food, watches, fabrics, tapped on the arm by beggar children. By a seafood shop, they got a taste of American music—"I Saw Mommy Kissing Santa Claus," being blasted on a loudspeaker. Christmas was a long way off; the boys knew nothing of Santa Claus. They were off their island for the first time. Everything was new to them, including the spices in the air.

That night they slept on the bare hard floor, grateful to be on familiar territory. Dan watched them drift off, knowing that in the morning they would again be hit by newness. Their world was upside down. Later, in the United States, they would face changes in virtually everything, family, weather, food, landscape, language, clothes, sports, humor. But first they had to adjust to Manila. They were going through culture shock in their own country.

One of Dan's hurdles was convincing the director of children's services in the Philippines that his family was the best one for Laura. The director, a hearty woman with artillery glasses, cautioned him that caring for Laura would require patience, that in a large family like his (becoming larger as time went by) Laura could easily be ignored.

He described the attention Laura would get in his family. He told about each of the children and adults. He explained that everyone was eager to have Laura join the family. He went on at length about the farm, the animals, the healthy life, the clean air.

The director would not approve his family for Laura.

She said she would seek a more suitable placement. Her agency kept a list of approved families in Sweden, the United States, Norway. She would be checking that list.

He could return to her office in five days for her decision.

141

* * *

When Dan and Nell finally connected, he could barely hear her. The line was staticky and uneven. Her voice came from deep inside a well.

He yelled, "*I said! . . . I! . . . love! . . . you!*" The only phone for guests' use was in the lobby. He imagined people up and down the hall with their ears pressed to their doors. "How's Arizona?"

Nell said she loved him too but she wasn't in Arizona. She was in North Dakota.

"What are you doing *there?*"

She said her uncle had called a family meeting at the homestead. She didn't say what the meeting was about. The omission rang in Dan's ears like a fire bell.

Nell asked him, Have you seen Max?"

"Not yet."

The line took on clanks and blank spots. Nell said words that Dan couldn't make out. He shouted, "There's interference! I can't hear you."

" . . . and leaks . . . rain . . . kids kept moving their sleeping bags upstairs. We put pails up there . . . more leaks . . . moved their sleeping bags down to the front room. Then we all . . . *flu!* When the kids got sick, we moved the pails down too so when they had to vomit or . . .? People all over the place, vomiting or, as Sigrid says, diarr-wheeing. . . ."

"Uh. I get the picture. Sorry about that." Dan made a rumble in his throat. "I have something to tell you," he said.

"Me, too."

"You first."

The sound on the line went off and on. He heard Nell say, ". . . trust me?"

"Sure."

"Okay. We're staying here! The place . . . learn farming. Jimmy Rinta . . ."

Dan paced a circle on the lobby floor, tugging the phone cord as far as it would go. "*Farming?* Who's Jimmy Rinta?"

142

The line improved. Nell was talking fast. "You're a quick study! You can do anything you put your mind to! Jimmy lives on the next place over. His Dad used to lease our farm and . . ."

"Wait . . . *Wait!* . . . *Farming?* Nell, this is nuts! There's a trend in farming, in case you haven't heard, and it's not good."

"I know. But we could live here rent-free, and Mom has pension and savings, and Daddy has retirement, and Sigrid can cut hair. We'll all pitch in."

Dan hated to ask it, but he needed one immutable fact. "How many bedrooms?"

"One. And an attic."

"One bedroom. Augh." He rolled his head around his shoulders.

"I *know*," Nell said, misunderstanding his concern. She didn't know the first thing about his concern! One bedroom for nine children and five adults?

"It *is* small," she went on, "but we can use the bus for sleeping and add a wing to the house . . . ."

"Just like that, add a wing? Nell. I'm not a carpenter. I'm not a farmer."

"We can *learn*. Honey? This is the first thing I've been excited about for ages!"

He made a hacking sound, like a microphone being tapped—an important sound that called for attention. "Well. We'll see. Are you ready for my news?"

"Ready."

"We have a few new kids."

"What on earth . . . !"

"I found a four-year-old girl to adopt. Her name is Laura."

"A little girl? Why didn't you call me? Tell me!" Dan told Nell about Laura. He said that they needed a new home study, that the Philippine authorities needed assurance, that it could take up to a year before he could go back to get her.

He took a breath and said, "And a friend died and left me his seven kids."

"A *friend?* What friend? . . . He *gave* you his *kids?* . . . Did you say *seven?*" The line quality was iffy again. Nell's words came out gargled. "Someone you just met? Why would he give you his *children?*"

"His name was Rafael. His father was a black American and his mother was from Luzon. He was born in the States."

"You've been gone *three weeks* and you've got this kind of *friend?* Someone who'd give you his *kids?*"

"He wanted them raised as Americans. He said I came along at the right time."

"He said that? And then he died?"

"Pretty much . . . Nell, he was a good man. He went to Manila and got it official. He signed the children over to me. You'll love them."

Nell let go of a one-syllable laugh. "Whooh! I wanted more kids, but this is *wild.*"

"Laura has hearing loss and learning problems, but she's great. Rafael's children are three older boys, eleven, eight, six, a girl who's five, twin boys who are three, and a baby girl. Abraham, Isaac, Jacob, Rachel, David, Jonathan, Rebecca."

"One thing about you, you're never boring! . . . What about the INS? Visas?"

"The kids are legal to go. I've signed the papers. We'll be home Tuesday."

"So soon!"

"Mike is the new director. My job is done, so we're coming home. I guess home is North Dakota."

* * *

Travelers appeared at the door of the tunnel, wearing the fatigue of international flight, shuffling up the ramp and scouting for familiar faces or having private thoughts. Jed jostled to the front of the waiting crowd, saying, "There he is!" But it was another redhead, not Dan.

Then Nell saw him. He came around the corner holding a bundle to his chest, a diaper bag on his shoulder, and the hand of a small girl with pretty brown eyes and curly dark hair. *Rachel.* Catching sight of Nell, Dan bent to whisper to the child. Urged ahead by Dan, the brothers too came forward— five handsome, dark-skinned boys with wavy black hair, wearing blue jeans and *barong tagalog*, the traditional white dress shirt of the Philippines. Nell sorted them by name. The tallest, the most somber, was Abraham. He held the hands of two toddlers, Jonathan and David. Isaac was the animated boy talking to his younger brother. The younger brother was Jacob. Each child old enough to walk was carrying a small duffel bag.

Dan herded the group to a row of seats and made introductions. He kissed Nell and handed her the baby in a blanket. Rebecca was thistledown light and the skin below her eyes was discolored. Nell felt an instant bond with this sick baby. Nell's mother held Jonathan on her lap and passed around cookies to the children. Her father sat down, took David on his knee and petted his head. Jed talked to Abraham about topics that fascinated him— virtually everything in the natural world. Addie handed Rachel a purple stuffed monkey and showed her how to turn his reversible jacket inside out. Sigrid gave Jacob a kaleidoscope, put it to his eye, and turned it. Isaac resisted getting to know anyone. He stood in the center, laughing and waving his arms, saying, "Flenty children! Flenty children!"

Nell and Dan were signaling each other that it was time to leave when David fell to the carpet, screaming and wailing. Jonathan joined his twin, curled up beside him on the floor and he too cried. Jacob went to sit with them. Before long, he was sobbing and banging the floor with the kaleidoscope. Rachel sat on Dan's lap and watched her brothers cry, her mouth quavering. Soon she got down on the floor and kneeled by the boys and cried. Together they made an adult sound, a desperate high lament like keening.

Jed, Addie, and the adults tried to comfort them. The children pushed away anyone who tried to pick them up. Abraham explained, "They are tired." He massaged their backs and rubbed their legs and arms. Isaac alone ignored his siblings. He made silly faces at the adults and tried to make them laugh.

For ninety minutes, the children cried. Gradually, they stopped. Everyone went to the rest rooms, washed up, got drinks of water; Nell put fresh diapers on the baby; the twins let Dan and Abraham change them into dry clothes. Fourteen people then exited the airport, the younger children either holding someone's hand or being carried.

Dan slid into the driver's seat of the bus, smoothly, as if he had done it all his life. Before now, he had never been a bus driver, or a farmer, or the sudden father of nine (ten, if you included Max). Nell admired his poise. He made it look easy.

Addie and Rachel sat together in the front seat, Jonathan, David, Jed, Abraham on one bench, Sigrid, Isaac, Jacob, Nell, Rebecca on the second bench, the grandparents in the rear of the bus. On the ride home, Addie and Rachel giggled like sisters lost and found. Abraham and Jed discovered a shared passion for science. Isaac told Sigrid about animals in his village. Jacob moved his head yes and no to Nell's questions. The twins fell asleep against Abraham. The baby slept in Nell's arms.

It was dark when they got to the farm. Jed and Addie ran ahead and introduced the new children to Marcie and Harald—who had delayed their departure to meet them—and to the dog, the woodstove, the wood box, the games, the toys, the books, the attic. Nell was elated. She felt she was flying somewhere near the ceiling. This was the honeymoon phase of adoption, the euphoria of the first hours. Reality would set in soon enough. But this headiness was real—the surge of welcome, the late hour, the shouts and calls, the darkness outside, the brightness inside. Harald wanted to show his cartoons right then. Marcie talked him into waiting until the next day.

After sandwiches and cocoa and trips to the barn with flashlights and trips up and down the attic steps, the excitement finally burned itself out. Elsa, Isak, Sigrid, and Stanley went to the bus to sleep, Marcie and Harald to the Rintas' bunkhouse, the boys in sleeping bags upstairs, the girls on the fold-out couch in the front room, the baby in a laundry basket in the bedroom. Dan and Nell fell onto the one real bed in the house.

"Today was eighty-three hours long," he said, "or a year and a half."

She said, "The children are *great!* They were *mine* the minute I saw them! How do you think they're doing?"

"Better than I expected."

"What about Addie and Jed? They might feel shoved aside."

"Sure. And jealous. And the new kids might feel I abducted them. But let's think about that later." He rolled toward her. "Let's see now. Where did we leave off?"

She gave him a laden look. "Remember when I thought I had the flu?"

"You're pregnant."

She made her face a caricature of "You got it"—*x*'s for eyes and a zipper mouth.

Dan laughed, "Hoo-haw!" He gathered her up and gave her a side-rocking hug.

✼ ✼ ✼

Elsa ran the kitchen like a home café, rotating groups for pancakes, sausage links, scrambled eggs, and orange juice. The new children tasted pancakes for the first time and liked them. Dan stood at the table and cut up food for the smaller children while Isak ate his usual breakfast—grapefruit, porridge (*puuro*), and Elsa's homemade bread. As with anything else, Isak had a ritual for eating breakfast. He sectioned half a grapefruit with a grapefruit knife, easing the knife around the membrane so as not to tear it, sugared the wedges, very evenly, and spooned the wedges, one at time, into his mouth. That done, he picked up the empty shell, squeezed it over his spoon, and drank the juice. At this juncture, Elsa delivered a pitcher of milk, a bowl of oatmeal, and two slices of bread. Isak buried a tab of butter in the cereal to let it melt, then buttered his bread by dragging his knife to the extreme edge of the crust, buttering and buttering until no crumb was left unbuttered. He sprinkled sugar on his oatmeal, again very evenly, and spooned out a mote around the edge, turning the bowl and eating the mote as he went along. After pouring milk into the mote, he ate the cereal from the outside in. In the bump and stir of this day, Isak took comfort in his small routines.

When the breakfast dishes were done, Isak and Elsa disappeared into the bus. Harald, Sigrid, Jed, and Addie took the new children—the six big enough to walk—outdoors to see the farm. The baby slept on the couch, prevented from falling by a tall chair and a wall of pillows. Marcie stayed at the table with Dan and Nell—to ask questions, she had said. She jittered around on the bench, pulsating with energy.

Dan didn't want to answer questions unless they were Nell's. He had been away for three weeks and had brought back seven new children. He and Nell had a lot to talk about, but *alone*.

Marcie said to Dan, "Tell me about Asia!"

"Like what?"

"Your work, the people, politics, anything!" Flipping her hair off her neck, Marcie shouldered forward to hear what he would say.

Marcie was a non-Finn redhead, and so was he. Dan wondered if her hairstyle described her personality: feral, uncontrolled. He wasn't comfortable talking about his work, and the other topics she mentioned were too big.

He said, "We were in Manila for four years. Nell can tell you."

Before Nell could speak, Marcie spilled the reason she was jittering. "Kik wants to go to Thailand, something about weaving. I want to go with her! I want to take my kids and let them see how other people live. Life is more than hockey and shopping malls!"

Nell said, "I know. I don't want our kids thinking that more *things* make people happier."

"Your kids are lucky," said Marcie. "They've lived overseas. Now you have the new kids from another culture . . . ."

Dan jumped in. "Go third class. First class hotels are the same anywhere. Tell your contacts you want third class."

Nell asked, "How far along are Kik's plans?"

"She's just started."

"Has she been there before?"

148

"No."

"You'll need a travel agent who knows Thailand. I'll give you our agent's number. She can put you on track."

"Thanks!" Marcie seemed pleased with their answers, as brief as they were. "Listen. I want you to meet everyone. Come to Minneapolis!" She laced her fingers, flipped her hands inside out, stretched her arms forward, freed her hands, put them on the table, patted a drum beat, then rested them flat before her. Dan wondered if her motor ever slowed down. Even now, as she talked on, she let her fingers rise and fall like hammers on a piano being played. "You haven't met Adam," she said. "He's a poet dressed as a math teacher. Miia's eleven. She's a gymnast, and she does *archery*, if you can believe it. Coop is ten and can mimic *anyone.*"

Marcie stilled her hands. "We lost Michael three years ago. A motorcycle crash."

"We had heard," Nell said. "I'm so sorry."

"He was sixteen," Marcie said. "He was a prince." She realigned her back as if gathering strength for the first time and not all over again. "But you have to meet Kik and Jeff. He teaches college . . ."

"Guess what!" Jed was first to bang through the screen door. The others followed, making *ugh* faces and moaning as a group. Jed said, "Abraham ate a *slug!* We dared him to do it, and he *did!*"

Abraham, the most serious-minded of the new children, had already made a name for himself—slug-eater. He folded in his lips and frowned at the adults.

Marcie said, "Slugs? Ick!" She swung her legs over the bench, stood up and shook out her muscles. "Who's up for a run? Race you to the windmill!"

* * *

At five the next morning, Marcie and Harald left for Minneapolis and Dan reported to the barn. He was a city boy. He had to start from scratch on this farming stuff. Ever since his father's death, Jimmy Rinta had been doing chores on this farm as well as his own. Dan was about to learn what "doing chores" involved, starting with milking. Isak had offered to help, but

Dan had talked him out of it, for today, at least. He didn't want Isak seeing what an amateur he was. It was bad enough the day before when Jimmy gave them corn on the cob—a late crop, Jimmy said, but what did Dan know?—and Dan shucked an ear *wrong* in front of Isak. In the past, he had always been too busy at the barbecue to shuck corn. He'd let the kids do it. Yesterday he grabbed all of the silk and husk on one side of an ear of corn and yanked downward, a manly pull but wrong-headed. He got stuck half-way down, the same way he got stuck if he tried to take off his jeans, socks, and shorts at the same time. In each case he had to do it over, one layer at a time.

Jimmy arrived on horseback, carrying an extra saddle and a saddle blanket on the pommel of his saddle and leading a heavy brown mare. Until Dan could buy a horse, Jimmy was loaning him his oldest horse, Tess. Jimmy dismounted, walked the horses into the barn, and set about saddling Tess—a demonstration for Dan.

Standing to Tess's left, Jimmy ran his hand over her back and brushed off wads of dirt and hair, then he laid the blanket on her back and made it straight. Before placing the saddle on the horse, he laid the right-hand stirrup over the saddle and hooked it over the horn. "Don't leave the stirrup loose," he said, "and don't throw the saddle on. It'd spook her. Or hurt her." He raised the saddle and put it on Tess, centered it, took the stirrup off the horn, reached under her for the cinch and passed it through the ring on the saddle.

"You're about my height. We don't have to change the length. Here's how to check. You put your hand at the top of the fender. This is the fender." He patted the broad leather flap that hung over the stirrup straps. He held the stirrup parallel to the floor and mock-measured it. "It's the right length if it comes to your armpit." It came to Jimmy's armpit. It would come to Dan's as well.

The next step, Jimmy said, was getting the air out of Tess. "She's not too old to play horse tricks . . . See? She's holding her breath. She'd hold it till you're in the saddle, then she'd let it out later, maybe in the field. The saddle would slip down around her and you get dumped." Jimmy took the cinch in two hands and set his foot on Tess's side. Shoving his foot against her, he fell backward. She let out air. He tightened the cinch and flipped it into a flat, compact knot.

Dan gulped air and let it out, his contribution to this emptying of lungs. It was time to get on his horse. He'd never been near a horse. As far as he was concerned, horses were from another world.

Jimmy told him what to do. Grasping the neck muscles of the horse near the saddle, along with the short hairs of the mane (the withers, Jimmy said), Dan raised his left leg (insufferably high, it seemed to Dan, even for a man his height) and wedged his hiking boot into the stirrup. He bounced tentatively on his right foot, took a jump and climbed the wall that was Tess's side. Straining major muscle groups, he dragged himself up until he was standing on his left foot, threw his right leg over her back and sat in the saddle. Tess was bigger than she had seemed from the ground. Her back was so broad that it forced his legs into lateral splits.

Jimmy got onto his horse, Georgia. She tossed her head and whickered, eager to get going. As soon as Jimmy reined her toward the door, well before they left the barn, she started to trot. Tess followed suit, putting Dan in mortal pain. Her every motion caught him wrong. When she bounced up, he flew. When she bounced down, he was still airborne. On the next bounce, he landed late, painfully so—Wham! *Ouch.* He tried to adjust his actions to Tess's, but they never matched. In a misery of bad timing, he trailed Jimmy into the field—Wham! *Ouch.* Wham! *Ouch.*

In the pasture they rounded up a half-dozen cows—black-and-white animals with indifferent expressions. (You want me to come in? What for? Oh. Right. Milking.) After herding them into the barn, Jimmy got off his horse and urged the cows into stalls, aiming their heads at the hay manger and their bony rears at Dan.

Dan still had to get off his horse. He felt glued there, or broken in pieces and stacked there. He stood in the stirrups, shaking, and swung his right foot over Tess's back and set it on the floor. He still had to retrieve his left foot, which had twisted in the stirrup. After wrangling with it, he got it too on the floor. His legs shook severely enough for Jimmy to see. His inner thighs felt stretched beyond repair. His posterior seemed to be missing. He said, "Well, *that* was fun."

Jimmy grinned and said it would get easier.

Dan said he certainly hoped so.

Jimmy carried a pail with him and sat on a short stool beside a cow. He took a teat between the thumb and forefinger of one hand. Squeezing, he stroked downward. A milk stream blasted into the pail, steaming in the chill of the morning. He did the same with the other hand, stroke, stroke, bringing milk with every pull. He showed Dan another grip, one that used all ten fingers. With any grip he used, he got milk to whistle into the pail. He got up and let Dan try.

Dan took hold of two teats. They were warm and soft, like flaccid human penises. He squeezed with one hand, then the other. No milk came out. He squeezed harder and pulled harder. Nothing happened.

He adjusted his hands, pulled again. He couldn't get a drop of milk to come out.

After suffering a dozen fruitless tugs to her nether parts, the cow swung her head toward her rear and leveled a dark look at Dan.

"Sorry," he told her. To Jimmy he said, "I guess you have to learn as a child, be born to milking, like being born to a mother tongue."

Jimmy said, "Next time we'll let the kids try. Some'll be naturals. You'll see!"

* * *

Isak felt like a cellist except that he had a pail between his knees and not a cello. He gave a performance for anyone who wanted one, zinging milk into the bucket, like music. Jed and Jacob had a gift for milking, and so did Elsa (of course she did, Isak thought; she had milked as a child). The others were like Dan—nonplussed but willing to try. In this hit-and-miss manner, the milking got done twice a day.

On this particular morning, Isak was alone in the barn. Elsa was in the house, baking bread. The others had something going on in town; he wasn't sure what. He sat on a stool by the smallest cow and looked around. Tess was there in the barn, that cranky old mare of Jimmy's. Isak liked sweet-natured horses, not stubborn ones like Tess. *Marigold.* His Palomino. He hadn't thought of her in eons. A better friend he could never have.

A familiar smell engulfed him. Ammonia. The cow was letting go of a stream of urine. He averted his head and breathed through his mouth until the urine molecules dissipated.

He took off his cap and stored it on his knee, then leaned into the cow, pressing his head on her belly. He had always milked this way, more or less asking the cow's permission to milk. He had learned the hard way not to take a cow for granted. As a boy, he once got kicked by an insulted cow—all the way across the barn.

Across *this* barn?

Isak pivoted and looked at the walls, the mangers, the stalls, the tack, the shovels.

In the manner of a man waking from a sixty-year sleep, he made a clucking noise with his tongue. "Can you beat that? I ended up on the home place."

* * *

Nell had waited for the new children to arrive before starting Jed and Addie at school. She registered the whole group on the same day. The new children spoke workable English, but the principal, Mr. Stenton, a joyous man built like Paul Bunyan, arranged extra help for them, anyway—individual tutoring in the library during group reading, less homework. To each Sanderson child he assigned a buddy, a student who knew how the school operated. Nell was touched by his concern.

When the children had been in school for three days, Nell got a call from Jacob's teacher, Mrs. Kettleworth, the only first grade teacher and thus Addie's teacher as well. The teacher seemed brittle on the phone. She said in clipped terms that Jacob never spoke in class. She insisted that Nell come in for a parent-teacher conference that very day.

So soon? For not talking? This seemed strange. Nell had seen Mrs. Kettleworth twice and hadn't like her either time. There was something about her eyes—more accurately, her eye, as Mrs. Kettleworth wore an eye patch. Nell didn't like the look of that eye. It seemed bent on blaming *someone* for *something.* Mrs. Kettleworth was the size of a ten-year-old, but, according to another mother, she was sixty-six, and this was her first year in the district. The regular first grade teacher, Mrs. Lyle, had quit her job after a personal crisis. Normally, the other mother said, the board snapped up teachers right out of college—"tweety young birds" was how she phrased it. In an unusual move, the school board hired an older teacher to replace Mrs. Lyle.

Unable to avoid a conference, Nell drove to the school at the end of the school day, found her children and asked them to wait for her in the library. She then reported to the first grade classroom.

The teacher was stiff as a clipboard. Her clothing looked strapped on—a dark belted dress that buttoned to the neck and grumpy pumps that laced and tied. Even her hair was a victim of her ferocity—a small gray remnant that she pulled back and screwed into a bun, then pinioned to the back of her neck. She ushered Nell into the room, talking as she walked, pointing her to a round, short-legged table on the far side of the room. She had an unpredictable pattern of speech, emphasizing words that didn't need emphasis and letting vital words slide with no energy behind them.

She said she *regretted* not *talking* with Nell *the day* she registered the children, that she hadn't felt *well,* and a substitute had had to take *her* class later *that* day as she *had contracted* the flu at a strange *time,* at the beginning *of* the flu season, and not in the middle of it, or *at the end,* when she usually got it, and that she had called Nell *because* she had *never* heard one word from Jacob, not a single word.

Hearing this spill of words, Nell wondered how anyone got a word in, much less Jacob. The teacher and the mother sat on stubby chairs made for first-graders. Nell's legs got in the way wherever she put them. She tried bending them to one side, but they cramped. She pushed her feet under the table, but they bumped the teacher's feet. She shrank and pulled her legs back.

She wanted no contact with this woman. She finally made her knees into mountains, over which she spoke to Mrs. Kettleworth.

"He talks fine at home," she said. "He talks slowly, but he does fine."

Mrs. Kettleworth said, "I have given him many chances! I spoke to him at my desk, *thinking* he might be afraid to speak in front of a group. He looked at me *all the while but* he didn't say a word. I tried having him write *out* a few words, or draw a picture, but he must not *have* learned to write or draw *in* his country. *So* that did not work!"

With a humph of triumph, she threw the trumped-up problem to Nell. Her one eye gleamed. This was one prickly teacher! Making an effort at getting along, Nell fixed on Mrs. Kettleworth's eye. "My husband and I think he might need oral surgery. He has a bad under bite, I'm sure you've noticed. His front teeth don't touch, so it's hard for him to make consonant sounds." In illustration, she thrust her lower jaw forward and made a fuzzy *S* sound.

Too late, she focused on Mrs. Kettleworth's mouth. The teacher had an under bite much worse than Jacob's. Mrs. Kettleworth pushed her jaw farther forward, out toward Nell, her eye burning bright.

Nell exclaimed, backpedaling, "But then again! He says *S* words just fine at home!" She cast an appeal at the wall clock. Isn't this meeting over *yet?* "Let's give him time," Nell suggested. "He needs more time."

The teacher said, "I can *find* a solution. I will be *watching* for retardation. He may be mentally incapable of learning or speaking."

Nell said carefully, "No, that's not the case. I'd like us all to step back and let him be quiet, see how that goes."

"It's a *matter* of stick-to-it-ive-ness," cried Mrs. Kettleworth. "*I'll* get him to talk! I have my ways. If a *student* sits under a chair for an hour, he usually gets the point."

"You would put a child under a chair?" Nell jumped to her feet. The teacher remained seated. "You would punish a child that way?"

"An adult chair, yes."

"Did you do that to Jacob?"

"No, but then I am not sure *how* much Jacob can learn. These mixed types? I always say they *lose something* in the mixing of blood."

"You can't be serious."

"Indeed I am. I've seen it too *many* times, generation after generation. Indians and missionaries? Mixed together *in* one family? It's not normal."

Nell made a hasty exit from the room, out of the atmosphere poisoned by Mrs. Kettleworth. Nell would teach Jacob and Addie at home! If necessary, she would do the same for the littler ones when they were ready for first grade.

Before she left the building, she told Mr. Stenton about Mrs. Kettleworth. He was distressed to hear her report. But firing a teacher took time. For now, Nell would protect her children from Mrs. Kettleworth.

At home after school, as the kids ate snacks, Jed said, "Abraham gave a report on Haley's Comet. Mr. Styveson *liked* it." Abraham reddened and smiled edgewise at Jed.

Nell said, "Wonderful, Abraham. Are you getting to know the other kids?"

"Yes," he said, glancing at Jed, "but I have Jed."

Peace bombinated between the two boys. Their teacher, Mr. Styveson—a soft-spoken engineer who after twenty years in Florida's space program retired to his hometown to teach fifth grade—had honed in on the two boys' intrigue with the natural world. He encouraged their questions and primed them with ideas for the science fair. A perfect match, in Nell's view, these two boys and Mr. Styveson.

Nell asked Isaac about his day. He said that he liked kickball and that his teacher, Mrs. Foote, made jokes about her name.

She hadn't yet told Addie and Jacob that she was taking them out of school. She would talk to Dan first. He was in Bismarck on adoption business, due back soon. She asked Jacob what he did at school. He said he had a hamburger for lunch. She asked Addie about school. Addie said, "It's okay," and sat at the table, not eating. She had nothing on her lap, no dolls or boxes. In the space of a few days, Mrs. Kettleworth had squashed her spirits.

Nell wanted to wring the neck of Mrs. Kettleworth.

✳ ✳ ✳

Dan snapped awake to thumps coming from the side yard. The male rabbit, Romeo, was having a rampage, clattering the door to the hutch and banging his food dishes. Before Dan got outdoors, Romeo had escaped. The children were tenting overnight at the Rintas', so it fell to the parents to catch Romeo.

Dan woke Nell and they got towels and went outside. The night was warm and inviting. A harvest moon hung in the trees—a mammoth orange ball with a genial face, giving a light bright enough for the task at hand. Dan and Nell spotted the rabbit in the vegetable garden, eating stubs of whatever Mr. Rinta had grown there, chewing in that reflective, circular fashion of rabbits. They guessed that when Romeo couldn't get into Juliet's cage he had crawled like Peter Rabbit under the garden fence. Dan ran after the rabbit with his towel, but the rabbit ran faster. Nell leaped to the chase, dodging and feinting, trying to trap Romeo. In her night shorts and T-shirt, she was charming in flight. Dan had trouble keeping his mind on the job.

He went to the house and took a blanket from the closet, went back outside and chased Romeo with it. Outsmarting the rabbit was impossible. Romeo high-tailed it out of reach whenever he got cornered, rick-racked through rows, evaded Dan's hands, and avoided the blanket when both Nell and Dan took edges of it and ran and took aim. In a riotous mood, they held the blanket in tandem and threw it at the rabbit again and again, in other words, throwing themselves and the blanket on the ground again and again.

After thirty minutes of chasing, Dan didn't think it was funny. It was futile to try to catch a rabbit outdoors.

Nell called, "Come *on!* We can do it! He's tired."

Dan knew how the rabbit felt. Between husband and wife, Nell was the better athlete on a long traipse like this. He was better on short runs. And when it came to *inner* strength he won every time. In a crisis, he never got worked up the way she did. He kept his head. He thought things through. Of course, when he did this, she complained that he was closing her out. She would demand that he talk to her. Well, he grumbled, chasing Romeo, he could talk just so much and *that* was *that.*

Finally Romeo gave up. He hopped behind the tool shed and hunched there, keeping eye contact with Dan. Dan got on his knees, reached around the shed, and pulled the rabbit out by the ears.

The next morning, Dan told Isak about chasing the rabbit. Isak said, "Kinda makes a fella wish he was young again, all that running around at night."

* * *

Too much went on in the kitchen—Nell's mother clinking pans, Sigrid and the little ones tramping in and out—and so Nell set up class in the front room. She found a table in the barn, scrubbed it clean, and set it under the window by the windbreak. She wanted Jacob and Addie to see trees when they looked up. Arborvitae had stood behind the house since her father was a boy, and the continuity pleased her. She wanted the children to have fresh air, so she opened the window and planned to leave it cracked open even in the winter. Fresh air, she believed, was as basic a need as the knowledge of letters and numbers.

Using the first grade guide she had bought in Seattle for Addie, she divided the morning into three sessions—reading, math, science—and between sessions Jacob and Addie played outdoors with the younger children, who were Sigrid's charges. After lunch, Nell read stories to the entire group. Then, while the little ones napped, Jacob and Addie did art projects or played math games.

Jacob spoke readily during lessons, if hesitantly, and with pauses. Nell had to wait him out. But he was talking. So much for Mrs. Kettleworth and her tantrums.

And Addie was back to normal, attended once more by her favorite things. She no longer had the downward gaze that had developed under the eye of Mrs. Kettleworth.

* * *

A castle with gardens. Trees. Clouds. Sky. Sheep. Most of the pieces had snips of pattern on them, the way he liked them. He was alone in the front room (a miracle, being alone in this whirligig), working on a jigsaw puzzle on the card table. When he had every piece turned face-up, he pulled aside the edge pieces. He liked to do the border first, so that he knew where he was going. Youngsters did puzzles any old way. He had seen them finish a row of geese before the border was even done! They went for the fun parts. They didn't worry about the *context*—the whole picture, one might say. They depended on grownups to take care of that in a jigsaw puzzle, same as in life. Isak learned a lot about people from the way they worked puzzles. Some made a tortuous job of it (even torturous) by not sorting colors up front. Sorting colors made sense, the browns and golds together, the sky-blue pieces, the red flowers. It saved time later, the same way it saved time when you kept string and pocket fuzz in your pocket. They were handy when you needed them. If a person lost patience while looking for a certain piece, Isak would say, "Don't think about it. Do something else. It'll show up. Usually right under your nose." If someone suspected a piece was missing from the puzzle, he'd say, "Don't waste time wishing you had it. Work with what you've got." There were truths in puzzles if you kept your eyes open.

His isolation didn't last long. But it was only Elsa, doing something in the drawers where she kept table linens. He took the opportunity to ask her a question.

"Who *is* that boy, anyway? The one they mean when they say my name. He's got those-kind *sneaky* eyes."

"It's Isaac. Spelled I-s-a-a-c. The second oldest boy from the Philippines."

Isak freed his lower denture with his tongue and adjusted it with a succession of clicks. "But they call him Isak."

"Same name, different spelling."

He thought about this. Could it be true?

She finished whatever it was she had come in to do. It was time for their rest. She said, "You all set then?"

"That boy is trouble," Isak said, gathering his crutches. "He laughs at the wrong times, and he laughs *mean*-like."

"It's just his way." She took her cardigan from the back of a chair and put it around her shoulders, picked up the thermos bottle and held the door open for Isak. He minced ahead of her on the crutches.

She said, "A sweater won't be enough pretty soon. We'll get frost one of these nights. We have to build a wing on the house or put a heater in the bus."

"Kerosene's dangerous."

"Mm. Are you cold?"

"I'm okay."

Inside the bus, he sat and waited while she poured coffee from the thermos. She brought two mugs to the table. He stirred sugar into his.

They sat across from each other like a dating couple, occasionally saying words that were private and insignificant. In Isak's opinion, this was needed from time to time, the saying of private, insignificant words.

* * *

It was nearly suppertime, but Dan brought out a slow comment, inviting offerings from Isak. They were in the repair shop, having put away tools they'd used on the porch swing; they had replaced the chains after one gave way. "I've been thinking about what needs doing before winter . . ." He had made many trips to the county dump, hauling off the detritus of forty years—a refrigerator with no door, moldy rugs, car parts long separated from cars, cardboard boxes dissolving into mush. Almost everyone—all of the kids except the baby and all of the adults except Elsa—had helped to clean the outbuildings, and everyone had ongoing jobs. Even the twins had jobs. They chased anything blowing around the yard, gum wrappers or tumbleweeds, and put them in a bag. In North Dakota, there was always something blowing around the yard.

Setting his chin into active mode, Isak said, "Oil the machines. Fix the west fence. Fix the rest of the roof." To Dan, Isak looked like a man who needed to fix *something*. He looked like a man of fifty-four, not seventy-four. He was

160

not the titan he was twenty years ago, but he was strong. Without the case he seemed expansive, relieved. His release from the cast had convinced him he wasn't ready yet to be old. The day he came home without the cast, he told the kids, "That Dr. Sawbones cut it off with a buzz-saw! *Zzzzzt!*" When the kids made puky faces and said, "Eeuw," Isak chuckled and made the sound again.

With an up-nod to the sky, Isak said, "We should do it before the weather turns."

"When might that be?"

"Any time. It could sneak up and you got yourself a blizzard."

The next morning, the adults tallied their sources of income. Isak's pension. Elsa's Social Security. Sigrid's stock dividends. Nell's column pay. Dan's consultant fees. Based on the numbers they came up with, they hacked out a budget for two months. Dan warned them that he'd be in Southeast Asia three weeks out of every six.

Later that day, Dan drove five miles south to see a man named Wally Frazier, who had a reputation for making-do. Dan stopped the bus by the garage on a well-kept farm. Inside an open sliding door, a man stood by a disemboweled truck. He had his hands on his hips as if he was taking time to scold the truck before checking to see who drove in. He came out and shook Dan's hand, smiling a welcome—or not so much smiling as tightening muscles around a toothpick in his mouth. When he tumbled the toothpick along his teeth, Dan saw that his teeth were stained brown. The toothpick was helping Wally to quit smoking. The bill on Wally's baseball cap pointed up.

After hearing that Dan wanted advice, Wally said, "What can I do-you-for?"

Dan asked his question.

Wally said, "How many rooms?"

"Three. No plumbing for now. We have a bathroom and an outhouse."

The toothpick made a quick jump, then stayed pointing up, like the bill on Wally's cap. Wally looked out at the pasture. "There's this building at the Matsons'. We could move it."

"Could we get it cheap?"

"Heck, he'd *give* it to you. He can't sell the place *no*-how."

They drove three miles west to a deserted farm. The building they had come to see was an unpainted storehouse, up on concrete blocks. Dan walked off the exterior walls. Fifteen by forty. He climbed the block steps, opened the door and stepped in. Trash and feed sacks littered the floor. There was evidence that small animals had nested here.

Wally entered the building and stamped his feet. "Floor's solid. You could make three rooms." He slashed his hand lengthwise and chopped the space into three pieces. Dan said, "Windows?"

"I know a guy who takes down buildings."

"Great . . . About moving it?"

"We'd cut it in half."

"How . . .?"

"My boys can help. Take it on a flatbed, two trips."

"You know someone with a flatbed?"

"Me."

"*You* have one?"

"Yup."

"What do you need, hydraulic lifts?"

"We got 'em."

There wasn't much, it seemed to Dan, that Wally could *not* do, or did *not* have, or didn't know how to do.

"We didn't name a price," Dan said uncomfortably. "Cutting it apart, moving it, setting it up again, putting in three rooms and windows."

Wally chewed his toothpick and found something else to see on the prairie.

"Say three hundred," Wally said.

Such a low price! Dan let his line of sight go out to the field. "Well, good," he said. "That's good."

* * *

162

Little-John galloped into the yard looking like a teen-aged cowboy rebel, which, Nell assumed, was what he hoped to look like. He reined in his horse and made it rear. The horse whinnied and pawed the air as Little-John waved his hat. Jed was first of the children to get outside.

Watching from the laundry room, Nell sighed. Jed wanted to be a cowboy—a scientist cowboy—but she and Dan couldn't afford a horse. They had Tess, of course, on loan from Jimmy. Tess didn't mind if children sat on her in the barn, but she didn't much care for actual riders. If she felt generous, she might let Jed ride her bareback to the nearest pasture where she stopped and grazed, ripping up grass with a sideways tug, ignoring Jed's prods with his heels. She was a well-padded horse, and Jed's prods did nothing to get her going. Tess had a multitude of horse jokes, and she tried them all on Jed. She might rub his legs on a barbed wire fence, or buck him off, or lie down for a roll and force him to jump off, or for no good reason head for home. If Tess started for the barn, nothing convinced her otherwise. "Going home" was the one event that made her hurry. Even then, she might ram Jed's legs against the door as she rushed into the barn. In spite of her abuse of him, Jed hadn't given up on horses. Little-John had a horse, and Little-John was his hero. Jed wanted a horse of his own.

Nell went outside. The children were clustered in front of the house, staying clear of the horse's hooves, surging back and forth as the horse danced toward them and away. Little-John made his horse go in circles on four legs and on two, walk backward, rear high in the air. Dust lifted from the yard in choking clouds.

"Hey, Little-John," Jed called. "Don't you ever slide off?"

"Naw." Little-John pranced the horse over to the children. "Wanna try?"

All the way down to the twins, they wanted to try. Little-John held David by the armpits and swung him into the saddle, and walked the horse while David clung to the pommel. Victoria and Jimmy were at wits' end with Little-John. He skipped school. He drank beer and stayed out too late. His friends were not of the best type. Yet, here he was, being kind to little children.

Nell went indoors to the laundry room. Occasionally checking on the kids through the window, she tackled a heap of dirty clothes. She thought she might do a column on laundry. She would advise readers, "Never count the jeans. It'll drive you nuts." There was no reason for nine children to put twelve pairs of jeans in the wash one day, fourteen the next day, twelve the day after (okay, she *had* been counting). The kids did their share of laundry—sorting, drying, folding, putting away—but the job was never done.

Starting the next load, she told herself, "Just stick 'em in. *Don't count!*"

* * *

Nell and Dan were in bed, recapping the day. She said, "Daddy had a jigsaw piece in his mouth. When I asked him what it was, he took it out and showed me. He said all it needed was a little soak and it would fit fine. Then he saw his mistake and got embarrassed. I said it was okay, we'd dry it, no problem. Poor Daddy! . . . Then there's Sigrid. She's always had a screwball side, but today it was worse."

He knew the first part of the Sigrid story. That morning, Sigrid asked to ride along to town with Nell and her parents. Nell said okay. Dan said he would stay home and watch the kids. In the kitchen, preparing to leave, Sigrid started teasing Elsa. That much was normal. What wasn't normal was the mean edge. She told Elsa she needed to loosen up, to have *fun* for a change. "Wear some lipstick, at least! You need color!" Sigrid swiveled open a scarlet lipstick and thrust it at Elsa. Elsa recoiled. Sigrid sneered, "Not your cup of forté, huh? Don't be such a *stuck*-in-the-mud!" Elsa looked stunned, as if she had been slapped. Nell said, "Mom, you look *fine*. Sigrid, be nice."

Now, in bed, Nell told Dan, "Sigrid eavesdrops, and she has trouble hearing, so she hears only part of what people say and makes off-the-wall guesses. We had just left the doctor's office and she said a man in the waiting room had a microphone in his dentures! Then, at the bank, she gave the teller her dividend check and a deposit slip, and he said, 'I'll be right back with your receipt,' and went away. Sigrid said in my ear, 'How does he know I have pleurisy?' I asked her what she meant. She scoffed as if I were being dense on purpose. She hissed at me, 'He said he has *ice packs* for my *pleurisy*! How does he know I have pleurisy?'"

Nell walleyed Dan.

He said, "Well? Did he bring her the ice packs?"

"*You.* I'm serious. Maybe she's losing it."

"What's the worst that could happen?"

"That she'll go blank and the kids will suffer."

"Do we need to watch her?"

"Maybe." Nell snuggled up to him. "Too many worries! Whose idea *was* it, anyway, so many people in this little house?"

* * *

November 1, 1979. "A Glimpse From Here" column submission. Nell Sanderson.

Today we had a small miracle—one of those ticks of the universal clock that puts everything in balance. The balance never lasts, but it should be memorialized.

Dan had left early with a neighbor, heading to the Bismarck airport and to Thailand for three weeks. We're used to separations. We know how they go. The first hours are fine, the last ones grueling.

But this first hour was not just fine. It sparkled.

The kids except for Jacob are eating Cream of Wheat. Jacob's allergic to wheat so he's having corn puffs. I say, "Corn puffs are round like a ball, not lumpy like popcorn. I wonder how they do that?" This is not a trick question. I have no idea how they do that.

Jacob, the shyest of the bunch, says, "I know! Foost they grow the corn on the cob on the ground. Nen they pit in a sheen, and nen—you ready? They pit the corn on the cob and sprinkle it with dots!"

The other kids laugh. So many words from quiet Jacob! He smiles

165

and glances at the others. Being the center of attention is new to him. He likes it.

Not to be outdone, Jed says, "How do you know when spaghetti is old? When it grows whiskers!" (In our previous house, he found fuzzy spaghetti in the refrigerator and thought it was hilarious. My mother cooks here at the farm. She never lets food go bad.)

Jacob wants to win back the limelight. "I know how to make a cake! Foost you pit in the butto. Nen na nilla. Nen na salt . . . Nen is 'at all?" He smiles at Rachel, his co-conspirator and co-inventor of recipes.

She says, "Flour?"

"Oh yeah, flour. *Nen* you pit it in na pan!" He's apparently watched my mother in the kitchen and invented his own recipe. He took a risk, telling us about it. A big advance.

Addie, wanting to read out loud: "'And be yeh kind to one another.'"

I: "'*Yee.*' It's old-fashioned for 'you.' It goes, 'Be yee kind to one another.'"

Addie: "'And be yeh . . .'"

Jed: "*No!* That's not right! It goes . . ."

Addie, turning red in the face: "*Sh!*"

Jed: "I was just trying to help."

Addie, grinding her teeth: "I DON'T WANT ANY HELP!"

Jed: "But it goes . . ."

Addie, jutting her head at Jed: "BE! . . . QUIET!"

I, laughing: "Gentle. The whole idea is being kind to one another."

Tooth-brushing. Jackets. Rubber boots. Jed, Abraham, and Isaac are to meet the school bus at the bottom of the hill. I'll feed the baby, Rebecca, while Sigrid, our helper friend, takes the younger kids to the barn to play—Jacob, Addie, Rachel, and the twins, Jonathan and David.

Rachel and Addie put on matching yellow rain pants, slickers, and wide-brimmed hats—gifts from our neighbor Victoria who claims she found herself with extras. I snap the straps under the girls' chins. Their cheeks pudge out from the pressure of the straps. The girls think that's funny. Addie shoves her hat brim up in front. Rachel does the same. Now they have big yellow half-circles on their heads, and they think *that's* funny. Abraham, the oldest of the kids from the Philippines, helps the twins into their coats and tucks their pants into their boots. Isaac puts on his jacket. The zipper won't zip. I use a little AI oil on it. As I work on the zipper, Isaac twists away, joking with Jed.

They finish early. I kiss them and they spill out the door, still joking.

Later I look outside. The rain has slacked off to a drizzle. Isaac and Abraham are squatting at the top of the hill. Jed stands back by the house. He calls something. Isaac comes to where Jed is. They're playing Red Light-Green Light. It's good they have extra time. All that stopping and starting over could take a while.

I move aside at the window to look for Sigrid and the little kids. They haven't gone inside the barn yet. They're standing in a clump outside the door. The barn is maybe a city block away, so I have to look carefully. But it's true. They all have their faces turned up to the mist.

See what I mean about sparkle?

Ten

The Flying In-box

Cracks in the outhouse wall let in air and stripes of light. Outside, a bird chip-chipped, waited a beat, chipped again. Dan left the outhouse and walked toward the field. He needed solitude. He had to think about Abraham.

In the tumble of family life, Abraham seemed to be coping well, but when Dan found him alone he seemed bereft, his face streaked—if not with tears, with grief. Abraham felt responsible for his siblings, but they were no longer just his. He looked stricken when someone else fed Rebecca, or picked up Jonathan or David, or decided it was time for them to do this or that. *He* used to be the one to decide. Abraham had suffered tremendous loss, the loss of his parents, his homeland, his island, the smells and sounds of home. He probably wanted to *go home* and take his brothers and sisters with him. But there was no home to go home to, except this one. When he first came to the States, he seemed relieved of some burden. Then he turned sorrowful, quietly resistant at times, even angry. In other words: culture shock. In Southeast Asia Dan had experienced a small degree of culture shock, and returning to the States he'd felt reverse culture shock. Everyday sights triggered contrasts and caused a diffused sadness, a sense of being in the wrong place. Abraham was likely going through this and much more.

One aspect of America was a boon for Abraham. Cars. Abraham loved cars. He wanted to learn everything he could learn about cars—about trains and planes, too, but cars were close at hand. He had an inborn knowledge of how machines worked. Already, at the farm, he had replaced two lamp switches, substituted a paper clip for the battery in the kitchen radio, and fixed the toilet flusher. He was currently trying to fix the bus, which would readily start but then go dead. Even Isak was stymied.

Now Dan remembered something. After school today, Rick Suomi, a teen-aged mechanical wizard, was coming to look at the bus. *That* should help Abraham feel better.

Three hours later, Rick and his father, Arvo, bent over the innards of the bus, located at the rear under a lift-up hood. They were generational copies of each other, gregarious brown-eyed blonds, the son destined to repeat the shape of his father, more or less a barrel on legs. Abraham, Dan, Isak, and Jed stretched around them to see the engine for themselves.

Arvo stepped back and shook his head. "Ya, *he's* better with these rigs," he said, meaning Rick. He took off his cap and pushed back his hair, managing by this act to convey pride in his son. "He'll figure it out."

Isak also backed away, his confidence siphoning off. "They did those-kind fancy things in there. A fella can't tell *which* way's up."

Abraham made a production of handing wrenches to Rick, and a mop rag, a flashlight, anything he needed. Maybe, Dan thought, after the bus was fixed, Rick would find another sick vehicle in some other place and Abraham could help him on that job as well. Auto repair might be one small answer for Abraham. If Dan could tack together enough small answers, the boy might feel less alien.

Dan made "Helping Rick" a chore for the week and gave it to Abraham. That left Jed afloat; the two boys usually worked together. So Dan asked Jed to help him in the hayloft. He had bought a supply of heavy rope for a new Tarzan swing plus a spider web and a rope ladder. Winter here meant forty below zero. But regardless of the weather kids needed to play. If they could play in the barn, the weather wouldn't matter so much. In the loft, they could jump in the hay, swing, climb. Downstairs, they could sit on Tess, who stood quietly for sitters if she had oats in front of her and shifted around if she didn't.

* * *

169

November 15, 1979

Dear everyone,

It's about time I wrote and found out what you're up to. I guess writing isn't easy for you guys, either, since I haven't heard a peep. I was glad to meet everyone, including the kids from the Philippines. You okay?

Are you coming for Christmas? We've got loads of room. The kids can sleep on the floor (thick rugs) and the grownups can find a bed somewhere. Kik thinks it would be great. This year Liisa and Bill are going to his folks', so that leaves space. Liisa makes up for Kik and me having only two kids each. She and Bill have <u>eleven,</u> I kid you not. They belong to the old Finnish church. Big families! We've had piles of people here. So start packing!

Our news. Adam is working too much as usual. The truth is he loves it. He lights up when he talks about his classes and students. The kids are fine. Miia's got this, what to call it? A fascination with old clothes and old movies. I take her to the thrift store and she whips through the racks, pops into the dressing room and steps out looking like a WAC from World War II, or a paperboy from the 1900s, or a schoolgirl from *our* days. Where did she get <u>that</u> from? The <u>drama</u>, I mean. She wants to be a pediatrician. Coop plays every sport that comes along. . . Hmmmm, <u>he's</u> dramatic, too. He tries out for school plays when he can work it around his ball games. He wants to be a sportscaster. Dad and Mom send snapshots and look like a typical Florida retired couple, sunglasses and Bermudas. My Mom teaches baking at a retirement center, which is the most fun she could have. For exercise, they walk up and down the beach. What's retirement for, if you can't do what you want? As for me, I'm getting ready for a show. I've got cameras going and the dark room steaming.

The rest of the Minneapolis tribe? Kik is head of a weavers' group in St. Paul, I think I told you. She actually makes money from weaving. She makes one-of-a-kind jackets and capes. She and Jeff have twins, Sadie and Ensio. They're twelve and have a language of their own. They're not as rowdy as our kids but the four are good friends. Ensio signs his name NCO. He's an amateur chemist and Sadie is a future teacher. Sadie's best talent is whistling with two fingers, you know, that sharp sound that hurts the ears? Kik and I tried to whistle like that when we were kids and never could. Kik and Jeff play handball. Don't ask. I'm not a handball player. Even with Jeff being so tall, he can't count on beating her. When I was little, I was the active one. The others wanted to sit down all the time. Now it's like they all decided to be athletes. Aarnie and Kaisa play ice hockey! Really. In a league for retired people. I've seen those old folks play. They're wicked with the sticks and pucks.

Time to go get Adam. His car's in the hospital. We'll pick up pizza on the way home. Let us know about Christmas.

Hugs, Marcie.

*　*　*

Three people had November birthdays—Elsa, Rachel, Jacob—and Nell wanted a balloon tree for the combined party. Dan found a fallen birch branch and anchored it in a pail of rocks, brought it to the kitchen table and draped the pail with a blue towel. Then he helped the children blow the balloons. The new children had never seen balloons. At first they breathed in both directions and swallowed back the blown air, getting their lips and the balloon lips wet and slippery. He dried the balloon lips and knotted them with string and helped the children tie them to the branch. The new children were too urgent. They kept snapping off twigs. "Easy does it," Dan said. Nell helped them scissor-edge ribbon to make long curls, which they hung on the tree. They cut out paper figures, one for each family member, drew on faces, names and clothes and hung them too on the tree.

Nell's mother, as a birthday person, wasn't allowed to cook, so Nell fixed the foods that the birthday people had chosen, hot dogs for Rachel, pizza for Jacob, ground beef casserole for her mother. Sigrid baked two cakes, her personal choices—a coconut cake with a white boiled frosting and a Three-Layer Slush. Three-Layer Slush was the rage in Bear Paw, she told the kids, made of crushed pineapple, yellow cake mix, and secret ingredients she did not wish to disclose.

Excitement was running high. The idea of a birthday party was new to the children from the Philippines. Even Isaac seemed uncertain. Rachel pressed her front teeth with one finger and said, "They're not *loose*. I'm *five*, and they're not loose!" The kids were still jumping around, getting settled at the table, when Sigrid opened the cupboard above Nell's father's head. He suddenly stood up, very fast, and hit his head on the point of the door. He grunted and sat down, piling his hands on his head. Blood showed between his fingers.

Nell pressed a towel to his head. Shifting his hair to see the wound, she said, "You need to see a doctor. I'll drive."

Elsa said, "I'll go-with."

Dan and Sigrid would stay back to run the festivities, or what were left of them. The party was winding down before getting started. The fun had faded and bickering had taken its place. As if one injury sponsored more, the kids started pinching and poking each other. At the door, Nell turned to Dan to say goodbye, but he was occupied with who was doing what to whom at the table.

Then the children looked up and watched Nell's father go out the door, their faces saying, "With Grandpa hurt, and Mom and Grandma leaving, too (and Grandma is a *birthday person*), what good is a party?"

✻ ✻ ✻

"We had to get to the barn to do the milking, but we couldn't see the barn. We had five feet of snow and it kept coming down." Isak stopped for a breath, taken off-guard by what he would say next.

"Father had us dig a path from the house to the barn. He set up ropes so we could pull ourselves there. We felt our way with ropes." He didn't say the whole of what he was thinking, that Father was a good man, after all—a good farmer, a good provider. Yes, he made the one big mistake. Killing Matilda. *That* mistake. But he was more than just that mistake. And his mother wasn't just fury at his father. Isak made an effort to reach back and reconstitute his Mum. She had been silent as long as he could recall, angry at her husband, cool to the children. She meant to love her children, he believed, but even before Matilda died she was consumed by some private grief. Losing Matilda crushed what was left of her. She kept her remaining children at a distance, as if she could avoid more pain when she lost them as well.

He sucked in air. *He needed more from her.* He wanted her to shine like the morning star whenever she caught sight of him! He wanted to be the best thing possible walking through her door!

"We're all children," he said. "We never grow up."

"Um," said Dan, obviously off-put by Isak's comment. "You think we'll have to do that, put up a rope?"

With effort, Isak returned to the here and now. He was in the barn with Dan, Abraham, Jed. The boys were shoveling manure. The wind was banging the sliding door, *batta-bat*, but Isak felt warm. The snow was deep (though not as deep as the time they needed ropes). Snow had drifted against the barn, insulating it, and the cows inside the barn were giving off heat. The electricity was working. If the power blew, he would get out the kerosene lamps. They were in a hinged box by the milk house. Or used to be.

"Naw," he said. "We probably won't get it that bad. Anyway, we can handle it. Lotta shovels, lotta kids."

He ruminated the way cows did, chewing at his thoughts, thinking that one advantage to a big family was a supply of hands. In a few months' time, these youngsters had shoveled garden dirt, manure, and snow, and kept the wood box full. In October, Isak told Dan they needed to stock firewood. (Dan might not have thought of it, left on his own.) Isak knew where there was wood free for the taking—at least when he was a boy—by Hazelton on the river banks where floods deposited branches and uprooted trees. Dan and he went there and got a pile of wood, but they needed more. About that same time, Jimmy Rinta brought a load of logs from his cousin's land in Minnesota. Dan bought several logs from Jimmy, enough for a winter supply of firewood. Isak, Dan, and the older boys sawed the logs, chopped them into stove-sized pieces, and stacked the pieces in the woodshed. (Isak let the others go to the woodshed. He dreaded the place.) When the woodshed was full, they used the hayloft. He didn't try getting up there, with his cast and all, but it came back to him fully formed. Spiked with sun. Heaven-high. Enough dust to croak a fellow. Some things never change.

"We have coal," he said, then closed his mouth, annoyed at his wrong insertion of words. He hadn't meant to speak. No one was talking about fuel. "In case we run out of wood," he finished lamely. "Lignite. It burns dirty, but it's okay in a pinch."

Trying to recover, he said, "Did I tell you I herded cows with my brothers? We'd round up cows from town and bring them to our pasture, back and forth every day, May 1 to September 1. We got a penny a cow."

Jed said, "Why would they have cows in *town*?"

"Everyone kept a cow."

"In town? They don't have any barns."

"The cow lived in a lean-to, a shed built onto the house, practically *in* the house."

"*Weird.*"

"And we hunted gophers," Isak said.

"But gophers are cool! Why would you hunt gophers?"

A weariness flooded Isak. Talking could be hard work. "They were pests," he said. "We got a penny a tail . . . ."

A mechanical roar broke into his words. The boys slid open the door, and there was Little-John, revving the motor on one of those new-fangled buzzers, Isak mused, those machines that young people rode on snow. It had shark's teeth painted in front. That lad was always charging into the yard on one beast or other, motorized or not, showing off and making the children's eyes big and giving them something else to covet.

Little-John said, "Want a ride?"

Isak, catching the caution behind Dan's greeting, thought, Man oh man! That Dan's got a job-and-a-half, keeping so many children straight for as many years as it'll take to raise them.

The same thought returned an hour later as he rode in the bus with Dan and the eight older children. Dan was fuming mad. Isak was sitting up front, trying to ignore Jed and the boy Isaac, who were behind the driver's seat.

174

Despite Dan's warnings, the two boys kept wrestling, punching, tee-heeing, and making crude sounds. The other children were peaceful. Abraham was studying something under a microscope—an eyelash, Isak recalled hearing. Rachel and Addie were playing "I Spy." Jacob was singing, "I been workin' on the railroad, all the rest have gone away." The twins had made up a game. When they heard the honk of a car horn—or heard nothing at all—they said, "'M-body *beep*-beep! Pooze *me*!'" Excuse me, Isak thought they meant.

Jed and Isaac continued to wrestle and laugh and poke each other. Dan pulled to the side of the road and turned off the engine. Turning to the two boys, he yelled, "When I say something, you listen! I can't drive if you jump around! It's *dangerous*! It takes my mind off driving and there's ice on the road! We could swerve!" He huffed through his nose, catching up on air. "I don't want to have to stop again!"

He got the bus back on the road, still in a blue funk. The bus rolled along. No one made any noise.

Finally Jed said, "Can I laugh just a *little*, Dad? It's awfully hard to hold it in."

Isak thought this was funny, but he kept it to himself. Dan wasn't ready yet to let the boys off the hook, so Isak lightened the mood. "We had a woodpecker," he said, "that pecked the side of the house all in one spot. He got through two layers of siding, nearly *into* the house! So I went to Will Storky's and borrowed his stuffed owl. It had *mean*-like eyes as big as your fist. I put it on a perch on the side of the house and hung a sheet of light metal by it. When the wind blew, the metal sheet made a big racket. We had plenty-wind, so it did the trick. Sent that woodpecker packing! He never bothered us again."

Jed and Isaac had questions. Did Isak *see* the woodpecker? Did it come there alone? What kind of bugs was it after? Is the perch still there?

Isak thought, See how I settled them down? It's a good thing I'm around! Dan should thank his lucky stars.

* * *

The little woman was in a temper. She stopped Nell in the hall after school, quaking with rage. She was shorter than Nell by a head, and her blonde topknot got a workout as she spoke. "I'm Wilma Johnson! I hate to say it, but that boy of yours? Isaac? He's a thief! He stole my Bethie's lunch money!"

Nell's spirits sagged. *Isaac. Again.* She had never met Wilma before this minute, but Wilma knew who Nell was. Nell guessed that she was well-known, pointed out by other mothers, "*That* one, with all the kids." She asked Wilma what had happened.

"Bethie came home crying yesterday, saying Isaac took her lunch money! It happened again today!"

"What made her think it was Isaac?"

"She saw him at her desk, touching her things! She told the teacher."

"Has the teacher talked to Isaac?"

"I don't know." Wilma touched the collar of her green wool coat. Finding it standing, she made it lie down. "But that boy needs *help*. He's a *menace*."

Nell apologized to Wilma and paid her for the lunches. She rounded up Jed, Abraham, and Isaac and took them with her to the bus. She would go ahead with her plans, take the boys to Hanson, do errands. She wasn't ready to talk to Isaac about the lunch money. She had thinking to do. Where was Dan when she needed him?

Isaac. It was something every day, at home or at school—Isaac fighting, Isaac pinching, Isaac hurting the hamster. Earlier that week he had come home from school and said, "We getta new locker! You vang a locker, you get a *little* locker!" Nell had surmised, rightly so, that he had mangled the first locker and the principal had issued him a smaller one. When Isaac first arrived from the Philippines, his problems were mostly invisible, disguised by a charm that he could call upon at will. Now they were in the open. He played with matches. He lied for no reason. He hurt the twins. He sat on the kittens. Caught in the act, he contrived innocence. The normal school setting didn't work for Isaac. No teacher could watch everything at once, and Isaac was slippery and smart. He needed a tight structure, soon, or he would end up as a charming, slippery con man.

Nell decided to teach Isaac at home along with Addie and Jacob. That way, she could keep an eye on him. She ran down the names of the other children.

Rachel sat in on Addie's and Jacob's lessons and called out words. She was teaching herself to read. She would do beautifully in kindergarten. But if Mrs. Kettleworth was still teaching when Rachel was ready for first grade, Nell would teach her too at home. She didn't want any of her kids near Mrs. Kettleworth.

Addie and Jacob had blossomed in home school, joshing with each other and speeding through their schoolwork. No problems there.

David and Jonathan were sweet little boys who faltered in their use of words. Mrs. Kettleworth would label them retarded. *No!* When the time came, Nell would add them too to the school at home.

Nell continued down the list of children. The baby? When she came to the States Rebecca was pale, thin, and weak. She had grown rosy on the farm, like Clara in Heidi's mountains. Thriving on Elsa's food and the fawning of thirteen people, she had turned out to be a saucy, humorous child.

Jed and Abraham were flourishing at school. Under Mr. Styveson's tutelage, they read everything they could find on the natural world. They did draftsman-like drawings. They collected bugs. When they heard that moon rocks had fallen in North Dakota, they scouted the fields for meteorites. At home, Abraham was cooperative and helpful. Usually that was also true of Jed. But lately Jed had been shrill, falling into giggles while bopping the other kids on the head with a cloth snake, and only pretending to stop when Nell told him to. When he caught a cold, he wanted Nell to take care of him—him alone. "Mom, you work too hard," he said. "You should rest! All you have to do is take care of *me*." She gave him a lozenge and suggested he lie down. He went up to the attic. In two minutes he was downstairs, asking for honey for his throat. Nell had her hands in soapsuds, so she told him to help himself. Grumpily, and half-heartedly, he pulled out the flatware drawer, took a spoon, reached across the open drawer to the cupboard for the honey jar, and spooned honey into his mouth, dribbling honey into the drawer. Nell shouted. He shouted back and went upstairs. Nell felt terrible. What Jed needed, more than honey, was her attention. She went to the attic and apologized for shouting. He apologized for spilling honey. She gave him a long hug. Peace ensued.

But that was a familiar sequence, kids pushing at her, Nell getting irritated, kids pushing more, Nell blowing up. Was that the pay-off, her blowing up? Were they getting attention any way they could? In a family this big, individuals had to vie for position, and vying could get *loud*. Nell had caused a few scenes herself, set off sparks and watched what happened—like an arsonist who slips into the crowd to watch his fire burn. Why did she do that? She didn't know. She recalled a 1960s T-shirt slogan: "I'm trying to find myself. Have you seen me lately?" She knew why that was funny. Or wasn't.

Ticking off her list of family members, Nell came to her father. He was tentative again, and cantankerous. One evening when he kept nodding off in the recliner, Nell's mother urged him to go to bed. He snapped, "There you go, pestering me! Just leave me alone!" This was not like him. Nell needed to talk to her mother about getting him to a doctor. He needed a checkup, but he would resist. Nell had her own resistance. Doctor visits were expensive and time-consuming. Besides, she didn't want to hear bad news about her father. On top of everything, her mother showed signs of confusion at only sixty-two. Nell had seen her standing in the pantry, making hand motions, reminding her muscles what she would do with an item when she found it—stir, wind in a circle, or mash. At what point would Nell need to be a parent to her parents?

As she drove, she watched out for deer. They sometimes leaped from bushes onto the road. She did the must-do jobs on autopilot—overseeing, arbitrating, protecting, responding, sweeping, mopping, doing laundry, swinging pot handles out of toddlers' reach, wiping toddlers' faces, keeping the surfaces cleared up—but she ignored deep-cleaning. She was expert at what her mother called a lick-and-a-promise. The difference was that her mother kept her promise, at least in her own house. At the farmhouse, Nell's mother did all of the cooking. Nell didn't want her to have to clean the house as well, so she snuck deep-cleaning onto the kids' chore list. She felt a tad guilty seeing toddlers wash windows, but they scrubbed away, chewing their tongues, thinking it was a game. Nell's ideal plan for housework: (1) Put everything that's out of place in a drawer, the washer, the sink, or the trash can. (2) Open the front door. (3) Tip the house in that direction. (4) Sweep up what falls out and throw it away. (5) Put a jelly jar of wildflowers on the table. Her job was too big! She upbraided herself. *Remember, kiddo, you asked for it. You wanted gobs of kids.* And she was glad she had them. But they took too much time, or she gave them too much time to the point of ignoring Dan. She was unreasonable when it came to Dan. She wanted him involved, but then she undercut him. She knew he disliked traveling for work—he would change places with her in a flash—and yet, when he got home from a trip, she might subtly punish him for leaving, try to keep the kids' loyalties with her, resist telling him their small stories. A trait she wasn't proud of! Her scheme never worked, anyway. The kids were wild about Dan. Their loyalties rested solidly with both parents. Within Dan's first hour back home, she would recant and tell him every story.

She pictured herself on Berit's stress scale, a horizontal continuum as she saw it. At position one, at the left, she stood like Wonder Woman, her feet wide apart, her hands at her waist, ready for anything. At position ten she was flat on the floor, mumbling and him-hawing, downed by an avalanche of domestic crumbs. Where was Nell at the moment? Seven? No. Eight.

Then there were the crank calls. Three times that week, the phone had rung at two in the morning. When Nell answered, she heard coarse male breathing, no words.

The calls never came when Dan was home. Someone knew he was gone.

* * *

That kid says a lot with a few words, Isak thought, meaning the boy Isaac. The boy had called from the kitchen, "Mom! Cinnamon not working on the toast! *Vurning!*" What better way was there to say that? None. Even if the boy stirred up trouble, Isak admired his gumption. Like that business with the rooster. Bill Hoosier had stopped on the road and given Isaac a rooster in a cage.

179

The boy rolled the cage up the hill with the rooster inside it, kuh-*lump*, kuh-*lump*, the rooster jumping around, trying to stay upright. And what did Isaac name the rooster? *Isaac!* As if there weren't enough of *those* around here already.

It was Saturday morning. The front room was full, Nell at the desk, writing something, Isak in the rocking chair, biding his time, the children watching a cooking show on television. Why this show instead of cartoons, Isak couldn't guess.

The TV chef was cooking tripe. Explaining that tripe was the lining of a cow's stomach, the chef held up a clumpy, off-white, honeycombed membrane that reminded Isak of a ladies' swimming cap, the old-fashioned kind made of rubber. Isak believed the clumps were globules of fat. The chef held the tripe as high as his arms could reach. It sagged onto the table.

The children called out, "Eeuw!" "You eat that?" "Nasty!" So *that's* why they chose this show, Isak thought. Because it's gruesome.

Jed wanted to write down the recipe. He got paper and a pen from the desk and went back to sit on the floor. The chef put down the tripe and held up two pigs' feet, shoving them in the camera's eye. Everything enlarged, the cleft hooves, the hair bristles, the thick rolled skin of the pigs' feet. The children gaped and snorted. The chef said he would cook the pigs' feet for gelatin. He put them down and again held up the tripe, like a merchant holding up a tapestry. He said something about garlic.

Jed said, "Did he say cowlick?"

"Garlic," Abraham said.

"Garlic." Jed wrote the word. The chef gave the rest of the recipe, which was long and complicated. Jed wrote as fast as he could.

Addie said, incredulous, "Did he say cook it *twelve to fourteen hours?*"

Jed said, "*How* long?"

Addie said, "Twelve to fourteen hours!"

Abraham asked, "Can you cook it that long?"

Addie said, "Grandma said we can't use the stove."

Isaac asked, "Do you have a fig?"

Addie said, "He means a pig. *Do* you?"

Isaac asked, "Can you cook a fig?"

Jed threw down his notes. "That's it! Forget it! I can't think with all these questions! I'm gonna make French toast."

Addie scolded, "Grandma said . . ."

"Grandma said we *could*," Jed said, aiming for the kitchen. The others got up and went with him. Nell followed.

To Isak, Nell looked tired. She needed more help with the children. Where was her husband? He was gone too often and he stayed away too long. Isak thought he might talk to Dan about that when he got home.

* * *

"Mohoganide," Sigrid said. "You know, that fake kind of leather?"

"Naugahyde?" Nell said.

Sigrid snapped her fingers. "That's it. We could cover the table with it, so we can wipe it up."

Elsa said, "I have oilcloth in the bus. We can use that."

Nell, Elsa, and Sigrid were at the table after supper with pencil and paper, totting up the hours and days before the bazaar. They figured that if they worked for three hours every weekday they could make eighty jars of refrigerated corn relish, twenty loaves of cranberry bread, and forty lace angels. The Rintas had left two working freezers and a refrigerator in the garage. They would come in handy.

Addie and Rachel showed up in pajamas at door to the front room. Addie was holding her stuffed animals—alligator, bear, giraffe, lion. Rachel was empty-armed. But at bedtime, Nell knew, Rachel would copy Addie and sleep under a zoo.

Addie said, "Can we help?"

Nell said, "Well . . ."

Sigrid said, "Sure you can! We'll start tomorrow. You can glue the lace."

181

Addie gave Rachel a glare of triumph. As their spokesperson, Addie pressed for more. "We want to *bake*, too." She aimed her ask at her grandmother who, as everyone knew, never let anyone help.

Elsa made a show of having been talked into it. Making marks on a piece of paper, she said, "I suppose you can butter pans."

The girls glistened at each other, smiling inside their mouths. As young as they were, they knew when to keep quiet. They didn't want to push their luck.

Addie said, "Okay then! Good night!" Like a vaudeville comic with a hooked cane, she pulled her sidekick off the stage.

❊ ❊ ❊

December 1, 1979

Dear Marcie,

I want to get a quick note to you so you'll know how to plan for Christmas. We can't come. Not this year, sorry! The bus isn't up to the trip. It's on blocks again. Until it's fixed, we troop around in the Rintas' pickup, taking this child and that one to the dentist, etc. We put everyone in the back for a school play or a trip to town. Around here, the cops don't mind. Stanley loves to ride back there. He puts his front paws outside the truck bed, <u>way</u> down on the fender, and stretches around the corner—a laughing dog about to fall on the road! Scares me to death.

We're getting ready for the bazaar, which is next week. Sigrid has made so many angels, she never wants to see one again. The corn relish and cranberry bread are in the refrigerator and freezer, respectively. We're sending you some of each, angel, bread, relish. Hope they get there without smooshing.

I'm pregnant! Can you believe it? Due in May. The more the merrier! We send our best for Christmas. I wish we could close our eyes and <u>be</u> there. Maybe next year.

Love, Nell

❊ ❊ ❊

"Spackle paddle." Isak rolled the words on his tongue. Jed had come in from the barn and asked Nell if she had a spackle paddle. Nell assumed he meant a putty knife, and she found one for him.

Jed said, "Thanks, Mom! You're a real pal."

Nell laughed and said, "If all I have to do to be your pal is find you a spackle paddle, I've got a pretty good deal." Jed went back outside and Nell took a basket of folded clothes upstairs. Where were the rest? Isak didn't know.

Alone at the table with coffee, Isak repeated, "Spackle paddle." He reviewed what the ladies had told him. He was going with them to a bazaar. The truth was, the ladies ran his life. They treated him like an invalid! He *was* an invalid, kind of; his leg still ached, even without the cast, and his mind went *kaput* when he least expected it, but he wished they'd let him in on things before they all got decided. That would help him to keep matters in order. This group moved *way* too fast—Elsa and her busy body, Nell and all those children. And that Sigrid? When she flares her nostrils, look out! It means she's going to say something crazy. Or sing. Her voice was deep, like a man's, and she liked radio commercials—"Cream of Wheat is so good to eat, and we have it every day!" and "Ha-*lo*, everybody! Ha-*lo*! Ha-*lo* is the *sham*poo that *glor*ifies your *hair*, so Ha-*lo*!" She'd get stuck on one song and that would be the only song for days on end, until he felt like pulling out his hair. There was a spell of thirteen days when all she sang was, "I've Got a Lovely Bunch of Coconuts," which was fine except she got stuck on the "Roll a bowl a ball" part, and that was all she sang. "Roll a bowl a ball, roll a bowl a ball, singin' roll a bowl a ball, a penny a pitch!" To his invisible audience, he said, "Try listening to *that* for thirteen days." Sigrid switched words around or made up new words whenever the mood hit her. If she was singing, she turned "Down by the Riverside," into "Don't Buy the Liverwurst." If she was talking, she might say, "I'm being calm, cool, and collective." *Collective?* Sigrid, calm and cool? Hot and bothered, more like it! Half a sandwich short of a picnic!

Isak had an axiom for almost any situation, some guideline for handling this or that, but he couldn't land on one for Sigrid.

Aha! He had it.

He poured coffee into his saucer and slurped it—loudly, on purpose, since he was alone—and gave himself advice in a waxy, preachy tone. "If you can't say anything nice, don't say anything at all."

* * *

Victoria had given Nell a gift certificate to the Ball Room, a Hanson warehouse that had been turned into a funhouse of balls—pinball machines, a miniature bowling alley, a batting cage, a glass room full of squishy plastic balls for toddlers to wallow in. Nell would use the certificate on the morning of the bazaar, which would be held in the school gym. She would take the kids to the Ball Room while Sigrid sold items. At noon, Nell and the kids would report to the gym. Jed and Abraham would man the table while Nell drove Sigrid and the kids back to the farm. Nell would pick up her parents, return with them, and the three of them plus Jed and Abraham would sell items until the bazaar closed at four o'clock. This was right during her parents' usual nap time. Nell hoped that her father's mind would stay lucid, that her mother's math genius would kick in, and that by the end of the bazaar neither parent would be confused or overtired.

The day arrived cold and still. A half-foot of snow had fallen during the night, giving the prairie a rough white blanket with weeds poking through. The sky was rocklike, the color of granite. At eight-thirty, Nell pulled into a parking lot so earnestly plowed that the asphalt showed in patches. An old man who seemed vigorous for his age, clean-shaven and sporty in a Russian fur hat, motioned them toward an empty parking spot. Nell stopped and rolled down her window, said she wasn't parking, just dropping off one person with sale items. The old man looked in at the children—at their dark skin, light skin, black curly hair, black wavy hair, reddish straight hair, brown straight hair, Asian features, African features, Nordic features—and pulled back ever so slightly. Nell wondered if he was thinking, "Half-breeds"—a term she had heard applied to children of a Sioux man and his Swedish wife. This region didn't have many non-white residents, and the Sandersons upped the percentage considerably. When Nell and

184

the children shopped in town, she saw curiosity on the faces of passersby, plus an occasional involuntary twitch that said, "How many men did she sleep with to get *that* bunch?" The children had a rambunctious time at the Ball Room, and by the time they and Nell got to the gym Sigrid had sold every angel and most of the relish and cranberry bread. Nell left Jed and Abraham there, drove Sigrid and the rest to the farm, and brought her parents back to the gym.

She need not have worried about her parents. They were in top shape. Her mother wowed customers by adding numbers in her head. Her father told North Dakota stories to anyone who stopped by. One person who stopped by was his boyhood friend, Sammy Koski, a short man with sunsets on his face. His farm was next door to the school. Isak asked him, "Do you still have that electric box?" Sammy nodded. Isak said he'd like to borrow it sometime. Without hurrying but with steady forward purpose, Sammy walked out of the gym, went home, and came back with the box.

At closing time, Victoria bought the last jar of relish. She patted Nell's arm. "You need anything, you let me know. You've got your hands full. I know what it's like."

Simple, good words. Victoria did this often , boosted Nell with a few good words.

* * *

Sigrid and Isak stood by the kitchen table, ready to try the box. The children pushed forward, ready to watch. On the table sat a businesslike oak box about ten inches square, with a hinged top, a crank handle, and two electrical leads with grips of coiled brass. As the children stared at the box and at him, Isak wrapped the leads in damp washcloths. Sammy had reminded him that the leads tended to bite when left bare since the current came to the high points of the coils, and that if a person put too much water on the cloth the holder got zapped. Isak swallowed the spit that had gathered in his mouth. He wasn't sure if this would work. When he was a kid, grownups used the box to ease arthritis pain. Sammy and Isak tried it, too, roaring at the *zuz-z-z* tickle that came through the leads. But the grownups were the ones with the aching joints, so it was mostly the grownups who used the box.

He told Sigrid, "Take the handles and hold on tight."

She did. She was being quiet, unusually so. He guessed she was nervous. He said, "Okay then," and slowly rotated the handle. The box made a low growl that corresponded in intensity with the force of his turning. Sigrid gave him a quick look at the start, then said nothing for many turns of the crank.

He said, "Does it help?"

"I think so. It makes my nerves jubbery. You know, rubbery, jumpy."

"Should I stop?"

"No. A little longer. You think we're doing it right? Shouldn't we hold hands so the current goes through us?"

Isak had no plans to hold hands with Sigrid! Not today, not ever. "Naw," he said. "This is fine."

Sigrid squeezed her eyes shut as he wound the crank. "I'm not talking while the flavor lasts," she said. But she opened her eyes and talked anyway. "Mrs. Meerson had one of these. We would've stayed there except . . . ? What happened was, we lost the rooming house and Hitch was out of work, and I found an ad that said free rent for cooking one meal a day for a lady in a wheelchair. I thought, *why not!* We went there in the morning and met Mrs. Meerson. She was old, and the house smelled of cooked cabbage, and she kept the place too warm, but we figured she was sick and needed it warm. She seemed nice, so we moved in and took our suitcases to our room upstairs. It was stuffy and had wallpaper with great big pink roses and an old dresser."

Sigrid was having a hard time sitting still, Isak noticed. She usually talked with her hands, and her hands were holding the leads. She said, "We went downstairs to fix supper for the lady. I knew we had a problem. The son was smoking."

Isak mistrusted Sigrid's way of talking, her habit of inflating words with pumped-up hype, but she had hooked him with this story. "The sun was smoking," he repeated. An alluring image—the sun misted over, the sun smoking. He liked any story that had fog and mystery in it.

Sigrid continued, "We could hardly see each other, the air was so thick. I'm allergic to smoke, and there he was, blowing smoke in my face!"

Oh. The *son.* Isak glanced at the children. Did they see his mistake?

Sigrid said, "We moved out that minute, without fixing any food. We said sorry to Mrs. Meerson and got our suitcases and left. But she had one of these boxes. I saw it on the way out."

Isak ground the crank, vowing to never trust her again. Sigrid had caught him at his word game and *she* had come out on top. He was so agitated that he cranked too fast, giving the leads a burst of heat.

Sigrid yelled, "*Stop!* I can't let go! I can't get my hands off!"

He remembered this too from the early days, how Sammy and he had cheated after promising to crank slowly. If the current got too strong, the holder's hands couldn't let go. Still, even after they knew this, Sammy and he had sent each other into spasms.

"Sorry," he said, "I'll go slow."

Afterwards, Sigrid said she would like a treatment every day at the same time. Then, of course, the children wanted to try it, one after another. So many children! Isak almost wished he'd never mentioned the box to Sammy.

✵ ✵ ✵

Two weeks before Christmas, Nell lay awake. Ready or not, Christmas would happen. They were definitely *not* ready. Too many medical bills, too many repairs, too little money. Christmas gifts for so many kids? Nell's mother was knitting socks and hats, but children needed toys, too. The only extra income that was expected was Dan's New Year's bonus check. But it might not arrive until January. Too late.

The next day, while the children ate noon dinner at the Rinta farm, Nell and Dan called a meeting of the adults.

Dan said, "We said this before, but let's agree. No gifts for grownups."

The others agreed.

"We need to assume my check will be late," he said.

Nell said, "Maybe we should wait for your check and have a late Christmas, even if it comes after New Year's."

Sigrid said, "No! Kids need to feel Christmasy at the right time!"

Nell said, "We don't have money to buy toys."

Elsa said, "We can *make* toys."

So, starting that night, the adults did shoemaker elf jobs while the children slept. Abel Sorenson, the grocer, had given Nell a strong wooden apple box. Placed on its side, it became a toy cabin. Dan and Isak built a loft and ladder from wood scraps, plus a kitchen counter, table, and chairs. Sigrid made bed frames of twigs and mattresses of woven twine. Elsa sewed curtains and quilts. Nell braided rugs and pasted pictures to the wall. Between work sessions, the box sat on end beside the bed under the cloth that normally draped the bed table; Dan had taken the bed table to the hay loft and put it among other stored items. Back in October, he had found a bird cage up there. Surprised that the kids hadn't seen it first, he had cleaned it, wrapped it in plastic sheeting, and placed it in the cedar chest beneath embroidered pillow cases. He figured that, as curious as kids were about hidden gifts, they wouldn't paw through fancy linens to find them. Nell lined it now with gold paper, put a red bow on it, and took it to Victoria's house.

In the daytime the kids got into the act. Sigrid helped them make paper chains and they swagged them around the house. Elsa baked gingerbread men and let the kids frost them. Nell saw her swallow objections when they made the faces purple or took forever painting on buttons. By the time they added candy sprinkles, the frosting was like concrete and the sprinkles bounced to the floor. The kids then stepped around on purpose to hear the crunch.

Days passed. No check. Nell's talks with God went something like, "*Help!*"

The day before Christmas Eve, Dan took the children to Tony Serritt's Christmas tree lot. Every year on that day, Tony gave away trees that hadn't sold. The tree the kids chose had a bare spot but was otherwise perfect. The bare spot could go against the wall.

While in storage, the strings of tree lights had tied themselves in knots. Dan had the kids stand in a line in the front room. He straightened one section of string and placed that section in a child's hands. Waiting was tedious, and Jonathan grew antsy. He dropped the string and put one leg over the playpen rail, intending to climb in with Rebecca.

Nell said, "No, Jonathan. You're too big. It's for Rebecca."

Jonathan shook the playpen, shouting, "Me a *bird*! This my *bird*house!"

Laughter burst from the group. The group was big, and the laughing made a big noise. Jonathan glanced around, terrified, and sobbed with his mouth wide open, a wet cry that brought liquid from his eyes, nose, and mouth. Abraham picked him up. Jonathan stopped crying, burped, gulped air, and smiled at him through saliva bubbles.

David wanted Abraham to pick *him* up, too. He pushed against Abraham's legs. Judging by an aroma and a droop to David's diapers, everyone knew that David's pants were full.

Jed said, "Hey, David. What's that you got in your pants?"

David said, "Chocolate."

Again the group laughed and again the laughter made a big noise. Like his twin, David got frightened and started crying. Nell came to his rescue, saying, "Don't worry, honey," and taking him by the hand toward the bathroom. She didn't know if he had made a joke on purpose or not, but he hadn't expected such an uproar in response.

When they got back, the light strings were untangled. The children still held the strings, though they were prancing or sitting down as they waited. Beginning at the tip of the tree, Dan and Nell placed the strings loosely on the branches.

Sigrid stood back and gave orders. "Too many blues there. Put that one lower." Dan put it lower.

She made a shooing motion with a forefinger. "That gold is too bright. Move it down to there."

Dan moved it down.

"The blue ones." Sigrid pointed to two blue bulbs next to each other. "Too close."

Nell lifted one string to another branch.

Sigrid said, "Now there's too many reds."

Nell said, "You want to do this yourself?"

"No, I'm the inspector. Hide the plug behind the trunk so you can't see it."

Dan did as she directed. He said, "Do we pass inspection?"

"Just this." Sigrid went to the tree and hooked one section of cord over a higher branch. "There. It didn't need much, just a little renouncement."

Nell's father, who had been whistle-snoring in the recliner, slept on as the kids took miniatures from egg cartons and hung them on the tree—skiers and sleigh riders, Swedish horses, Finnish elves. When the cartons were empty, Dan switched off the lamps and plugged in the tree lights.

The children said, "Wow," and advanced to identify the ornaments they had hung, retreated to see the whole, advanced more times, drank hot cocoa, got into pajamas, brushed their teeth, went to the tree again to see their ornaments, and went to bed.

The next day dawned. Christmas Eve.

This was the day. The check *had* to come.

Straight-up at noon, Nell walked along the driveway to the crest of the hill, rounded the corner past the small woods and followed the curve of the road down to the main road. Today the distance seemed very long.

She pulled the tab of the mailbox. The mailbox door was crooked, and it squeaked as she drew it down, but it opened to the right thing. *The check.*

"Thank You, thank You, thank You!" She ran to the house, hugged Dan and whooped and jumped, called goodbye to the others and ran to the blue bus. She had to hurry. Stores would close early on Christmas Eve. After cashing the check at the Kintyre bank, she drove to Hanson. At the toy store, she bought two three-inch stuffed brown bears, two yellow Tonka trucks, a red-blue-yellow stacking toy, and a black recorder. She took them to the bus and stored them behind the seat; she needed her hands free. She ran to the pet store. There she found the right green parakeet, the right brown mouse, and the right three goldfish. She bought them plus pet food, a mouse cage, and a fish bowl with a prince's castle and purple iridescent stones.

On her way back, Nell stopped and retrieved the bird cage. Victoria's house smelled like Christmas and looked like Christmas. Her children, even Little-John, were solemn and big-eyed, as if Christmas were too much to take in, as if their hopes were too urgent to come true. While at Victoria's house, Nell put the cage in a black plastic bag. At home, before going to the house, she hid the bag in the barn.

Dan took the kids to Kintyre to see Christmas lights. While her mother fixed supper, Nell went to the barn and brought back the cage, took the parakeet from its travel box and set it in the cage, gave it food and water, then started wrapping toys. Sigrid took the fish from their plastic bag of water and the mouse from its box and settled them in permanent homes. While they worked in the front room, Nell's father watched the goings-on from the recliner, smiling distractedly at whatever gag this was—some tricky plan concocted by the women.

When Dan and the kids returned, they washed up and Elsa served Sloppy Joes, which were such a hit that Dan declared a new tradition—Sloppy Joes every Christmas Eve. The group then sat around the Christmas tree on rocker, couch, and rug, small children on grownups' laps, and Dan read Luke 2, the story of Jesus' birth. The wind screamed at the corners, but the people were safe. Nell thought it was a miracle they had found this place. She had a surge of everything-is-fine—this burgeoning group, the carols on the radio, prinks of color on the tree, the Franklin stove waving heat.

Jed said, "It's warm in here!"

Nell said, "Too warm for a fire in the stove?"

"Not that kind of warm," Jed said. "*Family* warm."

"That's a nice thing to say," she told him.

When Nell was a child, she and her parents opened gifts on Christmas Eve. Beginning with their first Christmas as a married couple, Nell and Dan had followed suit. This year Sigrid played Santa. Without a costume, but with dash and buffoonery, she handed out gifts with a trumpeted flair.

All of a sudden Nell felt nervous. Each child would get only one toy or pet! Mittens too, and a knitted cap, thanks to her mother, and crayons and coloring books, but only one toy or pet. Would one be enough?

Rebecca picked at the wrapping paper with pincer fingers, fascinated with the designs and the twisted ribbons. When she found the stacking doughnut toy inside, she whacked it on the floor, then whacked it again. She got the idea slowly, aided by Dan, that the rings fit over the post and came off again. The possibilities enthralled her.

David and Jonathan loaded their Tonka trucks with alphabet blocks and drove them across the room, growling, "*Brrrmm! Brrrmm!*" They dumped them, reloaded them, drove them back, dumped them again. All the while, they never let up on the growling.

Nell asked Dan, "How do boys know how to *do* that, make that noise? Even these two? From a fishing island in the Philippines?" Dan said, "It's a boy thing."

Rachel and Addie hovered above their toy cabin, discussed the pictures, rearranged the furniture, cuddled their bears, asked Nell to help them sew bear clothes.

Jacob was possessive over his goldfish. He didn't want anyone else to look at them. He called them One, Two, Three, and kept his nose against the bowl, trying to tell them apart.

Isaac picked out notes on his recorder, playing the first line of "Jingle Bells" again and again. A perfect choice, Nell thought. The first seven notes were identical. Isaac had a knack for quick success. Follow-through was harder. Each time, the eighth note was off.

Jed named his mouse Seeds and held the mouse to his cheek, talking in mouse words and becoming Seeds' best friend.

Abraham called his parakeet Moses and tried to teach him to sit on his finger. Moses climbed up Abraham's arm, hopped onto his head, dug into his hair, and hid.

In every case, one toy or pet was enough!

An hour before midnight, the adults—except for Isak, who had gone to bed—carried the younger children into the church and herded the rest, sliding into pews beside neighbors and their families, including college-aged sons and daughters home for the holidays, and visitors from out of the area. Candlelight pulled in the walls and made the company tight. The place smelled of evergreen. The congregation sang, "Hark the Herald Angels Sing" and "We Three Kings" as a man behind the Sandersons hiccupped and snored, snorting himself awake only to fall asleep again. The Sanderson kids snickered at him until, one by one, they too fell asleep.

Afterwards, Dan, Nell, Elsa, and Sigrid picked up the younger children, woke the others, and made their way outdoors, wishing a merry Christmas to people they knew and to people they didn't know. The planet was frozen stiff. The parking lot was icy and flat, like the night. The sky was black velvet. Only one star showed. Doing its share for the occasion, the star winked at Nell.

* * *

On a sunny February day, Nell, Sigrid, and eight children waited at the international gate at the Bismarck airport and watched for Dan. He had fought through hindrances, refusals, dismissals, and delays, and he was bringing Laura home.

He was the tallest person among the passengers. He rounded the corner and came up the ramp carrying a small girl in a yellow dress. No braces, no orthopedic shoes. Dan put her down and pointed out the family. Laura ran to Nell—a staccato run due to a stiff leg—and grabbed Nell's knees, then bent back to look at her. She said, "You my *mudder*?" She turned to the boys. "You my *brudder*?" To Addie and Rachel, "You my *sisser*?" Her smile went from ear to ear, a smile a young leprechaun might have. Nell experienced one of the rushes that came with adoption, a joy so profound she could hardly see. She felt a crushing affection for this little girl.

They walked through the airport in a long, wide formation, Nell in front with the baby, Dan in back with the twins. Jed was near the middle with Laura, holding her hand as she talked about Sister Mary Clare (Jed later told

Nell), the babies, a blind boy, the ride on the airplane, acting out stories with the hand Jed wasn't holding. Dragging Laura with him, Jed caught up to Nell and whispered, "I knew she'd be small, but not *this* small! Or this *cool!*"

In the bedroom at the farm, Laura narrated a letter to the nuns, doing somersaults on the bed as she dictated. Nell typed Laura's words. "Fish are fimming! Sissers they take me to pancakes! I take care of babies! Cows they bang the fence!" Nell added a note, "These are Laura's memories of the Philippines. She thinks of you all very fondly. She is doing beautifully. She fits right in."

Laura did flips on the bed. "I jump! I go in a car with Daddy!"

＊　＊　＊

After the others had gone to bed, Dan and Nell sat at the table with candlelight and Chianti. If they had looked outside the window, they would have seen—in the square of light that fell from the kitchen to the back yard— three inches of new snow on a foot of old snow, and something else, a slide of silent people.

The flames made them look outside—a fire in the shape of a small cross.

Dan jumped up, shouting, "Call the police!" He ran out the door and around the north side of the house. In back, two sets of footprints led to and from the driveway on the south side. Dan stumbled after the prints, having to step high in the snow, topping the hill in time to hear a truck start its engine down on the main road. As the truck drove away, the headlights bounced off clouds.

He doused the fire with snow. What he carried to the kitchen was a charred wooden cross, eight inches tall. A baby cross.

He laid it on a newspaper on the table. It reeked of kerosene. It had been skillfully crafted from a single piece of wood. Someone had taken the time and effort to carve this cross, nail it to a platform that would float on snow, bring it here with a cohort, douse it with fuel, light it, and escape—all to send Dan and Nell an unmistakable message: We want you and your babies gone.

Within minutes, police lights streaked the yard, red and blue strobes. Two officers filled the kitchen with a clanking presence. The older cop was stocky and swollen, with spongy cheeks that deflated as he spoke. The younger cop was fit, athletic, his main pose a military stance. The older cop seemed fatherly and kind. The younger cop seemed not to be present, or, if present, only superficially.

Elsa and Sigrid appeared in housecoats, looking in from the front room. Behind them, three boys tried to see past the barricade formed by the two women.

The policemen asked questions and wrote down answers. Acting more the concerned neighbor than a cop, the older man dropped his official guise. "It's the same guys," he said, shaking his head, apologizing for a few ignorant locals. "It happened twice before, to Sioux who live off the reservation. Most people around here are good folks, not like this." He grimaced at the cross.

When the officers went outside, Dan went with them. The police car waited in front, flashier and more important than other cars its size, police radio crackling, a woman droning codes in police talk. The cops inspected the scene, spoke into equipment, put more footsteps in the snow, wrote more notes, said good night and drove off.

Dan and Nell were left to answer the boys' questions—and later, in bed, their own. Now what? Do we move? A cross-burning by itself couldn't chase them off—they didn't want the black-hearts to think their tactics had worked. But long before this night's events, Dan had doubts about staying on. As much as the family liked it here, and as friendly as 99.99% of the neighbors were, he had to consider relocating.

"It boils down to money," he told Nell. "We're losing ground, you know we are."

"But we live here rent-free!"

"My work's too far away. If we stayed, I'd have to keep traveling." He let his shoulders sag, giving Nell notice that he had more news, not necessarily welcome news.

"You got something in the mail, didn't you?"

"I'm being asked back to Seattle."

"Seattle?" Nell sat up and stared pins and needles at him. "We just *left* Seattle."

Dan sat up and raised his knees and hung his arms over them. "I can't earn enough by just consulting."

"But we just *got* here!"

"I could go alone and get the ball rolling. You could come later."

"Move back?" She fought free of the covers, pulled on her robe, and sat on the straight wooden chair by the window. Her feet tapped a tattoo on the floor. "*Move back?*"

"George is retiring," he said. "They want me to run the office."

She was so irked that her mouth jerked. "Do you want to?"

"It's better than staying here and sinking deeper."

"How much would you have to travel?"

"Some. Less than from here."

"I don't *want* you to travel!"

"Me neither."

An interval passed during which he counted the photos on the dresser. Five of Sandersons, three of Halonens, one of an Albertson. No Rintas.

She said, "I know we're tumbleweeds, but I don't want to move again! How could we move *anywhere* with all these kids? They love it here. *I* love it. Besides, the bus couldn't make the trip again."

"Sure it could, with a new engine. We could be the Tumbleweed Rest Home on wheels."

"No jokes."

"Let's talk about it in the morning. C'me 'ere, let me rub your back."

Petulantly, she got into bed and sat with her back to him. He massaged her neck and shoulders and worked down her arms to her hands and fingers, crooning in a plummy accent based on no true language. "Ah, Mrs. S.! So gracious you come to me! You are dee-leecious person, innyone ever told you? . . . I em your servant . . . I *fix* you."

196

He slid the band off her hair and unwound her braid, making fluffing motions to fan out the strands. "I fix your hair, I fix this, I fix that."

He put his mouth to her ear. "I fix *everything*. You have ecks and penns? I heal you with my hands . . . See? . . . The kiss? No charge."

* * *

When Nell looked for Isaac, she found him in the attic, squatting by his sleeping bag and trying to tie a dishtowel to a stick. He had chunks of bread and cheese beside him. Where had he learned about hobo sticks? In the Philippines? She didn't think so.

She asked him what he was doing. He didn't answer. Jed, who had followed Nell upstairs, said, "Hey, Isaac! You can use the towel for a blanket when you sleep outside! Just keep going south. Then you won't get so cold."

Isaac said, "None ob your vusiness!" He tugged at the dishtowel, but it was too thick to form a knot.

Nell tipped her head at Jed. He went downstairs. She sat on a chair and said to Isaac, "Would you like to talk?"

His eyes were like high tide in a hurricane. "You hate me! You like *Jed and Avraham*! Not *me*. You like me to go vack to Pilippines!" He made important work of wrapping his bread. "You think the little kids so *cute*. You like the little kids, not *me*. You say, '*Wonderpul* little kids!'" He said the final three words in a siren voice.

Nell was moved by his complaints, yet she felt an urge to defend herself. "Isaac! Honey! What's got you so upset?"

He blazed at her, "Jed and Avraham, same-same! All the time they lapp at me! They make me vee punny and they lapp and lapp!"

"They like jokes, and so do you," Nell said reasonably. "What happened?"

He shouted, "You don't like me!"

"Why do you say that? Because I get mad at you sometimes?"

"Yes." Vindication made his face glow.

Nell said, "*Why* do I get mad?"

"Vecause I tell lies and take toys."

Isaac didn't always tell the truth, but he was doing it now. "Yes," she said. "What do you suppose I need from you?"

"Don't tell lies. Don't take things."

She nodded and held his gaze. "What would *you* like from *me*?"

"Take my ficture! Jed and Addie hab a whole vuncha fictures. I don't hab *any*!"

He had a point. She had forgotten where the camera was. "I'm sorry, Isaac. I'll take your picture. You can have your own album, a book of pictures like Jed and Addie's. The others can, too."

When she said he could have his own album, his face had opened in victory. When she said the others could, too, his face shut down.

He said, "How come eberyone?"

"That's how it works. Everyone gets good things, maybe at different times."

"Jacov gets you *more*."

Not for the first time, Nell heard in a child's complaint an appeal for more of *her*. This show of emotion from Isaac was an improvement. Too often, he seemed frozen over—or, at the other extreme, too charming to be real.

Nell got to her feet and urged him into her arms. He was a bag of boards. She made herself a pillowy place and held him while he wriggled and fought to free himself. Slowly, as if risking a great deal, he relaxed one set of muscles after another until he was letting Nell hug him. This hug was *good*. It was happening on *her* terms. Isaac was cagey when it came to hugs, arching away if she reached for him or running up behind her when she wasn't expecting a hug, crashing into her, locking his arms around her, pummeling her in the process—more of a flying tackle than a hug. This gentler hug meant progress.

She said, "I like your hugs *so much*."

Isaac slid out of her embrace and stood before her, smiling a hero's smile. "When I'm big and you call me on the telepone, I'll come ober in one minute on the airflane! With a sfaceshiff fushing it! I'll get there in the nick of time!"

198

How touching, and how sweet.

But his problems were severe. On any given day, they could throw her off-stride. Neighbors called to report what Isaac had done—stolen something, or hit someone, or set a fire, or maimed a pet. Every time the phone rang, her stomach clenched. After picking up the receiver, she was silent for a beat, hoping it wasn't more bad news about Isaac.

That night she had two odd dreams. (This pregnancy gave her the *oddest* dreams.) In one, she was driving foster children from place to place. A small girl refused to talk. In a playroom at a social services office, Nell got her to talk with her. The girl let Nell hold her. The supervisor, a large, businesslike woman, said, "*I* need that, too," and fell on her face in tears. Nell knelt and hugged the woman's shoulders. The scene changed to Nell breast-feeding a foster baby. The baby tried to swallow her breast. Nell was shocked to see a deep crevasse in the baby's head. A caseworker said, "That's *nothing*. You should have seen it when we got him, before we put grass seed in there!"

What did *that* mean?

In the second dream, she and Dan were attending a conference in a foreign land—hotels, boardwalks, crowds. Nell was walking outdoors with friends when she realized Dan was missing. She asked the others if they knew where he was. They pointed to the sky, to an aircraft made of three stacked rectangles—a flying in-box. She stepped into a plaza and the in-box tipped in her direction. She knew it was Dan saying hello; he had recognized her blue dress. The flying machine disappeared in a fog. Nell went with the others into the hotel, furious at Dan. He wasn't in danger, just *absent*—doing what he wanted to do regardless of what she needed. The lights dimmed. Dinner was served. Nell didn't want food. She wanted a whiskey sour. She never drank hard alcohol, but she thought now was the time for a whiskey sour. She left the room to find Dan and got lost in the hotel. An East Indian concierge gave her a nod, motioning up. She got to the next level by convoluted means, no stairs or elevators, just a tight tunnel. In sluggish dream-time, she snaked upward for a long time and came to a hole above a swimming pool. The opening was too small for her shoulders. Then she saw that snips fanned outward around the hole, allowing flaps to open to let a body through. She dropped into the pool, swam to the edge, climbed out, and came upon college friends. When she said that Dan had disappeared, they told her not to worry; Dan was such a sweet man. Yes, he *was* sweet, but why did he always leave? She found herself in a small empty office at a private airfield. Dan came in the door wearing a flight jacket. He smiled and said, "And so this jacket . . ." She shouted, "You disappear without a word! Then you show up out of nowhere, talking about a jacket?" She grabbed his lapels—or what would be lapels on another coat—and shook them. He waited her out, smiling.

She woke up clutching her blanket. She snapped on the bedside light. The flying in-box would be funny if she weren't so mad at Dan. His disappearing act wasn't just traveling for work, but being impossible to find at home. Whenever she needed help, he was someplace else, in the barn or on the other side of the farm or *inside his head,* giving energy to objects or ideas when what she needed was his person, his total presence. The flaps above the pool signified birth—the actual birth due soon, plus other breakthroughs badly needed. There was promise in the image. The answer was right there. The flaps were designed to open. All it took was a little push.

But where was Dan?

He was in Washington state, where, any minute, a volcano might explode and bury her parents' house in boiling lava.

Which would explode first, Nell wondered, Mount St. Helens or Nell?

* * *

Before supper, Isak took a length of red thread and aimed it at the eye of a needle. He was in the bedroom that was once his Mum's. He didn't think Nell and Dan would mind, since he was doing his own mending. He could do this job himself, he didn't need to bother Elsa or anyone else. Did they make the needle eyes smaller nowadays? He adjusted his grasp of the needle. His fingers were big and the needle was small. Seated in the straight chair by the standing lamp, he had his red flannel shirt on his lap and Elsa's sewing kit at his feet. He missed the eye of the needle four times. The thread was too fuzzy to go through the needle. He took scissors from the kit and trimmed the end of the thread. He used to enjoy fixing things, but as time went on he found less pleasure in fixing. He had noticed other changes as well. He didn't drive these days (which was okay, as the pedals of the bus perplexed him), he slept more, and Elsa hid his cash. He still had his billfold, but he couldn't find any bills in it. As for money, all he had was a pot of pennies that he kept under this very bed.

They treat me like a kid, he sighed. But they need me. Otherwise, how would they know how to farm? *That Dan? He's a tenderfoot if I ever saw one!* Still and all, he thought, I'm getting old. He said in his daytime voice, "'Old age comes at a bad time.'" He had seen the saying on a church sign long ago. He enjoyed it now again, then tried once more to thread the needle.

He got the thread through the eye, extended the thread to double length, licked his thumb and forefinger, rolled the ends into a knot and yanked the knot tight. Threads were like problems, he figured. You have to go easy, get affairs in order before yanking tight, undo tangles when they're loose enough to handle. If you yank too soon, you get a knot you can't undo.

After taking a break to flex his hands, he stored the needle in a fold in the knee of his pants. He picked up the shirt. One sleeve had an *L*-shaped tear, the result of his having fallen (just a little) against the interior barn wall. A nail sticking out of the wall had ripped the sleeve. How could the *sharp* end of a nail be sticking out of a wall? How could he reinforce the tear? Lap the *L* over and sew it up? No. It wouldn't have enough strength. He tried folding the edges of the tear, twice, as for hems. That wouldn't work, either. The sleeve would pucker.

Old age comes at a bad time, yes, and the sleeve had ripped in a bad place. There wasn't enough cloth to go around. He pulled the needle from his pants, unthreaded it, and dropped the thread into the waste basket. He put away the needle, making sure it went in and out of the pin cushion so that it wouldn't disappear. He then balled up the shirt and put it too in the waste basket.

Moving slowly, he went down on his knees, drew out the money jar, and poured the pennies on the bedspread. He spread them out in a hexagon, pleased to have the right amount of pennies. At first they looked alike, but as he studied them they proved to be new or old, sparkling or dull, dark or light, mottled or smooth, and to have a variety of colors—copper, pewter, brown, gray, orangey, almost black.

Isak pulled the wooden chair over to the bed and sat down to get a good look. He moved his head from side to side to see how daylight changed the pennies. He covered one eye, then the other. He was enjoying this; the hexagon had his allegiance. Every penny was unique. By itself, a penny might go unnoticed, but placed alongside others it added contrast or relief or repetition. Together they were beautiful. Ordinary pennies!

He was a little surprised. All of the pennies were needed to make the pattern, even the ugly ones.

✵ ✵ ✵

"Hello, this is Addie, speaking from the farm. We have Isaac here to sing for you." Addie handed the megaphone to Isaac. He delivered a wet belch and stretched his mouth into geometrical shapes, then checked to see if the others thought he was funny. He sang, "This yo man *island*! This my man *island*! This man was made for you and me!" He sang the first line of "O Christmas Tree." He made duck sounds, "Raakk-raakk."

Jed grabbed the megaphone and sang, "My country, 'tis of thee . . ."

Addie said, "No fair grabbing," and grabbed back the megaphone. Trying to keep from laughing, she said, "David? You wanta tell about the chickens?" She giggled and bent near David, cupping her hand as if telling him a secret. "*You* know," she said, loudly enough for the others to hear, "when you said you hoped Jimmy's chickens would *lick your arms?*" She doubled over in giggles. "Or when Jonathan said he couldn't use the potty chair 'cause he was a *butterfly?*" She fell onto the couch, laughing and holding her stomach, forcing laughs when she ran out of natural ones.

Jed commandeered the megaphone. He put the bell end on his head like a hat, took it down, and held it to his mouth. "Here's the news," he said in a broadcaster's voice. "We have duck poop all over the yard. We have a duck poop landfill. Next we have Abraham, who makes a neat pig sound. Here. *Do* it." He held the megaphone toward Abraham, who shook his head.

Isaac said, "You porgot the Fledge Allegiance." Covering his heart with his hand, he recited the pledge. He took the megaphone and sang, "Ah-*mer-i-ca!* Ah-*mer-i-ca!*"

Addie sat up. "Remember when Rachel fell out of bed and she was standing there holding her pillow? And Mom asked her if she wanted to sleep on the floor? And Rachel said yes, she would, but she was trying to *find* it?" Addie howled and lopped over again on the couch. Rachel, sitting on the floor by Addie's feet, seemed pleased; being teased meant being included.

At her end of the couch, Nell supported her back and baby-belly with pillows. She was glad for this break in the fighting. The noise had been deafening for days.

"*I* know," Jed said. "Let's play robot. Addie and Rachel, you be robots. The boys are the bosses . . . Walk! . . . Raise your arm! . . . Get that book!"

Addie made a rotten egg face at Jed, gathered her rag dolls and moved toward Nell. She put her head on Nell's shoulder. "Mom? Will I still have birthdays even after I'm *seven*?"

Nell said, "Sure, even after you're a hundred and seven."

The telephone rang, and Nell unpacked herself from the pillows and went to answer it. Harald shouted in her ear, "So how you guys doin'?"

"Fine. We're . . . ."

"Say! I'm in Minneapolis and I'm wondering about the mountain. The one Isak and them live on? Does he know it might explode? What about their house?"

Recently, as she heard about earthquakes and steam on Mount St. Helens, Nell had asked herself these identical questions. She said, "Dan called this morning—he's in Seattle for six weeks. He's going to check on the Cougar house. We'll call you when we know more."

She put her father on the line to say hello. He seldom used a phone, and he treated the hand-piece like a time bomb, had trouble placing it to his ear. He experimented with a few words and gave the receiver back to Nell. His face said he'd rather deal with people face to face, not at the end of a phone line.

After the call, Nell asked him, "What do you think about the Cougar place?"

He said only, "We'll see." Mount St. Helens was threatening to ruin his house, but he didn't want to talk about it.

She went to the bedroom and lay flat on the bed, mentally listing problems. Harald had brought up another one—the Cougar house—and there were already too many. The roof was leaking, again. She and Dan were in a financial pinch, again. The kids were in a spin and she was big with child. Everyone in the house needed something from her—caution, help, encouragement. The twins were in perpetual motion, either outdoors pushing their Tonka trucks and plowing dirt with their heads, or indoors running through the house screaming. Before noon that day, they had broken a bowl of cereal (the one time she hadn't used plastic bowls), dipped a roll of stamps in apple juice, flooded the bathroom with bath water, and spilled orange juice three times. She'd had to take David to the hospital two days ago when he passed out at the table with his head in his plate. Dan called the hospital after she left, saying he had found the green mouthwash bottle empty; it had been a quarter-full. Nell was angered to learn from the medics that that brand of mouthwash was 19% alcohol. How could it still be on the market? David could have died! The medics checked him and said he would doze it off without ill effect. David now seemed fine. Isaac ("the *boy* Isaac," she thought, in deference to her father) was being altogether too friendly. As soon as she looked away, he punched someone. She had to watch everyone all the time. Even Abraham, the most conscientious of the kids, made plaster of Paris in the bathroom sink one day. Only by chance did Nell find it before it set. And Jed was in a mood for practical jokes. Two nights earlier, as Abraham poured water for supper, Jed walked behind him adding ice cubes to the glasses. He tee-heed when Addie found a fly in her ice cube, and Sigrid found one in hers, and

204

Isak found one in his. He had frozen a fly in every cube. Among the boys, Jacob was the only one who required no watching. He was a water-color painter who took his paints up to the attic or outside under a tree and got lost in his art. Rachel, Addie, and Laura needed supplies—buttons, tape, glitter, glue, ribbon, sparkles, paper, cardboard—and Nell had to stop what she was doing and tell the girls where to find the items, or find them herself, or say she couldn't go to town right then to buy them (in fact, couldn't afford to buy them), or suggest they find alternatives. The baby, Rebecca, was at an exploratory stage, crawling into cupboards and pulling out pans and banging them for the fun of it. Nell's mother seemed to blame Nell for the bedlam.

When Dan was at home, he was her sounding board. They debriefed in bed at the end of a day, talking about what had happened since breakfast, laughing if they could, coming up with plans of action. He was in Southeast Asia. She had to talk to *someone*. Missing Dan, she called a meeting of the grownups.

They gathered on Saturday morning when the kids were having waffles at Victoria's. Her mother sat down reluctantly, not a fan of face-to-face gatherings. She ironed the tablecloth in front of her with her hands. Nell wasn't sure if what she saw in Sigrid's eyes was hilarity or not. (Hilarity? As tired as they all were?) Her father wasn't giving away his thoughts or looking anywhere except at his hands.

Nell took a start-up breath. "I need ideas! We've got too much to do! We have too many problems, and the kids are out of hand." She looked from person to person.

Sigrid, the only person who responded, moved her mouth but hesitated before speaking, as if waiting for her elders to first say their piece. Nell said to her, "What are you thinking?"

"I think we're doing *fine*," Sigrid said. "The kids are fine. They're a big job, but they're healthy. We'll get through."

Nell's father sputtered, "That boy Isaac! He's a pesky one."

He was right, Nell thought. Isaac bucked every rule, tested everyone's patience. But instead of commiserating with her father, Nell gave an explanation.

"He got sick when he was little, was in the hospital with terrible pain. He almost died. After that, he changed. He didn't trust anyone. That's what Abraham says."

Sigrid said, "That's too bad, but it's like he *wants* us to feel bad. We have a nice day? He hits the baby. We laugh? He makes someone cry. I'm glad I take care of the little kids. They're easy, compared to him."

"But *you're* worn out, too," Nell said.

"I'll be okay."

Elsa made an indistinct sound. "We could take days off," she said. "Work four days and get a day off. Like at the restaurant."

A pleasant sense came over Nell, a freedom, like a breeze. She said, "Let's do it!" She smiled the way a carnival barker smiles, selling something right from the start. Realizing this, she smiled a lesser smile, this one, unfortunately, a facial whimper. Still, she barged ahead. "I like it when you talk, Mom. I wish you'd talk more often."

Her mother retreated into silence. She did not enjoy personal talk. Nell regretted having said anything about talking.

Sigrid said to Nell, "People don't always have to talk. They show how they feel by what they *do*."

Nell tensed. Was Sigrid siding with her mother, against her? Uncomfortably, she said, "Do I depend too much on words? Do I ask too much when it comes to talking?" This was a new idea to Nell. True, she counted on words for balance. Words helped her to sort out issues. She regularly pushed others to talk things through. And it worked, at least with Dan . . . Or did he feel hounded by her demand for words?

"It's okay to let some things go," Sigrid said. "No one's perfect. Notice what a person does, not just what a person says."

Isak said, "A picture is worth a thousand words."

The focus had turned, and it pointed at Nell. *She* was part of the problem. She was too demanding. Her self-righteousness was a burden. And her exclusive grab on the kids wasn't fair. She did the same thing to Sigrid and her parents that she did to Dan. She wanted help, but when the helpers got too close to the kids she pushed them away.

No one had actually said these things, but she knew they were true. She held back tears. "What do you want me to do?"

Sigrid said, "Go easy on us. You're great with the kids. Do the same for us."

"For instance?" Having trapped the others into using words, Nell felt obliged to ask the question. But she dreaded the answer. She didn't want to hear any for-instance words. Words could end up being her downfall!

Sigrid said, "Stand up for *us*, like you do for the kids. If your dad's mad at Isaac, let him *say* it. Take it in. Don't lecture him about Isaac's childhood."

There was a thrumming in Nell's ears, the ratchety noise of correction. Her father studied something in midair.

Nell said, "I'm sorry, Daddy. He makes me mad, too."

"He's that-kind *sneaky* boy."

"I know."

Isak spoke to his hands, which rested on the table in a two-hand pile. "'Raise up a child in the way he should go, and when he is old he will not depart from it.'"

Nell said, "But I try! We all do! It's not working!"

Her father smiled a small smile. "I guess he's not old *enough*," he said.

The women chuckled and shifted position. His levity had taken the pressure off.

Sigrid said, "We agree then. Isaac makes us mad. He needs us to be firm."

Nell said, "He scares me! He needs more help than we can give him."

"Maybe, but we'll solve that later," Sigrid said. "For now, let's be a wall he can butt against. He needs to butt *something*. We'll keep him safe and tight, like in a circle. We'll catch him doing good and make a hullaballoo and give him some freedom. Then, when he goes out of bounds again, we bring him back in close."

Nell took in a large amount of air and let it out. She felt accompanied, not solitary. She had three strong adults to help figure things out. Why had it taken her so long to simply sit down with them and be honest?

Her mother took over leadership of the meeting. She told Nell, "You make a chart for days off. I'll go make some coffee."

✻ ✻ ✻

Sigrid had made birch bark boats with the twins and it was time to launch them. As she walked with the boys to the windmill tank, her thoughts felt muffled, as if they had to pass through lambs' wool to reach the surface. Her eyes wanted to close and stay closed for a long time. The boys put their boats in the tank and slapped the water to make them go. It took some doing, but Sigrid got herself down on the ground and sat with her back against the tank. She extended her legs, crossing them at the ankles. The spring thaw was over. The sun was alluring and warm. Spots twirled behind her eyes, an image-play in red and orange.

When she opened her eyes, the twins were gone. She shambled up awkwardly and hurried toward the house. After a few steps, she stopped, horrified. In a panic, she returned to the tank. The rim was three feet high—low enough for three-year-olds to climb over. She made a stumbling circuit of the tank, peering into the black water. They hadn't drowned.

She got to the house and said, "Has anyone seen David and Jonathan?"

Nell paled. "The tank."

Sigrid said, "No. I looked."

Nell said, "Everyone look! The barn, the silo." On an impulse, she picked up the phone, dialed O, and told Ava Nelson, the operator, "We've lost the twins. At the Halonen place. Have you heard anything?"

Ava said, "Well, you wouldn't believe it, but I just talked to Betty Paulsen, and her Craig saw them playing at the bottom of your hill. He would've put them in the car and brought them home to you, but he didn't want to scare them, so he drove to his place and told Betty, and she didn't know your number so she rang me. I was just getting ready to call you. Isn't that a coincidence? They didn't have any clothes on."

208

Nell thanked her and hung up. Jed ran down the hill and returned with two muddy, naked little boys. Sigrid wept in guilty relief.

"They were playing in the ditch," Jed said.

Nell filled a bucket with warm water and placed it on towels on the kitchen floor. "Let's get you cleaned up. Did you leave your clothes in the ditch?"

David glanced at Jonathan, then said, "No!"

Jonathan shook his head, *no*.

Nell said, "Maybe you took them off to play and left them in the ditch?"

This time it was Jonathan who said, "No!"

David shook his head, *no*.

Nell smiled. "*I* think you left them in the ditch."

"No!" they said.

"It's okay," she said. "*Jed* can find them. *He'll* know where to look."

David said brightly, as if the idea had just occurred to him, "Dey're inna ditch!"

Jonathan too lit up. He nodded and said, "Dey're inna ditch!"

The others laughed. Sigrid didn't. She sat where she was and tore at a cuticle. If she could fix the cuticle, she might be able to transfer the skill to other raggy parts, like her patience and strength. She didn't have much left of either one.

* * *

May 13, 1980. "A Glimpse From Here" column submission. Nell Sanderson.

Mind-Jangled Jingle

Let a few take up residence,
or even one, and you'll see evidence
that your carefree days have up and flown.
Starting sweetly—charming, wooing—

they control you with their cooing.
You can guess their thoughts but can't recall your own.

They proceed on the assumption
that you're there for their consumption,
every second, every minute, year by year.
Example? Till they're very, very grown,
they hate to see you use the phone,
so they keep talking to your one free ear.

If you try to take reprieve
with tea or book, you will receive
an invitation to attend a fresh emergency.
You try to nap. You haven't rested.
Help! Your presence is requested!
They call you back with manufactured urgency.

Or you step into the shower,
and plan to hide in there an hour.
But now they're yelling questions through the curtain.
If your person's on the premises,
you *will* be hounded by your nemeses.
They'll track you down, of that you can be certain.

So you plan a step ahead.
Before dawn, sneak out of bed!
They're sound asleep, so none of them can find you!
But as you tiptoe down the hall,
you know you're not alone at all.
They tiptoe down the hallway right behind you.

Eleven

Like Summer Rain

In an elongated sunset, Nell had proclaimed a reading night, and the plan seemed to be working. Everyone was quiet, boys upstairs in sleeping bags, girls on the fold-out couch in the front room. They all had new library books, and if they weren't actually reading they were thumbing through pictures. She was climbing into bed, eager to read her own book, when she heard the boys shouting overhead.

Jed ran down the steps and to the bedroom door. "There's a *bat* flying around!"

Nell wasn't eager to solve this problem, but she put on her housecoat (which didn't quite reach around her pregnant body), scooted into her slippers, and followed Jed to the attic. The boys were bunched at the top of the steps, having retreated to the stairwell to evade the bat but to also watch it. A reading lamp gave light to one area of the attic, in the corner by the sleeping bags. The rest of the attic was lost in dusk. By keeping her eyes on one spot, she caught sight of the bat as it flew by. It was *fast*. It swooped and dived and seemed confused. The loft window, the door-swinging kind, was open a half-inch. Apparently, that was where the bat had come in. There was no chance it could find its way out the same way.

Every time the bat flew by, skimming low to the floor and thus low to the stairwell, the boys yelled and shrank back down the stairs. "They land on your head!" Jed said. "They get tangled in your hair!"

This was a fine mess. The two naturalists, Jed and Abraham, were shrinking on the steps along with everyone else, and Jed was telling old wives' tales. Bats didn't really tangle your hair, did they?

211

The bat came to rest on the curtain rod. Like a chicken on a roost, Nell thought. No, bats didn't *sit*. They hung upside down. She couldn't see the bat very well. It remained in place, a dark lump near the top of the curtain. Normally, Dan would handle a predicament like this. She had no idea what to do.

Isaac said, "Ebryone out! You got a towel?"

Jed ran downstairs and brought back a bath towel.

Isaac went to the toy chest and shook the Tinker Toys from their box. The box was a cardboard cylinder, eight inches in diameter and fourteen inches tall. He closed the toy chest. With his foot he nudged it to the window. He opened the window wide. Improbably, through all of Isaac's maneuverings, the bat stayed where it was.

Clutching the towel and the Tinker Toy box, Isaac climbed onto the toy chest. Lightning-fast, he threw the towel over the bat, stuffed the towel and the bat inside the Tinker Toy box, threw the box outdoors, and shut and locked the window.

The others cheered and ran to Isaac and clapped him on the back. He had done what no one else could do, what no one else had even thought of doing. Isaac had saved the day!

Nell held this victory as a snapshot of the future. Isaac, the Conqueror.

✻ ✻ ✻

In another twilight, in another time zone, Dan descended the long steps of Hillclimb just to sniff salt air. He was going out of his way, to a bus stop farther down, in order to see the waterfront. The sun was refusing to sink, clinging to the horizon and bronzing Elliot Bay. A riffle of wind pecked the surface into coin-sized dots: tangerine, baby blue, pink. Any added motion—a leaping fish or a passing boat—tipped the dots to and fro—pastel nickels and dimes flashing at Dan. Passing by restaurants, he smelled other people's dinners. He missed his family. This six-week job was six weeks too long.

He unlocked the door to his half-basement sublet and threw his keys on the kitchen counter. The landlord had gone to extremes to make the basement dry, encasing it in steel and concrete. The result was cold and efficient. Dan snapped on the TV and went to the refrigerator. Five Pepsis. Brown mustard. Cheddar slices in deli paper. An apple that didn't look so good. He reached for the cheese and a can of Pepsi, got a knife from a drawer and a box of crackers from the cupboard and spread his supper on the coffee table.

He settled on the couch and popped the Pepsi cap. Lions crept up on gazelles and raced them to the ground. Snarl! Snatch! He got up and turned the channel. He didn't want to see *that* while he was eating. Now a man was grilling steaks and seafood. Dan got up and turned the channel. He didn't want to see any steaks right now. Or any lobster, shrimp, or salmon, either. He bit into a cracker while a TV family ate spaghetti and meatballs. He wanted spaghetti and meatballs. Or mashed potatoes and gravy. He was considering walking to the café on the next block when the TV broke news of Mount St. Helens.

Strong earthquakes. Loud booms. Threat of avalanche. Scientists moving from the crater's edge to a safer distance.

The volcano registered earthquakes off and on during March, Dan had heard, and this month, April, it was shaking almost daily. Today KING TV was reporting the presence of harmonic tremors, indication that lava was stirring. Eruptions of steam and ash had increased. The north flank was identified as the site of most of the earthquakes. The ash—a powdered pumice, sulfuric, abrasive, slightly acidic—was dangerous to breathe. Residents were being advised to hose it off their vehicles.

Two names were familiar to Dan from earlier reports. United States Geological Service geologist Dave Johnston, who worked near the crater, was predicting that the only way the north flank could stabilize itself would be to come down, and lodge owner Harry Truman, who had lived on the north face of Mount St. Helens for fifty years, was renewing his pledge not to leave home even if the volcano exploded.

Roadblocks had been set up around the Red Zone, the reporter said. Residents were required to show passes at the barricade. Evacuation routes were being published. People living near the mountain were urged to leave the area.

Dan took note of the map on TV. Cougar was inside the Red Zone.

He called the farm and asked Elsa about the Cougar house. She said she had phoned their neighbor, Joe Nichols, the day before. Joe had told her that some residents were evacuating but most were staying. He was staying. He felt sure that his house, and theirs, would still be standing when the shaking was done.

Dan called Joe Nichols, explained who he was and asked Joe how he was doing.

Joe said, "Fine, except for the *ash*. My horses were eating it off the fence posts! I got 'em out last week. I took 'em to my brother's place, down by Tillamook."

"What about the roadblock?"

"It's a pain in the caboose! Can't hardly get through, myself! They got white permits and yellow permits, all kinda permits. The guards say no to everyone! This one logger was on his way to work and he got into it with a guard. Almost came to blows! They wouldn't let the guy through to do his *job*. But they can't really *do* anything. They've got all these rules, but they can't put you in jail."

"Could I get past the barricade?"

"They'd give you a hard time. They wore guns for a while, like *commandos*! People complained, so they started wearing baseball caps and jumpsuits. I guess they've still got guns, but they don't advertise it. But, heck, what're they gonna *do*? Say some guys break through the roadblock. What're they gonna do? *Shoot* 'em?"

On a sunny Saturday morning, Dan left Seattle in a rented car, drove under Tacoma's circling planes, swept downhill past Olympia's gold dome, and settled in for the long straight haul through the fruit-and-tulip interior of western Washington. Once in a while, he checked the southeastern sky. No sign of eruption.

After three hours, he exited at Woodland and turned east, following, in general terms, the curves of the Lewis River, named for Meriwether Lewis—crystalline waters that spread to the sun, overhung with alders and flicks of fog. The drive was a travelogue, even with ash on every surface. Gulliver hills and storybook lanes. Cattle on high rolling pastures. Dan wondered how the cattle found clean grass to eat. After ten minutes in rolling farmland, he came to the foothills of Mount St. Helens. The peak itself was not visible. The road took repeated S turns, rose and dropped in elevation, did sky-drives over rivers and creeks, occasionally cut through rock and left a sculpted wall high to Dan's left. In places the forest moved close to the road, reducing the sky to a bolt of blue. Around a bend, without warning, Mount St. Helens appeared—an imposing white mound filling half the sky, streaked in purple where snow had melted, topped with a dollop of steam. To Dan—now, and earlier when he and Nell and the kids visited Isak and Elsa—the mountain looked like an ice cream sundae with blackberry syrup, including the plop of whipped cream on top. At the next turn, it vanished.

He got through the roadblock with ease and drove on until he came to Cougar, a town of five hundred, situated on a cliff above Yale Lake, surrounded by green giant hills. Most of town's houses seemed to be in the forest, as not many could be seen from the main road. The business section had a post office, two campgrounds, a gas station, a motel, a coin laundry, a tavern, and two cafés. Dan drove a mile past town, turned left on a gravel road, and stopped at an unpainted wood house. Ash capped the roofs of the house and the garage.

Joe Nichols seemed eager to talk. Cooped up too long, Dan guessed. "We're supposed to leave," Joe said, "but, Hector, I'm staying! I'll take my chances." He brought Dan into his living room—a gathering place for elk and deer heads. Dan didn't think he could relax in this room with so many eyes on him. The interior wall was made of rough-sawn boards; the fireplace, of river rock; the mantel, of a long chunk of wood. Joe had built the house ten years back, he said, six years before his wife died. His wife did the sewing, he told Dan, the red cushions on the slat couch and the cross-stitched pictures on the wall, a kitten in a watering can and a puppy chewing a sock. The house was orderly and clean. Dan thought Joe's wife would be proud of him.

The coffee had been keeping warm at the back of the stove. When Dan took a taste, the hairs in his nose saluted. The men sat on benches at the kitchen table to drink their coffee. Joe had put out some Oreo cookies. "The pummy's the worst part," he said. "It gets so bad you can't see a thing. So thick, it's like night in the daytime. It stops the windshield wipers and grinds into the glass. You can't even see the road. You have to drive with your door open just to see the ditch, to know where you *are!*"

This sounded drastic. Dan thought Joe was brave to stay on. If Dan were Joe, he would hightail it for Tillamook and stay with his horses and his brother.

Dan walked up the hill to Isak's place, a two-story cabin with a garage downhill in a small dip. A layer of ash covered the roofs of both buildings. The windows were blank, curtains drawn. The house looked shut down, crouched, bracing for a blow. He found the key and let himself in. After snapping on the kitchen light, he looked around. Kettles, key rack, *Popular Mechanics.* The place looked dead.

He found the sewing bag that Elsa had requested, turned off the light, went outside to the porch, locked the door, re-hid the key, got into the rented car, and drove back to Seattle. He hadn't stayed long. When he was at the house before, Isak and Elsa were there. It was eery, seeing just their belongings.

* * *

Isak had found a wordsmith (a term he admired because it turned a hobby into a work skill) among the grandchildren, surprisingly not in his blood line—Abraham. The boy managed to be in the workshop when Isak was putzing in there, or in the barn when Isak was milking. He asked Isak about garden bugs, engine parts, flax seeds, groupings of stars, American slang words. He asked his questions with intelligence and courtesy and seemed determined to find answers.

216

One day, as Isak tinkered with the push mower (Abraham had helped him to get it up onto the workbench), Abraham asked, "What does 'indicted' mean?"

Isak sensed a bigger topic behind the question. "Accused of a crime. Why?"

At first Abraham didn't want to say. "Little-John," he said finally. "He was indicted for robbery. He got into a house through a window."

This was news to Isak. That Rinta boy? You never know! Only three children in that family, and yet they have their grief.

Isak waited for several heartbeats. Then he said, "'The world is too much with us, late and soon; getting and spending, we lay waste our powers.'" This wasn't the whole piece, but it said what he hoped to say.

Without facial expression, Abraham digested the words.

That's what Isak liked about the boy. He didn't raise his eyebrows at Isak's sayings, the way some people did when they signaled each other, "There he goes again." Isak believed that words had special powers, that at times they lifted above their normal meanings and became more than they'd started out to be. Words could tumble in space between speaker and receiver and land in altered form, fit for the moment. Abraham understood that.

"Maybe my brother will be indicted," Abraham said. "Isaac. *He* steals."

Oh, thought Isak, the boy Isaac. "You worry about him," he said.

Abraham said nothing.

Isak waited for the right words. "You can't help him more than you already help him," he said. "He has to learn for himself."

After a silence, Abraham asked, "Did *you* ever get in trouble?"

Isak didn't like to talk about that. But Abraham was new. He didn't know. "Not with the law," Isak said. "But, sure, I got in trouble. Everyone gets in trouble, or *has* trouble. We . . . had some trouble when I young." He coughed. "In the woodshed."

Isak hadn't known this would come out. What had he started?

Abraham was silent, watchful. In a voice unused to harsh words, Isak said, "Father got drunk and killed the baby. He didn't mean to."

Such bald words! *Can I ever forgive Father? Or Mum, the way she clammed up?* He tried to see through the window above the workbench, but it was layered with wood dust. He wiped it with his hand and brushed his hand on his pants.

Abraham said, "My mother died. And my father."

Isak said, "Yes." He did a neck stretch, lolling his head in every direction. He left his head bowed, deeply forward. "Yes." He chanced a look at Abraham. The boy's eyes were shaded from so much frowning.

For the space of a minute, Isak stayed bent and sorrowful.

Then he released them both. Raising his head, he said, "How about we go to the house and get some toast?"

The next day Abraham showed Isak what he had written for class. Asked to describe an important person, Abraham had described Isak. Isak was astounded to read about a "looming, stoic giant," who was himself.

"This is about my Grandpa, a looming, stoic giant, always building something, taking something apart, or grinding something into obscurity through clouds of smoke and flying sparks, an ancient man built like an eighteen-wheel Mack truck, covered in gasoline and wheel grease and smelling like a mix of both. He is an amazing presence. He knows more than anyone else but he is humble in his wiseness. He came from someplace else and knows more than all of us, and he knows he is headed back there."

Isak was touched—but he wasn't a giant, especially now that he was old. He was smaller than he used to be. Maybe Abraham meant a giant as to his mind? His mind was smaller these days, too.

He *did* like to grind things and make sparks fly, but mostly long ago. Strange that the boy knew.

* * *

Elsa dreamed she was in a theater with the grandchildren, waiting for a movie to start. She didn't often go to movies and she didn't usually dream. Nell was the one who dreamed. If she paid attention to dreams the way Nell did, she would say that this dream's meaning was clear as day. Organ music played, the curtains drew back, and a title came on the screen: "My Best Times." Who should *roller-skate* to the front of the theater, in person? Isak! He made a circle, one of those foot-splayed rotations, then stopped and smiled like a sneaky boy. The wardrobe people had dressed him in strap overalls (which he never wore in real life) and a farmer's straw hat (again, something he never wore). He seemed happy to wear whatever they wanted him to wear. When credits appeared on the screen, he glanced up at them, then at Elsa, wanting her to see that *his* name was up there. An announcer gave the movie's title and said, "Starring . . . Isak Halonen!" The movie started, and there he was on the screen, grinning, dressed in the same get-up, roller-skating under trees. As if a person *could* roller-skate under trees!

That Isak!

The dream meant that Isak was doing fine, even if he had to do what other people wanted him to do. He was confused some days, but overall better. North Dakota was good for him. The cows, the air, the barn. Mostly the children. They piled on top of him and kept him safe, like in a blanket, and let him go when he got warm.

* * *

Nell's head felt like Mount St. Helens—ready to blow. On Berit's stress scale, she was approaching ten. She sat with her elbows on the table, holding her head to keep it from soaring around the room. The roof was leaking again. Most of the kids had colds. Jacob was being clingy. He wanted Nell to sit with him all the time and sing "Sweetheart in the Bushes" ("Rock-a-bye Baby in the Treetop"). David and Jonathan wanted her to sit with *them*, instead. Even while coming down with colds, the twins insisted on wearing six T-shirts and seven pairs of sock each, at the same time. Jonathan had a new obsession. He kept saying, "Unca Haral' come in a *new red truck!*" He clung to the story even when everyone told him Harald wasn't coming and, besides, he didn't have a red truck. Addie and Rachel normally doted on the twins, made them peanut butter sandwiches, helped them tie their shoes, but lately they had ignored them and turned screechy themselves. Laura had reverted to bedwetting. Isaac ate everything in sight. He didn't gain weight, but his appetite was never satisfied. He went around the table after meals and ate any food left on plates. After breakfast one day, he consumed (Nell wrote down the list, hardly believing it) two pieces of bread, a hard-boiled egg, a banana, two oatmeal raisin cookies, a carrot, an apple, and two glasses of orange juice. He then sat on Nell's desk, sneezed, and said, "What can I *eat*? I need something to *eat!*" She needed to ask a doctor about that boy! It wasn't just the kids who needed her. Earlier that morning, her father had tripped on a toy and timbered forward like a falling tree, crashing to the floor. He wasn't hurt, but the fall had scared Nell. She had to watch everyone at the same time!

Her father was drinking coffee in his usual spot. He cleared his throat and said, "Accident no come bell neck." He wasn't blenching the way he usually did when he talked to her. He sat coolly at the table, alternating his gaze between the wall and Nell. His eyes had lights in them, pinpoint reflections of the kitchen bulbs.

"I've never heard that one," she said.

"Trouble gives no warning. No bell around the neck." Light came to the caves of his face as he said, "'Be of good cheer. This too will pass.'" He nodded, agreeing with himself. "'They had nothing more than the birds of the air, or the flowers of the field—yet they could not sleep for joy.'"

Nell took her hands off her head and put them on the table, and she looked with interest at her father. How did he come up with this stuff? At times like this, he seemed younger than she was, naïve, overly optimistic—or else timeless and eternally wise.

Later that day, he again gave his counsel. The boy Isaac, playing with the other kids in the barn, went out of control. He exploded over *nothing*, Jed later told Nell, raged and cursed and swung buckets at the smaller children, threw a wrench at Jed and threatened to burn down the barn. Jed and Abraham got the other children out of the barn and into the house. Isaac stayed in the barn and screamed.

Nell's father advised Nell, "Call the police."

She did.

Then she went to the barn to try to talk to Isaac. He yelled, "Go away! I can kill you!" She stepped back. He picked up a pitchfork and swung it at her.

Trembling, she retreated to the house.

The two policemen who had handled the cross-burning came to the farm. After hearing the story, they walked toward the barn, calling Isaac's name.

After a few minutes, Isaac appeared at the barn door. He gazed at family members grouped on the porch, smiled at the cops, and came outside, acting as if nothing had happened.

The policemen asked Nell if she wished to press charges. If she did, they said, they would take him to juvenile hall. If not, there was nothing they could do.

She did not press charges.

She called Dan in Seattle. He offered to fly home early. Nell said no. She felt sure that Isaac would be calm until Dan came home at the regular time. She and Dan had seen the pattern before. Isaac would be genial for a while, then tease-lie-steal, then explode, then become genial, then slowly build up again to tease-lie-steal. She told Dan he should finish his job so he wouldn't have to go back later and finish it.

Isaac went upstairs. Nell kept the other children downstairs. She didn't know what he was doing in the attic, but she wasn't going to check.

That night, the other boys slept at the Rintas' house. Isaac came downstairs to eat and to use the bathroom, but he otherwise stayed upstairs. He played at remorse, a variant type of manipulation.

He was a master at manipulation.

* * *

The lock was sticking again. Grace Ann slid in the key, but it wouldn't move. She removed the key, put it near her mouth and breathed on it, back and front. She put it in the lock again. This time the door opened. Why one type of heat (Arizona sun) would jam a lock and another type (her breath) would loosen it, she had no idea.

She stepped into her apartment and nearly fell backward. The silence hit her like a body blow. What *was* this? After Herb died, she had made a new life, found new friends, taken up swimming and volunteer work. She had everything she needed.

Why, then, was she so miserable? Ever since Elsa and her group drove off, Grace Ann had been fidgety, without focus.

She dropped her keys on the half-circle table by the door. The table collected keys, mail, her errand book. All at once her prissy ways offended her. Everything in its place. Nothing to ruffle her or trip her up. Nothing to suggest reliance on anyone but herself.

She ached for something she didn't currently have—a sense of belonging. She shared a level of camaraderie with her Suomi Circle friends, but there were limits to even that. Increasingly, any feeling of belonging existed on the surface only. The other circle members had known each other far longer than she had. They shared memories that she had no part in. Lately, during circle meetings, she had felt definitely *outside* the circle. She tried to fit in, but she didn't.

Inside her apartment, the problem was worse. The solitude was killing her.

She went to the kitchen and started tea, automatically connecting "tea" with "Elsa." Elsa normally liked coffee, but when she was having a bad day she drank tea. Lately, it seemed that *all* of Grace Ann's days were bad.

She missed . . . what? She missed having women beside her, shoulder to shoulder, cooking, talking, making jokes, deciding what to do next. When had she experienced that? Certainly not during her marriage. She hadn't missed it then. Life with Herb was full and companionable. While he was alive, she hadn't needed anyone else.

As she fixed her tea, she realized what she missed. The kitchens of her youth. Spaces crowded with women—her aunts, her mother, her grandmother, Elsa.

Elsa.

That was *it.* She missed Elsa.

* * *

A soft noise brought Nell awake. She snapped on the bedside lamp. Isaac stood above her holding a sledge hammer in the air, ready to strike. His expression was unlike any she had ever seen. Pure evil.

He said, "I could kill you any time."

Visualizing the quickest escape (climb over the bed to reach the door), Nell murmured anything she could think of. "Isaac, it's okay, let me put on my robe, we can talk, let me get my robe." She didn't feel as brave as she pretended to be.

After one faked swing, Isaac lowered the hammer and let it hang in his hand. He looked absent behind the eyes.

Slowly, he seemed to come to himself. She asked him to go to the kitchen with her. The talk she had with him was a repeat of others she had had with him. She and Dan had talked with Isaac countless times. Talking didn't work. Praise didn't work. Point systems didn't work. Groundings didn't work. Nothing normal worked with Isaac. Even his normal pattern of geniality and anger was broken. Only yesterday he had terrorized the children in the barn. She had thought he would stay placid after that.

Nell put the girls in her bed and had Isaac sleep on the fold-out couch in the front room. She did not go back to bed.

She called Dan in Seattle in the middle of the night. They agreed. For everyone's safety, Isaac had to be removed from the house. He needed professional help.

Early the next morning, Nell called Marcie in Minneapolis. "You and Adam are good with children. What would *you* do if you had an Isaac?"

"Same as you, protect the others," Marcie said, "which is protecting *him*, too. Listen. Adam knows about special programs. Let me talk to him."

Marcie called back. "There's a school for boys near Duluth. They do great work. I called them and they happen to have an opening! That's amazing!

The wait list is usually a mile long. They test for allergies, learning problems, attachment problems, brain injury, you name it. They use natural remedies before drugs, but they can do either or both, whatever works for that one boy. Call them. Then call me. I'll drive him there and have him screened. Send me his medical records and a notarized letter giving me permission. If Isaac's accepted, Adam and I want to pay for it. In the meantime, take the pressure off. Send him to *us!* We'll be fine. As you say, he'll be good as gold for a while."

By coincidence, Jimmy Rinta was driving to Minnesota the next day to see his brother. He would take Isaac to Marcie's house.

Isaac left home with a pack over his shoulder, eagerly, like a boy off to camp.

* * *

Harald roared into the yard in a red Ford pickup and came to a sudden stop, bringing up a storm of dust. Isak thought: Jonathan knew Harald was coming. Driving a red truck! How did he know? Isak had been sitting on the porch, watching the birds fly by and having a day-vision of Elsa. When she said she had dreamed he was roller-skating under trees, he had fancied the idea and improved on it in dreams of his own, some at night, some in the daytime. By now he had the two of them up on skates, although she had known how to skate from the start. That first Sunday on the ice river? He was twirling and reaching for her, wanting her to spin with him. But, typical Elsa, she was holding back. She was too modest to show affection in public. He had just this minute come up with a new vision, a cartoony sight. No roller-skates, not yet. If they twirled for practice on the ground, without skates, he might be able to talk her into twirling on skates. Harald's interruption was not particularly welcome.

Harald shouted, "Brother Isak! You old scallywag!" He got out of the truck and limped toward the house. Isak had a feeling that Harald put on a show any time he felt like it and made his limp worse than it was. This was one of those times.

Isak didn't feel any need to get out of his chair. He said, "You lost?"

"I was in Minnesota. Came to see what you're up to!" Harald came up onto the porch and sat on the other metal armchair. The springs bounced and squeaked beneath him, more so because he continued to bounce on purpose. "You doin' okay?"

Not waiting for an answer, Harald scooted forward and stopped the action of the chair. He peeked around Isak's shoulder. "I got this idea. I don't want the others to hear."

"They're gone." Isak figured Harald could see perfectly well that they were gone. Otherwise, the minute he drove up, children would have poured out of the house or the barn. No one could miss his arrival, what with all the dust and noise.

"Okay then. You know about Mount St. Helens? That it's gonna blow?"

Isak quailed. Yes, he knew.

Harald asked, "What about your house?"

That very question had been seeping into Isak's mind. "Wish I knew."

Harald whooped, "That's just it! That's my idea! Let's go *see!*" He had Isak by the forearm and was whanging it on the armrest of Isak's chair.

"Let go my arm," Isak said.

Harald let it go and rocked back and forth in his chair. "The more I think of it, the more I say we go *now*, before the others get home. They'd just try and stop us."

Isak wrinkled his eyes at Harald. He didn't say the words, but he thought them. *Go? Now? Take what? Stay where?* He had too many questions, so he said nothing. He got up and went to the bus and came back with a paper bag filled with clothes.

Harald went to the pantry and loaded up on food. Isak wrote a note for Elsa. "Harald came by. We went to Cougar to check on the house. He has a red truck."

* * *

When Nell found the note, she talked with her mother and Sigrid. They considered calling the police, but what would they report? That two retired brothers were driving to the West Coast? They found proof that the men wouldn't starve. Missing from the pantry were the jam and peanut butter jars, several loaves of bread, and Mason jars of Elsa's canned peaches, pears, beef, and chicken.

Nell called Dan in Seattle. He said, "Do they have enough money?"

"They should be fine. Daddy took his stash. He hides twenties in the navy beans."

Dan said, "Then let them have their fun. It'll take them two, three days, depending on where they stop at night. I can meet them at the roadblock."

Nell hung up and told her mother and Sigrid what Dan had said, then wondered out loud, "How on earth did Jonathan know about Harald's red truck?"

＊　＊　＊

Isak woke up, saying, "Don't!" He didn't know why he had said it. He ran his hands over his eyes and looked around. Harald's left hand held the wheel while his right hand turned the radio knob. The landscape had changed. Isak could see mountains in the distance—purple, like in the song. The peaks had snow on them. Or was it ash? Had Mount St. Helens erupted?

"Anything new?"

For some reason, the question irritated Harald. He groused, "You sleep more 'n any six people I know! I was talking to you and I kept talking and talking—and then I see you've been sleeping the whole time!"

"*Well*," Isak said. He didn't appreciate Harald's tone. "If I could help drive, I would. But I can't, with my bum leg. Even if could, I couldn't figure out your car. How can you drive with those gadgets in the way?"

Harald yelled at him, "That's what makes it so I *can* drive it, the *gadgets*! For my fake leg! Holy Moly!"

"I forgot." Something teased at Isak, something from his memory box. When he got hold of it, he said, "'There is so much good in the worst of us, and so much bad in the best of us, that it hardly behooves any of us to talk about the rest of us.'"

Harald barked, "*What?*"

Isak felt justified to ride along without responding. He had raised the level of talk to an honorable track and he wanted his brother to acknowledge it.

Instead, Harald growled like a mad dog.

Isak sent his thinking far away, over to the mountains, to the most distant spot he could see. After counting one-two-three on his way to ten, he said, "How long until we get to Cougar?"

Harald rumpled his hair with the hand that wasn't driving. "Tomorrow noon." He didn't sound any nicer.

Isak thought, Well, *that's* a relief, anyway. I won't have to be in the car any longer with this owly guy. Is this guy *Harald?*

* * *

Nell was so big she had trouble getting off the bed. She had been counting contractions when she heard a scream. A thunderstorm was keeping the kids indoors, and the decibel level was high—but a scream? As she reached the doorway, Addie tumbled into her, laughing and puffing. The front room was a blur, kids in motion, Seth and Mark Rinta involved in the flurry, David and Jonathan jumping on the couch, flapping their arms and shouting, "I'm a *chicken*, I'm a *chicken!*"

Nell said, "What's going on?"

Addie gasped, "I'm the best bulldog. I chase 'em and I can't strangle 'em." She turned and rejoined the cause.

Jacob was hanging onto the arm of the rocking chair, catching his breath. Nell said, "This is a pretty loud game. I think I'm going deaf."

"I think *I'm* getting the giggles," he said.

Nell felt a strong pull down through the center of her body. She said to Jacob, "Go get Grandma!"

Nell's mother drove. The others stayed home. Nell did Lamaze breathing on the way to Wishek Hospital, *in* at the start of a contraction. Twenty minutes after they got there, Minda Marie Sanderson was born.

When Nell brought the baby home, the other children pushed forward to see Minda. Unbothered by being watched, and in fact giving her siblings something to watch, she screwed up her face, turned radish red, opened her mouth as far as it would go and bawled, gasping between syllables, "*Waa!-*(augh)-*aa!-*(augh)-*aa!*" Her cry was wavery and urgent, inspiring imitations by the other children. They couldn't come close to matching Minda's volume.

"Nice pipes," Nell told her. "With this crowd, you're going to need them."

Mount St. Helens hadn't exploded yet, but Nell had, and her explosion had produced Minda—funny, deafening, lovely Minda.

✻ ✻ ✻

Dan sat at a window with a cup of coffee, looking out for a red Ford pickup. He exulted, *I have a new daughter!* Minda was squally as babies went, Nell had told him, but she was healthy and had a symmetrical face. He was eager to get home.

First, though, he had to find Isak and Harald. The day before, he had finished his job in Seattle, packed his belongings, given back the sublet keys, rented a car, and driven south to Jack's Grill at the south edge of the Red Zone. In an orchestrated plan, he sent his rented car to Woodland with Bill Morse, a District 7 fireman, Joe Nichols drove his smaller truck to the roadblock for Dan to use, and Joe's neighbor, Shorty Magistrate, gave Joe a ride back to his house. Dan spent the night in the truck in Jack's parking lot.

Under normal conditions, Jack's Grill was the hikers' registry for the south side of Mount St. Helens. Now it was headquarters for the Red Zone. The road was barricaded in front of Jack's and manned by members of the National Guard. Cougar was seven miles farther inside the Red Zone. Cougar residents had to pass through this funnel on their way to Woodland, Amboy,

Battle Ground, Kelso, Longview, Vancouver, Portland, or virtually anywhere else. Returning, they had to stop, show their permits, and convince the guards they had reason to go through. When allowed to pass, they went home to pick up vital documents or goats or cats or dogs—or, against official advice, to stay there.

Jack's drew residents like a magnet, especially now that the mountain was threatening to blow. Neighbors stopped by to compare notes. When they spotted an outsider among them, namely Dan Sanderson, they gravitated to him and told him stories. A frizzled eighty-year-old logger slid into Dan's booth and leaned across the table with tales of the woods. Other residents joined in from time to time. Dan learned that the stretch of foothills between Woodland and Cougar was called Ariel, that local residents were can-do folks who chose to "live upriver" (on the north fork of the Lewis River) despite hardships. Some years, they said, they got stranded for weeks due to ten-foot snows or flooded roads or a washed-out bridge. Quite a few stories featured animals—the deer that liked to ride in the family car, the elk that kicked a dog to death, the cougar that crossed the school yard, the goats that got milked in a cart in downtown Portland by their Ariel owner between her business meetings. One couple saw a Sasquatch standing by their barn, staring at them, then roaring and raising a terrible stink (a very bad smell, they said) and walking into their woods. Recently, residents had taken to sitting on roofs or picnicking at Yale Lake to watch the mountain puff steam. Describing the scene at the lake, a woman said, "It looked like Seuratt's 'Sunday in the Afternoon.'" Her husband said they had their own Richter scale. "It's a plant at the house, and our dresser. If the plant moves, we figure it's a 2.5. We get a lot of those. One day, the dresser got to rattling—*bangedy-bangedy!*—against the wall. We figured *that* was over a 5."

About noon on the second day, Dan spotted Harald's pickup. He drove to meet Harald, hand-motioning to him to turn around and follow him. Over a small hill, out of sight of the National Guard, Dan pulled into the driveway at Yale School and parked beside the gym.

Getting out of the car, Harald and Isak seemed creaky but otherwise unharmed. Dan shook their hands and asked them if they'd had a good trip. They said they had. "Are you hungry?"

Harald said, "Naw, we had steak the whole way! It was *beef* country." He made his eyebrows jump as if he had made a joke. The joy slid off his face. "Say, what's the scoop? How's the house?"

"I haven't been there yet, this trip, but I talked to Joe Nichols. He says it's okay. It's hard to get through the roadblock. I saved my permit until you got here."

Dan took down the tailgate on Joe's pickup and pulled aside two khaki blankets to expose a leather saddle, a tool box, pieces of scrap wood, and half a dozen tires. He said, "You can ride back here under the blankets."

Isak said, "What in the Sam Hill!"

"I have to hide you," Dan said. "Cougar's in the Red Zone. They don't want us going in there."

Dan's plan fired Harald's imagination. He said to Isak, "You have to be *real quiet* now. No peeking!"

Isak ignored him. "We can sit in front. Three can fit there, easy."

Dan said, "I can't let them see you. They don't want outsiders in the Red Zone."

"Outsiders?" Isak was indignant. "I *live* here! . . . or used to."

Dan said, "I hate to ask it, but can you prove it?"

No, he couldn't. Isak didn't have a driver's license or a billfold or any form of identification.

"People have to argue with the guards," Dan said. "They have to prove they have a right to go through."

He helped Isak into the pickup's bed, Isak involuntarily mewing as he crept on hands and knees. Dan thought back to his childhood and to rides in the back of a pickup. The steel ribs were murder on a kid's knees. They would be that much worse on an old man's. Dan wished he had put cushions back there. He slid two tires together, and Isak got on top of them and lay on his side, one tire cupping his rear, the other, his right arm. Dan rolled a blanket and put it under Isak's head.

Harald tried using the saddle as a pillow for his head, or a lift for his legs, or a rest for his chin. He ended up hanging his armpit over the saddle and pressing his head to his shoulder. He lifted his head and said, "Hey, brother Isak! You all cozy?"

Isak said nothing.

Dan pulled a blanket over the humps of saddle, tires, Harald, and Isak. He stepped back to check the effect. The pickup looked about the same as before. "The guards won't see any difference. Besides, they know Joe's truck. They won't check the back."

He drove to the blockade and stopped the truck but kept the motor running. In the past fifteen minutes, a new National Guard officer had come on duty—a baby-faced boy who took his job very seriously. Dan rolled down his window. The new guard swaggered to the window and said, officiously, "No traffic to Cougar."

The new guard had a tic in one eye. It twitched and pulled his left eyelid downward. Dan wondered if the tic was permanent or if it happened just when this boy lied. For he was surely lying now. From Jack's window, Dan had seen people get through the blockade and drive toward Cougar. Still, he guessed that *this* guard would do his best to keep Dan from doing the same.

Dan handed him the permit. It was rumpled from riding in the rear pocket of his jeans, but it was yellow, the right color.

The guard emitted suspicion. "This is a *resident's* pass. Are you a resident?"

"No, but I'm helping one."

The guard perused the pass, front and back. His tic worsened.

Dan added, "He needs me to get things from the house."

Packing his words with accusation, the guard said, "Who is this 'he'?"

"Isak Halonen, my father-in-law. He has a house by Cougar."

The guard let it be known, by means of facial contortions, that he had caught himself a base criminal. "And where is this 'he'? Why isn't 'he' here?"

A sound came from underneath the blankets, a cross between a horse laugh and a snuffle. Harald was having a coughing fit and couldn't contain it. Dan revved the engine, veered around the barricade, slammed his foot on the gas pedal, and drove pell-mell toward Cougar.

The guard called, "STOP! STOP!"

Dan yelled back at him, adding his shouts to Harald's and Isak's, "What're you gonna do? *Shoot* us?" The laughter of two old men and a son-in-law rose to the ashy sky.

After their joy-ride to Cougar, the men made two transactions. First, Isak sold his house to Joe. Joe was buying cabins as summer rentals, reasoning that, after the mountain blew, tourist traffic would skyrocket. He wanted *in* on the boom. Second, Dan bought Joe's smaller truck. Later he could use it at the farm, and now he could fill it with items from the Cougar house. Elsa had described on the phone what she wanted, photos, cooking utensils. Isak had walked around the garage and pointed at tools.

Two loaded trucks left the Cougar house. Isak rode with Dan, and as they came out of the driveway Isak looked straight ahead—the habit of a lifetime, Dan assumed: no looking back. But that wasn't exactly true, Dan thought. At the farm, Isak did look back, to the brink of his manhood. To the day his father killed his baby sister.

The mountain erupted the next day, Sunday, May 18, 1980, at 8:32 a.m. Driving east, the men listened to the news on their radios. They listened all day on different stations.

The blast killed at least six people. Twenty-one went missing. More deaths were reported as the day went on. The explosion was heard hundreds of miles away in Canada, but not by local residents.

The swath of the blast was eight miles long and fifteen miles wide. It destroyed everything in its path.

The heat blistered paint on trucks parked miles from the site. Chunks of ice and rock dropped from the sky. Hot cinders triggered forest fires. The sky rained mud. The air in some places turned a purplish ultramarine, like a gas.

Mudflows rampaged the Toutle River, took out a dozen bridges and swept away homes, livestock, logging equipment. Farmers ferried stranded cattle out of the mud on metal roofing sheets. Spirit Lake, once a vacation paradise, was now a pit of mud and floating logs.

Ash accumulated to a depth of many feet. It stank like sulphur. Clouds of ash floated east, turning daytime dark. By evening, ash had reached Montana and Colorado. (Dan and Harald drove through ash in the air for most of a day.)

It was the north flank that had given way.

Among the dead were Dave Johnston, the geologist who had predicted that the north flank would give way, and Harry Truman, the lodge owner who had refused to leave his home on the north flank.

Communities south of Mount St. Helens went nearly unscathed.

Cougar and Ariel were on the south side.

Twelve

Maybe So

Ronnie Jakes cornered Dan at Grady's Hardware Store. It was a gentle cornering, but a cornering, still. Dan had met Ronnie once before, at the farm, after the kitchen sink developed a clog that even Isak couldn't extract. It intrigued Dan that someone like Ronnie, a bashful man with a football player's body, was willing to roll around on the floor in full sight of the homeowners, reaching into dark places for hard-to-reach pipes which, even when found, would not want to budge. At Grady's, Ronnie apparently had something to say to Dan. Being a North Dakota man, he mentioned the weather before he broached the reason for this get-together at Grady's.

"I heard you might be wanting work," he said. He paused, having spent his gusto. This topic was too blunt for his taste. Yet he plowed on. "You could maybe try plumbing," he said. He glanced at Dan and then at a lineup of kitchen sinks.

Plumbing? Dan didn't think so. Plumbers worked with tangible things, objects made of metal and hard plastic. Dan worked with ideas. He didn't have much experience with tangible things.

Ronnie said. "I'm retiring. My back can't take it any more." He said he'd made a good living as a plumber, and that if Dan felt like it he could follow him for a week and see what he thought of plumbing. When the week was over, if Dan was okay with it, Ronnie could take him on and teach him the trade.

Dan considered the invitation and accepted. Even if he didn't become a plumber, he could at least learn how to fix leaks. That would come in handy, no matter what.

* * *

Jed and Abraham were popping with news. Mr. Styveson had taken the class to a sheep farm, and the boys were ecstatic. Everyone was in the kitchen, either serving snacks or consuming them. Abraham said, "The babies are *black*! They have curly black coats! They're *nice*!"

Jed said, "They have white feet and white faces and black circles around their eyes, like raccoons!" He wanted to say more, but he let Abraham say it.

Abraham looked meaningfully at Isak and Elsa. "They're *Finn* sheep," he said.

Isak, seated at the table, raised his eyebrows. Elsa, standing at the stove, raised hers as well. It was clear to Dan that they had never heard of Finn sheep.

Jed clarified matters. "They come from Finland."

Abraham said, "They're different, not like other sheep. The mothers have lots of babies at one time."

"Yeah! They have *litters*," Jed said, "and they're *strong*. They get up right after they're born and start nursing!" He shut his mouth with his hand, removed it, and said to Abraham, "You talk."

"They're born white, or black, or both," said Abraham, "but they all have the black . . ." He fumbled for the right word, vertically patting the air to decline Jed's offer to fill in the word. "They all have the black *gene*. Finn sheep have, are, sweet by nature."

"Their wool is great for spinning," Jed said.

"What's spinning?" Addie asked.

Jed didn't want to have to stop and explain. "*You* know. They spin the wool to make yarn. And they use it for felting."

Addie said, "What's felting?"

"You felt it, you know, press it down, to . . . to make other stuff." Jed flopped one hand, side to side, meaning "other stuff."

Addie said, "What other stuff?"

Jed glowered at her.

To avert a spitting contest, Dan asked Jed, "Did you get to pet the lambs?"

Jed said, "Yeah! They're *soft!* The sheep have real thick wool, but the lambs are soft, like baby blankets." He told the smaller kids, "I'll show you my baby blanket sometime. It's lambs' wool."

Abraham said, "We should get some Finn sheep."

Like 4-H club members, the boys had a plan for raising Finn sheep. They would start with a small herd, twenty-five lambs, and raise them, breed them. They would learn how to sheer and vaccinate, how to worm, trim feet. They needed a lamb barn and enclosures. After they placed their order, the lambs would arrive in three to five days.

Dan drooped, listening to the boys. He couldn't afford to buy lambs or build a lamb barn. He said, "There's the part about paying for it."

Elsa said, "We have money from selling the Cougar place. We can use that. And Grace Ann knows sheep. She worked with Father. She can come and help us get started."

Jed yipped. Abraham smiled. Dan saw shock on Nell's face. Her mother was offering funds, no argument or hold-back, no hint that the sheep idea was risky, and she wanted Grace Ann to help with the sheep. Dan hadn't witnessed the sputter fight in Mesa, but Nell had described it to him. Grace Ann had a perfect set-up in Mesa, it seemed to Dan, the Finnish women's coffee group, the shows at the Tumbleweed. What had Elsa found offensive? No matter. Elsa was ready to patch relations with her sister. Now, thanks to the boys, she had her chance. She wouldn't even have to fake a reason.

But Dan had qualms. He didn't feel like starting from scratch again. He didn't want to learn something new. What did he know about sheep? Nothing. Were Nell's parents too old to tackle a project this big? No. Isak was ready for anything that had to do with farming, and Elsa had a biological need for hard work.

In a fleeting hunch, he saw the group's new enterprise. Raising Finn sheep.

He had another fleeting thought. Going broke raising Finn sheep.

He had to consider the Seattle offer. With this bunch to support, he couldn't afford to be foolhardy. They all might have to move back to Seattle.

But "moving" was not a popular notion. Last week when Victoria heard the Sandersons might move, she had taken two cowbells to the bottom of their hill and walked back and forth on the road, ringing the bells and calling, "Don't go!" At the time, Nell had said to Dan, "See? No one wants us to leave except you."

❉ ❉ ❉

Isak figured that his game might help. He thought the grownups (the children too) could sit in the kitchen and put their ideas on the table (so to speak), discuss their ideas, then vote (this is the step he wasn't sure about, considering the large number of people). That should tell them what to do, move to Seattle or stay at the farm.

Dan had called a meeting at the kitchen table. Everyone was there. Isak scratched his ear, afraid that his game might fail. "You should wait till after your birthday to make decisions," he said.

Dan laughed. "It's okay. It's always *someone's* birthday around here. Tell us about the pieces."

Isak patted the three piles of game pieces that he had grouped by size. The largest pieces were cardboard circle tops from glass milk bottles, washed and collected over the years and rescued from the Cougar house. The middle-sized pieces were pop bottle caps, the metal, star-edged kind. The smallest ones were shirt buttons from Elsa's box. He explained that the biggest ones were for the most important ideas, the middle-sized ones for middle-sized ideas, the smallest ones for small ideas.

He slid the piles to the center of the table. "Take some of each." He passed paper scraps and pencils to those who knew how to write. "These, too." He adjusted his lower denture with his tongue, then stopped, recalling that he wasn't alone. He didn't like to fix his teeth in public.

"Think about the next ten years," he said, "about what you want to do, what you want around you. Animals, work, weather, anything. Chose your

237

best idea, then the next best, then the last idea. Write them down and fold the paper slips and cover them with game pieces. Arrange them from most important to not so important."

Like a horse in a stall, he pushed air through his lips. He wasn't sure about his game. It seemed convoluted.

Nell said, "First, though, we need to talk? So we know what we're voting on?"

Isak nodded yes.

Dan said, "I could tell about the Seattle job and Ronnie Jakes and plumbing."

Sigrid said, "We should start with what we *need*, like quality of life and infinity to the place."

"Affinity," Nell said.

"And enough bedrooms," Sigrid said.

Elsa said, "If we stay, we can build bunks."

Jed said, "Yeah, let's *stay* and raise sheep!"

Abraham's eyes stayed on Dan, willing him to side with Jed and him, to say they could stay on the farm and raise sheep.

Dan said, "Seattle means a steady income. We *need* a steady income."

Nell said, "But if we lived in Seattle, you'd have to travel. I don't *want* you to!"

In the absence of noise that followed her words, Isak said, "'If, of thy mortal goods, thou art bereft, and from thy slender store two loaves alone to thee are left, sell one, and with the dole buy hyacinths to feed thy soul.'"

Jed said, "Grandpa? What the heck does *that* mean?"

Isak wondered that, too. Or he wondered why he had said the lines just then.

Nell smiled—the way she did when she was little, Isak thought. "That's nice, Daddy," she said.

"We need a steady income," Dan repeated. "That's the most important."

Sigrid said, "Wait. We're not voting on most important yet."

The adults talked. The children talked. Nell kept notes. Twenty minutes passed.

They took a vote.

When the answers came they fell like summer rain. Isak felt restful on the inside. They would stay on the farm. Abraham and Ned would raise Finn sheep. The others could help, too, but the boys would be the managers, along with Elsa and Isak, and Grace Ann too if she decided to come and help. The boys would do research and find out what they needed to do first.

Dan would become a plumber. He had mostly made up his mind before the meeting, he told the group, but he'd wanted everyone to have a say. Plumbing was puzzle-solving, he said—locating, getting to, and fixing items in tight squeezes. He had found that fitting things together was satisfying. That's what plumbing was, he said, the fitting together of elbow joints and C-rings. He was going to give up his shyness and roll around on floors to help people. After years of doing invisible work, he liked the idea of giving immediate, visible help—stopping a spurt or preventing a flood. And he liked the idea of working from home.

"You can't teach an old Finn new tricks," Isak said.

No, thought Isak. That's not what I meant. I meant to say *my game worked.*

Thirteen

A Reason to Hum

The fence was high enough to keep lambs corralled and strong enough to hold a row of children standing on the rails. Feeding time was over, but the lambs were curious, saying, "M-baa" and "A-a-a" and crowding the fence. When the children offered their fingers, the lambs nibbled them. Grace Ann pictured a lamb barn that would maintain a constant fifty degrees. She would ask for a bedroom at one end, with a heater. She would want her bedroom a little warmer than fifty degrees.

After Elsa called, Grace Ann had contacted the extension service at Arizona State University, collected free materials, and bought books on raising sheep. Much had changed since she was a girl. A few terms were still in use—"skirting," the removal of stained edges from the fleece, "yolk," the wool's natural grease, "lanolin," what the yolk was called after it was purified—but she hadn't known that coarse wool from the hindquarters was "britch wool" or that the first fleece shorn from a one-year-old sheep was "hoggett wool." Sheep were still fed alfalfa hay and oats, but nutrition was more scientific, vaccinations more precise. Wool-grading terms were new to her—"the American Blood System" (once used to describe breeding, the writer said, now used to describe fiber diameter), "spinning count" (the number of hanks of yarn, each hank measuring 560 yards long, which could be spun from a pound of clean wool), "micron diameter" (a micron being 1/25,400 of an inch). When she came to the farm, she brought along her sheep books. They sat on a shelf in the bus, near where she slept.

Nell called the children in for supper, and they ran to the house. They would eat on the first round, leaving Grace Ann time to herself. She removed her barn boots and slid into clogs, thinking her Suomi Circle friends wouldn't recognize her in flannel shirts and bib overalls. They were practical for the barn, the most comfortable clothes she had ever worn. The lambs were aa-aa-ing so loudly that she couldn't hear the radio. She reached up to the shelf to her birthday gift from the Suomi Circle—a red battery-operated radio the size of a paperback book, chromed and shiny as a new tractor, with a crank for recharging the battery, an extendable antenna, and a suitcase grip for carrying—and she increased the volume. A woman gave the recipe for Mimi's Apple Cake, a really moist cake, she said, due to the fact that it called for applesauce as well as chopped apples. A man read classified ads, pausing between ads to crackle papers—a washer for sale, two pregnant pigs, a baler, a dresser.

She snapped off the radio and went to the fenced area. Lambs pushed toward her, and the one she called Belle poked her head between the rails. Grace Ann stroked the lamb's face. The wool was silky to the touch. Like the others and yet unique in herself, Belle had a sturdy black body with tall white socks and a white head with black circles around the eyes. Surveying the group, Grace Ann made an executive call. "Belle, we're going to keep you," she said. "You'll be the old lady of the sheep barn."

She hadn't told anyone she wanted to stay. She needed to do that soon. She needed to see what Elsa and the others thought about her plan. For her, it was a natural next step. Her other life, her Arizona life, had closed like a morning glory whose time was done.

* * *

Sigrid helped Elsa serve breakfast, then put on her sweat suit and Keds and set off on her walk. Stanley came along and so did the mother cat, Missus. Sigrid didn't know how to tell Missus that cats didn't normally take walks with people. The cat maintained a distance of a car-length behind Sigrid, lifting her feet high when she came to tall grass and spitting at Stanley when he wanted to play. The first light of day skimmered in the weeds and made them shine. Game birds flushed out of bushes as Sigrid walked by. Small birds flicked white in the sky. One little brown bird flew a solo for Sigrid, did corkscrews and zigzags and looped in the air, then made himself a streamlined thing and aimed straight down, scooping up at the last second. Dakota mornings were like pictures in little kids' books. (Once when she told Isak what she saw on her walks, he said, "'The morning stars sing together and angels shout for joy.'" It was from the Bible, he said. She didn't know much about that, but it described her walks to a *T*.) She walked the same route every day but she never got bored. The view across hills *called* her outdoors. What was it about unfenced fields that spoke to her? Maybe the fact that they *were* unfenced—or mostly, anyway. The fences here were safe to climb through. No electric zaps. Thinking of zaps, the emotional kind, she realized she hadn't had any for quite a while—only now and then when she thought about Hitch.

The thinking that she did on her walks was thinking she couldn't do at any other time. This morning she was rating the move to North Dakota. Here out in the country the kids could run free and learn to work, both. They had lambs, chickens, and ducks to take care of, and two pigs, a slew of rabbits, the cat and her kittens. The kids acted like born sisters and brothers, argued and got silly like regular kids, played hard and did chores. The new ones were learning American ways. Nell and Dan were looking for the Roosevelts, starting in Jersey City. Sigrid thought it was a good idea. It would be nice for the new kids to meet their American relatives. A nice conjunction, she thought. Nell was crazy about the farm. Sigrid had seen Nell count her chicks at the table, looking all girl-scouty and taking courage from their faces. Elsa was back to her old tricks—cooking for globs of people and loving it—and now, with Grace Ann staying for who knows how long, Elsa couldn't be happier. Though, if you didn't know her, you'd never guess she was happy. Elsa kept a straight face better than anyone. And Isak? That man was brand-new! She hadn't seen a bit of confusion in him for weeks. Maybe it was the turmeric. He'd heard that turmeric and curry helped the brain, so he had Elsa put them in everything. (But just for him. The others, including Sigrid, preferred *regular* food.) And he wasn't touchy like he used to be. A nurse had told Nell that any shock, say, a broken bone, could make a person grumpy, and that when Isak's leg felt better he wouldn't be so growly. That's how it had turned out. But Sigrid gave *some* credit to the B12 shots. And the hydraulic acid. No, she corrected herself, the hydrochloric acid.

Stanley had made a big circle and come back, and he stood by, panting, waiting for her to tell him to run on, his tongue going long and short as he took in air. She said to him, "That Isak is recapitulated," and waved him off.

Then there was Dan. Man oh man, he was at a loss there at first! The cows wouldn't let down for him for the *longest* time. Lucky for him, Isak knew how to milk. And the sheep deal was going fine. And the kids were healthy and the blue bus was running. The roof had even stopped leaking (stopped leaking because the rain had stopped, but, still, stopped leaking). Life was pretty sweet.

Two problems, though, still bothered her.

One, Nell still sometimes gave her the look she gave her when she was little, the look that meant, "What fool-crazy thing did you just say?" Stanley was out in the field, so Sigrid couldn't talk to him. She talked instead to Missus the cat, who was walking soberly in the weeds beside the path. "Like when Addie had a rash and I said I had a bottle of comatose? Well *of course* I meant calamine. *Anyone* would get mixed up with so many kids around, even a proper oh-pair. Those kids are a piece of cake!" The cat stepped along with a pursed face. Sigrid scrubbed her cheeks with two hands. "I mean a piece of work. Those kids are a piece of work." In Alaska, she had thought she might stay in Arizona. If she *had*, and if she didn't have all these kids to drive her coo-coo, what would she be doing? Dying of yawning, that's what!

Two, Hitch still made her mad. That *fink!* She hadn't seen him for years, but he could still get her storming mad. Why! If she let him, he could make her really, truly sick—so sick she'd have to go to bed, or to the hospital! . . . Hmp, she thought. Maybe I shouldn't *let* him. She'd have to give that some thought.

She said to the cat, "Isak says not to waste time being mad. But *he's* a fine one to talk. He can't get *close* to that woodshed without turning beet red."

* * *

Dan said, "Ready, set, go!" Jed and Abraham gave the woodshed a push. Not much effort was needed. It had been preparing to fall for years. It tilted, hesitated, and collapsed. Earlier in the day, Dan and the boys had emptied it, put the firewood in the barn, the sawhorse in Isak's shop. They had found no old tools, in particular, no axes.

The planks were rotted and full of holes. They would burn well. The kids could make a bonfire that night, a snapping fire that would shoot off sparks: red dots flying to the sky, taking the poison with them. It was the right thing to do, Dan thought. Cook hot dogs on the site! Burn marshmallows papery black! Let the kids have their fun. Let them holler and shout at the expense of the departing ghosts.

The kids were innocents. They had no link to the woodshed. In the end, they would win. They—maybe *only* they—could ease the pain that held the old man hostage.

* * *

The plan had been brewing in Elsa for a day or two, something to help the boys and to also stop the flutter in her belly. She added wood to the cook stove, went to the hutch and got her recipe for "South of the Border Bundt Cake." She would make this cake, then instigate her plan. She had to compose a proposal that could not fail. She had to convince everyone, including Grace Ann, that Grace Ann should stay.

Not go back to Arizona.

Stay.

Grace Ann was who she was. It was okay to let her be. Truth to tell, it was more than okay. Grace Ann was history to Elsa, continuity; she was there at the start.

Elsa found the bundt pan, gathered ingredients, and assembled the cake in raw form. She buttered the pan, which had a tower in the middle, and spooned the heavy batter around the sides. The pan's shape was soothing—

fluted and flowerlike, a step up from a regular pan. The recipe was a regular chocolate bundt cake recipe with one added ingredient, cinnamon.

That's really all she was proposing. One added ingredient.

❊ ❊ ❊

June 14, Flag Day, was Rebecca's first birthday. Nell could have delayed the June party until the following day—Rebecca was the only June birthday person and *she* wouldn't know the difference—but Marcie and Adam and their kids would arrive in two days, and Nell and her mother needed time to get ready. So the parade and the party would happen on the same day.

The Sandersons, Nell's parents, and Sigrid found a stretch of grass beside the curb, set out chairs for the adults in back and blankets for the kids in front, and unpacked picnic coolers, diaper bags, insulated jugs. Dan held Rebecca on his lap, Sigrid held Minda on hers. Nell settled into a low chair and a took out a notebook and a pen. She would document the parade for her column. A baby cried a block away from the Sandersons. More people arrived, looked down the street, and milled around for better spots. Nothing much happened for restless minutes. United States flags flew on most of the buildings, thrown about by the wind. Red, white, and blue balloons bounced on streetlight poles. A banner spanned the street: "Flag Day 1980, Hanson, North Dakota." The weather was overcast, moderately warm, a light wind blowing (North Dakota is a windy state, Nell wrote for readers who didn't know). The parade would assemble by the firehouse, according to the newspaper. The firehouse wasn't visible from where Nell sat—it was down the block to her left—but interest was generating in that direction. Corly Cray, the weight-lifter cook for Donna's Luncheonette, stood on the sidewalk in a white canvas apron, his arms folded across his chest. His arms were so bulky they hardly made space for each other. The fabric shop had a "Closed" sign on the door, as did the Chevy dealership. Someone had made caramel corn and brought it to the parade. Nell waited for her kids to catch a whiff and ask for food, but they were engaged in looking down the street. Sounds escaped from the firehouse area, car honks and police whistles, riffs on a clarinet, tentative toots from tubas and trumpets.

Then came a clang of cymbals and a band started playing—"The Washington Post March," Nell guessed. It was hard to tell since the bass drum obliterated the tune. Before the band actually showed up, an antique fire truck drove by bearing a sign that read, "1940 USA." A Dalmatian sat haughtily in a high seat, trained to sit there in the biggest tumult. The Sanderson children called to the dog, but he didn't move. Firemen threw wrapped candies to the crowd. Most landed in the street. Jed and Abraham ran onto pavement and got enough for themselves and their siblings.

The band marched around the far side of the firehouse and entered the parade route. A large banner, carried by girls in white majorette boots and uniforms similar to one-piece swimsuits, announced the Hanson High School marching band. Nell's feet kept time with the drums, *left* on the downbeat. The band members wore blue jackets with silver buttons down the front, blue trousers with silver stripes on the side, and red fezzes with silver pom-poms on top. They had many things to do—play music, march in formation, bow and dip their instruments, sway on their feet, and, when the drum major gave a signal, run a number of steps to the right or left, being careful not to step on anyone's feet, then put their instruments at rest and march to the patter of the snares. Nell felt sorry for the heavier players. They were already red in the face. After passing the Sandersons, the band resumed playing. Notes turned flips in the wind and came out flickery. For a few measures, the trombones drowned out other instruments. Then the clarinets took a turn, squealing and triumphant. Five small girls clopped by on horseback. Behind them came three clowns carrying shovels and pushing a trash barrel on wheels. A man in a business suit rode a bicycle down the street, carrying flowers in his handlebar basket. His sign read, "Randy Shandor, Mayor." The parade had officially started.

A modern red fire truck, one firemen driving, six hanging on.

An antique yellow Chevrolet honking a steam horn, advertising an auction to benefit the community center.

A green Bobcat tractor, a dealer's name and phone number printed on the side.

Six horses draped in Arabian robes, the riders in desert garb.

Truck displaying the American flag and a sign for a hair salon.

Candidate for sheriff, Nelson Graddimer, seated on the folded top of a 1957 tan Oldsmobile convertible, two small girls, presumably his daughters, beside him.

Little League pickup, Little Leaguers standing in the back, waving flags.

White Toyota with "Acts 29" painted on the side.

An apple green 1935 John Deere tractor.

A Girl Scout troop on foot.

Six teen-aged girls on a flatbed float in dresses the colors and shapes of flowers.

Jed pointed up the street, laughing. "Look!" A clown was driving a jalopy and acting mystified. The steering wheel kept coming off in his hands. A sign on the jalopy read, "Student Driver."

There was a gap—an empty street—and the parade started up again.

A blue Ford announcing, "Trinity Lutheran Vacation Bible School."

Another candidate for sheriff. The sign said, "Sing Bob-white for Bob White."

A girls' baseball team on foot, cheering and singing.

The singing reminded Nell that she hadn't seen any bands after the first one. "I expected more bands," she told Dan. He said, "It's a small town. Maybe there's only one band." Countering his words, twenty old men in Sunday suits—walking in no particular order—took kazoos from their pockets and played a sea chantey. Nell laughed and clapped. A sea chantey in North Dakota!

Next came a truck containing (the sign claimed) a superior water filter. The driver honked his horn and waved. A hometown parade is democratic, Nell wrote. Everyone gets a chance to show off.

Farm truck pulling a flatbed of milk cans filled with fresh daisies.

White Cadillac convertible, three Dairy Princesses seated on the folded-back top.

Two go-carts covered in paper flowers.

Car carrying a poster, "See Your Native Land! Join Our Nordic Nights Tour."

Garden Magic Nursery truck pulling a greenhouse on wheels.

Pickup truck advertising Stevens' Well Drilling.

Sedan with roses in holders, a large card: "In memory of Gladys Shaker."

Jimmy Rinta drove by in a horse-drawn hay wagon. Victoria sat on the haystack dressed in a sun bonnet and an ankle-length polka-dot dress. She smiled and waved at the Sandersons. The sign on the wagon read, "Rinta Rugs. Finnish designs. Hand-made."

Two pigs riding in a push-cart, pushed by two young boys.

Water ski boat with six people in it, pulled by a silver pickup.

Motorcycle with a sign, "Beauty and the Beast," the rider in a pig mask.

Five dune buggies.

Six military trucks.

State representative Margaret Unger in a car decorated with streamers.

A collie pulling a red wagon with a boy in it.

A Conestoga wagon.

A truck labeled "Frisky Towing." Dan said, "I'm not sure I'd want a frisky tow."

A '43 Plymouth driven by a man in winged sunglasses.

Candidate for sheriff, Norman Sunovich. "Unfortunate name," Dan said.

Six women in aprons carrying bowls, spoons, a sign: "Ladies of the Morning."

The Hanson Historical Society van.

A truck representing Germantown Local Produce.

A hometown parade tells people who they are, Nell wrote. It celebrates the past and defines the present. It's unique to one locale. A parade brings a community together, literally, for a display of itself. Hanson presented itself as civic-minded, family-oriented, hard-working—its people descendants of immigrants, Germans, Swedes, Finns. . . .

She stopped writing and looked up at the parade. One group was missing. The Sioux. The Standing Rock Indian Reservation was less than fifty miles from Hanson. But nothing of Indian life showed in the parade, nothing of Hanson's history with the Sioux. On rare occasions, Nell had seen Indians in town. They traveled in groups of four or five and kept to themselves. She had heard of poor conditions on the reservation, a level of the poverty partly brought on, some non-Indians claimed, by the Standing Rock tribes themselves, who had never fully complied with the Indian Reorganization Act of 1935 and thus had never received full government funds.

There had to be more to the story, Nell thought. The only local nod to Indians that she had seen was the print on the wall at home, "The End of the Trail," the bowed Indian on his bowed horse. She had seen it in other homes as well, and in offices and shops—a scene of displacement, widely displayed by the displacers.

Seven police cars drove by very slowly, signaling the end of the parade.

* * *

Minda sneezed and vomited simultaneously—a white torpedo aimed at the wall. Dan said, "How do you do that, do both at the same time? Minda with the hazel eyes?"

Her expulsion upset no one, Isak noted. The baby threw up on a regular basis. Isak knew why. She drank her milk *way* too fast. Nell stopped what she was doing to clean up the mess. Setting aside the baby bottle, Dan mopped Minda's face with a towel. She gave him a sloppy smile. Milk oozed from the sides of her mouth. Dan dabbed at her chin and said, "Messy baby."

Isak asked Jed, "What's that you got there?"

Jed made a show of nonchalance. "Well, I had this frog," he said loudly. When he was sure he had an audience, children and adults, he held up a squashed frog with two fingers. Innards oozed from the frog the way milk had oozed from the baby.

The children said, "*Eeeeuw*."

Jed said, "I forgot it was in my pocket and it went through the wash!" He paused for effect, giving radar signals to his siblings: heads up, get this, here it comes.

"I guess I brainwashed my frog," he said.

Almost everyone laughed. The new children didn't get the joke. In fact, the boy Isaac took offense, as if he suspected he was being hoodwinked. He was visiting at home for a week, and Isak hoped the days would go smoothly without trouble.

The boy Isaac said, "That prog is *dead*!"

Jed said, "Of course it's dead! Brainwashing means . . ."

"Put it away," Nell told him. "Go wash your hands."

Jed left the table, clowning for the other boys and for Laura, who could always be counted on to giggle. Nell brought two plates to the table—tomato wedges and cucumber slices. Isak had caught her running a fork down the cucumber before slicing it, to make it scalloped when she sliced it. She hadn't seen him watching. Sigrid set down two bowls of mashed potatoes and returned for snap beans with bacon. Elsa made two trips and brought back meat loaf slices and buttered bread. Isak checked to see what was already on the table—a lettuce salad, sweet pickles, a red berry jam. Before any food had gone on the table, Grace Ann had spread a white tablecloth and scattered flecks of yellow and green paper. "Corn-fetti," he had said at the time. He said it again now. "Corn-fetti."

Jacob, seated to Isak's left across the corner, moved toward Isak and said softly, "Do you know the secret of how to be an elf?" Isak said no. Flushed with inside knowledge, Jacob whispered, "The best way is, you're born one. Or you can get to *be* one. Ding! And you're an elf."

Isak considered this. Maybe so, he thought.

Dan passed out paper party hats. The children from the Philippines had never seen party hats. They were skeptical, not sure how to put them on, not sure they wanted to put them on. Dan demonstrated. Holding Minda in one arm, he put an alligator hat on his own head and a princess cone with streamers on Minda's. She batted off the hat and tried to put the tip of it in her mouth. Dan made a switch, first offering her a baby rattle, and, when she reached for it, snitching away the princess hat. Minda tried to put the rattle—shaped like an oversized lollypop—in her mouth. Isak mentally told her, "You won't make it. It's too big." The boy Isaac put on a fireman's hat and snapped the rubber band under his chin, over and over, as if he didn't feel the sting—or, if he felt it, as if he *liked* it. That was the problem, Isak reasoned. The boy Isaac didn't feel pain—his own or anyone else's. Or else he felt too much pain. Isak was glad the boy was going back to that school. Better for everyone, safer. The school said he had "attachment disorder." That sounded right. He didn't connect with anyone. Elsa's white nurse cap sat on her hair like a sailboat. An appropriate choice, it seemed to Isak, considering how she liked to sail around and serve people. Isak had said no thanks when Dan offered him a hat, then accepted a Smoky the Bear hat. He assumed he looked righteous but friendly in it. Elsa's sister had chosen a tiara and she wasn't even a birthday person. Sigrid's hat suited her well, he thought—a jester's cap. When Jed returned, he put on a Frankenstein hat that was half-hat, half-mask.

It was too much for Isak. Around the table sat children in bird-bills, rabbit ears, and stovepipes. The dog was wearing a cowboy hat. Isak formed a word: *risible*. To his right, Rebecca—the birthday girl, one year today—had slid into a corner of her highchair and propped a bare foot on the food tray. A black beret slanted over one eye. She looked very cocky indeed. She was chewing a piece of apple, getting ready, Isak knew, to eject the apple skin. It was her special talent. Her lips stayed shut but kept active as they helped her tongue isolate the apple skin. Isak had advised Nell to make applesauce for her. Nell said Rebecca did fine with slices, that she chewed them into applesauce herself.

Rebecca spit out a blop of apple skin and put her lips in an *O*. Out came a whistle. She turned to Isak and said, "Wha da?"

He laughed, one or two arfs—an incidental comment. A baby who could whistle!

Nell's sombrero had bobbles around the rim, and when she reached for Rebecca, to set her straight in the highchair, the bobbles went every which way. She said, "What's so funny, Daddy?"

He had no idea. He flailed in his mind for something to say. He joggled his head to say never-mind, then he got out, "Just some laughter left over."

Nell smiled at him in a certain way. *She thinks I'm daffy.* Maybe so. But I found the farm, didn't I? And taught them how to milk?

Isak took in the vast numbers of people at the table. *Imagine that,* he thought. *We had to come all the way across the country to find each other!* Across the globe, more like it. It didn't make sense. But he had seen with his own eyes that things that didn't make sense turned out just as well as if they did.

He addressed the group. "Every hour you sleep before midnight equals two hours after." He thought about this and added, "Keep your hand on your horse when you walk behind him. Let him know where you are."

Satisfied that he'd said what needed to be said, he looked around for Elsa. She had her back to him, stirring a pot at the stove. She hadn't turned when he spoke, but she had heard him. He knew her quirks. Elsa caught everything that was said or done, even if she pretended she didn't.

Out of the blue, he saw a truth he had never seen before. *His wife was a lot like his Mum.* Elsa, Emma, four letters, *E* at the start, *a* at the end. Elsa worked harder than anyone else around. Same with his Mum. Elsa's best work went on inside of her, and she kept it there. Same with his Mum. Elsa thought that *he* was great. Maybe his Mum did, too? This was a notion that left him humming.

Isak set his fork, knife, and spoon in straighter lines and said, "There's calm in knowing another person's quirks and having that person know yours."

THE END

Acknowledgements

Many people contributed to this book, whether or not they meant to. I handle their gifts with joy. Years ago my husband, Burt Chamberlin, dashed off the drawing that's now on the cover. His inspiration? I don't know. But it's perfect as Isak's daydream. Our adult kids will recognize bits from their growing-up. Jordan actually did freeze flies in the ice cubes. Jamie wrote the "looming, stoic giant" piece about my father. Lindsey's toy bear cabin was made from an apple box, and Tucker gave us his recipe for corn puffs. Like Abraham in the novel, Benjamin felt responsible for his younger siblings, in his case, his Korean sisters. Like Laura, Sherry spent her first years in Manila, well-loved by nuns. Like Jed, Annie threw a football so fast it could knock down the catcher. And, like Addie, Katie once told her cat to sit there in his bathwater while she got a flea comb from the next room, and he did.

My late parents, Lillian and Eino Jutila, lived out a wisdom of simple things and made magic in kitchen and garage. I borrow their talents for characters Elsa and Isak Halonen. After Mount St. Helens blew on May 18, 1980, my mother gave me newspapers that tracked the volcano starting months before the eruption. These accounts helped me to plot the novel. I am indebted to her for this archive and to writers and photographers at *The Columbian* (Vancouver, Washington) for their excellent journalistic record.

Our former neighbors near Mount St. Helens, in the long valleys of Amboy, Ariel, Cougar, told tales about living in the mountains and I've used them in the book; their stories, stirred together or seen in glimpses, celebrate a richness of place and a solidity of neighbors: Kathi and Bill Wheeler, Pat and Jim Stepp, Kathy and John Huffman, Julia Stoll and Fearon (Smitty) Smith, the late Virgil Wallace, Dixie White, the late Dave White, Rob and Linda Dore, the late Theodora Appling, Bob Appling, Becky Huesties, Alice and Don Merkle, Lorene and Don Stuart, Carol and Bill Foss, Millie and Dick Slayton, Dennese and Buddy Kelsay, Sue and Leonard Reese, Bert Roberts, Sharon and Gary Stuart, Keith Stuart, Cheryl and Paul Cline, Morgan (Morgine) and Jerry Jurdan, Ilene and Walt Black, Vonnie and Larry Houglum, Donnie and Jack Kelley (Donnie was also my Alaska expert), Kennen and Grant McNeal (parents of Andrew McNeal, whose birth nearly coincided with the eruption of Mount St. Helens), Carol and Frank Springer, Vicki and Arvid Anderson, Bernice Adams, Mariah and Eric Reese, Ira Lee Kelsay, Evelyn Brill, and Jody and Judy, the mail ladies.

My cousin Edward and his wife, Sharon, who farm the Jutila homestead in North Dakota, filled in background on cattle and the town of Kintyre. In my childhood, Edward and his siblings, Donald, Elsie, Raymond, Vernon, Helen, with their parents, Esther and George Jutila, hosted my family for dreamy visits on the farm; Helen was my buddy on horseback, a witness to horse antics named in the novel. The "eye palls" comment originated with Eino Juola. Nancy Thomas generously shared her expertise on attachment disorder. My publishers, Corinne Dwyer and Cecelia Dwyer, helped me to stay on track when life turned frowsy. My brothers, Morris Jutila, Calvin Jutila, Dale Jutila, came up with details I'd forgotten, such as secrets of the arthritis box. My sisters-in-law, Jacquie Jutila, Teresa Arden, Barb Jutila, provided coffee, hugs, and fond sisterhood.

I extend my warm thanks to all.